GONE WITH THE
WINDSORS

Also by Laurie Graham

FICTION
The Man for the Job
The Ten O'Clock Horses
Perfect Meringues
The Dress Circle
Dog Days, Glenn Miller Nights
The Future Homemakers of America
The Unfortunates
Mr Starlight

NON-FICTION
The Parent's Survival Guide
The Marriage Survival Guide
Teenagers

LAURIE GRAHAM

Gone With the Windsors

FOURTH ESTATE · *London*

First published in Great Britain in 2005 by
Fourth Estate
An imprint of HarperCollins*Publishers*
77–85 Fulham Palace Road
London W6 8JB
www.4thestate.co.uk

Copyright © Laurie Graham 2005

1

The right of Laurie Graham to be identified as the author
of this work has been asserted by her in accordance
with the Copyright, Designs and Patents Act 1988

A catalogue record for this book is
available from the British Library

ISBN 0-00-714675-2

Typeset in Sabon by Palimpsest Book Production Limited,
Polmont, Stirlingshire

Printed in Great Britain by Clays Ltd, St Ives plc

To Howard

March 10, 1932, Sweet Air, Baltimore
Six months since Danforth Brumby surrendered to the first
hint of kidney failure and left me a widow. It always was
the risk, in marrying an older man. Yesterday his head-
stone was raised, so now it's time to look to the future.
I still have my youth and my looks. Men are already
flocking to my side and women are pursuing me as always
for my advice and my vivacious presence at their dinner
tables. *Le tout* Baltimore is impatient for my return to
society, so tomorrow I shall drive into town, place my
chinchilla in cold storage, and order a selection of spring
outfits from Madame Lucille. A new chapter opens.

March 13, 1932
A letter from sister Violet. *Why not come to London,
Maybell?* she begs. *It will lift you out of yourself. It's
impossible to remain sad for long in a house full of children.*

Well, that is a matter of opinion.

Pips Waldo is here, she writes. *You always liked Pips.
And Judson Erlanger. Remember him? He's married to
one of the Chandos girls.*

I'll say I remember him! Judson Erlanger took me to
the Princeton Ball.

1

It's getting to be a real Little Baltimore over here, she concludes. *And who knows, we may even find you another husband. Melhuish knows quite everyone.*

I have already endured thirteen years of Violet's condescension, brought on by her marriage to Donald Melhuish, *Lord* Melhuish as she reminds me with tedious regularity. The truth is, I could have snagged Melhuish for myself, had my tastes run to cold castles and men in skirts, but I allowed Violet to have him and I've said nothing since to disturb her smug satisfaction in her title and her connections and her lumpen Melhuish offspring. To some it is given to tread the wilder track, to risk the ravine in order to conquer more majestic peaks, and I have always had a head for heights.

PS, she adds. *You might think of spending some time with Doopie. She has missed you dreadfully.*

So there we have it. Violet doesn't want me in London for the zest I would undoubtedly bring to her life, nor does she particularly intend to find me a lord. Tired of playing the angel of mercy, she hopes simply to palm me off with the retard.

What a trial Doopie has been to us all, a regrettable afterthought in a family already perfectly adorned by Violet and myself. If people must have children, two is certainly enough. But our misguided parents would have her, and they would allow her to arrive on my birthday too.

'Maybell,' Father said, 'you have the best birthday gift a girl could ask for.'

I had hoped for a new donkey cart, not an attention-seeking brat of a sister.

They named her Eveline and doted on every smile she smiled and every mew she mewed, but sister Eveline didn't

2

impress me. Over and over she'd allow a person to take away her pacifier, then look injured and start her sobbing. She never learned to say No. Then, after she caught inflammation of the brain, there could be no doubt about it. The child was a vegetable.

'Slow' was the word Mother used. 'Slow, but special.'

The fact is, Eveline is stupid. Always was, always will be. I renamed her Stupid, but she's so dumb she can't even say it. 'Doopie' is the best she has ever managed.

They tried her at elementary school, but she was an embarrassment to us all, and it was soon decided that she would do just as well at home. She's handy with a needle, I suppose. She can knit and crochet. And she's quite the green-thumb, which used to endear her to Father.

'I had given up that ficus for lost,' he'd say, 'but Eveline has raised it from the dead.'

He claimed she knew every plant in the conservatory and talked to them like friends. Well, that says it all about Doopie's powers of communication. 'Bayba', she used to call me. And 'Vite' was the best she ever managed for 'Violet'. 'She does love you so,' Mother used to tell me. 'Her eyes don't leave you for an instant when you come into the room.'

There has never been any question of Doopie marrying, though I believe I am the only one who ever took the trouble to inform her of this. When Violet was coming 'out', there was the threat of war, so it was decided I had better be brought 'out' too. Just as well because the Prussians quite ruined the 1915 season. Doopie helped with the trimming of our gowns.

'We're invited to the Bachelors' Club Cotillion,' I explained to her, 'which is something that will never happen to you.'

She just smiled. How much of what one says penetrates her brain one never can tell, but she always seems contented enough. The only question was what would become of her. Father seemed to think that two sisters and a trust fund answered the case, but I was never consulted. And when Danforth Brumby asked for my hand, nobody asked him if he'd mind having a halfwit in the attic some day. Violet thought she'd made her escape, I guess, settling overseas. I suppose she thought an idiot couldn't be sent on a sea voyage. But when the time came, after Father passed over and Mother had to be placed in the care of a full-time nurse, it so happened that Brumby and I were much burdened with the renovations at Sweet Air. It would have been most unsuitable for Doopie to move in with us. She might have bumped into a marble pillar awaiting installation and brought it tumbling on top of her, or wandered into the path of some falling beam. It was safer by far to send her to Violet. We provided her with a chaperone and they travelled first class and everything has worked out for the best. From their army of peasant retainers Violet and Melhuish have been able to provide her with the simple companionship she requires and then, with the arrival of the babies, she has gained a nursery full of playmates.

So I will not fall for Violet's sly attempt at luring me to England. I see her little game. She hopes to catch me while I'm weakened by grief and change the arrangements for Doopie. Well, they seem perfectly satisfactory to me. I shall stay where I am and reign over Baltimore.

March 20, 1932
Stepsons are sent to try us. The earth has barely settled on his father's grave and Junior is demanding to know

my plans for Sweet Air. Do I expect to stay on, alone, in such a large and isolated house? And if I were to think of selling he knows his father would have wanted the place kept in the family. Junior has never liked me. He's never forgiven me for replacing his sainted mother and making Danforth smile again. He obviously hopes to spook me out of the place and then pick it up at a knockdown price. He'll probably come around tapping on windows and making hooty owl noises. Well, he'll find Maybell Brumby is made of sterner stuff than that.

March 24, 1932
Randolph Putnam pressed me to join him for luncheon today but I declined. I find him too eager, and anyway, I'd already agreed to take tea with Nora Sedley Cordle. One social obligation a day is enough for anyone, especially where Nora is involved. She sat behind her Gorham teapot pretending friendship, but I can read her like a book. She's hoping I'll give up Sweet Air too. I always was a challenge to her social ambitions and now I suppose she's hoping I'll get me to a nunnery. Well, I can tell her one thing. She may be a Daughter of the American Revolution, but she had better learn to leave the ruffled neckline to those of us who can carry it off.

April 1, 1932
The telephone keeps ringing and no one speaks. Today a package arrived, *The World's Most Chilling Ghost Stories*. Junior must take me for a fool.

April 3, 1932
Not sleeping well. I've instructed Missie not to answer the telephone after 10 p.m.

April 7, 1932

Randolph Putnam crossed the street to tell me how strained I look and to recommend I take myself off to Palm Beach for awhile. And leave Nora Sedley Cordle to consolidate the gains she made while I was in mourning? I think not!

April 10, 1932

A quantity of horse manure was deposited on the front steps during the night. Missie says she was wakened by the sound of unearthly laughter and didn't close her eyes again till morning. Much theatrical yawning when she brought in my breakfast tray. Just what one needs at a time like this: the help falling asleep on their feet.

April 12, 1932

Another letter from Violet. *The most extraordinary thing,* she writes. *You'll never guess who has appeared on the scene.* She then digresses, recounting in unnecessary detail various antics of the brood. Ulick won a trophy for shooting. Flora wet her drawers at Lady Londonderry's. Rory fell off his new pony and knocked out two teeth. On and on it went without at all getting to the point. Violet's meanderings are so fatiguing. I had to turn two pages before I learned who it was who had so extraordinarily appeared on the scene. Minnehaha, no less. Wally Warfield! Well!

I ran into Pips Waldo, she writes, *who told me all she knew. Apparently, she's married to someone who was in the Guards but is now in business. They have a little place somewhere north of Marble Arch and from what Pips has heard she's quite on the make.*

I can imagine. Her mother didn't have a dime, but Wally

never allowed that to hold her back. She had sharp elbows and a calculating mind and she didn't miss a trick. Great fun though. School was much more interesting once Wally was around.

She came to Oldfields in 1911 and only because an uncle was paying for her. One didn't expect a new girl to start throwing her weight around, especially a girl who was a charity case, but on her first day she warned everyone that although her given name was Bessie Wallis she only answered to Wallis or Wally. I could see her point. Bessie's more a name for a cow or a mammy.

But more often than not we called her Minnehaha, because of her cheekbones and the way she braided her hair, and she quite liked it. She reckoned she was descended from Pocahontas, but then so do a lot of people. Pips Waldo and Mary Kirk and I were her main friends. Lucie Mallett was a hanger-on but she never invited Wally to her home because Mrs Mallett knew all the dirt, about Wally's mother taking in boarders and wearing lip rouge, and the Malletts had very closed minds. But we Pattersons were raised differently.

'Let me not judge my brother,' Father always said.

Anyway, it was Lucie Mallett's loss. Wally and I used to have such fun. Inventing pains so we could stay in and read fashion tips instead of playing basketball. Drinking ginger ale and eating butter cookies after lights out. I was always sorry we drifted out of touch. So now she's in London. Perhaps I'll reconsider. It would be nice to see Pips. It might be interesting to pick up the threads with Judson Erlanger. And with Wally around livening things up I think I could even endure a few weeks of dull old Violet.

April 15, 1932

Dead crows nailed to the gateposts this morning and yesterday. I leave for England next week. And if Randolph Putnam is so anxious to be of service to me he can arrange for the locks to be changed. I don't want to come back and find Junior has taken possession of Sweet Air.

May 11, 1932, Carlton Gardens, London

A whole month since I have found the energy for my diary. Can there be anything more prostrating than travel? And my recovery is being made a thousand times harder by the chaos in Violet's establishment. She and Melhuish had been in the country, so when I arrived Carlton Gardens wasn't properly aired and my bed was distinctly damp. I threatened to move to Claridge's. Violet eventually asked a rebellious-looking domestic if she might find the time to fill a rubber bottle with hot water and rub it between my sheets, and seemed to think that addressed the problem. Said rubber bottle finally delivered with heavy sighs an hour after I had fallen exhausted into my bed. If this house is anything to go by, England is on the very edge of revolution.

Violet has grown stouter and probably hasn't had her hair attended to since the day she left Baltimore. She clips it up and she's no sooner clipped it than it escapes. Melhuish's hair, on the other hand, is now in the final stages of retreat. One thing I will say for Danforth Brumby, he kept a fine head of hair till the very last.

Of the children I have so far met only Flora. She is eight years old and has occasional lessons from a spinster who comes to the house whenever she can be spared by her sick relations. Otherwise the child seems to tag along with whatever Doopie is doing, which cannot be very much. They take each other for walks in St James's Park and make tiny coverlets for a dollshouse. My arrival caused great excitement and the child immediately showed signs of wishing to attach herself to me, so today I was forced to establish some rules. She is not to visit my room. She is not to lurk in doorways spying on me. She is not to play her drum within a country mile of me. One must start as one intends to go on.

As for Doopie, she never seems to age. She stared and stared at my face, then smiled and said, 'Ids Bayba!' but I'm not convinced anything really registered with her. Violet credits her with understanding, but a person may smile in an aimless way without at all understanding whether there's anything to smile about. Nora Sedley Cordle springs to mind.

I haven't yet sighted the two boys. They are normally kept at a school called Pilgrims but are being allowed out tomorrow night for something called an *exeat*. Not on my account, I hope.

A sweet note of welcome waiting for me from Pips Waldo, now Crosbie. She and her husband Freddie are in Halkin Street, just off Belgrave Square. We lunch on Monday.

May 14, 1932

Besieged. The house is filled with boys wearing hobnail boots. They were brought down to the drawing room to meet me last evening. All Violet's children have Melhuish's carroty hair and freckled skin. Ulick is tall, I'd say, for twelve, Rory is like a skinned rabbit. According to Violet, he suffers from night terrors. According to one of the housemaids, who offers unsought opinions on everything while dust gathers in drifts inches deep, he sees 'imaginings'. Well, all children are prone to imaginings and the less intelligence they have the more susceptible they are. I remember I used only to have to snake my arm out of bed and set a rocking chair in unexplained motion for Violet to start howling, followed rapidly by Doopie. Anyway, both boys shook me nicely by the hand and Ulick asked me how many acres I have at Sweet Air. Rory was gazing at me with his mouth open and Ulick nudged him in the ribs. When he still stood catching flies, Ulick said, 'And how was the crossing? Agreeable, I hope.'

Rory said, 'You beast! I was going to ask that. You know I was. Now what shall I ask?' Quite droll.

But they've all been tramping overhead since the crack of nine and now, just as I thought I'd found peace in the morning room, Violet has appeared with her book of lists and the child Flora has bounded in, draped in a tartan traveling rug. She says they're playing Highland Clearances and she is It.

This evening Violet and Melhuish are dining with the Bertie Yorks. He's a brother of the Prince of Wales. Violet said, 'I'll have Smith prepare you a tray. I hope you understand. It's not the kind of dinner where one can arrive with an extra.'

Extra indeed! I have no great desire to dine with royalties, not even junior ones. I can think of nothing worse for the digestion.

May 15, 1932

The boys Ulick and Rory were driven back to their school after luncheon, Rory sobbing pitifully when the moment came to leave, begging to be allowed to have lessons at home like Flora. Ulick was in a fury with him. He kept saying, 'Stop it at once. Melhuishes don't blub.'

Violet busied herself in the library with committee papers while he was being bundled into the car. She says he always cries, but once he's back with his friends he soon cheers up. She said, 'He'll toughen up. And someday he'll thank us for it. Imagine if a boy went into Officer Training still soft from home life.'

May 16, 1932

Lunch with Pips. She now has a red tint and bangs and looks adorably modern. She goes to Monsieur Jules in Bruton Street and is going to introduce me. Her husband, whom she can't wait for me to meet, is in Parliament, although not in the same section as Melhuish. They seem to see quite a bit of Judson Erlanger. She said, 'As I recall you had quite a pash for him.'

Pips is misremembering. Judson was the one who pursued me.

Another name from the past. Ida Coote is in town, living some kind of artistic life in a rooming house full of White Russians. Extraordinary. I hadn't realized Russians came in any other color.

I don't believe I've seen Ida since Gunpowder River Summer Camp. It must be twenty years. She was another unusual girl. I can't wait.

Wally is now married to someone called Simpson and I have her address from Pips. George Street. They've seen each other in passing at several receptions, but so far they haven't managed to get together for lunch. I sense Pips is dragging her heels. She said, 'I don't know. Maybe the years have improved her, but didn't you always find her rather mouthy?'

Actually, I liked that in her. I had the face and the figure but Wally had the patter. We'd take a slow walk down to the Chesapeake tearooms on a Sunday and collect ourselves quite an escort of good-looking navy boys, in from Annapolis for the afternoon. We made a good team. Perhaps we will again. Me, Wally, Pips, Ida. At this rate we belles of Baltimore will be taking over London.

Violet says Ida's address is in West Kensington which hardly counts as London. Also that she'd hesitate to classify Wally Warfield as a belle.

Tomorrow to Swan & Edgar for woolen camisoles.

May 18, 1932
Swan & Edgar's store knows nothing of customer service. They told me there was no demand for woolen camisoles at this time of year, when only two minutes earlier *I* had demanded them. They advised me that their next supply will arrive toward the end of August and asked would I care to leave my name and number. I said, 'I see no point. I shall be dead of the cold.'

A long wait while Ida was fetched to the telephone by one of her Russians. She screamed for joy when she heard my voice. Lunch tomorrow.

May 19, 1932
Treated Ida to the Dorchester. She has dyed her hair black and wears costume jewelry, having lost everything in the Crash, but seems very gay. She said, 'Money's a curse, Maybell. I'm a free spirit these days.'

Of course, I don't know that Ida ever had *that* much money.

She's taking me to the Argentine Embassy on Monday.

She says attendance at one cocktail party begets invitations to ten more so there's no faster way to meet people, and canapés also solve the question of dinner.

No call from Wally.

May 21, 1932
To the Crosbies'. Freddie Crosbie is very sweet in that dithering English way. He has no chin and makes only four hundred a year as Member of Parliament, but Pips obviously adores him. They must be very glad of her money.

The house is all beige and cream, what Pips calls 'neutrals', and is run in the modern style. There's no withdrawing after dinner, which I very much applaud. I've never liked all that sitting round drinking tea, waiting for the men to finish their cigars.

The great shock of the evening was seeing Judson Erlanger after all these years. He never had what one could call chiseled features but he did once have a certain amount of dash. Now he looks like a big, pink man in the moon and is married to Hattie, formerly Chandos, who has crooked teeth and a permanent wave. Pips says her people go back years. But surely everybody's people go back years?

Still nothing from Wally. I begin to wonder whether Pips copied down the address correctly.

May 24, 1932
How I missed Danforth Brumby last evening. Ida and I had no sooner arrived at the Argentines than she set off across the room in search of potato chips and left me at the mercy of a Latin with shiny hair and built-up shoes. What is one supposed to say to these people? Brumby

would have struck up a conversation about silver mines or the price of beef, but I felt quite at a loss. Was finally rescued by an American press attaché called Whitlow Trilling, also married to an English girl. He knows Judson and Pips but Wally's name meant nothing to him. Perhaps this whole Wally business is a red herring.

Violet came in before I was dressed wanting to discuss something called Royal Ascot. Ascot is a racetrack and there's a week of races there next month. I wouldn't mind going. Brumby and I went to Saratoga once and it was quite fun. Violet said, 'Oh, I'm afraid it's not that simple, Maybell. Melhuish and I will be in the royal party, you see. And I'm just not sure what best to do with you.'

I said, 'You make me sound like a surplus chair. It's very simple. I'll join the royal party too.'

But she says that's out of the question. That one cannot invite oneself along, nor even propose that one's dearest sister, recently bereaved and newly arrived in a foreign land, be added to the invitation list.

She said, 'Let me have a word with Lady Desborough. She's always very sweet about accommodating an extra.'

That word 'extra' again.

I said, 'As a matter of fact, now I reconsider, I expect to be rather busy that week, so don't give it another thought.'

She said, 'Will you? Nobody'll be in town, you know? But it'll be a great weight off my mind. Their Majesties absolutely depend on us for Ascot, you see. Well, Melhuish has known them all his life.'

Violet never tires of displaying her tired old stock of claims to grandeur. How she met Melhuish when he was traveling with the Prince of Wales. How Melhuish's father was equerry to two kings. How Melhuish has known the

14

Duchess of York since she was a baby in her bassinet. She forgets how differently things might have turned out. If I hadn't stayed home to represent us at Lucie Mallett's wedding shower I'd have been at Sulphur Springs myself. Who knows, I might have caught the royal eye, never mind Donald Melhuish's. Not that I'd have wanted either of them. They say that crowns are unbearably heavy to wear. I notice anyway that the Prince of Wales seems to have dropped Melhuish. Violet says it's not a question of 'dropping'. She says friends grow apart when one of them becomes a family man and the other continues to run with a fast set.

I said, 'I assume you'll leave me with a cook at least, and a maid, while you're being indispensable to Their Majesties?'

She said, 'I'll leave you with everything but a driver. And you'll have Flora and Doopie for company.'

So there it is. It doesn't bother me. I'm sure royalties must be death to the natural gaiety of friendship. Better to stay at home and be one's true self, even if it does mean being left with a child to supervise and an imbecile and a staff of Bolshevik insurgents.

May 25, 1932
Minnehaha at last! She said, 'Maybell, you must think me such a slouch, but I've been sick. This is my first good day for a week.'

Stomach ulcers, apparently. I didn't think she looked too bad, though. Still skinny, still parting her hair in the middle, still as tidy as a tinker. Little gray suit, white shirt-waist, good shoes. Her skin isn't brilliant but then it never was.

Lunch was a riot, we had so much to talk about. She's

been married to Simpson for four years, his name is Ernest and she's never been happier. Of course, she said that when she married the aviator but it was all far too hasty.

The first summer we were 'out', she got an invitation to visit a cousin who was stationed at Pensacola, Florida, and she was off like a shot. Wally always adored a uniform. The next thing we knew, she was back with a diamond on her finger, engaged to a lieutenant in the Aviation Corps. That was Win Spencer. The wedding was at Christ Church and I was supposed to be a bridesmaid, along with Mary Kirk, but then Grandma Patterson died and I had to go to the burying, so Lucie Mallett stepped in at short notice. I wasn't altogether sorry. The gowns were yellow, which has never been my color and our bouquets were snapdragons. Somehow whenever I see a snapdragon I think of Wally.

We lost touch after that. I said, 'You could have written.'

'Well,' she said, 'it wouldn't have made an edifying read. I knew the first week I'd made a mistake.'

I think the honeymoon comes as a shock to every bride. It was years before I felt able to enjoy the Pocono Mountains again. But with Win Spencer there was the additional problem of drink. They went to a resort in West Virginia, which was dry, but apparently he'd thought to bring along his own supplies.

She said it was the stress of flying that had turned him to alcohol. It was the usual thing to toast the flag before anyone went up in one of those crates, but Win would always have a couple more shots, to settle the first one.

She sounds to have had a pretty good war, though. He was posted to California and they say the beaches at Coronado are divine. Then he was sent to China and she thought it'd be more fun to tag along than sit it out on

Soapsuds Row with all the other navy wives, so she followed him. There was never any stopping Wally. In fact, advising her against something only made her all the more set on doing it. Like the time she borrowed Nugent Wilson's suit and crashed a Bachelors' Club ball dressed as a buck.

She says China was a real adventure. Hong Kong, Shanghai. There was a war going on, people getting shot in the streets, heads appearing on pikes, and there was typhoid. She ended up in Peking, had an affair that didn't work out and then decided to call it a day with Win. He was drinking more than ever. She went back to the States, got a divorce, and was staying with Mary Kirk for awhile, getting back on her feet, when she met Ernest, who has business interests in London. So here she is.

I said, 'You never looked up Violet? She's Lady Melhuish, you know, in Carlton Gardens?'

'Yes,' she said, 'I know. But I don't think Violet ever really approved of me and these days she's so grand. Frankly, I'm looking to create a livelier circle. I'm more interested in what people *are* than who their grandfathers were.'

I'm invited for Saturday. She says I'll find Ernest very knowledgeable on wine and literature.

The Westminsters to dinner at Carlton Gardens. Poached salmon again. Violet might take time off from her committees one of these days to review her recipe book.

May 26, 1932
Flora fell crossing the Mall, and came in crying. Even Doopie couldn't soothe her. 'Mummy, I crazed my knee,'

17

she kept sobbing, but there was cold comfort to be had from Violet.

'Did you, darling?' she said. 'Jolly good. Now off you skip. I have Fishermen's Orphans this afternoon.'

Every day there's something. Consumptives, Highland Crafts, Unmarried Mothers.

A note pushed under my door when I woke from my nap. HURRO written in wax crayon. The poor child spends too much time around Doopie.

May 28, 1932

Bryanston Court is a dull building in a dull street. Wally's on the second floor with a cook, one live-in maid, a daily, and a driver for Ernest. A claustrophobic entrance hall filled with white flowers and ivory elephants. A modest drawing room, mahogany and striped silk mainly, but one glorious lacquered Chinese screen and a table full of gorgeous little jade doodads. All bought for a song, I'm sure. Her China years may be glossed over whenever Ernest is around but she doesn't make any effort to hide the booty.

Ernest came home at seven and presided over the drinks tray. He's pleasant enough, dapper, a little too fat in the face to be handsome and he almost certainly dyes his moustaches. To hear him speak you'd take him for an Englishman. He showed me some of his first editions while Wally interfered in the kitchen. She always did love to cook. After her mother remarried she'd often come home with me during vacation and one time she took over our kitchen and made terrapin stew, because she heard Father saying it was his favorite dish in the whole world and nobody ever cooked it for him.

I reminded her about that. She laughed.

'It was 1912,' she said, 'I can tell you exactly. After Mama moved to Atlantic City with that four-flusher.'

Her stepfather was a drinker and an idler called Rasin. Goodness knows what Mrs Warfield saw in him. Wally used to say she prayed he was a seedless Rasin because she was in no mood for any baby sisters and brothers. He was dead within two years anyway.

Ernest said, 'You two certainly do go back a long way.'

Indeed we do. Back as far as her mother's sad little boarding house, though I'd never dream of bringing up that kind of embarrassment now.

May 29, 1932

Another note under my door. HURRO ARNT.

I placed a call to Lucie Mallett Norman this evening, Violet fretting in the background about expense, quite unable to understand why a letter wouldn't do just as well. She knows I always pay my way. I just wanted to find out if Lucie knew anything about Ernest.

She said, 'All I know is, Wally came back from China with her insides in some kind of disarray, crossed the state line to get a divorce and wasted no time in helping herself to someone else's husband. She met him at Mary Kirk's.'

I said, 'I know that. But who is he?'

'A nobody,' she said. 'And he left a child and an invalid wife, just because Wally Warfield snapped her fingers. Scandalous.'

I said, 'I'll tell her you said hello.'

'Please don't,' she said.

May 30, 1932

Lunched with Pips and Wally at the Criterion. They were a little stiff with each other at first, but a bottle of hock wine soon got them talking about past times. Pips remembered something I'd quite forgotten: how Wally talked Homer Chute into masquerading as her cousin and picking her up from Oldfields in his Lagonda one Sunday. They were gone all day at the pleasure beach and Wally came back with a tintype portrait of herself sitting on Homer's knee. Not that Pips was backward with the boys. She had more fraternity pins than any of us. Wally says she doesn't know how long she and Ernest will be in London but she'd really like to liven things up while she's here and leave her mark. Pips suggested costume parties, but she hasn't seen Bryanston Court. It's far too small for a crush. Anyway, Wally says unlimited drink is death to conversation. She prefers elegant little dinners where she can draw people out.

Wally believes the secret of success as a hostess is to mix important people with a sprinkling of interesting types from lower levels. Also, in the matter of food and presentation and entertainment, to have the courage to season the expected with the unexpected. She says the King of England would be happy to come to dinner if he thought he might meet Mahatma Gandhi and be served a good tasty hamburger on a Minton plate. Pips says Mahatma Gandhi doesn't eat hamburger.

After lunch Wally took us to see an adorable gramophone she'd found in Wigmore Street, completely portable, in a lizard-skin case. I couldn't resist. But I've entrusted it to Wally because if I bring it to Carlton Gardens Flora will expect to play with it and it will soon be broken.

Pips was on the telephone the instant I got home. She said, 'Minnehaha's as slow as ever to pick up a check, I see. And I hope you're not going to buy her every toy in the store. You're too generous, Maybell. Always were.'

Well, what's a little money between friends? And I'm only *lending* her my gramophone.

June 2, 1932
Shopping with Wally. Ernest seems to keep her on a very strict allowance and goes through the account books at the end of each month. Thank heavens Brumby was never so particular.

Flora sitting on the stairs watching for my return. She announced that she'd been making 'gakes' and had one saved for me up in the nursery, but I was too exhausted to climb more stairs. I said, 'I'll come tomorrow.'

A hammering on my door five minutes later and there she stood with a lump of warm gray dough in a paper case.

Tonight dinner with Violet and Melhuish's friends, the Belchesters, who can't wait to know me.

June 3, 1932
Anne Belchester's busybodying and charitable works make Violet look like a positive lady of leisure. She wanted to know about my Baltimore committees, but I told her, it isn't everyone who's suited to committees. There are talkers and there are doers, and I'm a doer. All that time spent shuffling papers and drinking tea. I'd sooner sign a check.

Billy Belchester said, 'Careful now, Maybell. You'll have writer's cramp by the time Anne's finished with you!'

Melhuish said, 'Violet gives her time, that's the thing, and her expertise. All the money in the world is no use if it's not wisely marshaled and the thing about Vee is, she's terribly good with lists.'

Anne Belchester said, 'She is. She sometimes mislays

them, but when they come to hand they're absolutely first-rate.'

Oh well, glory in the highest to Violet and her lists. I do my bit. I sort through my closets every fall and give to Christmas Goodwill. Quality woolens, shoes hardly worn, hats that aren't keepers. I just don't make a fuss about it.

Pips is getting up a party to go to Ciro's tomorrow night. So far the Judson Erlangers and Wally and Ernest. Ida is an unknown.

June 5, 1932
We closed Ciro's. Judson and Hattie brought along the little press attaché, Whitlow Trilling, and his wife Gladys. Ida turned up with an Argentine who smelled of brilliantine. Ernest had business papers to peruse so cried off at the last minute. No great loss. He's so serious. People don't always want to be discussing Pluto's *Republic*.

According to Whitlow a new First Secretary just arrived and it's someone Wally knows from her navy days in San Diego. Benny Thaw.

Pips said, 'Is he an old flame?'

Wally says absolutely not, but she's going to look him up.

The birds were singing as I arrived home so I looked forward to a restful day in bed, but Wally was on the telephone at ten, slave-driving me to go shopping for lingerie, and then a military parade started up. Violet says it was the Major General's Review. Men and horses tramping across Horse Guards Parade. Drums, bugles, shouting, all bad enough in themselves, but Doopie and Flora came back from watching and proceeded to reenact it in the corridor outside my room. Doopie always did get over-excited by military bands.

Violet is walking around with a furrowed brow because the Rutlands and the Bismarcks are dining tonight but someone has chucked, leaving her with thirteen, and I'm far too tired to make up the numbers. I don't have the strength to lift a soup spoon.

Caught my heel in the hem of my charcoal silk getting out of the car this morning and there is apparently no girl among the overfed rabble of servants in this house who knows how to mend. Not one.

Light rain.

June 6, 1932

I am completely recovered. Dr Collis Browne's linctus certainly lives up to its promises. Now I've tried it I shall never be without it. And while I slept Doopie quite expertly repaired my ripped hem. I shall buy her a box of candy.

Wally on the phone first thing. She sent a message of welcome to Benny Thaw and he replied immediately with an invitation for drinks. She seemed particularly excited about his being married to Connie Morgan.

I said, 'Do you know her?'

'No,' she said, 'but I soon will. This should get the American scene here fizzing. Those Morgan girls all have money and style.'

Lunched with Pips who says she doesn't know anything about Connie Morgan, but what her sisters have is money and reputations. Gloria Morgan was married to Reggie Vanderbilt until he drank himself to death, and Thelma Morgan was Mrs Bell Telephone but is now Lady Furness.

She said, 'And we all know about her!' Then Ida turned up, raving about a miraculous new oxygenated face cream

23

and we somehow never got back to the subject of Thelma Furness and what it is we're all supposed to know.

Took a tray of fruit fondants for Doopie.

Violet was out at her Distressed Pit Ponies. Flora knows the days of the week by her mother's committees.

'Bunday, Pit Ponies, Doosday, Blood, Wesday, Falling Women and Not Forgottens.' She was stuck for a minute with Thursday but Doopie helped her out. Something called 'Lebbers'.

They seem to be great friends and have a most amusing sign language they use from time to time. How simple their lives are! I have to dine with the Angleseys and Violet's gruesome in-laws, while they can play with their dolls and have sugar sandwiches for tea. There is something enviable about the life of an imbecile.

Of course, Flora will never learn to speak clearly listening to Doopie's version of things. I may take her in hand.

Violet finally came home at six.

I said, 'Don't you think Flora's rather backward with her speaking? She just copies Doopie, you know.'

'Oh,' she said, 'they'll sort that out when she goes to school. They did Rory.'

I said, 'Well, I feel sorry for her. She never goes anywhere.'

Violet said, 'Nonsense. Doopie walks her to Duck Island almost every day. And she was invited to the Yorks' for tea yesterday but would she get dressed?'

I said, 'That's because no one has taught her properly. She sees you running out to committee meetings, hair uncombed, egg yolk on your blouse. It's no wonder she thinks she can go to tea parties in bloomers and a liberty bodice.'

'Maybell,' she said, 'will you please go and bathe? Salty and Elspeth are coming at seven.'

I said, 'First tell me if you ever heard of Thelma Furness and, if so, what's her scandalous story?'

She made a great business of closing the door to the drawing room, then said, 'Lady Furness is a friend of the Prince of Wales, but not the kind we mention in front of the children. Why do you ask?'

I said, 'No reason. Wally knows the husband of one of her sisters. She probably thinks this is going to be her entrée to royal circles. She's as ambitious as ever. She keeps quizzing me about our connections with the throne.'

'Well,' she said, 'first of all, *you* have no connections. Secondly, those who do have them never speak of them. And thirdly, I would say it's a very steep climb from acquaintance with the husband of a certain person's sister to meeting royalties, too steep even for Minnehaha.'

Violet has always taken herself far too seriously.

She said, 'I hope it goes without saying, Lady F is never to be mentioned in this house. And please don't have your bath too hot.'

Chance would be a fine thing.

June 7, 1932
Flora has renamed one of her dolls 'Lady Furness' and has banished it to the backstairs. I grow fonder of the child.

June 9, 1932
All the talk is of Race Week. Violet said someone called Lightfoot might be willing to escort me to the Guards' luncheon tent but I recognize crumbs when I see them falling from my sister's table. Three times today she's

asked, 'Are you sure you won't let Ettie Desborough squeeze you in?' Guilt.

Wally says without a white badge Royal Ascot isn't royal at all, so why bother? We may borrow Ernest's driver and go shopping for bibelots in forgotten backwaters.

June 12, 1932

Wally and Ernest went to drinks with the Benny Thaws and met the unmentionable Thelma F. Wally says Connie and Thelma are both adorable and she's meeting them for lunch on Monday. Pips says if they're lunching with Wally someone had better warn them to take along a fistful of their Morgan dollars.

Violet and Melhuish's luggage has been taken to Windsor, not a great amount of it for three days of banquets and royal carriage rides. Wally says fashion is everything at Ascot but I'm certain Violet hasn't bought a single new gown. We might have had such fun shopping together, but no. She didn't even ask my advice about hats. Wally would have been much more fun as a sister.

June 13, 1932

Violet and Melhuish left after lunch for Windsor. Ida Coote has been angling to stay with me while they're out of town. She seems to have become some kind of nomad since she lost her money, always offering to air people's villas or walk their dogs. She said, 'You won't want to be alone in that great big house.' But I'm not going to be alone. I'm going to be in charge. Anyway, Ida has only two topics of conversation, Ida and men. It's all right for the occasional lunch but a slumber party would be unendurable.

To Gamages for galoshes, then home for a nursery tea.

Jello, toasted cheese and gingerbread. Afterwards we played at Royal Ascot, with dolls strapped to Ulick's spaniel and Melhuish's little ratting dog.

Flora wanted to know if I was going to live with them forever!

June 14, 1932

I'm a great hit with my niece, not least because I've decreed no fish will be served as long as I'm in command. I told her she could choose her favorite dinner and she came down in her nightgown to deliver her decision: LAB SHOPS. SIRUB TART. GUSTARD.

I said, 'Flora, wouldn't you like to go to school?'

'No thank you,' she said.

I said, 'Other little girls do.'

She said, 'Lilibet York doesn't.'

A lot of huffing and puffing from the housekeeper over my menus. Flora's choice tonight, then tomorrow a rib roast and ice cream.

She said, 'I don't know, madam. Her Ladyship didn't say anything about specials. This kind of thing isn't customary.'

I said, 'I know it isn't customary. That's precisely why I'm ordering it.'

Such a fuss. All she has to do is telephone Harrold's. They have everything.

'Carry on like this,' she said, half out of the door, 'Her Ladyship won't know the place when she gets back. We shall be all upside down with bilious attacks and overspending.'

I'll deem it a failure if Violet *doesn't* see a difference. I've already put a stop to Trotman's discussions. She now understands that if I say the tea is too strong I'm not inviting her to pour herself a cup to see whether she agrees. Give me a little longer and I'll break that footman of breathing through his mouth.

Tomorrow to Cotswoldshire with Wally.

June 15, 1932

Doopie was on good form last evening, chatting away in that funny snuffly style of hers. Flora seems to understand all of it. We looked through Doopie's albums, pictures I'd quite forgotten. Mother and Father with baby Violet, posed beside a potted palm. Me in a little cotton pinafore, with Doopie in her crib. That would have been before she lost her mind. Several photographs of our Season too. Pips and Violet setting off for Mary Kirk's tea dance. Me, Pips, Violet, and Wally in our finery before the Bachelors' Club Cotillion. What a production that was. Wally and I used to practice our one-step together. 'I'll be the man,' she'd say. Homer Chute had taught her the tango too, but that was far too racy for the Baltimore Bachelors'. It looked at first as though Wally wouldn't be able to attend because her uncle refused to help her out. He said it wasn't seemly to be giving balls when young men were laying down their lives in Flanders. But then he relented and gave her a gown allowance and she spent it all on one fabulous white satin. She reckoned she'd rather star at one important ball than blend with the masses at half a dozen. Flora wanted to know why there were no pictures of Doopie going to a ball. I told her there was a war and left it at that. I supposed having been cooped up with Doopie in that nursery all her life, she thinks of her as normal. I must say though, they both sat up so nicely and ate so daintily I've ordered dinner served in the dining room tonight.

A profitable day in Chipping Norton. We found Wally a set of silver-plate vanity boxes, quite good enough for a guest room. Also a bone-china compote dish, with the tiniest hairline crack, and a very pretty set of Victorian creamers. Bryanston Court is the kind of apartment that needs all the help it can get. It has no features. Wally's done the best she can with her Chinese pieces, but the place still looks half dressed. I suppose when Ernest got his divorce the invalid wife was awarded all his good things.

Wally's going to give a dinner for the Benny Thaws and invite Thelma Furness too. I can't wait.

June 16, 1932
Unexpected company last evening. We were about to go in to dinner when Melhuish's friend, George Lightfoot, called in on his way back from Windsor. He said, 'I thought I'd look in on my favorite girls.' Flora clambered on to his knee immediately so I offered him a sherry wine and he stayed to carve the beef. He's a tall drink of water, rosy cheeks, tangled hair. He had a brother who was in the Grenadiers with Melhuish, lost at Passchendaele.

He said, 'I would never have taken you and Violet for sisters, but you and Doopie, yes. I see a definite resemblance.' I don't think so.

He said it was a criminal waste to eat such a fine-looking roast without a drop of wine, raced off to his cellars in South Audley Street and came back with a bottle he described as 'toothsome but sincere'. I don't know that it was advisable to allow Doopie a glass, but afterwards she kept us quite entertained with her impersonations of Theda Bara and poor Fatty Arbuckle.

June 17, 1932

Violet and Melhuish got back just as I was leaving to meet Pips for lunch. Flora came thundering down the stairs to greet them. 'Mummy!' she said, 'I've had a splendid time with Aunt Bayba. We had lab shops and ice cream and Doopie had red drink. Smith says she's never seen such garryings-on in her life.'

'Not now, darling,' Violet said. 'I have to talk to Lady Habberley about raffle tickets.'

Pips thinks Wally's only inviting Thelma Furness to dinner in the hope she'll bring the Prince of Wales, but I'm sure Wally knows that's out of the question. Theirs is a very private affair.

Pips said, 'I suppose having the Prince's sweetie to dinner is still more than a little fly-up-the-creek girl like Wally ever dreamed of.'

Poor Wally, tarred for life, even by a friend like Pips. It's not that there was anything particularly inferior about the Warfields. Her Uncle Sol had a very good house on Preston Street and her Aunt Bessie is still well thought of. It was her mother who lowered the tone of things with one foolish marriage after another. Too many husbands and too much rouge. No wonder Wally's so determined to start over and make something of herself.

Tonight to the Embassy Club with the Benny Thaws.

June 18, 1932

Violet says what I had Smith spend on meat for two days would feed an African for a year. Ridiculous. I don't believe Violet knows any Africans.

Interesting people at the Benny Thaws' party last night. Boss and Ethel Croker from Michigan. Ethel was a navy wife before she met Boss. She knew Wally from China.

Somehow Ethel seemed more pleased to see Wally than Wally did to see Ethel.

June 20, 1932
Wally's birthday. I gave her a calfskin guest book and lunch at the Dorch. Ernest gave her a fountain pen. What a dull old stick he is.

We've been worked off our feet all afternoon planning her dinner party. There's so much to do. The menu to be decided and the placement, new table linens and stemware to be purchased, conversational topics to be studied. Wally reads the newspapers cover to cover every day and she's skimmed through centuries of history and philosophy while having her hair done. She says one hardly ever needs to plod through an entire book.

June 21, 1932
Lunch with Pips, who had invited along Ethel Croker, as she put it, 'to help us join up a few more dots in Minnehaha's Chinese period'.

Ethel's nice. Overdressed and hair an unhappy shade of brass, but very sweet and chatty. Ethel was in Panama, waiting for a transport to Hong Kong. When she joined the ship they berthed her with Wally and they became friends.

She said, 'God knows, you needed a friend. It was hell in a sardine can. Heat and storms and doughboys fighting with knives. Five weeks of it.'

She and Wally both got navy quarters on Kowloon when they arrived.

She said, 'She did try with Win Spencer, you know? She really did. I don't know why because he was a bastard. If I'd been her I'd have left him. But then he left her, added

31

insult to injury. She went off the deep end a bit after that. Man-crazy. And travel-crazy. I went with her on a trip to Shanghai, to take her mind off Win, but I couldn't keep pace with her. I was a married woman, you know? There was a lot of talk about Wally. Still, it's all a long time ago now.'

Ethel's made a good marriage with Boss Croker. They say he's Mr Frozen Fish.

She said, 'It'd be nice to catch up with Wally again. He seems all right, the new husband? A bit serious, but he doesn't look like a drinker. I'll bet he doesn't hit her.'

Poor Wally. No wonder she grabbed Ernest when he came along.

She's still a man short for Tuesday's dinner. Pips says the obvious solution is to drop a lone woman, the prime candidate being me. She predicts Wally will ask me to fall on my sword, but I shall absolutely refuse. Given my outlay on guest towels from Liberty the very least I'm owed is dinner with the fabled Lady Furness. If the situation is desperate I'll suggest George Lightfoot. He seemed to me the kind of man who could fit in anywhere.

June 23, 1932
Pips was quite wrong. Wally couldn't care less about odd numbers.

She said, 'This may be London but aren't we Americans, Maybell? Don't we do things our own way? More women than men, so what? Anyhow, Nada Milford Haven is coming and to all intents and purposes she's a man. It's going to give my table a rather avant-garde complexion.'

One thing about Wally, she's always made necessity the mother of invention. The menu is now decided. We're to have caviar, followed by grilled squab, iced Camembert, and then strawberry sherbet. It remains to be seen, though, whether Ernest will cough up for caviar. He seems to keep Wally very short.

I said, 'Well, if it doesn't run to caviar, you can always serve soup.'

'Never,' she said. 'Take it from me, Maybell, soup is the ruin of a good dinner.'

I'm quite agog to meet this Milford Haven person. I wonder whether she wears pants!

June 26, 1932
Violet's put out because she assumed I'd be free on Tuesday evening and now finds I'm engaged. The Nicholases of Greece and the Harewoods are dining. She said, 'Now who am I going to pair with Lightfoot? I was depending on you. Surely, if it's only Minnehaha, you can chuck?'

I have agreed to stay for one drink provided Melhuish has his driver at the ready, engine ticking over, to whisk me to Bryanston Court. It's like Baltimore all over again. Everyone wants me.

June 27, 1932
A working lunch with Wally, putting the final touches. We'll be eleven. An interesting number. She's placing me between a decorator called MacMullen and a German commercial attaché. She promises me he speaks English.

Ernest telephoned while I was there. I heard her say, 'Of course we must. First impressions! There's nothing worse than being offered caviar and then needing a magnifying glass to see it on your plate.'

I must say, when it came to paying I was rather shocked at her lavishness. Beluga, sevruga *and* ossetra! She calls it an overture of caviars, but I could hear Ernest worrying away at the other end.

'Ernest,' she barked, 'think of it as an investment in our future. Do you want to meet the Prince of Wales or not?'

Pips says she doesn't eat caviar anyway, so there's one economy that could have been made.

June 29, 1932

Flora came hammering on my door at some unearthly hour, found me prostrated by migraine, and fetched Doopie to minister to me. Cold compresses and a draft of something pleasantly medicinal. Flora said it's called Dog Hair. Whatever it was, it made me sleep and I woke restored. I think my headache must have been brought on by an unhappy mixture of beverages. A whiskey and soda with Violet and her guests, and then two deceptively strong Russian cocktails at Wally's.

The dinner was a qualified success. I found the squab a little dry, but the sherbet was delicious and my linens and crystal looked superb. The German did speak English but seemed to find Thelma Furness so fascinating he omitted to turn between courses and Freddie Crosbie became engrossed in conversation with Benny Thaw, which left me easy prey for Nada Milford Haven who was seated across the table. Wally says she's not only a marchioness but also a Romanov. I can well believe it. She may have been wearing a gown but that didn't prevent her foot from romanoving up and down between my knees.

Thelma Furness and her sister both have pale, pale complexions and wild black eyebrows. They're exotic rather than pretty. The Prince of Wales can surely take his pick of the most beautiful women in the world so he obviously has a taste for the unusual. They're both very sweet though, and Thelma doesn't at all trade on her special position. She has a child apparently. I wonder whose it is? Pips says Lord Furness stays in the South of France with a tootsie, so as to leave the field clear for the Prince.

Flora has been tiptoeing in and out waiting for me to be awake enough to inspect a little story she wrote this morning. It was about a good aunt who buys candy and ice cream but then gets sent away by the bad aunts.

She said, 'Daddy said you were a loose cannon. Why did he?'

That's because I uttered the forbidden F word in the drawing room last evening. Henry Harewood asked where I was off to in such a hurry and I told him I was dining with Lady Furness. I only said it to provoke Violet. How was I to know Mary Harewood is the Prince of Wales's sister? Homely little creature. Not my idea of a princess at all.

The boys will be home from school on Friday.

June 30, 1932

To Fortman's for a post-mortem with Wally. She's already had a warm note of thanks from Thelma so she feels she's established another useful friendship.

I said, 'You're very keen to meet the Prince of Wales.'

'Not especially,' she said. 'I've already met him. But Ernest would be very thrilled, and anyway, who ever knows where these things may lead?'

She claims she met His Royal Highness at a reception in Coronado in 1920 when he was on his way to Australia and his battleship refueled at San Diego. Strange she never mentioned it before. And she doesn't remember what he said to her. I'll bet she didn't actually *meet* him at all.

I said, 'So what happens next?'

She said, 'We wait and see. But I'll be very surprised if we don't get an invitation to Thelma's country house in the fall.'

That's where the royal *affaire* takes place, apparently.

I said, 'Why the fall? That's months away.'

'Well,' she said, 'after the middle of July nothing important happens till September. We're going to the Tyrol.'

Pips wasn't impressed by Thelma Furness. She found her doe-eyed and vapid.

I said, 'What else would she need to be? The Prince of Wales is heir to the throne. He's used to giving out edicts and laying down the law. He'd hardly choose a sweetie who answered back.'

She said, 'Oh, I don't know. I've heard he's pretty vapid himself.'

She and Freddie are going to Italy for the month of August.

July 1, 1932

Even Ida seems to be fixed up for summer, caretaking someone's house in Gloucestershire. When I asked Violet if she planned to remain in London she looked at me as though I'd asked whether she intended jumping into the Thames.

'Maybell,' she said, '*no one* stays in London in August. We go to Drumcanna of course, and this year you'll come with us.'

We'll see about that.

Wally and Ernest are dining with Boss and Ethel Croker before they leave London.

I said, 'You and Ethel must have so much to catch up on.'

'Not really,' she said. 'We were never close. But Ernest and Boss will find lots to talk about. They have a house on Long Island, you know? And they travel all over, first class. Ethel's certainly landed on her feet. Traded in a midshipman for a multimillionaire.'

Hardly 'traded in'. Ethel's husband was killed in Canton, friendly fire.

July 3, 1932

Ulick and Rory are home. Doopie has been flapping around all morning, unpacking trunks and examining socks for holes and shirt collars for turning. After the summer Ulick will be going to Melhuish's old school, Eton College, and so has to have his name stitched into dozens of new garments. A simple, repetitive task that would drive a normal person insane, but Doopie is clearly in her element.

Violet says the entertainments at Drumcanna will be simple, outdoor pursuits. Fishing, deerstalking, shooting. She says they don't keep late nights because of making an early start, but they do play parlor games after dinner and they always give a ball, where the help and the guests mingle and dance. I told her I didn't think it was for me.

'Nonsense,' she said. 'You'll have a wonderful time. The mountain air will do you good, and you'll strike up new friendships. Jane Habberley is coming, and Penelope Blythe. Anyway, you can't stay here. Smith and the maids go to their families for August.'

The butler and the driver go north with them apparently, but Drumcanna is otherwise run by a staff of locals, even more wayward than the London tribe no doubt, left to their own Scottish devices for months at a time.

I said, 'Then I'll go to an hotel.'

'You'll come to Drumcanna, Maybell!' she said, 'and do what normal people do.'

A note under my door at bedtime.

Dear Aunt Maybell,
Please come to Scotland. Flora and I will be very sad if you do not.
Yours truly,

Rory Melhuish

July 4, 1932

To the Legation for luncheon. 'The Star-Spangled Banner' brought a tear to my eye and made me think of going home. But to what? Sweet Air will seem so quiet after the madhouse at Carlton Gardens. To be alone in Baltimore or alone in London? Everyone is paired off, making their gay plans. No one considers you when you're a widow.

July 5, 1932

Violet says I've relieved her of a great worry by agreeing to go to Drumcanna and she promises me I won't regret my decision.

She said, 'We'll go for lovely walks. It'll lift your spirits. And I think I can promise you you'll get to meet Bertie and Elizabeth York. They'll be at Birkhall and may very well invite you over. It's even possible you'll be presented to Their Majesties!'

I asked about the Prince of Wales. That'd be one in the eye for Wally, but Violet thinks it unlikely.

She said, 'Wales comes and goes. He's like a flea at a fair. Never settles to anything for long.'

I said, 'Thelma Furness calls him "David".'

Pursed lips. 'Does she indeed?' she said. 'Well, in the

38

unlikely event of your being in his company, don't think of imitating her. Be on your guard, Maybell. Don't let Wally and her set lead you into regrettable habits.'

I'm going to retrieve my gramophone and my tango record from Wally before she leaves for the Tyrol. It sounds as though it may be the saving of those Drumcanna evenings and Violet thinks a guest called Tommy Minskip might enjoy the novelty of it. He's a viscount, unattached, and prefers indoor diversions to the hearty outdoor activities Melhuish's other friends seem to enjoy.

Violet said, 'Who knows, perhaps you'll hit it off!'

I do believe she's matchmaking.

Less than three weeks till we leave for Scotland, which allows very little time for purchasing mountain wear. Violet has offered me a green waterproof cloak she uses for Ascot, but I have no intention of meeting Viscount Minskip dressed as a cucumber.

July 7, 1932
To Peter Jones department store for cardigan sets, warm nightgowns, and bed socks. Violet says we're not going to the North Pole. Life here may have thickened her blood but so far it hasn't affected mine. In addition to Viscount Minskip, the guests at Drumcanna will be the Habberleys, the Blythes, the Anstruther-Brodies, George Lightfoot, and ex-Queen Ena of Spain. Melhuish's sisters and their encumbrances will be at Birkhall, staying with the Bertie Yorks.

Next Tuesday is Rory's eleventh birthday. I'm granting him his dearest wish and taking him to a cafeteria for poached eggs on toast. I said he could invite a friend too, but he says he'll just bring Flora. Ulick has declined and Doopie gets anxious in tearooms.

July 8, 1932

With Wally to collect her vacation outfits. What she does is, buy one good thing each season and then have it copied. She has a little woman in Cromwell Road who does it for a song and also remodels gowns, if they still have wear in them but have been seen rather too often. Wally's accustomed to this kind of thing, of course. All her life she's had to make a little go a long way, but still, how depressing! I felt compelled to take her to Derry and Toms and treat her to a new day dress.

She says it's not that Ernest's poor but he's in the family shipping business which went through shaky times when his father was in charge, so even though it's now quite successful, Ernest has a fear of financial reversals.

I said, 'Did you know this when you agreed to marry him?'

She said she didn't know very much about him at all except that he had nice manners and good taste. Also, he offered to divorce his wife so he seemed like a better prospect than working as a stenographer and living in a walk-up which was the bleak future she faced after things didn't work out with Win Spencer. I still think she rushed into things. I made Brumby wait two years for my answer.

She insists they're well suited, though. She says that apart from being a stickler over the accounts Ernest is very quiet and undemanding. He's quite happy to smoke his pipe and read his books and leave the decisions to her.

July 10, 1932

Last evening to the Crosbies'. Came, Judson and Hattie Erlanger, Whitlow and Gladys Trilling, and an English couple, Prosper and Daphne Frith. Prosper is in Parliament with Freddie. Much talk about vicious street fighting in

Germany. The Communists are behind it, of course, picking on the National Socialists. Prosper Frith says the situation is particularly tense in Hamburg, which is precisely Wally and Ernest's first port of call. Ernest has an office there. I must warn her.

July 11, 1932
Wally says Germany is a wonderful law-abiding country and she isn't the least bit nervous about her trip. After Hamburg they'll be motoring south to stay with an American friend called Lily. She has a small castle.

July 12, 1932
Rory's birthday. My success as an aunt knows no bounds. It was such a hot afternoon we went first to the Serpentine Lido where Rory and Flora took off their shoes and stockings and paddled, then to Oxford Street to Lyons Corner House for tea. Flora wanted to know whether we have Red Indians at Sweet Air. Rory quizzed me about Wally. So much for Violet's whispering. Children don't miss a trick.

I said, 'She's a friend who went to school with your mommy and me and she's had a rather hard life. Her people didn't have any money.'

'Gracious,' he said, 'that must have been jolly hard. Couldn't they have sold one of their houses or something?'

I said, 'There wasn't anything to sell. Imagine. But your Grandma and Grandpa Patterson were always kind to her. She used to come to our house all the time in school vacation. She was like an extra sister. And now she's in London and so am I, so we can be friends again.'

He wanted to know if she's still poor. I said, 'Well, she's certainly not rich.'

He said, 'I expect Mummy hasn't invited her to tea because she wears raggedy clothes.'

Flora said, 'That's not why. It's because she's vast. I heard Mummy say so.'

I said, 'No, she's not. She's small and slender.'

'Well,' she said, 'Mummy told Aunt Elspeth the Wally was as vast and bushy as ever.'

Extraordinary.

I pumped Rory for information about this Viscount Minskip Violet has lined up for me.

He said, 'I don't know really. He always comes to Drumcanna but he never asks me or Ulick to play with him. Uncle George Lightfoot says he doesn't have both oars in the water.'

I'm surprised to hear he rows. Violet gave me the impression he's more of a drawing-room man.

July 18, 1932

Wally gave up my portable gramophone very reluctantly, but she and Ernest leave tomorrow so she can't have any possible use for it. I also had to ask for my tango record and she wouldn't let me borrow the two she bought. She said Ernest is very particular about lending things.

July 21, 1932

The car, the luggage, and the butler have left for the long drive north and what remains of the staff seems to be in premature holiday mood. Bells go unanswered, baths are run late, and dinner has been pared down to soup, an entrée, and a dessert composed from stale cake and canned fruits. Violet says we'll be glutted with good food once we get to Drumcanna. I suppose that means more salmon.

July 27, 1932, Drumcanna, Aberdeenshire

We are at Melhuish's Scottish seat, by some miracle. Now I know how our great pioneers lived as they forged west. We had to change trains at Edinburgh and again at Aberdeen, into ever more spartan carriages, so that we arrived at Aboyne with every tooth shaken loose. There we were met by cars for another bone-rattling ride. Fifteen miles on rutted tracks and in sweltering heat. I've been put in a turret room below the nursery, pleasantly furnished but one can only reach it by way of a perilous staircase, one narrow, winding climb for everyone, people and servants alike. In the mornings when the night potties are being taken down and the breakfast trays are being brought up it must be like Oxford Street. Melhuish is in a jovial mood and has been very attentive to me, teaching me a dance called the strathspey and savoring those moments when the lurching of the train threw us into each other's arms. I wonder if he has regrets about Violet? She's become so stout and plain.

The first guests arrive tomorrow, Ralph and Jane Habberley and Fergus and Penelope Blythe. The shooting doesn't start till August 12 but they're coming to fish. George Lightfoot is expected at the weekend and Queen Ena on Monday. There'll also be some local people, the Anstruther-Brodies, but they only come for the start of the shooting. Violet says it's impossible to predict when Tommy Minskip may arrive as he's a law unto himself. I begin to like him already.

July 28, 1932

No breakfast trays allowed. Violet says it's too much for the help when they have to get luncheon ready, and anyway it's nicer if everyone comes down and starts the day sociably over a kippered herring. But nobody's here yet, and anyway, what is help for if not to help? We'll be expected to carry up our own hot water next. I hardly slept. When Violet enthused about the cornucopia of wildlife in the Highlands she omitted to mention the miniature mosquitoes that have eaten me to the bone.

Rory says they're called 'midges'. He and Flora have been running wild all morning, building a camp in a coppice beyond the vegetable garden. I'm to be invited to view it the moment it's fixed up. Violet doesn't seem to care what they drag outside, pillows, teacups, a meat safe.

I said, 'Do you realize Doopie's allowed them to take a good coverlet?'

'Not now, Maybell,' she said. 'I must catch our Consumptives secretary before she leaves for Glendochrie.'

The Habberleys and the Blythes have just arrived. Lady Habberley dresses like a stablehand, the Hon. Mrs Blythe wears nail polish.

July 29, 1932

The men and Ulick went out to fish at five, banging doors, crunching on the gravel, and generally wakening the dead. I ventured down at nine hoping to organize a little tea and toast and tiptoe back to my room, but Doopie saw me pass the door and cried out 'Bayba!' so I had no choice but to go in and join the ladies.

Jane Habberley is a drab creature. Violet described her as 'the backbone of our Highland Crafts Association', and certainly, everything she wears appears to be hand-knitted. Penelope Blythe is definitely more promising. She'd already spotted my gramophone and suggested to Violet that we have dancing after dinner this evening.

44

Violet said she had no objection but we might find ourselves short of men. She said Melhuish doesn't do *that* kind of dancing. We'll see about that.

Penelope said, 'Who's at Balmoral? If Prince George is there I'm sure he'd adore to come over and dance.'

Violet says Prince George isn't there, nor the Prince of Wales. Only Prince Harry, and Bertie York and his little family at Birkhall.

Penelope said, 'Well, neither of them is any use. They only dance reels. Do you know them, Maybell? Violet won't like my saying it, but they're *such* a dull bunch.'

I said, 'No, I don't. But I do know Lady Furness.'

'Do you?!' she said. 'How thrilling! Well, of course, Thelma Furness is the *plat du jour* but she's only the latest in a long line, and Wales still keeps up with some of his old sweethearts, you know? He visits Freda Dudley Ward all the time.'

Violet sliced the top off her egg with a fearsome swipe.

She said, 'I hope you're coming out for a walk this morning, Maybell? I very much hope you're not going to sit around gossiping.'

She knows darned well I don't go for walks. One of my conditions of coming here was that I be left in peace to write my diary and peruse the great works of Sir Walter Scott and Rabbi Burns.

Penelope Blythe describes Viscount Minskip as *chétif*. Unfortunately, the library here is not equipped with foreign dictionaries.

July 30, 1932

George Lightfoot arrived at teatime and was pleased to find I'd set up my gramophone in the Long Gallery. Penelope and I took turns with him, then Ralph Habberley appeared, drawn by the sound of the music, as did Doopie, Rory, Flora, and several spaniels. I think we've managed to give them all the rudiments, except for Flora who won't apply herself to anything and made up her own wild Scottish steps. Ralph has more enthusiasm than ability but George moves rather well, for an Englishman. The help were so fascinated, peering round the door at us, that the dinner bell was late.

July 31, 1932
Jane Habberley stood on my tango record and destroyed it.

August 1, 1932
There is no store in either Aboyne or Ballater that sells gramophone records.

August 2, 1932
I now know the meaning of *chétif*. Tommy Minskip is insane. He drives himself in a Bentley motor car, and travels without even a valet. He arrived yesterday with one small valise and a trunk containing the Battle of Waterloo which he now has laid out in the smoking room. George Lightfoot has explained it all to me. Every afternoon, as close to 2 p.m. as social obligations allow, the Royal Scots Greys charge the French infantry, with sound effects, Minskip captures the enemy's eagle standard and then falls, mortally wounded.

'Still a boy at heart,' was George's explanation. I think he's too generous. If he were still a boy at heart he wouldn't have disappointed Rory and Flora by omitting to visit their sodden camp.

August 3, 1932

Penelope and I have taken up watercolor painting. We find we can run off half a dozen before luncheon and smudges don't at all matter; indeed, they add to a picture's talking points. Rain kept us indoors today but one doesn't need to be looking at a moor in order to paint an 'impression' of it. Penelope tosses hers away at the end of the day but mine might make interesting gifts for Christmas.

George Lightfoot is very amiable, playing at Dolls' Shooting Lunches with Rory and Flora in their hideaway and holding Doopie's skeins of knitting yarn while she winds them into balls. He's been chaffing Melhuish about his stags, keeps asking when he's going to 'do a Sassoon' on them. Sir Philip Sassoon, apparently, has had his stags' antlers gilded so they catch the sun. Shudders from Melhuish. I think it a rather wonderful idea.

I said, 'I think I'd like to know Sir Philip Sassoon.'

George said, 'You mean you haven't met him? Violet, what are you thinking of?'

She said, 'But we never see him. I see Sybil, of course. She's on my Blood Bank committee, but Philip, almost never.'

George said, 'Well, *I* shall introduce you, directly we get back to London.'

I said, 'And where do Sir Philip and Lady Sybil live?'

'Oh no,' he said, 'Syb's not his wife. She's his sister. She's the Marchionesss of Cholmondeley, married to Rocksavage, but Philip's not married to anyone.'

So much the better. Sir Philip sounds much more to my taste than Viscount Minskip. Penelope says Minskip owns practically half of Yorkshire but I don't care. Whatever it is, he can keep it.

August 5, 1932

Ena of Spain has arrived, wheezing and perspiring but all smiles. She has perfect English, being an actual grand-daughter of Queen Victoria and almost raised by her. She's an ex-queen though, so there's no need for those deep curtsies that put such a strain on the knees. The ex-King isn't with her. They take separate vacations.

More thunder. More insects. Tonight's much trumpeted treat for dinner was sea trout caught by Melhuish and Ulick. 'How wonderful,' Violet kept saying. 'Only an hour out of the water!' Still a fish though, when all's said and done. I long for a filet mignon.

Ena took my hand and said she hoped we'd be friends. She said, 'Violet has been my rock and Doopie's almost like a daughter to me, so I'm going to claim you too. Then I'll have the full set!'

August 6, 1932

Ena Spain is quite gay considering the circumstances of her life. Her children are all sickly, her husband goes with actresses, and last year, when the rebels drove them out of Spain, he left without her. Ran off to Paris, leaving her to take her chances and follow with the youngest of the brood once they were healthy enough to travel. She says there were rioters ramming the palace doors with trucks and if it hadn't been for two footmen helping them slip out the back way they'd have been murdered in their beds. I wonder whether she lost her jewels. No one dresses here so it's impossible to know whether she's been reduced to paste copies.

She's especially attached to Doopie because by an extraordinary coincidence one of her sons is the same kind of dullard. His name is Hymie but they spell it with a J in Spain. She said, 'Hymie and Doopie get along so well. They understand each other perfectly. It's a pity they're not closer in age because I think they'd have made a very happy couple.'

The very idea. I told her, they must never be allowed to breed.

She said, 'I don't see why. It's not an inherited kind of deafness. And in every other respect they're just like you and me. The Greeces have an aunt with exactly the same problem and she's led a very full life.'

Penelope Blythe agrees with me that Doopie doesn't seem all there, George Lightfoot says she's sharp as a tack but deaf as a post. I'm beginning to think information has been kept from me.

August 7, 1932

It's official. Doopie is deaf. I had it out with Violet while she was dressing. I said, 'Someone might have thought to mention it to me.'

She said, 'Mother told you. I know she did. You just never listen. And anyway, it couldn't matter less. Doopie manages very well and she's perfectly happy.'

I'd just like to know when it was decided she's not an idiot.

She said, 'You're the only one who ever said she was. Things take her longer, that's all. Some things.'

I suppose now I'll be expected to apologize. Violet says there's nothing can be done about her ears. Apparently, Prince Hymie with a J tried a hearing aid, an electrical box that hung round his neck and plugged into his ears, for when he had to go to receptions, but it didn't help him at all. I'm not surprised. No one at receptions can hear anything. The only thing to do is nod intelligently and move swiftly along.

Rory says Thomas Edison, inventor of the light bulb, was also deaf. Greek aunts, ex-Prince Hymie, Thomas Edison. Suddenly deafness is all the rage.

August 8, 1932
Flora is wearing an Atora suet carton hung on a string and is playing at Hearing Aids. George Lightfoot says there's no need to apologize to Doopie for thinking her an idiot all these years because there have been many times when she's thought the same of me. What a relief.

August 10, 1932
Melhuish's sisters motored over from Birkhall for luncheon. Jinty is even sourer than Elspeth, but she lives in the far, far north so I'm unlikely to be troubled by her company again. Elspeth may be reconciled to the idea of a foreign sister-in-law, in fact I think she's rather fond of Violet, but Jinty doesn't even approve of the English, so what hope for a patriotic American? The only time she addressed me was to ask me when I'd be returning to the United States. Worried I might stick around and bag one of those spare Scottish lords, I suppose. And she looked at the jug of iced water I requested as though I'd asked for a doggy whoops to be brought to the table.

I said, 'September. I'll be going back in September.'

I hadn't realized I'd decided until I'd said it.

Tears from Flora. She fled from the table, Doopie followed her and Rory followed Doopie.

Penelope said, 'Oh Maybell, don't go. I rather thought we might be chums. You'll find things much livelier after the summer. Balls, parties. Do stay. Violet has room for you.'

But I didn't say I was going back for good. Not at all.

50

I'll simply settle my affairs, let it be known to provincialites like Nora Sedley Cordle that Maybell Brumby has gone international, and then return. And Violet's having room or not won't enter into it because I shall take a house. I'll be one of the Baltimore Belles who are making their mark on London.

August 11, 1932
A boot boy has gone by bicycle down to Aboyne with a wire to Fishbone & Strong. I've instructed them to find a good tenant for Sweet Air. Flora is happy. She's been dancing up and down the Long Gallery singing, 'Aunt Bayba's staying for ever!'

Penelope seems very pleased too. She says there's a house that may be coming up across from them in Cadogan Square. I don't know. I'll have to see if it's my kind of neighborhood.

The Anstruther-Brodies have arrived, which signals the start of the shooting party. The quarry is a small bird called grice.

August 12, 1932
The guns went out early, Ailsa Anstruther-Brodie among them. It was all too obvious at dinner last night that Melhuish is very smitten. He kept gushing about her being a first-rate shot and bounding across the room to light her cigarette. It all seems to sail over Violet's head.

Everything now revolves around the shooting, even luncheon, so one has the choice of piling into motors and joining the guns, or going hungry. Even Viscount Minskip has been forced to reschedule his daily battle. Two long tables had been taken up to the moor and set with china and flatware kept especially for these occasions. Shooting lunches, they're called. The whole thing must be an enormous strain on Violet's struggling staff and it would be altogether simpler if sandwiches were sent up in a shooting brake and the rest of us were left in peace, but no. Ladies, children and Minskip at one table, men, loaders, beaters, and Ailsa Anstruther-Brodie at the other. Stag pie and salad and a cake decorated with flaked almonds which Rory calls Toenail Cake.

Jane Habberley is now sucking up to me, asking my advice about watercolor painting, feeling pangs of guilt about my tango record, I hope.

August 13, 1932
I now know everything there is to know about shooting parties. The guns come in at five and talk of nothing but the day's bag. More than sixty birds were taken today which means we shall be eating them till kingdom come, but at least it will make a change from fish. The guns also dash away after one Scotch whisky, help themselves to all the hot water, then commandeer the conversation at dinner. Weather prospects, heather bugs, gamekeepers droller than Beatrice Lillie, dogs smarter than Alfred Einstein.

Next year I shall summer with my own kind of people. The raspberries here are delicious, however.

Weather close and thundery. Poor Ena Spain is suffering. She perspires even on a cold day. Her age, I suppose. She'll be moving on to Balmoral on Tuesday. 'Home from home,' she calls it. She's been there every summer of her life. She said, 'Well, no one ever dared question it. Grandmama loved Balmoral, and wherever she went we followed. She never let Mama out of her sight. Even visited her on her honeymoon! But Mama doesn't come anymore. She had her fill of it, and she doesn't care for travel. She prefers to stay put.'

Ena's mother is Princess Baby, still going strong, with an apartment at Kensington Palace and a house on the Isle of Wight.

Violet said, 'And is she still beavering away at her diaries?'

Ena said, 'She is. Almost finished, I think.'

I told her I keep a diary.

'Well,' she said, 'these aren't Mama's own diaries. They're Grandmama's.'

Princess Baby is apparently going through Queen Victoria's diaries, taking out anything that might cause offense and rewriting them in fresh notebooks. It's called editing.

I said, 'No one had better change *my* diaries after I'm gone. I'll be very cross.'

Violet said, 'Maybell, rest assured, nobody will be interested in your diary.'

August 14, 1932

Rain beating against the windows all night, heavy snoring from Anstruther-Brodie who is in the room below mine and then, just as I'd dropped off to sleep, doors banging as the early birds went down to breakfast. When the party breaks up on Tuesday I may try the room Jane Habberley's been occupying. She claims she sleeps like the dead when she's at Drumcanna and I believe I can live with wall-to-wall tartan, for a few nights at any rate.

An extraordinary question from Penelope. Have I managed to enjoy a little romance while I've been here? Romance!

I said, 'I already told you what I think of Tommy Minskip.'

'Well, not Minskip, obviously,' she said. 'But Habberley perhaps, or Lightfoot? You seem quite "in" with him.'

George Lightfoot is certainly the best of a bad lot, but too young. If I were in a hurry to find a beau, which I am not, I'd be looking for a man with a little silver at his temples.

I said, 'No. I haven't had a romance. Have you?'

'No,' she said. 'I put it down to the quality of the shooting. Last year they were coming in with very small bags and I found Anstruther-Brodie quite in the mood for an adventure. But this year, not a nibble. Maybe I'll make a play for Lightfoot this evening, if you're sure I won't be trespassing.'

How desperate and how dangerous. A person could so easily fall and break their neck, tiptoeing up and down those turret stairs in a state of ardor.

August 16, 1932

Penelope winked at me over the kedgeree, signaling she made a conquest last night.

She said, 'Maybell, why don't I stay and keep you company when Violet and Melhuish go to Birkhall? Fergus won't mind going on to Glendochrie without me.'

I thanked her but pointed out that everyone else is moving on today. Including George Lightfoot. More winks. Then a lot of giggling in the morning room while she had me guess who she's seduced. Not Lightfoot, because he played billiards all evening and didn't tango with her once. Not Anstruther-Brodie because that would be like reading yesterday's newspaper. And not Ralph

Habberley because he's a drip and the last man on earth. So who? Angus.

I said, 'Who is Angus?'

'Shh,' she said. 'One of the housemaids is his sister. He's the under-gillie. Isn't it a lark?' She said she found him in the rod room.

Ena Spain, Doopie, George Lightfoot, and the Anstruther-Brodies have just left for Balmoral. The Blythes and the Habberleys are meant to be going to Perthshire but a major row blew up between Penelope and Fergus as to whether she should remain here instead. I'm afraid she got no support from me.

She said, 'Oh but, Maybell, what about Minskip? What if he makes a play for you? Shouldn't you like a chaperone?'

But Minskip is on his way home, and anyway, I believe I'd have been safe in his company. The only way to get Tommy Minskip's attention is to disarrange his cavalry. And as for Penelope, I want nothing of her complications. I think a little of Penelope Blythe goes a long way.

August 17, 1932
Violet, Melhuish, and Ulick have gone to Birkhall for three days. I am in charge. I explained to the help how to make French toast and it will now be served instead of oatmeal. Rory requested sausages for dinner and Flora has asked for 'gake with lots of jam' and they're now skipping up and down the gravel sweep crying 'Hurrah! Hurrah!'

A wire from Fishbone & Strong. They have people from Kentucky keen to take Sweet Air but they'd want it by October. Can I have it ready so soon? I most certainly can. As soon as ever I'm released from duties as Favorite Aunt I shall go to London and book my passage.

August 18, 1932
A little girl called Ellen MacNab, daughter of the head keeper, overcame her shyness and ventured up the drive to play with Flora. They are much of an age. We've had great fun, dancing tangos and reels and strathspeys, all without the benefit of phonograph music.

Rory asked to speak to me privately when it was time for Ellen to leave. He said, 'Should I walk her home?'

I said, 'Would you like to?'

'Oh yes,' he said, 'but it's rather tricky. Daddy says one should always take care of ladies, but MacNab works for us and Daddy also says one should be mindful of familiarity with servants.'

I said, 'We could get one of the maids to take her.'

But he did it himself, with Flora tagging along.

He said, 'I think it was the right thing, Aunt Maybell. I was very mindful.'

August 20, 1932
Violet returned from Birkhall bringing with her Duchess Bertie York and her elder daughter. They stayed to tea. Princess Lilibet is a year younger than Flora, but very pink and white and refined. She sat neatly beside her mother for the entire visit and ate her scone without dropping a crumb. Flora, wearing Rory's kilt and an ecru lace runner from the dining-room sideboard, and for whose benefit I'm sure the call was made, glowered at her little playmate and then hid behind a curtain. The Duchess and Violet are great friends and I can see why. They're both so homely.

August 21, 1932
Tomorrow to London and a midge-free suite at Claridge's. Violet is raising objections right and left. Why

the haste? Why spend money on accommodations when I could wait only two more weeks and travel back with her to Carlton Gardens? Isn't it a rash move, giving up my home and plunging into the unknown? It says everything about the differences between us. She clings to her lists and timetables and routines, whereas I'm not afraid to seize the moment. Why the haste? Because prospective tenants with good references and no children don't grow on trees and the *Lancastria* sails on August 30. And a rash move? Well, a two-year lease hardly amounts to burning my boats, and Belgravia isn't exactly darkest Africa.

I've reminded her it was her idea I should come to London in the first place. Gay diversions and eligible beaux were the inducements, as I remember it, neither of which Violet is in any position to provide, I now realize. She thought I'd be one of those wallflower widows, eager to meet a titled simpleton, grateful to be squeezed into Lady Desborough's guest attic. Now she knows better. I shall have my own coterie before Violet can say 'agenda'.

'Well, if you're absolutely sure it's what you want, Maybell,' she keeps saying.

I am.

August 25, 1932, Claridge's Hotel, London
Violet was right about one thing. London is dead. I woke a realtor from his August slumbers and have appointments to view three houses tomorrow, one of them catty-corner from Penelope and Fergus Blythe. What a surprise Pips and Wally are going to get when they come back and find me with my own establishment.

August 26, 1932

I am taking a house on Wilton Place. It's light and very prettily done out in the palest greens and blues. More important, the owners are Americans, so it has a good efficient furnace and a Kelvinator icebox. I didn't like the aspect of the Cadogan Square property and the one in Eaton Mews was too close for comfort to Melhuish's sister Elspeth. The last thing I need is her training the Rear Admiral's telescope on my front door.

September 2, 1932, RMS *Lancastria*

The ocean is as calm as a soup dish and I have unexpected company. The Erlangers came on board at the very last moment and I bumped into Hattie as I was taking a turn on deck this morning. She had a friend with her, Daisy Fellowes, and they were on their way to the gymnasium. They begged me to join them but I preferred to sit with a cup of bouillon and my own thoughts. They said they were going to bicycle all the way to New York and went off shrieking with laughter. It seemed too early in the day for them to be tight.

September 3, 1932

Judson tells me Hattie's friend Daisy Fellowes is immensely rich. From what I saw of her at dinner last evening she's certainly made inroads into the world's supply of pink diamonds. He's in a nice gossipy mood. He thinks Wally must have stampeded Ernest into marriage because he has the look of a man who's not quite sure where he is or what he's doing there.

I said, 'I think the appeal of Ernest was he was effectively a free ticket to London and a fresh start.'

He said, 'Yes, that makes sense. She'd fouled the nest too much to stay in Baltimore.'

He goes on and on about what a great girl Hattie is. Had he told me just once I'd have believed him, but three times leads me to think it's himself he's trying to convince. I find her gratingly tall.

September 8, 1932, Sweet Air, Baltimore
Sweet Air was bathed in sunlight as I arrived and it feels so roomy and bright after those London houses with their rooms stacked higgledy-piggledy four and five floors high. I almost picked up the telephone and told Fishbone to call everything off. But it is too big for me in my present circumstances. Too big, too quiet, too remote from invigorating company. I've grown accustomed to nightlife and the rattle of London trams. Also, Missie says Junior's wife stops her car outside every day and peers through the gates up to my pleasure porch. If I stayed she and Junior would surely rob me of my peace of mind and destroy my health.

September 19, 1932
The last of my boxes has gone and the ticker-tape machine has been removed, my final reminder of Brumby. Whatever Junior may say, we were contented. I didn't bother him and he didn't bother me, at least not in recent times.

I've put Nora Sedley Cordle out of her misery. She's been making hay in my absence, hosting musical soirees and raising funds for the veterans' hospital, and must have been anxious about my returning home, worried I'd confiscate her new little empire. By a great stroke of luck she arrived at Klein's just as the boy was loading my furs into the car. I said, 'Hello, Nora, and goodbye. You know, I find Baltimore so narrow now I live in London. I wonder if we shall ever meet again.'

I've always made good exits, though I do say so myself.

September 24, 1932, RMS *Rex*
Junior and that grasping creature he calls a wife had the nerve to send a basket of fruit to my stateroom. All poisoned, I'm sure. I've donated it to the stewards' mess.

A squall is forecast for tonight.

September 25, 1932
More than a squall. The girl from the infirmary ministered to me like an angel, but there are no hair appointments until tomorrow afternoon.

September 26, 1932
Connie Thaw is on board. She claimed me in the Palm Court as I was trying to regain my sea legs. We shared a pot of tea and when she heard of my difficulties she made a call and immediately, miraculously, a hair appointment opened up.

A wire from Violet. Melhuish is sending his car to meet me when we dock and she insists on my going to Carlton Gardens until my own house is aired. How kind everyone is.

September 30, 1932, Carlton Gardens, London
Ulick and Rory have returned to their schools and the pace of London life is quickening again. Violet already has a number of invitations on her mantel. I predict that by this time next year mine will make hers look sadly bare.

She said, 'Well, now you're here, what do you plan to do?'

My feet have hardly touched dry land. I said, 'I'm going to make telephone calls, to see who's back in town, and tomorrow night I'm going to Ciro's with Pips and Freddie and the Whitlow Trillings.'

'No,' she said, 'I mean, what are you going to *do*? There are more important things in life than going to niteries.'

She underestimates me. I'm perfectly aware I have to hire a cook and a driver, and pick out new drapes for my dining room, but one can't be slaving every hour of the day. Lunch with Ida.

October 1, 1932
Ida has a new beau, acquired in a lecture hall in Tewkesbury. He's an Acolyte of the Seventh Ray, drinks only camomile tea, and is showing her the path to inner vitality. The people one meets in Gloucestershire!

Wally's back. Shopping on Monday. Her friend Lily Drax-Pfaffenhof is coming to stay, so she's splashing out on a new rug for the guest bedroom.

October 3, 1932
Heal's had a selection of perfectly adequate rugs, but Wally insisted on going to a little Persian in Sackville Street and once those people have you in their clutches they won't let go until you've seen their entire stock. Wally, of course, went to his most expensive item like a homing pigeon. 'Oh,' he said, 'a most discerning choice. A most unique rug made in a mountain village to a pattern known only to one old man.' They always say that, but Wally's impossible to turn once she's decided on a thing. She's promised to get a check sent round to me first thing tomorrow. Another jolt to Ernest's careful budget.

She said, 'Ernest will be fine about it. He'd rather stretch himself to buy something good than settle for mediocrity. We're of one mind on that. And I won't have Lily stepping

61

out of bed on to the kind of thing a grocer's wife might buy. Lily's a landgravine, you know?'

A landgravine! Further complications. No doubt there will be the expense of special dietary requirements in addition to outlay on handmade rugs.

October 4, 1932
I've engaged a butler, a cook, and two housemaids but still no driver and no satisfactory lady's maid. Penelope Blythe says there may be servants going spare at the Orr-Tweedies' since Mrs O-T passed away. She's going to inquire.

Ructions in the nursery. It's Melhuish's birthday on Thursday and Flora had the idea of giving him a party. She said, 'We can make a gake and Daddy can blow out the gandles.'

Violet said it was a sweet idea but out of the question because he's speaking on the Pheasant Bill that afternoon and then going on to a January Club dinner.

Doopie said, 'Bedvus dime?'

Violet said, 'No, Doopie. Mornings are far too hectic, especially when he's working on a speech. Don't pout, Flora. You can have a little party without him. I'll ask Smith to find you something special. Now off you skip. Mommy has to look out some papers for Lady Strathnaver.'

Doopie looked at me, but there was really nothing I could do. The poor child was clearly disappointed and I'd have taken her out to Harrold's and bought her a new dolly but I was already committed to lunch with Pips and then a manicure. By the time I got back it was too late to save Flora from herself. She'd gone into the writing room and created a snowstorm of papers, from Violet's desk and from Melhuish's, scrambling them up with her grubby little hands and tossing them in the air. The floor was still covered when I looked in, Fishermen's Orphans mixed up with Unmarried Mothers and the Hedgerows Bill. Trotman had hauled her upstairs and she'd been sent to bed without any tea.

This must surely strengthen the case for sending her to school.

October 5, 1932

Penelope Blythe has come up trumps. I've taken on Padmore, formerly lady's maid to Mrs Orr-Tweedie, and also Kettle who was her driver for nineteen years.

He drove me along Piccadilly and the Haymarket and then back by Pall Mall to Carlton Gardens and he has a pleasingly smooth technique. He also carries a kind of Boy Scout emergency box which he showed me before he stowed it in the trunk: flashlight, bandages, medicinal brandy, magnesia tablets, and a miniature sewing kit. He said, 'In case of a loose button, madam, or laddered hosiery.'

There'll be no need for that. If I ladder my stocking I shall just have him drive me home so I can change it. Still, it does show he has the right attitude.

October 6, 1932

Wilton Place is ready for me. On Saturday I shall sleep my first night there. A fresh start, and how fitting. It will be a year to the day since I lost Brumby.

George Lightfoot was in the nursery when I returned from Monsieur Jules, helping Doopie and Flora fete the absent Melhuish with a rather dry marble cake.

'Ah,' he said, 'the very girl I was hoping to see. Come with me Monday next to Philip Sassoon's. He's asked me to Park Lane to see his new majolica urns.'

Over drinks I heard Melhuish say he didn't think Sir Philip was 'quite the thing'.

Lightfoot said, 'What can you mean?'

Melhuish said, 'I don't know. He strikes me as a bit of a Johnny-come-lately. Belchester told me he has a footman serve tea. Can you imagine!'

Violet said, 'But, dearest, he does raise a great deal of money for hospitals. And we're very fond of Sybil.'

Melhuish said, 'Oh quite so. Sybil's one hundred percent. I used to play polo with her husband. Never see him nowadays of course. Seems to spend most of his time in the South of France.'

All I said was, 'Like Thelma Furness's husband.'

Violet said, 'No, Maybell. Not at all like that. Rock Cholmondeley plays in tennis tournaments.'

Well, tennis, tootsies, whatever the excuse, it sounds to me as though the South of France is teeming with restless English husbands.

October 7, 1932
To the Cocoanut Grove. Wally and Ernest brought along Lily Drax-Pfaffenhof, who turns out to be much more fun than she sounds. Her first husband was in Manchester cotton and left her stony, but fortunately she made a good second marriage to a landgrave called Willi.

Wally thinks she may know the Sassoons. When she was in Hong Kong there was a family of that name and she's almost certain she went to a party at their house, but Hattie Erlanger says it must be a different lot because Philip and Sybil are Jews from Baghdad.

Freddie said, 'Yes, Hattie, but not recently. Sassoon's been in the Commons twenty years at least.'

According to Freddie he's something important at the Air Ministry, entertains lavishly and has a reputation as a firecracker, always sparkling and fizzing and dashing between his various wonderful homes. Sir Philip Firecracker Sassoon! I can't wait.

October 8, 1932, Wilton Place

My first year without Brumby. It seems longer, so much has happened. Well, I think I've conducted my period of mourning in a decorous manner. Violet may make her disparaging remarks about niteries but even widows have to while away their evenings somehow, and I can't believe Danforth Brumby would have wanted me to cover my phonograph with black crepe.

October 9, 1932

I've suggested to Padmore that we dispense with the customary black dress and white apron and get her something more modern. Dark blue, perhaps, or dove gray. 'Whatever you think, madam,' she said. That's the ticket!

October 10, 1932

I am in love! Philip Sassoon is delicious. He's the same age as Melhuish but you'd never think it, he's so svelte and so vibrant. Also, he has exquisite taste. Blood-red roses arranged against a panel of black glass. Twinned pewter buckets filled with forests of baby's breath. He dashed around showing us everything. The drawing room, *one* of the drawing rooms, all pink and gilt and tapestries. The dining room azure and silver. Everything done with a very sure touch. Only the ballroom was too hectic for my taste, no surface left unpainted. Camel trains, palm trees, sheikhs of Araby.

'The problem with owning a ballroom,' he said, 'is that one feels an obligation to use it.'

Lightfoot sang my praises as a dancer but sadly Sir Philip doesn't dance.

He said, 'One always feels obliged to buz-z-z around like a bumble bee, pollinating one's guests with gaiety, and then, when the evening's over, the room looks hor-r-ribly like Culloden Moor.'

A location from his Baghdad period, I suppose.

I said, 'What you need is a woman to hold your balls for you.'

'Maybell!' he said, 'I think I may thr-r-reaten you with an invitation to T-r-r-ent Park.'

I said, 'Invite away! You don't f-r-r-ighten me.' How we laughed.

A small point of accuracy for Melhuish. Sir Philip does *not* have a footman serve tea. He has foot*men*. And why not!

October 11, 1932

Wally was infuriatingly vague about her plans for the day and then when I walked into the Ivy to meet Pips, there she was, tête-à-tête with Thelma Furness. They waved but made no move to invite us over to join them.

Pips says she finds it horribly entertaining to watch Wally at work. 'Spinning her web', she called it.

She said, 'Look at her. I mean, Thelma's nice in her own sappy way, but Wally can't possibly find her *that* interesting. She's just cultivating her so she can get her foot in Wales's door.'

I said, 'There are worse projects. I wouldn't mind meeting him myself. They say he's a nifty dancer.'

Pips said, 'Well, I think it's all rather desperate and sad. It reminds me of the trouble she went to to snag a dance with Chevy Auburn. Remember? Cozying up to his sister. Memorizing all his sprint times. And men are so dumb. They fall for it every time. I'll bet she worked the same old business with Ernest. I'll bet she pumped Mary Kirk for useful tidbits, filed them under "Ernest" and then fed them right back to him.'

I think Wally just uses what little God gave her. She has a very plain face, no figure, and no fortune. It stands to reason she's had to develop her wits.

Pips could have shown more interest in my tea with Philip Sassoon. All she said was, 'But isn't he a fruit?'

October 12, 1932

Penelope Blythe says a fruit is a very useful, unmarried type of man friend and she's often thought of getting one herself.

To Carlton Gardens for drinks. The Billy Belchesters were there and Leo von Hoesch popped along from the German Embassy. *So* charming, and never married. I wonder if he's a fruit too.

A note had arrived for me from young Rory, to remind me he'll soon be coming home on his mid-term vacation. He writes, *I should very much like to take you to a Tea Room but I'm rather out of funds.*

No matter. What are aunts for if not the occasional piece of pie?

I've pinned down Violet and Melhuish to come to me today week. I want to throw a little party while the Crokers are still in town.

Violet said, 'Just drinks, Maybell. Melhuish will never manage your jazzed-up food. And please, no gangsters.'

I said, 'Boss Croker is *not* a gangster.'

She said, 'Well, he sounds like one.'

I've a good mind to invite Thelma Furness.

October 20, 1932

I am launched, and to great applause! Just champagne, whiskey, and salted almonds, but Padmore served them very nicely. I believe she's thrilled with her new livery.

Came, the Crosbies, the Erlangers, George Lightfoot, the Benny Thaws, the Whitlow Trillings, the Crokers, the Fergus Blythes who brought along with them a sweet creature called Cimmie Mosley, married to a mad revolutionary, Violet and Melhuish, and Wally and Ernest. Thelma sent regrets, as did Philip Sassoon who was unable to get away from the Ministry and Leo von Hoesch who had to give a little reception for some Hohenzollerns.

I omitted to invite Ida. I didn't want her arriving with a bagful of pamphlets or, worse still, with Mr Acolyte on her arm.

Much talk about Mr Mussolini. Ernest had read that he's a great all-rounder. He plays the violin and governs his country and yet he's not above rolling up his sleeves and helping with the corn harvest. A Renaissance man, Ernest called him. Also, he's electrificating the railroads. Freddie said that will be all very fine for the Italians but not so good for the Welsh miners whose coal the Italians will stop buying. Well, I'm behind Mr Mussolini on this. One has to look out for one's own.

Melhuish allowed Wally to flirt with him wickedly on the subject of trout fishing. He was quite pink by the time he and Violet had to leave for the Londonderrys'. He said,

68

'Come to Sunday luncheon, Maybell. Bring your Simpson chums with you.'

Violet was on the telephone first thing putting paid to that.

She said, 'I really don't want Wally here on Sunday. I'm sure her husband is perfectly pleasant but she's as raucous as ever. We'll have the Habberleys, and anyway, Wally's just not the kind of guest we'd want Flora to meet. Melhuish only suggested it because you'd given him far too much whiskey.'

I said, 'Don't worry. Wally and Ernest can't come anyway. They're going to a polo tournament. But I don't see why you have to be so against her. It was you who wrote excitedly to tell me she was in London.'

Violet said, 'I did *not* write excitedly. I mentioned her as one might report the arrival of a new dancing bear at the zoo. But I didn't mean you should pay to watch it day after day and I certainly didn't mean you should bring it home.'

October 23, 1932
Wally's in a state of great excitement. She and Ernest are invited to Thelma Furness's country house for a weekend. Leicestershire. This will undoubtedly involve a long, cold train journey because everything in this country does. It's a pity Mr Mussolini isn't an Englishman.

I said, 'And will the Prince of Wales be there?'

She said, 'I don't know. I could hardly ask. But we're going to be quite prepared for it.'

Ernest has a book on etiquette and Wally's practicing her curtsies, but the main thing on her mind is clothes. My advice was to buy every item of warm underwear Gamages have on sale, and fur-lined boots too, but she's talking about new dinner gowns. Crazy. Wherever Leicestershire is you may be sure it's nowhere near the frontiers of fashion.

Hattie Erlanger says Wally and Ernest will be expected to ride. She says it's inconceivable to go to Leicestershire without a hacking jacket at the very least. Wally says that's the trouble with people like Hattie. Their minds run along narrow muddy ruts and they fail to notice that thousands of civilized people go their whole lives without ever sitting on a horse.

October 25, 1932
Yesterday to Fuller's Tea Rooms with Rory and Flora. If you want to know what's being said on the backstairs, take your nephews and nieces out to tea. Prince George goes dancing with black girls. The Duke of Westminster shouts at his new wife. And Lady Furness is getting a divorce. Funny Wally never mentioned that. I brought them back to see my new house before Kettle drove them home. Both chiefly interested in which bedrooms they would have if I were to invite them to stay the night. I don't know that I would invite them. Tea is one thing, but not the complications of bedtime stories and prayers and night lights.

November 3, 1932
Found a dear little cashmere cardigan for Wally, edge to edge with a braid trim. If she follows my advice *that's* what she'll wear to dinner in Leicestershire. As a matter of fact I think she should avoid décolletage whenever possible. She has no bosom to speak of and the skin on her back is poor.

Dinner at the Crosbies'. Anne Belchester says she's heard

Thelma Furness keeps her country house ruinously hot for good paintings. Prosper Frith said he didn't realize the Furnesses had any good paintings.

November 4, 1932
To George Lightfoot's for a small supper party. Came, the Fergus Blythes, a Commons man called Boothby, and old Lady Ribblesdale. She's the one who paid lawyers to get her a good divorce settlement from John Astor when, had she but known it, she could have waited a little longer, waved him aboard the *Titanic* and inherited everything. They say it would be a curse to see into the future but I don't imagine Ava Ribblesdale thinks so.

All evening my mind kept drifting to Wally and Ernest. I wonder whether they had dinner with the Prince of Wales.

November 8, 1932
Wally is back from Leicestershire with bronchitis. She said she felt too ill to see anyone, but what are friends for if not comforting the sick? I hurried round with a bottle of Dr Collis Browne's chlorodyne and a jar of chicken essence.

She *did* meet the Prince of Wales. Also his brother, Prince George, the one who's reported to dance with black girls. The two Princes were staying at a nearby house but motored over each day in time for luncheon and stayed till late.

She said he's short, boyish and trim, and he calls Thelma 'darling'. He didn't hunt. No one did. Mainly they played old maid and watched movies.

The big question no one dared ask is what will happen after Thelma's divorce. Connie Thaw told Wally the Prince

71

leads a dog's life, bullied by the King, chastised by the Queen. She said weekends with Thelma are the only thing he has to look forward to. It seems to me it's quite straightforward. Thelma will get her divorce, the Prince will marry her and they'll live happily ever after.

I thought Wally seemed rather flat; aside from a hacking cough she doesn't have anything to show for her trouble. All that fussing at the beauty parlor and studying newspapers for topical subjects of conversation. So she met a couple of princes? I doubt she exchanged more than two words with either of them. I think Wally's gone about as far as she can go. Perhaps I should offer to introduce her to Ena Spain.

November 10, 1932
Franklin Roosevelt is the new President. Well, I'm glad Brumby didn't live to see it. He never cared for him. Brumby was a Hoover man, through and through. 'Never vote for a lawyer, Maybell,' he advised me. 'They'll have their hands in your pocket before you can say "dollar".'

November 13, 1932
Tea at Carlton Gardens. There was an unpleasant odor in Violet's drawing room. I do hope it wasn't dear Ena Spain. She was perspiring as usual, in spite of freezing fog. Went up to the nursery and found Flora playing Divorces with her dolls.

November 15, 1932
Lunch with Lightfoot. He dined at Carlton Gardens last evening and says there was an unaccountably awful smell in the drawing room. He said, 'I thought you might

bring it up with Violet. It would be better coming from you.'

Ena Spain wasn't present, apparently, so at least she's not to blame.

November 16, 1932
Carlton Gardens is in uproar. The smell is now so bad it greets you before you reach the drawing room. When I arrived a housemaid was flicking the pelmets with a feather duster – as though something like that could be dusted away! – Melhuish was pacing the floor and Violet had even canceled her meetings. The exterminator hadn't been sent for, however. I'd have thought that was the very first thing to do.

Violet said, 'To exterminate what? We don't have rats.'

Trotman said, 'Oh yes we do, Your Ladyship. I've seen 'em the size of cats outside the scullery.'

Thank heavens I've moved out. Melhuish took umbrage at my suggestion that the prime suspects must be the dogs. He said, 'My dogs do not smell.'

Well, they most certainly do, but I didn't particularly mean the dogs themselves, rather some little gift offering one of them might have left behind. My advice to them was to have the room stripped out, ceiling to floor. Dollars to donuts they'll find a doggy whoops.

Violet says it couldn't be more inconvenient. They have the Yugoslavias coming for the weekend.

November 17, 1932
To the Paradise Club for Hattie Erlanger's birthday. She and Judson are going to Jessie Woolworth's for Christmas, in Palm Beach. Wally and Ernest are going to Landgravine

73

Lily's, Pips and Freddie are going to the Prosper Friths'. No matter. Solitude holds no fears for me. I shall have delicious little meals served on a tray and immerse myself in the great thinkers of the day.

More fog.

November 18, 1932

Violet's smell has been run to earth. George Lightfoot called me with the news this morning. Seven pieces of kipper tucked into pillow covers and down the arms of chairs. The finger has been pointed at Flora but she maintains a 'purgler' must have done it.

Lunch with Wally. Connie Thaw told her that Thelma's divorce won't mean the Prince of Wales can marry her. Someday he'll be King and there are rules about who he can marry. Well, surely the answer to that is for them to continue as they are until he becomes King. Then once he's in charge he'll be able to *unmake* inconvenient rules. I shall ask Violet.

November 20, 1932

Violet says the Prince of Wales can never marry Thelma Furness, or any other divorced person. Neither can he change the rules when he becomes King. Only Parliament can do that. I begin to wonder if there are any advantages at all to being King.

I said, 'Well, it seems hard cheese for Thelma when her husband has gone off on tiger shoots and left the door very obviously ajar.'

Violet said Melhuish enjoys a good duck-hunt when he can get it, but they've never allowed his absences to lead to moral laxity.

Flora is to be tried at Hope House School as a weekly boarder after Christmas, to see if she's suited. She's not supposed to know till nearer the time, but she does know. It was the first thing she told me when I went up to the nursery.

She said, 'I won't be suited. I'll kick someone and then they'll send me home.'

Doopie was trying to explain to me about the business with the smell in the drawing room. She kept saying, 'Vora but a bees a gibber unna share.'

School can only be a good idea.

Melhuish said, 'Peculiar thing to do. Waste of a fine smokie too. Damned if I understand it. Never had any of that kind of carry-on with the boys.'

November 23, 1932

I am invited to Philip Sassoon's birthday luncheon at Trent Park. The question is, what to buy the man who has everything.

November 25, 1932

George Lightfoot is also going to the Trent Park party. He always tries to find a bottle of some unusual and undrinkable liqueur by way of a gift, but he says Philip is very keen on ducks and suggests I think along those lines. No help at all. What does he propose I do? Go to St James's Park and capture a pair?

November 28, 1932

Lunch with Wally, Hattie Erlanger, and Gladys Trilling. When Gladys heard about my invitation to Trent Park she said, 'Oh, Sassoon! The Court Jew! They say he's fabulously generous and if you admire something in one of his houses he's more than likely to give it to you. They say Her Majesty's done terribly well out of him.'

Wally said, 'Then I think Maybell had better introduce us all.'

I shall do no such thing.

To the Army & Navy. Bought a doorstop fashioned from a mallard duck decoy, very pretty.

December 5, 1932

Trent Park is a dream. Acres of parkland, lakes, tree-lined avenues, and dozens of dusky servants who glide around silently and appear the very moment they're needed. His sister, Sybil, attended, minus husband who was away at a tennis tournament. She looks haughty, very straight-backed with iron-gray hair and rather hooded eyes, but she's really very agreeable.

'Violet's sister!' she said. 'Of course! How very naughty of Violet not to have brought you to tea.'

The other guests were Mrs Belloc Lowndes, a Polish piano player called Rubinstein plus wife, a Sassoon cousin from Paris, and two Italian airmen with whom one could only gesticulate and offer the occasional 'olé'.

We had oysters, flown up from Kent, and roast guinea fowl dressed with homegrown oranges. In Hertfordshire! Then a blue cheese made on Sibyl's estate in Norfolk and a plum pudding carried flaming and aloft by a six-foot Ethiopian in silk livery. Everything was perfect.

Lightfoot said, 'Now, will you please set the record straight. Maybell doesn't believe you have stags with gilded antlers.'

Philip said, 'Oh, but I do, and if only it weren't such a gray day, you'd see for yourself. I've trained them to note the position of the sun and waggle their heads accordingly. Syb believes animals should be left *au naturel* but my stags are all tr-r-ragedians *manqué*. They'd have been deeply unhappy left naked on a moor.'

I'm sure he's right. And I may not have seen the stags this time but I did see his black swans. Very chic! I asked him how they were kept still long enough to dye their feathers but he refused to say.

He loved his mallard doorstop. Lightfoot took him a bottle of something made from roasted melon seeds.

December 7, 1932
To Harrold's Lending Library for my Christmas reading: Ethelda Bedford, Maysie Grieg, George Bertram Shaw, Alma Sioux Scarberry. Kettle had just carried them into the house when Violet telephoned. She said, 'What is this nonsense I hear about you spending Christmas alone?'

Lightfoot has said something.

I said, 'I shall be perfectly fine. I was alone last year, except for being frogmarched to church by Randolph Putnam and receiving an unsolicited visit from Junior, and no doubt I shall be alone in the future.'

'Not as long as I draw breath,' she said. 'You'll come to Carlton Gardens and be taken out of yourself.'

December 12, 1932
The whole day in and out of the car and up and down in elevators, searching for gifts. I'm beginning to agree with Penelope Blythe, Christmas takes all the joy out of shopping and should really just be left to the lower classes.

For Ulick, a Tri-ang Fort, for Rory, an Erector Set, which I'm assured is the gift of choice for boys aged twelve, and for Flora, a Betty Boop tea service. Whiskey for Melhuish, a gay Jacquard scarf for Violet, to help modernize her look, and for Doopie a copy of *301 Things for a Bright Girl to Do*. She needs to be stretched.

To Bryanston Court for dinner. Came, the Crosbies, the decorator MacMullen, with a woman I took to be his mother, but who turned out to be Lady Elsie Mendl. Also, friends of Ernest, the Rickatson Hatts. He runs a news agency, of all things. Wally certainly keeps her pledge to seat interesting mixes around her table. Pips says Elsie Mendl is an invert and only married Charlie Mendl for his title. If it's true I must say she hides her tendencies very well. She even paints her nails. There were no hackney cabs to be had so I gave Mr and Mrs Hatt a lift to Westbourne Terrace. They were shy about accepting but, as I told them, I'm aware of the punishing hours people in their business are obliged to keep. Melhuish's *Times* is always on the breakfast table by eight o'clock.

December 14, 1932

Johnnie MacMullen is going to advise Wally on the remodeling of her apartment after Christmas. She says he's hugely talented and has done Elsie Mendl's homes from A to Z. Well, he'll need to be hugely talented to make anything of Bryanston Court. I'd love to see her move somewhere with scope but Ernest is such a stick-in-the-mud.

She agrees with me that Mrs Hatt is dull but says she endures her because the husband is always good for whiling away an evening with Ernest. They often have macaroni cheese and peruse the Greek ancients, leaving her free to come dancing.

The Hatts' little shop is called Reuters but Wally has no idea where it is.

December 17, 1932

A festive evening at the Benny Thaws'. They had an adorable little chorale of children to sing us carols around the Christmas tree, American children from the compound, with proud deportment and straight teeth. It caused me a flicker of nostalgia for Sweet Air. Just a flicker.

Rory and Ulick are home from school.

December 23, 1932

Violet says luncheon will be served at twelve-thirty sharp on Christmas Day so the kitchen maids can get away to visit their mothers. It's going to make for a very long afternoon, unless of course we're expected to take our tea at three so the rest of the help can go gallivanting to Essex. I don't know why I don't just take us all to Claridge's.

December 24, 1932

Violet says they always do things this way, it suits them very well and this is how children learn about their responsibilities to servants. Before the family meal is served Melhuish goes below stairs to say a few words and carve the first slice of the servants' goose and this year Ulick will go with him, to see how it's done. She says we can have tea whenever we choose because Doopie will have charge of it, so as to allow Smith the rest of the day off.

All the more reason to go to Claridge's.

A greetings card from Randolph Putnam. His mother passed away. And I am missed in Baltimore. Of course.

December 26, 1932

The best-laid plans. Rory claimed Flora's tea service and performed a very clever trick with overturned cups and disappearing sugar lumps, Flora was only interested in

Rory's Erector Set, and Ulick remained disappointingly aloof from his fort. It would have remained in its box if Lightfoot and Doopie hadn't begun playing with it.

Violet gave me a calendar.

'So you can organize your time,' she said. 'You'll see the weeks laid out before you and be able to think how best to fill your days productively.'

Rory gave me a rough-hewn letter rack, made in his handicrafts class, Lightfoot gave me a coffret of candy, and Flora gave me a pink satin letter M, stitched quite nicely and filled with padding.

Violet said, 'How clever. Is it a scented sachet?'

'No,' said Flora, 'it's an M. We made it out of old ploomers.'

Elspeth and Salty Laird looked in during the afternoon. Elspeth said, 'Now, Flora, are ye looking forward to being a big girl and going to Hope House?'

Flora closed her eyes. She does that when you say something she doesn't want to hear. She gets that from Doopie.

Rory said, 'You'll like it when you get there, Flora. You'll make friends. And have cocoa every night. I used not to want to go to school but you get used to it, you see, and then it's really good fun.'

She said, 'Then I'll come to your school.'

Ulick said, 'You can't. You're a girl.'

She said, 'Well, I shan't stay at Hope House. I shall run away.'

Elspeth said, 'Do ye know what happens to girls who run away, Flora? The bogeyman comes after them and they're never seen again.'

Doopie and Lightfoot both got her with the peashooter cannons.

Ulick said, 'I really wonder why we're bothering with

all this. Why not have her taught at home until it's time for her to be finished? That's what they did with Pentlow's sister and she's now out and practically engaged to Gore-Cummings. Education seems to me to be quite wasted on girls.'

January 2, 1933
Gala night at the Savoy last night. Pips and Freddie, the Prosper Friths and Ida with an old Venezuelan *flâneur*. She said, 'Oh Maybell, no date?' I said, 'Oh Ida, no taste?' She was putting away Manhattans all night, so I guess she has tired of Mr Acolyte and camomile tea.

January 7, 1933
Wally and Ernest are back from the Alps. Landgravine Lily's house party had been quiet. Just the Benny Thaws, a couple called Rothschild, and Crown Princess Cecilie, a sad remnant of German royalty.

Ernest has a carbuncle on his neck. Wally needs dental work. She said, 'Don't you hate January? Nothing ever happens.'

Lunch tomorrow.

January 9, 1933
I'd given up on Wally and was about to order when she sauntered into the Fountain Room in that skimpy little mink of hers smiling like the cat that's had the cream. She said she was sorry to be late but had been delayed by an important telephone call from Connie Thaw. 'You see,' she said, taking forever to sit down and then starting to

nibble on a celery stick in the most annoying way, 'Ernest and I are invited to Fort Belvedere for the weekend. By the Prince of Wales.'

I'm very happy for her of course. This is something she's worked for tirelessly. I just hope she understands that the invitation doesn't spring from any desire on the part of the Prince of Wales. I'm sure he doesn't even remember who they are. But I expect he allows Thelma a certain number of her own friends and she and Wally seem to have hit it off. They're always screaming with laughter about something.

I said, 'But Ernest always seems to spend his weekends shuffling business papers. Are you sure he'll be allowed to take time off?'

She said, 'Of course he can. Ernest's a director, not an employee.'

If that's the case I wonder he doesn't open the safe and bring home a little more money. There are things she's going to need, but she said she'd better wait till tomorrow, till Ernest has agreed a budget. It only leaves her Wednesday and Thursday for all that shopping, not to mention hair, facials, and nails. What an impossible way to live. I offered her Kettle, to take them down to Windsor and bring them back on Sunday. It seemed the least I could do.

She said, 'Maybell, you're such a treasure. The thing about Ernest's car is, his driver doesn't like to work on Sundays.'

The thing about Ernest's car is, it isn't a Bentley.

January 11, 1933
Dinner at the Crosbies'. The Whitlow Trillings, Prosper and Daphne Frith, and Freddie Birkenhead. Everyone

83

very exercised about what Roosevelt may be planning to do with the gold standard. When I asked Mr Birkenhead if I had any cause for concern, he said, 'It rather depends how many double eagles you have under your mattress,' but gave no clue as to whether having them would be a good thing or bad. I may drop a line to Randolph Putnam.

Gladys Trilling said blizzards are forecast for tomorrow. Pips said, 'Friends of ours are going to Fort Belvedere for the weekend. I hope they'll be able to get through.'

Prosper said, 'Fort Belvedere! They'd be better off staying at home. Wales invites all kinds of nonentities. Get snowed in there, one could be sorry. Mediocre little house too. The kind of place someone who'd done well in trade might go for.'

Birkenhead said, 'Well, that's Wales really. Small and mediocre.'

January 12, 1933
Wally has borrowed a ruby choker from Pips. I'm not supposed to know. Cold, but no snow.

January 13, 1933
To the Fergus Blythes'. George Lightfoot came with a girl with a jutting jaw called Belinda, not at all pretty. Penelope Blythe says the Prince of Wales generally wears a kilt in the evening and keeps his cigarette case in his sporran. Lightfoot says he likes to embroider after dinner and could bore for England. Well, I'm sure that after a week of ceremonial splendor all he craves is the quiet life. I just hope Wally remembers not to try too hard. She does so love to outshine everyone.

January 16, 1933

Kettle had instructions to bring Wally and Ernest back here so I could hear all about their weekend, but he returned with an empty car, Ernest having business papers to attend to and Wally being in pain from her ulcers. That's what comes of starving yourself into new dinner gowns.

I caught Ernest on the telephone. Wally was in bed and not to be disturbed. He said, 'We've had a thoroughly enjoyable time, but it would be indiscreet of me to say more.'

Pompous ass.

January 17, 1933

Wally recovered enough to be lunching with Thelma Furness and Connie Thaw, but not to have called me, and not a word of thanks for the use of my car and driver. She said, 'Well, of course we're grateful, Maybell, but we didn't *ask* for your car. You almost insisted on our taking it. But do stop sulking, I want to tell you all about our weekend.'

Tea tomorrow.

January 18, 1933

Wally says Fort Belvedere is comfortable, full of good furniture and generously hung with Canalettos, but lacking a woman's touch, except in the love nest itself where Thelma had been allowed a free hand with pink silk. Also that the Prince did wear a kilt to dinner and has good legs.

She said, 'David's very informal. He even mixes his own drinks.'

So already it's 'David'. She says she only *refers* to him as David. When she addresses him she calls him 'Sir'.

She said, 'He is the future King, Maybell. Never forget that.'

January 20, 1933
Freddie Crosbie, Judson Erlanger, Fergus Blythe, and Whitlow Trilling have gone to Klosters, so Pips is giving a ski-widows lunch party. Do I think she should also invite Wally Simpson and Ida Coote? Well, ordinarily I'd say no, because Wally demands opinions of people and tries to belittle them with her grasp of current affairs and the only thing Ida brings to the table is a love life peopled by freaks, but on this occasion I think the case for two extra Americans is strong. Hattie Erlanger and Gladys Trilling can be so overbearing, braying on about people one neither knows nor cares about, ancient British families who've been lords of the manor since the Stone Age.

January 26, 1933
Penelope Blythe and Ida Coote got along famously yesterday. They both have men on the brain. I ought to have thought of introducing them sooner. Wally sparred with Gladys, each trying to outdo the other with inside information about the domestic arrangements of royalties. What a pity Violet didn't attend. I'm sure she could have topped them both.

February 5, 1933
Tea at Carlton Gardens, where I was most surprised to find Flora, sent home from Hope House. She had apparently taken to lying on the floor and holding her breath until blue in the face, so the school nurse advised withdrawing her before she damaged her brain. Too late for that, I fear. The situation is to be reviewed after Easter.

Mr Adolf Hitler has been hired as the new Chancellor of Germany. Melhuish says this can only be a good thing because a properly run Germany is all that stands between us and world Communism. How worrying.

A delicious new nail polish from Elizabeth Arden.

February 6, 1933

Lunch with Pips. She thinks getting in with Thelma and the Prince has turned Wally's head. She said, 'I can hear that brain of hers whirring away. I reckon she's out to scalp herself a duke at the very least.'

I said, 'What about Ernest?'

'Ernest?' she said. 'Oh please!'

But Pips doesn't know Wally like I do. All she ever wanted was to rise above that awful mother of hers, to settle down and have nice things, and in his modest way Ernest has made that possible. Now she's making her contribution, using her wits and vivacity to carry them into higher circles. I find them a very well-suited couple. And as for snagging a duke! Wally has certain talents but I feel entitled to say, as a friend who knows her better than any, beneath all that careful grooming she's still far too coarse to be a duchess.

February 8, 1933

A crisis at Bryanston Court. Ernest has gone to New York on business and left Wally seriously short. She says it's all a silly mix-up but her cook is threatening to quit and anyway there's the humiliation of it. She's meant to be giving a dinner for Lily Drax-Pfaffenhof and her friends the Eugene Rothschilds, and what's she supposed to do? Offer them bread and water? If she didn't have me to turn to she'd be in an impossible position.

Randolph Putnam writes that I have nothing to fear from Franklin Roosevelt. He says Brumby Steel and Chemical has weathered the worst of things and is in good health thanks to our Burma operations. He says my adventurous attitude to life has made him think of visiting London himself sometime. I do hope not. I haven't come all this way to see his shiny face beaming at me across a crowded Grill Room. I've written back immediately to warn him that London is wet and sooty.

Ten to dinner tonight. Philip Sassoon, Wally, Pips and Freddie Crosbie, Anne and Billy Belchester, Fergus and Penelope Blythe, George Lightfoot.

February 9, 1933

My dining room looked superb last evening. Ivory candles, Brussels lace laid over a gold undercloth. Mushrooms on toast, saddle of lamb, nougat parfait. I could see Wally noting every detail.

All the talk was of Mr Hitler. Freddie says he's the man to destroy the Communists, root and branch. George Lightfoot predicts the working man will rise up, but as Freddie says, with six million unemployed the working man will do well to keep his nose to the grindstone. Wally said England has nothing to fear from German rearmament. It was the French and the Poles who appropriated all that German soil so they're the ones who'd better watch out. I noticed a little twitch in dear Philip's cheek. He has tribes of French cousins. He said nothing but I don't think he took to Wally. I must make sure not to mix them in future.

Belchester said if Adolf Hitler wants to reduce the number of men out of work he can advise him exactly how to do it. One million can be set to paint the Black

Forest white, one million can be sent to lay linoleum along the Polish corridor, and another million can busy themselves building a one-way railroad to Jerusalem. Much hilarity over this, but by my reckoning that would still leave three million. Philip was very quiet all evening. He pleaded a sore throat and left early. I believe he may be the kind of man who only sparkles in his own milieu.

February 15, 1933
Flora's birthday. Her ninth. Gave her a silver-mounted hairbrush with her initials. Now someone needs to get her into the habit of using it. To a matinee performance of *Giselle* with Lightfoot, Doopie, and Flora. He's Flora's godfather and Doopie is one of her godmothers, so he takes them to a ballet every year. Of course, if Doopie's as deaf as they say she is, it seems rather a waste. Flora was in a very cheery mood and properly dressed too for a change, in a good wool pinafore and Mary Janes. There's talk of a day school after Easter, but it's to be sprung on her at the last moment.

She quite stuck to my side all afternoon, one hand in mine, the other clutching her hairbrush. She said, 'I wish you could be my other gobmother instead of Aunt Elsbeth.'

February 16, 1933
Have loaned Wally my sable. She's going to Leicestershire, to Thelma Furness's and will surely freeze without a decent fur.

To the Florida Club with Judson and Hattie, Pips and Freddie. Pips said, 'Typical Wally. She hates country, she hates horses, but she'll go and endure it because she just might meet someone useful. I'm telling you, she's on the prowl for someone with a title.'

Hattie said, 'The idea is beyond bizarre. She doesn't even ride. And why would any man look at her twice? She always looks so . . . corseted. And that frightful grimacing mouth. I mean, she's quite fun, but really . . . Anyway, no one important ever *goes* to the Furness house. One simply sniggers about it.'

February 20, 1933
According to the maid, Wally and my sable have gone direct from the country to the Cedars, for mud baths and facials. She might have asked.

Tonight to the Yugoslavs'. I shall have to wear my mink.

February 23, 1933
Wally says the Cedars wasn't her idea. She got dragged along by Thelma and Connie but is glad she went because she feels greatly rejuvenated. She described the weekend as low-key and cozy. She met some new people, the Bernie Cavetts from New Jersey, Humphrey Butler who equerries for fun-loving Prince George, and the Perry Brownlows who have a house near Thelma's. And the Prince of Wales joined her by the fireside and chatted to her for half an hour at least. She says she wasn't a bit nervous.

She said, 'I didn't even think about it. I was just myself, Maybell. I just treated him like I would any other interesting man.'

I bet she didn't.

She said, 'Strictly between you and me, I think he finds Thelma rather limited. She's sweet, but she doesn't have any conversation, and His Royal Highness has a wide-ranging mind. He wants to know about the lives of ordinary people and who better to enlighten him on that subject than me.'

She'd even told him about her mother's boarding house.

She said, 'He was fascinated. He's never met anyone like me before, not socially. He found it refreshing.'

Perhaps so, but I don't think Ernest will thank her for making such a feature of her regrettable background.

Philip Sassoon's sister has invited me to a musical soiree.

February 26, 1933
To tea at Carlton Gardens. Duchess Bertie York was there with Ena Spain and a couple of Greek princesses who never smile.

Flora was allowed down briefly to say 'Good day'. She doesn't appear to be using her new hairbrush.

February 27, 1933
To Sibyl Cholmondeley's. Her husband Rock was present, charming and dashingly handsome but impatient to get away, it seemed. He kept popping open his Hunter to check the time. And dear Philip wasn't able to attend, being horribly busy with something called Air Estimates. Lucky Philip. It was such a long program and then, as if we hadn't had quite enough, one of Sybil's cronies asked Mr Rubinstein for an encore, as if he needed any further encouragement. It didn't seem to occur to them that some of us had had a strenuous day and still weren't finished. I had the Erlangers and the Trillings waiting for me at the Paradise Club.

February 28, 1933
The German parliament has been burned down by Red agitators. Boss and Ethel Croker are taking a house for Royal Ascot this year and I am invited, as are Wally and Ernest. I'll just keep the information up my sleeve until

Violet starts talking about squeezing me into Lady Desborough's attic. Ernest is expected home at any moment and the sooner the better. Wally's going to need gowns, hats, everything.

March 4, 1933
Lunch with George Lightfoot. He was at the Century Club last night and saw Wally and Ernest at the Prince of Wales's table. Poor Ernest. He's not a night person at the best of times and he's only been back on dry land for five minutes.

March 6, 1933
Five hours of shopping. We've decided on a soft bias-cut for summer, which we'll follow with a more tailored look for the fall. Wally is *so* particular. She examines linings and seams practically with a magnifying glass. She says if she had my money she'd have everything hand-finished. Our needs are different, of course. I have a womanly figure and a pretty face. I'd look good in a sugar sack, whereas Wally has to rely on good window dressing. At any rate, Ernest is so thrilled by their growing closeness to the Prince of Wales that he's lifted the latch on his cash box and told Wally to buy whatever she needs.

We didn't even stop for lunch and then she dashed away in a cab. She's suddenly very assiduous about being at home with a welcoming drinks tray when Ernest comes in from business. That's the deal, I suppose. She's paying for her Ascot gowns with wifely attention.

Called in at Carlton Gardens. Violet was running out to a Soup Kitchen committee. She said, 'You should come with me. Do something useful. This has been a hard winter, Maybell. People are cold and hungry.'

Well, I was in no condition. I'd been on my feet since ten o'clock.

I said, 'I'll write you a check. I'm going up to the nursery to have tea with Flora and Doopie.'

She said, 'Then be aware that Flora is being punished. She stuck out her tongue at Lady Londonderry, so be stern with her and please don't give her candy.'

I must say Flora seemed to have forgotten she was in disgrace. We found some chocolate in my purse and made chocolate sandwiches and then she and Doopie danced *Giselle* for me in their bedroom slippers. I don't think chocolate counts as candy. Chocolate is chocolate.

March 10, 1933

Dinner at Judson and Hattie Erlanger's. According to Pips, Hattie's family owns much of Eccleston Square. All the more regrettable then that she doesn't invest some of her wealth in getting her teeth straightened. And why don't the English keep their diamonds clean?

The talk turned to Wally. I only mentioned that she longs to be presented at court and Gladys Trilling practically leapt out of her seat. She said, 'Oh, but that can never happen. Surely Wally and Ernest are both divorced?'

According to Gladys and Hattie, divorce is death to any court ambitions.

I said, 'What about Thelma Furness? She's about to get her second divorce but that doesn't seem to deter the Prince of Wales.'

Hattie said, 'There's all the difference in the world between sharing Wales's bed and being brought into the presence of Their Majesties and I'm sure Thelma Furness has always understood her position.'

If that's the case I'm surprised she hasn't explained it

to Wally. They're such friends these days they must surely commiserate with each other about the taint of divorce. How frustrating. A youthful error with Win Spencer and now Wally's greatest desire is forever beyond her reach. Well, *I'm* not going to be the one who tells her.

March 14, 1933
Philip Sasson has invited me to Port Lympne for Easter. A *fête champêtre*! Whatever it is, I can't wait.

March 16, 1933
The most extraordinary thing. I was with Wally at Bryanston Court early last evening when the door opened and in walked the Prince of Wales. He said, 'You didn't invite me, but here I am anyway.'

Wally didn't miss a beat. She said, 'Why, sir! I hope you know you're welcome anytime. We're very informal tonight, just an old school friend, Maybell Brumby.' She was pulling faces at me behind, reminding me to curtsy. She doesn't understand that when I was at Carlton Gardens Violet had royalties trooping through on an almost daily basis.

His Royal Highness has very blue eyes and a rather high-pitched voice.

'Brumby?' he said. 'A big name in Baltimore, I seem to remember. Iron, was it?' Iron, coal, nickel, cobalt, silver, bauxite. Wherever it was in the world Danforth Brumby would find it and have it grubbed out of the ground and turned into dollars.

I said, 'Yes, sir, Brumby Steel and Chemical, founded by my late husband. And you may have heard of my late father too. John Patterson was a legend for his worker housing.'

'Is that so?' he said. 'Well, you must tell me about it someday. I'm awfully keen on worker housing.'

Wally didn't like that. She thinks she's the only one who knows how to draw people out. She thinks I'm just a pretty face.

The Prince made us all Scotch and sodas, very much at home. He'd obviously done it before. Wally's a sly one. He told us about his week. He'd been in the North cheering up paupers. Wally plying him with questions, but he really wanted to know about me, what brought me to London.

I said, 'Well, funnily enough, sir, *you* did. I came last year, after my bereavement, to visit my sister Violet. And if it weren't for you, I very much doubt my sister would be here. If you hadn't gone to Sulphur Springs with Donald Melhuish all those years ago, Violet wouldn't have met him and married him and moved to London. So in a roundabout way you're entirely responsible.'

He has a funny little laugh.

'Melhuish!' he said. 'Of course! When was that?'

It was 1919.

He said, 'And you're Violet Melhuish's sister? Remarkable! You look nothing like her. A fine soldier, Melhuish. We were together at Verdun, you know?'

When Ernest came home he didn't seem particularly surprised to find the Prince of Wales sitting on his couch, so I wonder how long this has been going on. Great shows of affability, but I believe I noticed Ernest relax when the Prince said he couldn't stay to dinner.

He said, 'No, Ernest. As comfortable as I am, I can't stay, not even for Wally's goulash. I have to dine with Their Majesties.'

He kissed Wally on the cheek as he left.

She said, 'Oh Maybell, your face when the Prince walked in! I wish I could have snapped it.'

I said, 'You might have warned me. You were obviously expecting him.'

She said, 'Not really. He's dropped by a few times, but he never calls ahead.'

I said, 'You didn't even tell me he'd been here. Why the big secret? You were shouting it from the rooftops when he invited you to Fort Belvedere.'

Ernest said, 'We certainly did not. We've always been discreet about our friendship, and so must you be. Please don't go telling all and sundry about this evening. His Royal Highness feels at home here, thanks to Wally. She has the right touch. Clever girl.'

So that's why she's been shopping with such abandon. Ernest's paid her a good dividend for hauling in the Prince of Wales. Well, their secret is safe with me. Apart from Pips and Violet I won't tell a soul. And Hattie, of course.

March 17, 1933

I made a point of speaking to Melhuish on the telephone this morning. He said, 'You've missed Violet. She had a meeting at nine and then she's going directly to the Habberleys'. We're there for the weekend.'

I said, 'It was you I wanted. I was with the Prince of Wales last evening and he most particularly asked to be remembered to you.'

Stopped him in his tracks. 'Wales?' he said. 'Really? Were you at the Belchesters'?'

I said, 'No, at the Ernest Simpsons'.'

'Simpson, Simpson?' he said. 'Know the name, but can't place him.'

I said, 'You met him at my soiree. He was in the Guards

and his wife is called Wally. She talked to you about salmon flies. She was a school friend, but these days Violet disapproves of her.'

He said, 'Does she? Well, Vee's a good judge of people. As for Wales, these days I'm not entirely sure how sound he is. We had a good war together, but he doesn't appear to have done much since. From what I hear all he does nowadays is plague his tailor and run his valets ragged. He's a bloody clotheshorse, Maybell. If you ask me we're going to get a dandy for a king.'

It says it all. The Prince is so modern and unstuffy, and Melhuish is so set in his ways. How left behind he must feel.

Stood Wally lunch at the Dorch. Penelope Blythe came to our table and said, 'Oh Wally, I hear His Royal Highness is back from Northumberland. How is he?' I could have killed her. I'd sworn Pips and Hattie to absolute secrecy.

Wally doesn't seem as anxious about things as Ernest, though. She said, 'Well, of course, *nothing* the Prince of Wales does goes unnoticed. And why shouldn't he call in on friends at the cocktail hour?'

I said, 'I suppose what's remarkable is that he comes to an address like Bryanston Court.'

'Not at all,' she said. 'That's the kind of Prince he is.'

The Erlangers want me to dinner. The Trillings are begging me. Pips absolutely insists on having me. Wally's schedule may suddenly be full but they know they can get the story from me, and without earnest Ernest, sucking on his pipe and pontificating about discretion.

March 20, 1933
To the Crosbies'. The Prosper Friths were there, also the Erlangers and the Belchesters. Billy Belchester said it didn't

surprise him to hear that the Prince of Wales had taken up with people in the suburbs. He said, 'It'll be his latest fad. That's Wales all over. Picks things up and then drops them. I hope your Simpson friends are prepared for that.'

Freddie said, 'Still, I think it was very astute of Maybell to get him on to worker housing. He's not the easiest of conversationalists but that is a subject dear to his heart. Golf too.'

Prosper Frith said it was all very well for Wales to be keen on worker housing when he didn't have to find the money for it. He said, 'Ask me, he should attend to his own affairs. Cut ribbons. Settle down and produce an heir. Leave politicking to those who understand it.'

Daphne Frith said, 'Well, I'd hate to have royalties suddenly proposing themselves for cockers. It'd be such a strain, always being prepared.'

Not for Wally, of course. Being prepared is what she does best. I do wonder about Violet and Melhuish, though. The Prince is so agreeable I can't think why they allowed the friendship to wither. Tea parties with the Bertie Yorks are all very well but Wales is the one who'll be King someday.

Freddie says he's also very strong on pithead baths.

March 21, 1933
To Harrold's Lending Library. They had nothing on pithead baths.

March 22, 1933
Lunched with Wally. The Prince of Wales has asked after me!

She and Ernest had dinner with him last evening at the Benny Thaws'. She said, 'He loves Americans, you know.

He finds us much more in tune with his thinking than those English stuffed shirts. And he's often at a loose end in the evening, especially when Thelma's in the country. Really, if we want him, he's ours for the taking.'

She's talking about offering him a dinner. Not a potluck with just her and Ernest, but a proper dinner where he can meet lively Americans. With only a cook and two maids it sounds overambitious to me. Wilton Place would be far more suitable, but she didn't like my saying so.

She said, 'I can manage perfectly well at Bryanston Court, thank you, and the Prince feels at home there. Obviously I'll get in extra help. But don't be disappointed, Maybell, if you're not invited. The guest list will be out of my hands. That's the protocol, you see. David will have to approve everything.'

Minnehaha Warfield lecturing me on protocol!

March 27, 1933
Lunch with George Lightfoot who didn't seem at all interested in the Simpsons and the Prince. He said, 'It's no great coup, Maybell. I could introduce you to any number of people who spend their lives avoiding royalties. They're costly to maintain and have the habit of encouraging familiarity, then suddenly frowning on it. Befriending them is like venturing on to creaking ice.'

Flora is in trouble again. Violet took her to an outfitter to buy her clothes for starting at Miss Hildred's Day School after Easter and when they got home with their purchases Flora hacked her new straw hat to pieces with Doopie's sewing scissors.

Lightfoot said, 'I'm afraid it won't save her from Miss Hildred's, though. She's going, bonnet or no bonnet. It's a shame really. I shall miss her singular ways. It's not often a child reaches the age of nine without being tamed.'

Disappointed to find he's not coming to Philip Sassoon's at Easter. We could have traveled together. He was invited but had already accepted for something in Gloucestershire. The girl named Belinda with the jutting jaw.

I said, 'Are you in love with her?'

'No,' he said, 'not noticeably.'

April 2, 1933

To Carlton Gardens. The boys are home from school. I'd promised Rory we'd go to a cartoon theater this vacation, but now we have the complication of Flora who was meant to come with us but is in the doghouse. He was pleading Flora's case with Violet and Flora was doing nothing to help herself, sitting on the stairs shouting, 'I'm not going to Miss Dread's and I'm not wearing a banama hat.'

Ulick said, 'It seems very clear to me that she hasn't yet learned her lesson. It'll do her no good at all to be let off scot-free. Melhuishes know how to take their punishment like a man.'

Rory said, 'But she's a girl. And if she can't come to see *The Three Little Pigs* I shan't feel decent about going.'

To be resolved.

April 4, 1933

Saw Lightfoot on my way to Monsieur Jules. He says Rory took his appeal to the House of Lords, but Melhuish told him he never overturns Violet's decisions.

He said, 'The only thing I can suggest is that I play the Christian mercy card. I am her gobfather after all. I'll see what I can do.'

April 5, 1933
Violet has agreed a compromise. Flora will be allowed to come out with Rory for a high tea, but there will be no cartoons until she has behaved herself for a full term at school. Lightfoot said, 'There are conditions, of course. We're not to indulge her too much or in any way let her forget her misdemeanors. I've asked Doopie to make sure we don't smile too much.'

I don't see why Doopie always has to tag along on these occasions.

April 7, 1933
To Ruddle's for a fried-fish supper. Flora behaved impeccably. I don't know why Violet has such problems with her.

Rory asked about Wally. I said, 'You may very well see her yourself at Easter. You'll be at Windsor and she'll be just along the road, at Fort Belvedere with the Prince of Wales.'

'Gosh,' he said, 'even though she's poor? Are you going too?'

I said, 'No, I'm going to Kent to stay with Sir Philip Sassoon.'

'Oh,' he said, 'the gaudy Semite.'

Lightfoot said, 'I say, Rory! Where did that come from?'

'Ulick,' he said, 'after Aunt Maybell told us he gave her luncheon on a lapis lazuli table. Ulick said he's a gaudy Semite and not our kind of person.'

Doopie not following things at all, looking perplexed, asking Lightfoot over and over, 'Who Horty Zeemide?'

We should leave her at home really. She never does well in restaurants.

Flora said, 'Gaudy Semite is a nice name.'

April 8, 1933

A wire from Randolph Putnam. Franklin Roosevelt has announced that in future only the government may own gold bullion and those of us who thought to put our hard-earned dollars into gold are going to have to sell it to the Federal Reserve. At a very poor price, you may be sure. How sound Brumby's judgment was. Never trust a lawyer.

April 10, 1933

Two days to reach Randolph by telephone, then when I did get through he did nothing to put my mind at rest. If I don't turn in my gold I can be prosecuted for hoarding and, as if that isn't bad enough, he's coming to England, in June. I said, 'I shall be at Royal Ascot.'

'So will I,' he said. 'I'll be staying in a town called Maiden Head. I have a Putnam cousin there, twice removed. Now Mother has passed over I'm going to start seeing the world and I'm holding you to dinner, Maybell. We have a lot to catch up on.'

I doubt that anything of interest to me has ever happened to Randolph Putnam.

April 15, 1933, Port Lympne, Kent

If Trent Park was a dream, Port Lympne is paradise. Terrace gives on to terrace, vista on to vista, and the lawns are carpeted with daffodils. The Dickie Mountbattens are here and Alex and Nelly Hardinge. He's the King's private secretary, but I don't suppose His Majesty dictates letters on a holiday weekend. Also here, Tom Mitford, Sir Philip's cousin Hannah, a Frenchman called Hippolyte who plays tennis, and Marthe Bibesco who is personally acquainted with Mr Mussolini. She says he has a magnificent manly jaw. Arriving tomorrow, the Winston Churchills – he's something in politics, an actor called Gielgud, and a coal porter! Sir Philip certainly doesn't give a damn for class distinctions.

April 16, 1933
This morning a treasure hunt for eggs, each couple being provided with a list of clues written in aquamarine ink. I was paired with young Tom Mitford, who's just back from Heidelberg and speaks very highly of the German nation. Our clues led us to the orangerie where, hanging from a tree, we found a perfect little egg-shaped crystal pendant for me and a tiny basket with a plover's egg for Tom. A simple rustic luncheon was served on the lawn; spit-roasted kid and pineapple ice. Then Philip took us up in his airplane, one at a time, for an aerial view of the estate. What an accomplished man! He makes one feel nothing is too much trouble, and he's tireless. Everything must be perfect. Last evening he had the Union flag hauled down because the red in it clashed so violently with the orange sunset.

Musical diversions after dinner. Philip's wonderful dusky servants brought in thimbles of coffee which they somehow set ablaze and then the coal porter, who, I must say, is very well scrubbed considering his trade, claimed the piano and played and sang for quite an hour. He was really rather good. I've advised him to think of taking it up professionally. There must be a great many people in London who'd be willing to pay him and it would surely be more agreeable than portering coal.

Philip said, 'Maybell, you're a r-r-riot!' He's so easy to amuse. I think I could very happily be Lady Sassoon.

April 17, 1933
Marthe Bibesco says the man who played for us last night was Mr Cole Porter. Philip might have made it clearer.

April 18, 1933

How drab Wilton Place seems after Port Lympne. I found the men rather standoffish, especially Johnny Gielgud. And Alex Hardinge didn't smile, even when he was hunting for eggs. They say the King enjoys a joke, but I suppose servants only smile when given leave and once a servant, always a servant. His wife was adorable though, and so was Clemmie Churchill, and I liked Philip's cousin once I grew accustomed to her swarthy appearance. She has very good emeralds and superb pearls, but without them one could quite imagine her selling fish from a barrow in Lombard Street. I couldn't warm to Marthe Bibesco. She's one of those predatory types who fastens on to the most important man in the room and allows no one else to get a word in.

But an exquisite weekend. R-r-ravishing, as dear Philip would say. I wonder why he never married. It may be Cousin Hannah and Sister Syb have stood guard over him too fiercely. Well, they don't deter me.

April 19, 1933

Wally and Ernest are back from Fort Belvedere, with the Prince's blessing to make him a dinner on May 2. We start work tomorrow.

Lunch with George Lightfoot. He says Marthe Bibesco is a *grande horizontale*.

Something else to look into at the Lending Library.

April 20, 1933

Wally says a *grande horizontale* is a ceiling expert.

For his dinner the Prince has requested a list of lively, interesting people with a good sprinkling of Americans. She's told him she can accommodate fourteen, which is stretching Bryanston Court to its absolute limit. Pips and Freddie are already on the master plan whereas I am scribbled in a side bar along with the Judson Erlangers, the substitutes' bench. She said, 'It's not that I don't want you there, Maybell. And you probably will be there. I just have to weigh every place very carefully. Pips and Freddie are a good combination. She's sparky, he's political.'

I said, 'Well, don't think I'm going to keep the date open indefinitely.'

She said, 'Go ahead. Fill it up if you must, but if His Royal Highness summons you to dinner you'll have to drop everything. One doesn't turn down royalties. I'd have thought you'd know that.'

Of course, if she'd only transfer the dinner to *my* dining room, there'd be seats for twenty.

April 21, 1933
Lunched with Pips. Told her she and Freddie are on Wally's A list. She said, 'Only because she owes me, I'm sure.' Not just the loan of a ruby choker, apparently. There have been opera pearls. And a crocodile bag.

April 25, 1933
Flora's first day at Miss Hildred's. Lightfoot had drinks with Melhuish this evening and says there were no reports of mayhem.

April 26, 1933
Wally called me to tell me her plans: only three courses, and no wines because she's going to serve curried chicken. There'll just be gin fizzes and then cold beer with dinner.

I said, 'It's of no interest to me. I've made arrangements to go to an operetta in aid of Navy Widows.'

She said, 'Then you'd better unmake them. I've just finished the placement and I've put you between Prince George and Prince Louis Ferdinand.'

I knew she wouldn't be able to manage without me! And Prince George! Naughty, rebellious Prince George. We're sure to get along. Prince Louis Ferdinand is a German but Wally says he speaks perfect English. His mother is Crown Princess Cecilie, a regular at Lily Drax-Pfaffenhof's house parties. Wally says it's quite on the cards that Mr Hitler will restore the monarchy and then Louis Ferdinand may reign someday.

I'm undecided between my magenta crepe and my copper silk.

April 28, 1933

To Carlton Gardens for drinks. Chatted with dear Leo von Hoesch, told him I was dining with a future Kaiser on Tuesday. He said, 'How astonishing. We don't have Kaisers anymore.'

I said, 'But surely the National Socialists say they'll bring them back?'

'Yes,' he said, 'they do say that, don't they?'

I fear Ambassador von Hoesch is losing touch with things.

Violet says Wally mustn't feel too let down if the Princes don't appear. She says neither of them is known for their punctuality or reliability. Sour grapes, I'm sure.

Flora has apparently gone to school like a lamb every morning.

April 29, 1933

Wally's guest list is finalized. No room for Judson and Hattie because His Royal Highness wanted Thelma's friends, the Bernie Cavetts, and he's keen to meet Boss and Ethel Croker. Pips says she'd happily give up her seat. She thinks the idea of Ernest bowing and scraping all evening is excruciating.

I said, 'Don't you want to know the Princes?'

She said, 'Not particularly. They're not like real people. And anyway, I'll bet Wally's going to seat me way down the table. I hope so. I'll probably get the truck man.'

Bernie Cavett made his fortune in road freight, apparently.

April 30, 1933

To Bryanston Court to help with the finishing touches. The menu is decided: avocado ice cream, curried chicken, apple fritters.

Ernest has cold sores. He's anxious about Wally's idea of serving beer and keeps bringing out bottles of his cherished claret to try and persuade her, but as she says, the Prince of Wales has access to the finest cellars in the world, and anyway, he's no great wine drinker. He'll much prefer the novelty of beer.

One thing Ernest doesn't need to worry about this time is the expense. Funny how an overture of caviars was deemed necessary to reel in Thelma Furness, but the Prince of Wales is getting something more akin to a porch brunch.

May 3, 1933

Last evening I danced with two princes, three if you count an exile, which I think I do. More, anyway, than Nora Sedley Cordle will do if she lives to be a hundred, and I shall make sure she hears about it from Randolph Putnam.

The two Princes are very different. Wales fidgets a lot and allows his gaze to wander when he's in conversation. Prince George seems more assured, much more attentive as a dinner partner and an excellent dancer. Freddie Crosbie had described him as 'lavender-toned' but he looked perfectly healthy to me.

And Prince Louis Ferdinand is delightful. He's been living in Michigan helping out Mr Ford at his automobile factory and adores our American way of life, but he may soon have to give it all up because his elder brother has chosen to marry a commoner, which places Louis next in line, should the Germans bring back royalties. His mother wants him to go home and find a suitable bride.

Zita Cavett said, 'Why go home? Why not choose a gorgeous American girl?'

He said, 'A wonderful idea, but your husband got there first.'

They all pant after Zita. It's her legs. Bernie Cavett found her in the chorus at the Chicago Majestic. A showgirl at a dinner for the Prince of Wales, and with seats at a premium! Hattie Erlanger would be furious if she knew.

There was no withdrawing. Boss and Ernest lingered over their cigars. The rest of us rolled back the rugs and played Thelma's latest hoochie-coochie records on my gramophone. It was the greatest fun. The royalties didn't leave till midnight and were effusive in their thanks. Ernest was quite pink with pleasure but Wally was as composed as ever. All that dancing and not a hair out of place. The whole thing an undoubted success. I must hand it to her.

The trouble with such an exceptional evening is what to do the day after. Ida Coote is between men and wanted lunch, but I'm going to remain in bed, place a few telephone calls, and recover my strength.

May 4, 1933

Wally got flowers from all three royalties and Ernest is overcome with pride.

I said, 'Well, what next?'

'Nothing in particular,' she said. 'We're just very happy to have David's friendship.'

Well, if a day comes when Minnehaha doesn't have a scheme it'll be the first.

May 15, 1933

Lunch with Pips. From what she saw at Wally's dinner she thinks Prince George is the star of the royal Princes; funny, gossipy, good-looking. They say Bertie York and Prince Harry are both dull and Pips doesn't rate Wales's looks at all.

She said, 'He's like a schoolboy, only with lines on his face. Small fry. I don't think I could ever take him seriously as King. And he's not very bright. I heard him agree with two completely opposite opinions in the space of five minutes. But I know exactly what Wally's after. She's playing the long game, hoping to hang in there till King David and Queen Thelma are on the throne.'

That could be a long wait. The King may look old but he's only sixty-eight.

May 8, 1933

Penelope Blythe says everyone is talking about Wally and Ernest as 'the awful American couple who served the Prince of Wales beer in a bottle'.

This can only have come from Hattie Erlanger, still aggrieved about not being invited. But how quickly the facts get distorted. Wally served the beer in lead crystal chalices. I should know. I helped pay for them. But Pips must have given half a story to Hattie, who never listens anyway, and before you know it Wally and Ernest's names are being dragged through the London mud.

Penelope said, 'I find Wally Simpson rather direct, don't you? I hope she didn't ask the royalties any impertinent questions.'

Not at all. Wally just likes to draw people out, and I for one found it fascinating to hear that if Prince George didn't have to be a prince what he'd most like in the world is to do something with fabrics.

Marthe Bibesco was seated a few tables away, face heavily powdered. We exchanged waves. Penelope said, 'How do you know that old harridan?'

I said, 'She was at Philip Sassoon's at Easter. I believe she's a connoisseur of ceilings.'

'Maybell!' she said. 'What a hoot! I've heard it called some things.'

According to Penelope, Marthe Bibesco is a pensioned-off trollop who's made deposed royals her specialty. 'Willy Hohenzollern and Fonso Spain, to name two and omit hundreds,' she said. 'Connoisseur of ceilings! I shall repeat that.'

May 13, 1933

Flora has been removed from Miss Hildred's. When I called in at Carlton Gardens today she was confined to the nursery and told me proudly, 'I don't go to school anymore. Miss Hildred said I was a little wild animal.'

Violet says she'll just have to stay at home now until September. She has two charity balls and then Royal Ascot, as well as her usual workload, so the last thing she has time for is trailing around interviewing schools.

May 16, 1933

Judson and Hattie Erlanger have been invited to Fort Belvedere for the weekend. Wally says Thelma's only done it because she knows how disappointed they were not to attend the dinner at Bryanston Court, but even so! I'd have thought I was a far worthier candidate. The problem is, people think only in terms of couples. It takes a host of Philip Sassoon's imagination to think of inviting a lone woman. And now the summer is looming. I'm sure Violet's assuming I'll go to Drumcanna but I absolutely cannot. A whole month of midges and Jane Habberley.

Wally and Ernest are going to Lily Drax-Pfaffenhof's. I know Lily would have me too.

May 18, 1933

Lunch with Ida. She has a vague offer of a villa at San Sebastian, but I've heard that kind of talk from Ida before. Dinner at the Crosbies'.

May 20, 1933

Freddie and Pips won't hear of me going to the Tyrol with the Simpsons. Pips says I spend far too much time around Wally as it is. 'And not just time,' she said. 'Money too. I've seen you. You're too generous, Maybell. You must come to Italy with us. We pay our own way.'

The only drawback to this is Gladys Trilling, whom I can take in small lunch-sized doses, but a whole month? Hattie Erlanger is more bearable. She's careful around me, mindful that Judson and I have a history, but Gladys! Well, perhaps Hattie and Gladys will stick together.

May 21, 1933

Penelope Blythe's friend Cimmie Mosley has passed away after having her appendix removed. So young. How fragile life is.

To Monsieur Jules for a tint.

May 25, 1933

Thelma Furness has obtained her divorce. Wally says it merely frees Marmaduke Furness to marry his new sweetie and will make no difference to Thelma's end of things.

May 27, 1933

According to Padmore's *Daily Sketch*, the Prince of Wales has been seen several times in the company of Mrs Amelia Earhart, the aviatrix. Perhaps Thelma's days as Special Friend are numbered. That would be bad news for Wally and Ernest. Bad news for all of us really, just when everything is going along so nicely.

May 28, 1933

To Carlton Gardens for tea. Lightfoot was there.

I mentioned the story about Wales and Mrs Earhart. Lightfoot said, 'Yes, everyone's talking about it.'

Violet said, 'No, George, only silly people are talking about it and it's of no consequence anyway, because he's about announce his engagement.'

Lightfoot said, 'Who? Not Ingrid Sweden?'

Violet was shaking her head, lips sealed, refusing to say more, but Doopie was nodding wildly.

Lightfoot said, 'Ingrid Sweden! Not that old story! He won't marry her.'

Violet said, 'It's his duty to marry, therefore he will marry and soon. Even Wales understands that.'

May 30, 1933

Wally says the Amelia Earhart story is a spiteful fabrication and that HRH is as in love as ever with Thelma. She says when they're at the Fort the King telephones all the time, wanting to know who he's got there and what they're up to that's so fascinating he can't spare a little time to go visit with his mother like Bertie York does. She says Bertie York is the blue-eyed boy in that family and poor David Wales can't do anything right.

Wondering what to do about Philip Sassoon. He seems to need encouragement.

June 2, 1933

Lunch with George Lightfoot. He says Flora has made a bridal veil for Melhuish's terrier and renamed it Princess Ingrid. Advises me against making any claims on Philip Sassoon. He said, 'He's a particular type, Maybell. Do you understand? A dynamo of a man and a superb host, but an elusive friend. And not cut out for romance. I think they missed that piece out when they were making him.'

And Lightfoot still sees that Belinda but isn't 'seeing her', whatever that means. What is wrong with these Englishmen? Well, whatever, I'm going to have Sir Philip over for drinks. A little pre-Ascot cockers, as Hattie would call it. But not when Wally's around. She'd be sure to mug up on Chippendale porcelain and all kinds of subjects just to get her foot in his door.

June 5, 1933

Lunch with Connie Thaw and Ethel Croker. They're planning a surprise birthday party for Wally and my mission will be to waylay her and bring her to Quaglino's. Hattie

Erlanger and Gladys Trilling saw us and invited themselves to join us for dessert.

Hattie said, 'Ethel, tell us about Wally in China. We hear there was talk.'

Ethel said, 'There's always talk among expats. They've nothing better to do. She was young, that's all. Young and lonely and she liked gambling. She was good at it. Baccarat, blackjack. She used to make herself quite a bit of pin money.'

Hattie said, 'No, something else. Connie, do you know? Something she told Thelma? Tricks she learned to do for men?'

Connie said, 'Sort of. She knows this thing you can do, to slow a man down, if he's one of those hair-trigger operators. I don't know if that was China though, was it?'

Hattie said, 'Hong Kong. Ask Thelma. I heard she learned it in a whorehouse. It's called Ching Chong or Fong Wing or something like that. Ethel, you must know.'

Ethel said, 'Well, I never went to any whorehouses and I don't think Wally did either. There was a place at Repulse Bay she reckoned she went to once, a singsong house, but I didn't believe her. Even Wally wouldn't have been that crazy.'

I agree with Ethel. And what on earth is a hair-trigger operator? Something else beyond the scope of Harrold's Lending Library, you may be sure.

June 6, 1933

Philip Sassoon has accepted for drinks on Friday. Also Lightfoot, the Crokers, Pips and Freddie. I'm not having anyone who calls Philip 'the Babylonian' and Wally will be in Lincolnshire so he'll be safe from her attentions. She and Ernest are going with Thelma and HRH to the Perry

Brownlows' for the weekend. Quite the cozy foursome these days.

June 7, 1933

A wire from Randolph Putnam whose boat is about to dock. Dinner on Saturday? Does he think I'm sitting around with nothing in my appointment book? I shall go to Leake Priory and weekend with the Blythes. Penelope Blythe has been pestering me for long enough.

June 8, 1933

Penelope can be so infuriating. She has begged me and begged me to go to their place in the country and now, when it's convenient to me, she and Fergus are going to Hampshire for polo. Freddie and Pips are leaving for his constituency first thing on Saturday, Lightfoot is going to the Hon. Belinda's, and even Ida Coote has commitments. Dog-walking commitments, more than likely, or Buddhism. That's her latest thing. Well, I'm sure Buddha wouldn't mind her helping out a friend and having dinner on Saturday.

June 9, 1933

Still at my breakfast tray and I've received the inevitable call. Randolph Putnam. 'Surprise, surprise!' Not really. I know far more than I need to of his movements while he's in London. I've agreed dinner tomorrow. May as well get it over and done with. I suppose he's feeling rather lost and overwhelmed, his first time away from the United States. His feet kept him out of the war, or possibly his mother. When one has traveled and forged a new life one easily forgets how limited some people's worlds are. Well, charity, Maybell. Christian charity.

This evening, an elegant little coterie from *my* new world. Daiquiris, shrimp toasts, prunes in bacon, knackwurst, and pickles.

June 10, 1933
Randolph Putnam pretty much ruined my party. Philip Sassoon was the last to arrive and when he was shown in he had Putnam at his side. He said, 'I found your friend outside.' Randolph, bright-eyed and annoying as ever, said, 'Didn't intend crashing in, Maybell, but I couldn't wait to see you.'

He fairly took over, yarning with Boss Croker as though he'd known him all his life, attempting to stroll down memory lane with Pips. After three daiquiris Pips Crosbie misremembers *every* story about me. And to top it all, Randolph gave Philip the distinct impression that he has some kind of claim on me. I heard him say, 'She's a wild one. I've had to chase her halfway across the world. But she looks younger and more darling every time I see her.'

If it hadn't been my own party I'd have fled. Ethel Croker squeezing my elbow. George Lightfoot raising his eyebrow. Tonight Randolph Putnam has to be told, straight.

June 11, 1933
Randolph Putnam is impossible. He proposed marriage and appeared not to notice the firmness of my refusal. He said, 'I'm a patient man, Maybell.' He envisions us living out our days together at Sweet Air, me in a rocking chair, no doubt, while he goes around winding all his clocks.

I said, 'My life's in London now.'

'Yes,' he said, 'I see that. But times change, and they say wanderers eventually return to the place they started out.'

I believe the end of the world would have to be nigh for me to think of going back to America. He wanted to know am I seeing anyone.

I said, 'I see lots of people. You were lucky to find me at home.'

'Well,' he said, 'London's gain is Baltimore's loss.'

He seemed to be under the impression that crayfish are an aphrodisiac. *Au contraire.* Butter on his chin.

June 14, 1933
At the Shim-Sham till dawn. Whitlow Trilling got very tight on vermouth. Gladys was livid. Shopping with Wally this afternoon. We need gay umbrellas for Ascot and Wally is due a birthday gift.

June 15, 1933
Wally chose a silver punchbowl. Pips says it was too much. She said, 'You're a fool, Maybell. You should have ushered her toward the embroidered handkerchiefs. Well, I'm afraid all she's getting from us is a box of crystallized fruits.'

We wonder whether she'll get something from Thelma and the Prince. Pips doubts he sends birthday cards. She thinks he'd get the Lord Chamberlain to do it. *I am commanded by His Royal Highness to send you hugs and kisses!*

She said, 'Did Ethel say anything to you?'

I said, 'What about?'

'Nothing,' she said. 'Absolutely nothing.'

June 19, 1933
Wally did indeed get a birthday gift from Thelma and HRH. She'd guessed about the party but pretended very well. The Prince is at Windsor but Thelma had brought along a twig in a terracotta pot. Ernest says it's a rare orchid. He'd given Wally ear studs. Amber, supposedly, although they're so small it's not easy to see what they're made of.

It's the Prince's birthday this week too, but according to Connie Thaw they're born under very different signs. David Wales is Cancer the Crab. He clings to the things he loves and hates to leave his shell. Whereas Wally is an adventurous, quick-thinking Gemini. I'd have loved her to tell me what I am, but then the cabaret started.

I notice Wally's dropped a year from her age. It couldn't matter less to me, except that if she does it again I shall be forced to do likewise.

To Sunninghills.

June 20, 1933, Sunninghills, Berkshire
Sunninghills has neither sun nor hills but the beds are comfortable and Ethel Croker has hired an excellent staff. I traveled down with Pips and Freddie. The Trillings and the Erlangers were here ahead of us, also a Canadian couple called Bedaux. Tomorrow the cars take us to the racetrack at noon. The big race is the Prince of Wales Cup. *Our* Prince of Wales! Wally says Thelma is at Fort Belvedere, but it's all hush-hush because Their Majesties expect the Prince to toe the line during Ascot Week. Ethel says she has a surprise for me tomorrow. So *that's* what Pips was hinting at. Philip Sassoon, I'll bet. I saw them in a huddle about something at my soiree.

The forecast: warm but overcast.

June 21, 1933

A mixed day. Ethel's surprise was Randolph Putnam. He arrived, creaking in new shoes, in a taxicab. He's staying over.

She said, 'I never can resist a little matchmaking.'

I'd love to wipe that smirk off Pips Crosbie's face.

Wore my caramel spot with a black straw coolie hat. Wally was all in grapefruit. Charlie Bedaux wore salt-and-pepper trousers with his morning coat, which scandalized Ernest, but Fern Bedaux says that's Charlie. Tell him the rules and he won't rest till he's broken them. He's an ugly little man, like a prizefighter, but worth millions.

The royal parade was very pretty. Queen Mary was in shell pink, Elizabeth York in forget-me-not, and the Princess Royal in kingfisher. Melhuish was in the third carriage with Ena Spain, Bertie York, and the Duchess of Buccleuch. Violet was in carriage number 4 with the Nicholases of Greece and Prince Harry.

No sign of Thelma. I expect she stayed at the Fort and read magazines.

Ethel got Wally reminiscing about China over dinner. She said, 'Remember the smell, Wally, when we disembarked at Hong Kong?'

Wally said, 'Oh yes! Cinnamon. And sandalwood.'

Ethel said, 'Was that what it was! I thought it was rotten fish and pee pee. And Shanghai. What a shambles. Remember that hotel?'

Wally laughed. She said, 'It was called the Astor House, but it wasn't like it sounded. Your shoes stuck to the rugs. And run by a madman. He was ex-navy and when dinner was served he sounded Cook House on an old bugle.'

Ernest said, 'But still, a great cultural experience.'

Ethel said, 'Oh yes. Definitely that.'

Every time I look in Randolph Putnam's direction he's smiling at me. I suppose I have to be thankful he hasn't tried to steal a kiss.

June 22, 1933
Ladies' Day. Elizabeth York was in primrose, Queen Mary in ice blue. Freddie said she looked like the Jungfrau, whoever she is when she's at home. I wore my lilac crepe de chine and a cabbage-rose homburg. Wally very severe in a beige turban. Violet was promoted to second carriage today, but I believe I've seen that peppermint toque before. Several times.

Ernest left to go to his office immediately after the Gold Cup, as did Freddie, the Trillings, and Fern and Charlie Bedaux. Fern is so gracious and Charlie's so florid and common-looking. They make an odd couple. I have an open invitation to visit them in any of their many lovely homes. Ethel says their French chateau is divine. Randolph is staying on in Maidenhead for a further week and hopes we'll have time for another talk. Oh dear.

June 24, 1933
Having begged a ride with me and Pips, Wally has now taken off to Fort Belvedere. There's a lunch party for the Prince's birthday.

June 26, 1933, Wilton Place
Wally says Connie and Thelma are very concerned about their sister Gloria, who stands to lose her only child. Gloria lives in Paris and always has a very hectic schedule, so she left the little girl with her sister-in-law in New York, for safekeeping. But now the sister-in-law is refusing to give the child back and it may come to a court case. No

faster way to beggar yourself. And I wonder why Gloria wants the child back all of a sudden. Better to leave her where she's settled, I'd have thought.

Daphne Frith on the telephone. She and Prosper want me at Hoxney Court for a weekend before everyone disperses for the summer. Pips and Freddie are also invited.

June 27, 1933
Lunch with Randolph. He said, 'I've so enjoyed seeing you in your new life, Maybell. I can quite see you're not ready to leave it just yet. But we Putnams know a good thing when we see it, and I'm prepared to wait.'

My only consolation is that he's cheerful in his disappointment. He sails on Friday.

June 28, 1933
Dinner at the Crosbies'. Freddie says Hoxney Court will give me a true taste of rustic England. I already hear the clank and splutter of ancient plumbing.

July 1, 1933, Hoxney Court, Kent
Hoxney Court is a great creaking hull of a place. Daphne says it's been in Prosper's family for more than three hundred years and still has many of its original features. Indeed, I believe the mattress on my bed may be one of them. A sultry night forced me to risk an open window, until I heard a band of lunatics cackling out there in the dark. Prosper says it was only frogs, but my window will now remain locked.

Today we meet the natives. Pips and I are assisting Daphne in the judging of an embroidered tablecloth competition. Freddie and Prosper have to crown the Carnival Queen.

We're only fifteen miles from Lympne. I put a call through to Philip, who was expected although no one seemed to know when.

July 2, 1933
Freddie is laid up with an ankle sprained during yesterday's sack race and Daphne and Prosper had to put in an obligatory appearance at church, so Pips and I motored over to Port Lympne on the off chance. Philip was at home and made us very welcome. He gave us champagne and took us down to watch the dragonflies dancing on his new pond. Not his usual bubbling self though. Her Majesty the Queen has proposed herself for tea this afternoon, so he'd been up till very late painting modesty shorts on those saucy Egyptians in his dining-room frieze, in case she decides to tour the house.

What a chore. After all that I hope she doesn't cancel.

Daphne has been quizzing me about Wally and Ernest, but never when Prosper's within earshot, I notice. She said, 'How thrilling for two such ordinary people suddenly to find themselves whisked into the Prince of Wales's circle. And how odd that he should choose such people. He's certainly going to be a very different style of King to his father. If he ever becomes King.'

I said, 'Why wouldn't he?'

She said, 'Because he may burn himself out with fast women and smoky niteries. Prosper believes, and he's not alone in this, that Bertie York should be our next King.'

July 4, 1933
To the US compound for drinks. Ernest yawning constantly because Thelma and the Prince kept them out until three last night. As Wally says, he has no pep. At

thirty-six a man should be good for a little dancing after dinner.

July 6, 1933

To the Army & Navy store for beach pajamas. Padmore is so excited about the promise of foreign travel. Mrs Orr-Tweedie never ventured farther than the Suffolk coast.

Rory says he'd like to go to the circus for his birthday treat but doesn't think Flora will be allowed and then there'll be a scene. He said, 'We could pretend you're taking me to the dentist.'

I don't think I'm inclined to tell a lie. Better to say nothing and proceed by stealth.

July 12, 1933

To Bertram Mills's Circus and to a Corner House for high tea. I simply waited until Violet had left for her Fallen Women committee and then collected them all. Rory, Flora, and Doopie. It was the greatest fun. They had chimpanzees dressed in adorable little romper suits and when they brought them out into the audience one of them tried to climb on to Doopie's lap.

Flora kept saying, 'Won't Mummy be surprised.'

Rory was anxious though. He said, 'Mummy might be surprised in a bad way, Flora. I think it'd be better if we didn't say too much about it.'

That was what was agreed. Even Doopie understood. Then when I dropped them off Flora burst straight into the drawing room crying, 'Mummy! Aunt Bayba took us to the cirgus and then to the Gorner House but we're not going to say too much about it.'

Ulick said, 'I thought she was gated until further notice?'

Rory said, 'It was for my birthday.'

Ulick said, 'The whole point of a gating is to make one realize the error of one's ways, not to have exceptions made because it's someone's birthday.'

Flora said, 'Anyway, a bunkey sat on Doopie.'

Violet said, 'No more fibs please, Flora. Now run upstairs.'

Rory said, 'Aunt Maybell's going to the Venice Lido, Ulick. Don't you wish we could go?'

Ulick said, 'No, I do not.'

July 13, 1933

George Lightfoot has gone to Yorkshire. He's visiting Viscount Minskip, then traveling with him to Drumcanna. Wally is taking a pre-vacation cure at the Cedars with Thelma and Connie. She and Ernest leave for the Tyrol on the 20th. Thelma and her Prince will be apart through August. Thelma's going to Biarritz and HRH has to go yachting with the King and then hurry up to Balmoral for the shooting. Penelope Blythe is pleased. She says if Wales is going to be around there'll be a good chance of some proper dancing. 'And if not,' she said, 'next summer I shall tag along with you to foreign parts. I couldn't be more bored with Drumcanna.'

July 15, 1933

Lunch with Pips. She says Gladys has bought a very daring bathing suit. I'd say any style of bathing suit would be risky on Gladys. When a person has been delivered of two children she'd do well to keep herself artfully draped.

July 17, 1933

Gladys Trilling on the telephone. I seem to have drawn a shared berth with her in the *wagons-lits* to Nice. Whitlow can't get away for another week at least.

She said, 'Isn't it a lark? We can get to know each other much better.'

I said, 'Do you snore?'

'Like an old sow,' she said, 'but don't worry. I'm sure we'll be too busy chatting to do much sleeping.'

July 18, 1933
The kitchen maid has revealed herself to be in the family way, put there by the outdoors boy. Just what I need on the eve of my departure. A major domestic crisis.

July 19, 1933
The kitchen maid and the outdoors boy have been sent packing. They can argue about their nuptials in their own time. As Padmore says, it's a saving. There'll be no fires needed and no entertaining, so we can make a fresh start with new help in September. What a sensible girl she is.

July 21, 1933
Violet predicts that come September I'll be looking for a new lady's maid too. She said, 'Taking a girl like that to Italy. She's bound to fall into the clutches of some oily Romeo and that'll be the last you'll see of her. I don't know why you insist on keeping a lady's maid anyway. I've managed without one for years.'

All too obviously. And a smoothing iron. And a clothes brush.

July 23, 1933
Zita and Bernie Cavett have taken a villa in San Remo. They've invited us all to visit on our way back from Venice. The Trillings won't be able to, of course. They have children to attend to.

July 28, 1933, a train, approaching Genoa

No sleep. Pips and Hattie were in and out in their pajamas and face cream, tight on champagne, and then Gladys kept me awake with her latest notion about Wally. She thinks she's a man masquerading as a woman.

I said, 'I was at school with her. She used to sleep over at our house. I've known her since she was fifteen.'

She said, 'Yes, but did you ever see her in the altogether?'

I don't need to have.

She said, 'You must admit, she does look terribly manly. Those great big hands. And no bosom at all.'

I said, 'You seem to be forgetting she's had two husbands and quite a number of sweethearts.'

She said, 'That doesn't signify. Some men like that kind of thing.'

Some men may, but not Ernest Simpson I'm sure. I never met a more vanilla character.

She said, 'Well, I shan't be convinced until I've seen what she's got inside her bloomers.'

And they call Wally 'vulgar'.

July 30, 1933, Venice Lido

I adore Italy. Sunshine, smiling porters at the railroad station, and a sleek shiny launch to whisk us to the Excelsior. The chandeliers are exquisite. The linens are sumptuous and the sands are kept immaculately raked. All I ask is to be left in peace beneath this perfect blue sky.

August 1, 1933

Pips and Hattie are attacking the sights of Venice and Freddie and Judson keep disappearing to the tennis courts, which leaves me with Gladys, who insists on reading aloud from an Italian phrase book. I wish Ambassador Bingham would hurry up and release Whitlow from his desk.

August 4, 1933

Freddie had promised us drinks in a real Venetian palace, with an old college friend, Bobo Farinacci, but Bobo turns out to be in Switzerland. Pips says his palace is locked and shuttered. Gladys's monumental thighs have turned pink. She's convinced she has a poolside admirer. I hate to disappoint her.

Whitlow is rumored to be on a train heading toward Nice.

August 7, 1933

Pips seems to have wrung the city dry of Tipolettos and Tintiolos and has now moved on to mosaics, but Hattie has had enough. She's offered to help me improve my game of tennis, which will certainly be preferable to listening to Gladys's fevered fantasies every time a pool boy lights her cigarette.

August 8, 1933

I have sacked Hattie and hired a professional tennis instructor. She deliberately tried to befuddle me with technicalities: tram lines, backward forehands, lets, lets-not. Surely the main thing is that the ball travel back and forth over the net at an agreeable pace, without people yelling 'out!' all the time.

August 10, 1933

A very exciting development. The Prince of Wales arrived this morning. He's not yachting in the Solent, not shooting grice on Deeside, but right here on Venice Lido. And not with Thelma. The concierge told Padmore he's traveling alone, apart from two detectives and a valet and an equerry.

Hattie has sent him a note. When we reckoned up she has known him longest.

August 11, 1933
We heard nothing from HRH. So much for Hattie Erlanger's credentials as an acquaintance of many years' standing! Then as I was going up to change for luncheon I bumped into him coming out of an elevator. He greeted me very warmly. 'How splendid,' he kept saying. 'How splendid!'

He's in Italy on a fact-finding tour, apparently. The conditions of the working man. He's proposed himself for dinner. Joey Legh is equerrying, a man who should be told that a smile costs nothing.

August 12, 1933
HRH looked for Wally and Ernest when he joined our table last evening. I think he was disappointed not to find them. And then Hattie and Gladys would gush so. Little wonder he became rather subdued. I've seen it happen before. It takes someone like Thelma or Wally to draw him out when he's in that mood.

Sometimes I sense a very lonely man.

There had been talk of going to the casino, but he suddenly decided to turn in early. Freddie stayed down and had a nightcap with Joey Legh. Legh doesn't care for Italy. He told Freddie he couldn't understand why HRH couldn't just go to Balmoral like a normal prince. Captain Legh has obviously never felt the prick of a Deeside midge.

This morning they left without even saying goodbye. I suppose he's had to hurry on with his tour of working conditions. Next stop, Monte Carlo. A prince's work is never done.

August 17, 1933
Barbara Hutton is in town honeymooning with her Russian prince. She's throwing a little cocktail party on Saturday and has invited all of us on the basis of Judson's connections with her Aunt Jessie Woolworth.

Pips said, 'What a sad sack. Imagine inviting a bunch of strangers round when you're on your honeymoon.'

It depends on the length of the honeymoon. When a husband is in business, as Brumby was, he gets back into harness before boredom sets in, but I suppose all Prince Mdivani has to do is count Barbara's money. Anyway, it's nice to meet new people, even on a honeymoon.

August 19, 1933
The Hutton party was pleasant enough. Little Barbara looked so young, so bewildered. I think she was grateful to those of us who braved the thunderstorms. Gladys wore a print day dress and no jewelry. Hattie, a run in her stockings and a sad little topaz brooch. These English girls!

Tuesday, to San Remo. It will be a relief to be around someone like Zita Cavett, someone else who has a sense of elegance. The Trillings are going straight back to London and Freddie is going to Ireland to fish with Lord Templemore, so there'll be just me, Pips, Hattie, and Judson.

August 23, 1933, San Remo

The Cavetts' villa is heavenly. Corn lilies everywhere, and wild thyme and basil and the sea is midnight blue. Zita and Pips went for a swim in the buff.

Another couple are arriving tomorrow. Herman and Kath Rogers, Americans, but they've made their home in France. And why not. If Randolph Putnam could see me now, relaxing beneath a fig tree, sipping a glass of pretty pink wine, he'd realize there'll be no luring me back to Baltimore.

August 25, 1933

Herman and Kath Rogers are not only great company, they also know Wally Simpson, or perhaps *knew* is the word. They were in Peking in '24. Herman was attached to the US Embassy. Kath said, 'I'll say we knew her. We practically adopted her. Actually, I knew her slightly from San Diego, before I married Herm. But then she turned up in Peking, no husband, no chaperone, and it was such a dangerous time. Fighting in the streets, foreigners being kidnapped, and Wally was wandering around, like a kid at Luna Park. She didn't seem to have any sense of danger. In the end we persuaded her to move in with us, inside the Legation compound.'

They didn't know about Ernest. They haven't heard from Wally since she went back to the States.

Kath said, 'I'm glad she met someone. I hope he's nice. She was a mess when we knew her. Tell her all the best from us.'

Hattie said, 'What I want to know is, did she really learn "secret Chinese arts"?'

Pips said, 'Yes. The secret art of never picking up the check.'

August 27, 1933

The Rogerses left this morning. They have a house near Cannes which Herman says 'makes up with charm what it lacks in amenities' and they hope to see me there someday. I offered Kath Wally's London number but she said she wasn't sure she wanted to get involved again. Apparently, after Wally moved in with them, she developed a crush on Herman. Well, he is a very attractive man. Yale, Phi Beta Kappa, but with muscles and a wicked smile.

Kath said, 'I always felt with Wally it wasn't that she particularly wanted Herman or any of the other men she went after. She just seemed to want to prove she could get them.'

I said, 'Did she go after lots of men?'

'Several,' she said. 'I shouldn't gossip like this. Please don't tell her. She was young. She made a few mistakes.'

I said, 'One of our English friends has got it into her head that Wally's really a man. Can you imagine?'

Kath laughed. She said, 'I don't think so. I remember at least two Italians she was involved with. I don't think they'd settle for a fake, do you?'

September 4, 1933, Wilton Place

Flora was to have started at St Audrey's this week but has the chickenpox.

Tomorrow to Fuller's with Rory. A boy needs a cream meringue to set him up for a new school year.

September 5, 1933

I have all the Drumcanna news from Rory. Prince George came to tea and so did little Ellen MacNab. Their Majesties were disappointed the Prince of Wales spent so little time at Balmoral. Flora caught her first fish. And Ailsa Anstruther-Brodie had a mishap and discharged her shotgun into George Lightfoot's butt. No wonder I haven't heard from George. Apparently, Ulick has announced that when the moor belongs to him he won't allow girls to shoot.

But the great *scandale* centres on Penelope Blythe, though Rory told it with such innocence. He said, 'Lord Habberley got confused in the dark and went into Mrs Blythe's bedroom by mistake and kicked her potty and broke it. Mummy was furious because of the mess but the maids thought it was jolly funny. I suggested to Lord Habberley that he could have my old night light and then he wouldn't get confused anymore.'

Penelope Blythe and Ralph Habberley! Well! I can't say I'm surprised about Ralph. I remember how stimulated he was by our tango sessions last August, and of course Jane Habberley has no allure. But for him to choose Penelope! Well, in my absence she was the best of a dreary crowd, I guess.

September 6, 1933

George Lightfoot says Ailsa Anstruther-Brodie didn't make a very good effort at killing him, but would only laugh when I asked him about Ralph Habberley and Penelope Blythe. He said, 'When I go to bed I go to sleep, Maybell. I don't lie awake waiting for the sound of breaking potties.'

I think I'd better have lunch with Penelope.

He says Tommy Minskip has lost a few more spots off his dice.

We both received, in this morning's post, invitations from Ida Coote to a lecture on Reincarnation, and from Sir Philip to a charity ball at Park Lane, both on September

20. Lightfoot says this affords us the opportunity to go from the ridiculous to the sublime all in one evening, though how he expects me to attend a lecture *and* have time to dress for a ball I can't imagine.

September 8, 1933

Wally is back and filling up her schedule like a demon. She was in the chair next to mine at Monsieur Jules.

She said, 'I need you to get Philip Sassoon to invite us to his ball.'

I said, 'He doesn't know you.'

She said, 'What rot. It's a charity ball. Does he want to raise money for this pet hospital of his or not?'

Well, I'm not asking. Philip is *my* friend. How would she feel if I elbowed my way into Fort Belvedere? Besides, what use can she be to a raiser of funds? She doesn't have a nickel.

I said, 'I met some old friends of yours. Herman and Kath Rogers? They asked to be remembered to you.'

'Oh yes?' she said. 'Are they still together? I wonder he didn't tire of her long ago.'

I said, 'They seem devoted. I liked them both very much. And he's so good-looking.'

'Is he?' she said. 'That's not my recollection.'

I guess he turned her down. How humiliating.

I said, 'And while we're on the subject of China, what's this I hear about secret bedroom arts?'

The girls who were doing us were all ears.

She said, 'We weren't on the subject of China. And there's only one bedroom art a woman needs. The art of keeping her husband otherwise occupied.'

Of course, Ernest *always* brings home business papers.

September 11, 1933

Lunch with Penelope Blythe. She says Ralph Habberley was just one of those things. More questions about Wally and her 'secret power over men'. Hattie Erlanger and Gladys Trilling have evidently been gossiping. It's too ridiculous.

I said, 'If Wally acquired secret powers and the best she could do with them was seduce Ernest Simpson, she'd better go back and take the class again.'

She said, 'Oh, I don't know. I think Ernest is rather a darling.'

Of course, Penelope has already established her want of discrimination by allowing Ralph Habberley to enter her room and kick her potty.

September 13, 1933

Wally called to thank me for getting her an invitation to the Sassoon ball.

I said, 'I didn't. I haven't spoken to him since I got back from Italy.'

'Oh Maybell!' she said. 'Well, thank you anyway, for fixing it by telepathy!'

Lightfoot. It has to be.

September 14, 1933

Lightfoot it was. He asked Sybil Cholmondeley if it was possible the Simpsons' invitation had gone astray in the mails. I do wish he hadn't.

I said, 'If Philip's invalids in Clacton on Sea have to rely on the benefaction of Ernest and Wally they'll be in a poor way.'

He said, 'Oh, what does it matter? Wally's happy and I'm sure Philip Sassoon couldn't care less. Syb says Wales and Prince George may look in.'

So *that's* what it's about.
To Shriner's for evening pumps.

September 15, 1933
Lunch with Ida who has learned that she was formerly a princess in eighteenth-dynasty Egypt. With the Friths to a reception at the Austrian Legation, then on to dinner at the Belchesters'. Also came, the Dickie Mountbattens, the Perry Brownlows, and Anne Belchester's brother, Seb.

Game soup, boiled capon, mushroom savory. I was longing to leave and the men sat for far too long. I feel a chill coming on.

September 17, 1933
All day in bed and still feverish.

September 18, 1933
No improvement. Canceled Wally. Canceled Monsieur Jules. All these days without eating, my ball gown is going to look even more divine.

September 19, 1933
Chickenpox.

September 29, 1933
Back from the grave's edge. I'm as weak as a kitten and must be at least ten pounds lighter. Padmore has been an angel. Darling Philip sent grapes from Lympne and a Jasmine de Coree pillow spray. Lightfoot says neither of the Princes put in an appearance at the ball. Violet brought an egg custard and books, which I made her take away again. I'm too frail to turn a page. Doopie has shingles.

September 30, 1933

When Wally visits a sickbed she certainly doesn't outstay her welcome. She stayed only long enough to tell me what a fabulous ball I missed, that Philip Sassoon is going to invite her to Trent to show her his collection of porringers, and to promise that in the next few days I may learn something to my advantage.

She said, 'Now do buck up, Maybell. It's time we shopped for gloves.'

October 2, 1933

Wally has produced the promised rabbit from the hat. I'm invited to Thelma Furness's for the weekend of the 13th. She said, 'I can't guarantee that His Royal Highness will be there, but there's a very good chance.'

Well, anyway, I do like Thelma.

October 3, 1933

Monsieur Jules couldn't do a thing with my hair. He says it's the fever. I may go to the Cedars to recuperate.

October 8, 1933

Violet said, 'If you're going to a convalescent home you might think of taking Doopie with you. She's still far from well.'

I said, 'It's not a convalescent home. It's a rest cure, with beauty treatments. There's nothing for Doopie there.'

She said, 'Why not? She enjoys a little lip rouge.'

I said, 'Okay, let her come. But I'm going with Wally and Lady Furness and her sister.'

That was the end of that.

She said, 'I do wish you wouldn't. Associating with

those people may cost you the friendship of others who are more worthy.'

I said, 'Surely, what's good enough for the Prince of Wales is good enough for Violet Melhuish?'

'Don't test me, Maybell,' she said. 'The Prince of Wales may think he can afford scandal but that doesn't mean the rest of us should follow him like a herd of swine.'

Poor Violet. She just doesn't know Thelma and the Prince as I do.

Two years today since Brumby passed over. May he rest in peace.

October 9, 1933, The Cedars, Hertfordshire
Connie Thaw and I have been wrapped in steaming hay all afternoon and I certainly feel the better for it. Connie told me that Thelma didn't at all set out to seduce the Prince. It was he who pursued her and he was seeing Freda Dudley Ward at the time, so it was all rather awkward. When it was clear how smitten the Prince was, Mrs Dudley Ward offered to retire gracefully, but her children were terribly upset because they'd grown very fond of the Prince and regarded him as a special kind of uncle.

Connie said, 'There's only one reason David still keeps in touch with Freda Dudley Ward. Thelma insisted on it, for the sake of the children. She never monopolizes him, you know. You must have noticed. Thelma has a big heart.'

She does. I think she'd make a very good queen.

October 11, 1933
Wally says Thelma has had a moving-picture projector installed at Borough Court. She said, 'But I hope you're preparing conversational topics, Maybell. You don't always pull your weight at table, I've noticed.'

The ginger of it!

I said, 'And what kind of conversational topics do you recommend for Leicestershire?'

'Range widely,' she said. 'Be unexpected. Gertrude Stein, perhaps. Or *Ulysses*. Those are lively topics.'

The names meant nothing to me or to Pips. I shall make World Affairs my subject. Connie and Benny Thaw will be there, also Poots and Humphrey Butler, and the Perry Brownlows.

October 13, 1933, Melton Mowbray, Leicestershire

Wet leaves blown against the windowpanes but Borough Court is warm and has every modern convenience. The Prince is staying nearby at Craven Lodge but motored over for dinner with an equerry called Oxer Bettenbrooke. Wore my oyster silk. Much talk about Germany leaving the League of Nations. I made a knowledgeable showing, though I do say so myself. Humphrey Butler agrees with me that the Germans simply feel they've been punished quite enough. The war has been over for fifteen years and all they're doing is standing up for themselves a little.

Brownlow said, 'Well, I wonder whether Mr Hitler's motives are quite as peaceable as he promises.'

But as HRH reminded us, sometimes you have to prepare for war in order to keep the peace. He said, 'If there's another showdown it'll be against the Communists, and if it comes to it we'd better align ourselves with the Germans because no one else seems willing to take on the Red Menace. Except possibly Mussolini.'

Poots Butler said, 'I don't know. Mr Hitler. Mr Mussolini. Mr Stalin. Dictators seem to be all the rage.'

Ernest, who has another carbuncle which is making him

138

feverish and disagreeable, said, 'Yes, who knows, maybe we'll get one in England before long.'

There was a deathly silence until Thelma picked up the gayer subject of Mediterranean cruises. Wally gave Ernest a look to chill the blood.

We adjourned to watch Mickey Mouse cartoons, but Wally went straight up to bed. Not really *comme il faut* when royalties are present but she pleaded a headache, brought on I'm sure by Ernest's gaffe. As Oxer Bettenbrooke pointed out, it was tantamount to treason. Ernest hurried away to the billiard room with Benny Thaw.

October 14, 1933

The Brownlows, Humphrey Butler, the Prince, and Oxer B went cubbing. I drove with Thelma and her little boy to watch the meet at Kneilthorpe House. Hounds milling everywhere and hunters rearing and frisking. Lady Merrick, who looks like a washerwoman, was shouting orders and her sister, just as ruddy-cheeked, was thundering around with trays of stirrup cup. Thelma says there's an interesting American sister-in-law, a Jewess, but all we saw of her was her dog, trotting up and down the terrace with a little Hermès scarf round his neck.

Thelma says she may give up country life now she's divorced. Her son likes the horses, but she says he could have all this and more in the Argentine.

I said, 'But what about the Prince?'

'Oh,' she said, 'I won't run out on him. I'll wait till my time's up.'

I said, 'Has he found a princess? Is there a wedding on the cards?'

She said, 'Oh, not *that*. I expect he will marry soon,

139

but that won't make any difference to us. No, I mean when he finds someone new.'

I said, 'But he adores you.'

'Yes,' she said, 'but he adored others before me and I'm sure there'll be many after me. My Little Man has a restless soul.'

I wonder what happens to his circle when he moves on. Wally won't be happy if the Thelma connection is severed, after all the hard work she's put in. A scratch lunch. Thelma's resting, Benny's making heavy weather of a crossword puzzle, Ernest is dozing with a book. The dressing needs changing on his carbuncle. Wally ought to see to it, but she's in the morning room with Connie and Poots and causing great shrieks of laughter. Sharing further advice on the secret bedroom art of Pang Chung, I suppose.

How slowly time passes in Leicestershire. Prince George is dining this evening.

I think my ox-blood crepe and an angora wrap.

October 15, 1933

A narrowly averted disaster, for which I blame the Chinese, with their mischievously confusing language, and Hattie Erlanger, who sowed the seeds of a dangerous misconstruction. First Thelma's boiler failed, and it being Sunday nothing can be done to repair it. Then Poots Butler insisted we play bridge, but I left the table at the earliest opportunity. Bridge can bring out such unpleasantness in people. I'm sure anyone can mislay a silly card, especially when they're playing in gloves.

The Prince doesn't care for bridge either and was working on his needlepoint. He patted the seat beside him. 'Maybell,' he said, 'I'm chilled to the bone. How about warming up with a spot of ping-pong?'

I believe I blushed. One hears of *droit du seigneur* but he was so matter-of-fact about it, and we were fully within earshot of Thelma, and thank goodness. She saved me from myself.

She said, 'Darling, don't drag Maybell off to the games room. It's like an icebox in there. I'm already worried she'll go home with pneumonia. I'll ring for tea. We can watch some more Mickey, if you like.'

Wally said, 'Anyway, sir, Maybell never hit a ball in her life.'

He said, 'I think you're mistaken, Wally. When we were at the Lido this summer she was the talk of the tennis courts.'

That silenced her!

He left after tea. He has to go to Birmingham tomorrow to visit a bicycle factory, then on to South Wales.

October 16, 1933

Sad farewells to Thelma. She's leaving for the States on Wednesday, going to help her sister Gloria get back the child that's rightfully hers.

She said, 'Maybell, I'm depending on you and Wally to take care of my Little Man while I'm gone. He's sure to be lonely.'

October 17, 1933, Wilton Place

With Wally to Asprey for an urgent belt. She said, 'Thelma's going to be gone for months so this is our chance to become indispensable. As soon as David gets back from visiting his coal mines we're going to give him the most wonderful time. Cozy suppers. Lively people. It's a pity you don't have a country house, Maybell. If you were to get one I could help you do wonderful house parties. Not

141

like those dull little affairs at Borough Court. Thelma's sweet, but for an American she really doesn't have much idea.'

I think HRH seems perfectly contented with Thelma's weekends. Anyway, I'm not interested in getting a country house. More staff to subdue. More cold corridors to heat. Violet is a perfect example of the dangers of spreading oneself too thin.

Rory has an exeat this weekend.

October 21, 1933

To Lyons in the Strand for a Viennese whirl. Flora was allowed to join us because she's notched up a full week at St Audrey's without any misdemeanors. She doesn't appear to have made any friends yet. Rory said, 'You soon will. You should pick out a girl who looks nice and start chatting to her during recreation time.'

She said, 'I don't want to. I like torging to myself.'

To the opera with the Friths and the Belchesters. Something by Strauss, but not his usual hummable waltzes. Lightfoot was in a box with that Belinda.

October 25, 1933

Zita and Bernie Cavett are taking a house on Mount Street till January. Zita says the first thing they're going to do is throw a costume party.

To the Century Club with the Crosbies and the Erlangers. The Simpsons promised but never showed up.

October 27, 1933

Wally says the Prince has dined with them three evenings this week. I said, 'We expected you on Monday evening. Why didn't you bring him to the Century?'

She said, 'He was too comfortable to move.'

I said, 'And who have you invited to dine with him? Aren't your old friends good enough anymore?'

She says Benny Thaw came one evening, but otherwise they've just been a threesome. She said, 'It's not at all that you aren't good enough, Maybell. But sometimes he likes to relax and not be with lots of people.'

Surely, that's what a tray supper for one is for.

November 1, 1933

Lily Drax-Pfaffenhof wants me for Christmas and won't take no for an answer. Wally and Ernest will be going and Wally's keen to have me along. Once Ernest gets his head in a book he's no company.

Lunch with Pips who is very tense waiting to hear whether Freddie's got promoted to PPS. Whatever it is, I hope it means more money for them. Daphne Frith says they're living on their capital.

November 3, 1933

To Bryanston Court, where there are now *three* armchairs arranged round the fireplace. They never know if the Prince is coming until he appears, sometimes as early as five, sometimes as late as nine. Tonight we knew he definitely wouldn't come because he's gone to Norfolk to shoot with Bertie York.

I said, 'Don't you waste an awful lot of food?'

Ernest said, 'We waste nothing. Wally's very thrifty in the kitchen.'

I said, 'But it must be so unsettling, waiting around for hours.'

'Maybell,' he said, 'I can think of nothing more rewarding than entertaining the future King of England.'

Some kind of stew followed by crepes, filled with the Prince of Wales's leftovers.

November 7, 1933
Freddie Crosbie didn't get the new job. Daphne Frith says the problem with Freddie is everyone likes him, which is all very well on the golf course but useless in the Commons. He completely lacks the killer instinct.

November 10, 1933
A small dinner at South Audley Street. Came, Fergus and Penelope Blythe and a couple called Metcalfe.

Penelope said, 'What's happened to your friend Wally? I haven't seen her anywhere lately.'

Baba Metcalfe said, 'Wally who?'

Penelope said, 'Simpson. A little American. Before the summer she and her husband were all over London like a rash.'

Lightfoot said, 'It's true. Wherever two or three were gathered together and a small bottle of tonic wine was opened, Wally Simpson was guaranteed to appear, but not recently. What's she up to, Maybell?'

I said, 'She's taking care of the Prince of Wales.'

Uproar. Fruity Metcalfe said, 'Bugger me. I thought Bettenbrooke was supposed to be doing that.'

Much laughter. Apparently, Major Metcalfe also equerries from time to time.

Baba said, 'But why should Wales need looking after?'

I said, 'Because Thelma Furness is in America and she particularly asked Wally and me to make sure he wasn't lonely.'

'I see,' she said. I don't think she did though. According to Lightfoot she's from a top-drawer family, the Curzons, but I've never heard of her. He says she was reckoned to be a great beauty in her day. Fruity cuts a good figure, tall, commanding. I can see he was a catch.

Lightfoot suggests I go to the Cavetts' party as Little Bo-Peep. He's offered to accompany me as a pet lamb.

November 11, 1933

Remembrance Sunday. Melhuish laid a wreath at the Cenotaph. Lest we forget. I wonder how healthy it is to keep harping back. The world is surely a better place than it was, except for those Roosevelts and the Reds. We're all friends now. And if you start brooding over all the people who've gone to their rest you can end up feeling too depressed even to face the breakfast tray.

Tea at Carlton Gardens. Flora didn't say a word. Just sat on a couch swinging her legs and gazing vacantly.

Doopie said, 'Vora's nod abby.'

Violet said, 'Flora's perfectly happy, thank you, Doopie. Please don't interfere. She's been a very good girl this week.'

I went up to the nursery to see how Doopie's getting on with my shepherdess gown. She said, 'Bayba, Vora's nod abby adall.'

This was always likely to happen. Doopie's had the child to herself since the day she was born and she doesn't like it now Flora's going to school and learning how to behave like a young lady. I'd say it's Doopie who's 'nod abby'.

My gown is looking very well indeed.

November 12, 1933

Wally has asked to borrow my diamond stomacher for the Cavetts' party. She's going as the Snow Queen. Pips is undecided between the Little Match Seller or the Pied

Piper of Hamelin. Lightfoot is being very perplexing about his costume. He said, 'I shall be a wolf in sheep's clothing. Or is it the other way round?' There also remains the problem of a shepherd's crook.

November 15, 1933
Ernest is worried about insurance for my diamonds. He turned quite pale when I told him they were worth ten thousand at the last valuation, not to mention their sentimental value. He said, 'In that case I think they'd better remain in your bank. Wally can wear paste.'

Wally was furious. She said, 'Wally cannot wear paste. And I'm not ruining my costume because you lack nerve, Ernest. Maybell's diamonds will be quite safe with me.'

Personally I think she's overdoing things. It's only a party in a vacation home, after all. It's not as though she's going to Londonderry House.

November 16, 1933
Monsieur Jules wants me to try a finger wave. Not sure.
Drinks at the Yugoslav Legation.

November 17, 1933
I'm invited to a gala ball at Lancaster House, in aid of Anne Belchester's orphanages. Offered to make arrangements for Violet to get something done with her hair but she declined. I bet she's going to turn up in that ancient eau de Nil too. Tired brocade and day shoes. No wonder people never believe we're sisters.

November 19, 1933
A wonderful party! Zita and Bernie spared no expense and my Bo-Peep gown looked darling. George Lightfoot

seemed to have forgotten he was meant to be a Lost Sheep and turned up as the Tin Man, but I forgave him because he'd managed to borrow me a divine crozier from one of his little bishop friends. The Erlangers were Humpty Dumpty and Miss Muffet, Pips was the Pied Piper because Freddie had told her she has good legs and should show them to advantage. I don't think they're all *that* good. Freddie himself was in a yellow vest, making absurd noises all evening, supposed to be a motoring character called Mr Toad. Ernest wore a muffler and carried a jar of honey. A feeble effort, I thought. He said he was Pooh Bear. Daisy Fellowes came as Tinkerbell. Tinkerbag, Lightfoot kept calling her. Not sure who Bernie was meant to be. Some kind of gnome. But Zita looked very pretty as the Sugar Plum Fairy, in froths of pink net hung with candy. HRH looked in briefly and was asked to judge the best costume. I'm sure it was a close-run thing between me and Zita, but Wally pushed herself forward beneath a chandelier so my diamonds would sparkle to advantage. I suppose after all those dinners she's made for him recently, he felt obliged to choose her. She got a magnum of champagne and a kiss on the cheek.

Zita said, 'We hoped you'd come in costume yourself, sir.'

He said, 'Lord, no, I spend enough of my life in fancy dress.'

She said, 'But if you had to, who would you be?'

'No idea,' he said. 'What do you suggest?'

She said, 'Peter Pan.'

Wally said, 'Oh no, sir! I don't agree. I'd make you the King of Hearts.'

Pips said, 'Oh please! Take me somewhere I can throw up.'

November 20, 1933

Lunch with Penelope Blythe. She just had an 'adventure' with a man who came to rehang her dining-room doors and recommends the experience. 'None of those boring preliminaries,' she said. 'You know? Drinks. Dinner. Phone calls. You should try it. It'd take you out of yourself.'

I told her, I don't want to be out of myself. I'm quite happy where I am.

November 24, 1933

Philip Sassoon will be celebrating his birthday at Park Lane this year. A Sunday-afternoon tea party. Wally and Ernest have gone to Fort Belvedere for the weekend.

Pips said, 'What are they doing? Keeping Thelma's place warm for the King of Hearts?'

Since Freddie failed to get that position he'd hoped for, I notice Pips has become very bitter about the success of others.

November 29, 1933

Anne Belchester's ball. Violet wore full-length tartan and a limp white blouse. She said, 'I know it's not quite the thing, but Trotman forgot to freshen up my eau de Nil.'

Melhuish said, 'Stop fretting, Vee. You look ravishing.' Ha!

I thought the flowers rather skimped. Violet said, 'The idea is to raise money, not waste it on flowers that will be dead by midnight.'

I'm sure the orphans wouldn't have begrudged us a few hundred carnations.

December 4, 1933

Philip Sassoon's birthday. I gave him a walking stick with a duck's head handle, Lightfoot brought him a bottle of something made from Polish licorice.

Sybil was there, with two of her children. Also the dark-complexioned Cousin Hannah.

Philip said, 'Maybell, your friend Wally Simpson bombards me r-r-relentlessly with invitations. It's like being back in the Somme.'

I said, 'Yes, she's very keen to get you. She's taken charge of the social life of the Prince of Wales while Lady Furness is away. She wants to keep him entertained.'

'Ach,' he said, 'Wales! As well try to entertain a pet r-r-rodent. Tell her to put him inside a little r-r-running wheel.'

Smoked haddock sandwiches, an original touch. And delicious chocolate cake all the way from Austria.

Philip wore a long velvet jacket and zebra-hide slippers. Such a pity he doesn't think of marrying.

December 5, 1933

Lunch with Ida Coote. She's taken to blackening her eyes with a kohl pencil since learning of her ancient Egyptian lineage.

December 6, 1933

To the Adelphi Theatre with Lightfoot to see *Nymph Errant*.

He said he'll be relieved when school ends because he doesn't think St Audrey's is suiting Flora at all.

I said, 'But she's finally settled down. She hasn't done anything naughty since she started there.'

'Precisely,' he said. 'And she looks like a wan little candle. I think she's depressed.'

I said, 'You mean Doopie thinks she's depressed.'

'Yes,' he said. 'And I agree with her. We do know her rather well. We are her gobparents, after all.'

I see the start of a campaign. I shall warn Violet.

December 10, 1933

Violet says St Audrey's has been a great success and Flora has never been more amenable. She said, 'Lightfoot's a dear, but he's something of a theorist on the raising of children. Well, he'll find out someday.'

I said, 'Do you think he's going to marry that girl Belinda?'

'Very likely,' she said. 'It would be perfectly suitable.'

December 15, 1933

To Elspeth Laird's bazaar in aid of Life Boats. An entire stall filled with Doopie's handicrafts. Padded coat hangers, lavender sachets, little knitted hats for soft-boiled eggs. Flora was assisting her Uncle Salty on the bran tub. Violet was with Elspeth on the tea urn, Melhuish was selling prize-draw tickets, Rory and Ulick were circulating with Guess the Weight of the Cake. A real family affair.

Lady Strathnaver won the cake.

December 18, 1933

To Hamleys with Rory. Flora was obliged to go to a birthday party for one of the Belchester children but Rory picked out a hand puppet he believes she'll like: a pig. He didn't know what to suggest for Ulick, so I bought him a banjo. He has no interest in music, so it may be the very instrument for him.

Something from the Cussons range for Doopie and for Padmore. They're both fond of scented bath salts and dusting powder, but there's no sense in going overboard. No one ever smells them. I noted which model battleship Rory most admired and sent Kettle back to purchase it while we went to the Star Grill for sausages and creamed potatoes.

He said, 'I wish you were coming to our house at Christmas, like last year.'

I said, 'Well, there'll be other Christmases. I'm going to the Tyrolean mountains with my friend Wally.'

He said, 'I know. Mummy said The Wally is a climber.'

He got a good report card, except for geometry and gymnastics. I told him, math can be a puzzle to the best of brains, especially geometry which is of no use to anyone, and gymnastics don't matter either. They're an optional extra, like playing the violin or speaking French.

He said, 'Oh, but I'll need geometry when I go into the navy, so I can navigate. And I have to be able to climb up a rope. Uncle Salty told me.'

Such nonsense. They have people to do the navigating for you and I've been on many a boat and never seen any rope-climbing. There are staircases.

To the Cocoanut Grove. Came, Wally, Ernest and the Prince, Zita and Bernie, Hattie and Judson.

December 19, 1933
Drinks and Christmas caroling at the American compound. Benny Thaw says the news from Connie and Thelma isn't bright. Gloria's sister-in-law seems determined to hold on to the borrowed child and they're worried her lawyers have something up their sleeves. Benny says it's easy for a misconstruction to be placed on a person living in Paris. He also says the Prince of Wales

is pining for Thelma. Well, he seemed cheerful enough last night.

Dinner at the Crosbies'. Came, the Trillings, the Prosper Friths and Lord Birkenhead. Everyone is agreed that Mr Hitler is quite a phenomenon. He's pulled Germany out of its depression and now has the whole nation behind him. Freddie said, 'What Hitler needs now is a nice English wife, to remind him who his friends are. Or an American. How about you, Maybell? Shall we send you on a special mission to woo Mr H?'

I don't think so. Politics can be such a dangerous business, and anyway, they say he's very keen on women having babies.

Tomorrow to Paris, Thursday to Lily's.

December 23, 1933, Schloss Pfaffenhof, Bavaria

Lily's schloss is a real miniature castle and much better arranged than Drumcanna. At Lily's the help sleep in the turrets and the guests sleep in proper suites. Snow but blue skies. Dear Prince Louis Ferdinand is here with his mother, Crown Princess Cecilie. Ernest bows to her every time he sees her but I'm sure it isn't necessary. Strictly speaking, she's in the same category as Ena Spain: dispensed with as a royalty and dispensed with as a wife.

Arriving tonight, a couple from Milwaukee, the Gunters, and Baron and Baroness Rothschild.

December 24, 1933

Christmas shopping in Innsbruck with Kitty Rothschild and Wally. Wally was drooling over the displays of crystal but I bought scarves for all the girls and pocket silks for all the boys. Afterwards to Café Katzung for hot chocolate.

There's to be a Tyrolean ball on Friday and Lily has persuaded us all to buy Jacquard evening dirndls. Not my idea of a flattering garment, but no one can accuse me of not entering into the spirit of an occasion. Wally says I suit the look because I'm *zaftig*, which I certainly am not. Indeed, it's a rather juvenile fashion best suited to someone with no bosom, Wally being a perfect example.

The Gunters are tedious. They travel with photographs of their dogs and pass them around at every opportunity. The Rothschilds are nice, easygoing. Eugene kisses one's hand, just like Philip Sassoon. I suppose it's because they both have French blood mingled with the Oriental. Kitty is sporty-looking and plain-spoken in that refreshing American way. I don't think Wally likes her.

December 26, 1933
Slipped on freezing snow on Christmas morning and am bruised black and blue. Lily's doctor says there's nothing to do but rest. Of course, couch-bound one is easy prey for bores. Mrs Gunter taxed me for a full hour with her own medical history.

December 27, 1933
Everyone has gone to the casino in Garmisch, except for Cecilie Hohenzollern who went to bed early and Ernest who has insisted on keeping me company. I think the truth is he prefers not to see Wally gambling. Ernest isn't a risk-taker and according to Ethel Croker when Wally sits at a table she becomes a demon. He roasted chestnuts and grew sentimental on pear schnapps.

He said, 'I like nothing better than a cozy fireside. I'm afraid I hold Wally back sometimes. She has so much energy.'

The only respect in which he holds Wally back is money, but of course I couldn't say so.

I said, 'Yes, she was always a live wire.'

He said, 'I have no complaints, you understand. Wally's drawn us into illustrious circles and I'm very grateful to her. We don't broadcast it but His Royal Highness has become quite one of the family. It's more than I could ever have dreamed of.'

I got him talking about his people. English grandparents on his father's side, American on his mother's. He and his sister grew up in New York. They're not close. The business he's in now, ship brokerage, was started by his father. His first wife suffered from nerves. He said, 'Our splitting up was nothing to do with Wally, you know. Dorie and I were on the brink of divorce anyway.' She took the child and went back to her family in Massachusetts. He said, 'I have a daughter, nearly ten. I hope someday to be a father to her again. Have her to visit. She'd like London.'

I bet Wally hasn't been asked about that. I can't see her trailing round the Zoological Gardens with a child.

December 30, 1933
Too sore to dance but I made the effort and attended the Tyrolean ball. Actually, not so much a ball as a raucous evening of peasant-like simplicity. But fun. Lily, Wally, and Kitty polka'd all the men under the table.

The Gunters have moved on to another party in Salzburg. She said, 'If ever you find yourself in Wisconsin.'

I hardly think so.

January 1, 1934

Last evening we listened to Dr Goebbels on the wireless. Lily translated. It was a very uplifting speech about how much has changed in Germany in one year. Despair and civil unrest have been replaced by optimism and stability and the Bolshevik specter has been laid to rest. We all drank to that. My own private little wish is for a quiet year to come. Too much busyness is bad for the nerves.

January 8, 1934, Wilton Place

To the Victoria Palace Theatre with Rory, Flora, Lightfoot, and Doopie to see a children's show called *Goody Two Shoes*. We all joined in the singing and shouting and had great fun. Doopie's eyes never left the stage. I don't suppose she made much sense of what was going on but she enjoyed herself in her own little way. Her life is so sadly narrow.

Wally is talking about going to Paris to order gowns. Ernest doesn't have that kind of money.

I said, 'Can you really afford to?'

She said, 'The question is, Maybell, how can I afford not to? This is going to be our year. David's promised to get us presented to the King and Queen and I'm not going to do that wearing something from Derry & Toms.'

I said, 'But what about your divorces?'

She said, 'David says they're irrelevant because they were in America. They only count if they happen here.'

I must tell Violet.

January 10, 1934

An emergency at Carlton Gardens. Flora climbed out the nursery window on to a little roof rather than be sent back to St Audrey's. She had on her topcoat and mittens and took a bottle of milk and Pigster puppet, so it was all planned. The hook and ladder men were called out, but it was Lightfoot who persuaded her to climb back through the window. He promised he'd help find her another school where she'd be happy and she promised to do her lessons at home every day and try a new school when they find somewhere suitable.

All very well, but in the meanwhile she's falling further and further behind with her math. He said, 'Mathematics doesn't concern me. She'll catch up. She's perfectly bright. Doesn't miss a trick. But she doesn't have any friends. *That's* what school's about. And of course she didn't make any friends at St Audrey's because she was only there for six weeks, which isn't long for anybody to take to an odd little soul like Flora. I don't know. It was too awful. Doopie was crying, Violet was shouting at Melhuish, Melhuish was screaming at the firemen as though they were on a parade ground. She could have fallen and been killed.'

I said, 'I'll go and visit.'

He said, 'I wouldn't. Not yet. She's both in disgrace and being treasured like Lazarus back from the dead. It's a very strange atmosphere. I'd wait if I were you, till Violet returns to her committees and the normal chaos prevails.'

January 11, 1934

Benny Thaw was right, Connie and Thelma's sister does indeed have a battle on her hands. Gertrude Whitney's argument is that the child is better off on Long Island with a nurse and regular hours than she is in Paris with a lively, popular mother, and of course the judge is sure to see things her way. It's all a terrible worry to them and Wally says Gloria stands to lose thousands per month in child support. Meanwhile, HRH is deprived of Thelma's company and doesn't seem to know what to do with himself. I suppose courtiers direct him in every particular of his official life, but when it comes to a spare hour or two he has no idea how to fill it. That's why he allows Wally to monopolize him so.

January 12, 1934

Called at Carlton Gardens. Flora has a chill, caught sitting out on rooftops in January. She said, 'I wore my muvvler, Aunt Bayba, and so did Pigster. We were higher than the trees. It isn't hard. I can show you one day.'

Doopie said, 'You will nod. You gibben me nidemares.'

Trotman says a man is coming to fit bars tomorrow.

January 16, 1934

A bad start to the week. Ernest has put his foot down over Paris even though the Westminsters are giving a ball and for some unaccountable reason the Simpsons are invited but I am not.

Ernest said, 'Women of much greater means manage to dress without spending that kind of money. Look at Maybell.'

She said, 'I aim higher than Maybell.'

I agree with Ernest. Elegance is wasted here and Paris gowns are not the way to endear yourself to London.

January 18, 1934
Wally has asked to borrow Pips's sapphire bracelet.

Pips said, 'It was such a sob story. Ernest's imposed such a cruel budget it sounds as though she'll be going to the Westminsters' in rags.'

Of course, Pips was never as close to Wally as I was. She didn't see how she struggled to have any kind of Season. Her uncle kept her on pins till the very last moment about whether he'd loan her a car and a driver. She could never take anything for granted as we could.

I said, 'She just wants to shine.'

Pips said, 'And she will, in my sapphires. But honestly, what a fuss. I'll bet old Ernest had no idea he was marrying such a princess.'

January 20, 1934
Wally is getting a 'Paris gown' without going to Paris. Ida Coote's little woman in South Kensington is making her a copy of a Vionnet gown. Sepia silk velvet with a halter-neck, which saves her borrowing a necklace and will look very well with Connie Thaw's pageant tiara. She's satisfied and so is Ernest.

She said, 'What a pity the Westminsters didn't invite you. We could have shared a car.' If that was a hint about my Bentley I allowed it to pass unheeded.

Snow.

January 24, 1934
The Germans have executed the Bolshevik who fired their parliament. Mr Hitler is certainly showing the world he'll

stand for no nonsense. I think Brumby would have very much approved.

I'm going to give an impromptu dinner, but only for people who have topics of conversation other than balls.

February 3, 1934

If Loelia Westminster's ball was half as successful as my little dinner she must be a happy woman this morning. Came, Bernie and Zita Cavett, Marthe Bibesco, Benny Thaw, and Ida Coote. Marthe said I should have invited the Stanley Baldwins. She said, 'To create a salon is not so hard, Maybell. All you have to do is recognize nobodies who will one day be somebodies.' She said she always wished she'd thought to cultivate Ramsay MacDonald while he was an undesirable. My gamble on Ida paid off. Everyone enjoyed her reminiscences of ancient Egypt and Bernie confessed that for years he's been convinced he was formerly a Roman centurion on Hadrian's Wall.

February 6, 1934

Sir Philip hasn't forgotten me after all. I am invited to Trent to see the snowdrops. He said, 'Name your day, Maybell. One word from me and they'll pop up their heads.'

February 8, 1934

A 'little talk' from Violet. Why don't I find myself some useful work instead of lunching with drones every day? She can put me in touch with many worthy organizations. I defended myself. I'm sure I make more decisions over one lunch than her committees do after hours of discussion. And none of *my* friends drones. Well, Ida does, a bit.

February 12, 1934

Philip's snowdrops had indeed popped up their heads. He manages to have his gardens worth touring when everyone else's are nothing but wet leaves and frozen earth. I thought he looked fatigued but he dashed round showing me his latest acquisitions. A scarlet-and-silver japanned mirror, an antique pole lantern from Venice, and a new pair of king penguins for the lake. He said he's been feeling too cross for parties.

I asked him what he thinks of Mr Hitler. 'R-r-r-raving,' he said.

February 14, 1934

Valentine flowers from a secret admirer. They are Cellophane-wrapped so must *not* be from Philip Sassoon. I fear I detect the clumsy hand of Randolph Putnam.

February 18, 1934

The King of the Belgians is dead. We didn't know him.

February 19, 1934

At last! I am invited to Fort Belvedere. The Prince of Wales bids me for weekend of March 9. Pips and Freddie are also invited but that in no way diminishes the thrill. In fact, it will be fun to have someone to confer with about gowns.

Wally says she arranged it, but she can only arrange what she knows to be the Prince's wishes.

Violet tried to make light of my invitation. All she said was, 'The 9th? Oh, we'll be at Royal Lodge with Bertie and Elizabeth the very same weekend.'

I sense there must have been a big falling-out between Melhuish and the Prince. As young men they went everywhere together but now they never see one another.

Lunch with George Lightfoot. He says with Melhuish and the Prince it's been more a drifting apart than a rupture. He said, 'Wales still loves to do new things and meet new people, especially Americans, whereas Melhuish has become rather set in his ways. But Melhuish is loyalty itself, you know? If Wales asked for him he'd be there like a shot.'

February 23, 1934
To the Ham Bone Club with Wally, Ernest, HRH, and the Erlangers. A rather knowing little pansy sang at the piano. Wally and the Prince laughed loudly, but I can't say I found him so amusing. Gladys Trilling is expecting again. Poor Whitlow.

February 26, 1934
Wally recommends knitted jumper suits for day wear at the Fort. I just nodded politely. They may flatter a mannish figure like hers but they do nothing for us real women. I happen to know she's asked to borrow Hattie Erlanger's amethysts.

March 2, 1934
I have decided on a vine as my weekend gift to HRH. I know he's an avid gardener. The Crosbies are going to drive down with me on Friday afternoon. Boss and Ethel Croker are going to take Sunninghills again for Ascot Week.

March 6, 1934
Saw Benny Thaw at the Belchesters' cocktail. The court case has been heard and Gertrude Whitney has been granted custody of Gloria's child. He said it was a lost

cause once they called the child's nurse to the stand because she embroidered all kinds of exaggerations about Gloria's way of life. Drink, men, *women*. He said even Nada Milford Haven's name was uttered. All very hard cheese for Gloria because she'll now have to adjust to a lowered income. The good news is that Thelma and Connie will soon be on their way home. This weekend's party may turn out to be the last one Wally's asked to organize.

March 9, 1934, Fort Belvedere
The Fort looked enchanting as we approached, lights streaming from the windows, liveried footmen waiting like statues on the gravel, and then HRH himself came out to the car to greet us. I am in bedroom No. 3 with a view of the swimming pool. Pink sheets, pink drapes, even pink soap, in a wonderful American bathroom with a wonderful American shower. There's every sign that when he becomes King the Prince will do much to improve this country.

Also here, Fruity and Baba Metcalfe, Lord Templemore, and the Humphrey Butlers. He occasionally equerries for Prince George.

HRH is delighted with his vine. He asked me whether I cared for gardening.

I said 'Sir, I adore gardening. At Sweet Air I employed ten men.'

He said, 'Maybell, you must call me David.'

I wonder whether Violet's ears caught that up at Royal Lodge.

Wore my beaded celadon to dinner. Pips in biscuit satin, Poots Butler in lilac, Wally in black taffeta and diamonds. Excessive, I thought. The Fort isn't grand and we were very informal. HRH himself carved the roast lamb and then after the savory he entertained us on the bagpipes. No withdrawing. Just lots of jolly chatter around the table and then dancing to gramophone records in the Octagon Room.

March 10, 1934
By the time I came down this morning HRH had organized a working party and the men were all hacking at old shrubs, clearing an area he visualizes as a new rock garden. It was most amusing to see Freddie Crosbie armed with a machete. David and Fruity in ancient tweeds, having the greatest fun with billhooks. Ernest in a brand-new sweater, pecking at undergrowth as though it might peck back. He's not an outdoors person.

Wally and Poots Butler went to the kitchen and made club sandwiches for lunch. Baba Metcalfe says the chef and the major-domo were beside themselves, but HRH does love Wally's club sandwiches so they daren't complain.

Tonight I wore my peacock shantung. Wally was in forest green with Hattie Erlanger's amethysts. Baba Metcalfe wears practically no jewels at all. Prince George joined us for dinner and afterwards we played Assassin, spoiled for me by Ernest who accused me of extraneous winking. As I explained, I have a slight chill in my tear gland. 'Then you should disqualify yourself from playing,' he said. 'The rules of the game are clear.'

He can be a puffed-up little know-it-all for a man who allows his wife to wear borrowed jewels.

HRH received a telephone call just before midnight. Thelma, from New York. She sails on Monday. Pips said, 'There'll be rejoicing below stairs. No more club sandwiches. No more corn being popped at all hours. And as soon as the *Bremen* docks Wally'll be back in the chorus line.'

March 11, 1934

There has been a turn of affairs. Wally and HRH were missing for nearly two hours this afternoon. Heavy rain was falling so we knew they couldn't be inspecting the gardens. Ernest was asleep in an armchair, making annoying little whiffling noises, so he couldn't be questioned. Then Fruity found out that they'd taken a car and gone up to the Castle. Baba said, 'I hope they haven't dropped in at Royal Lodge. The Yorks would have a fit.'

People were just going up to dress when they reappeared, all jollity and dripping umbrellas. They'd been to a church service. Evensong in St George's Chapel. Well! I can understand that the Prince feels an obligation to do these things. Someday he'll be King and so must set an example to the lower classes. But Wally? She was enthusing about the spiritual uplift of the music, which was all embarrassing enough, but then she completely overstepped the mark.

She said, 'Oh, look how muddy my shoes are. David, take them off for me, would you?' and HRH got down on his knees and undid her laces.

Fruity and Ernest both studied the floor and the major-domo turned quite white.

Pips came along to my room the minute she was dressed. She said, 'There goes Wally's career as royal apple-polisher. Enjoy the evening, Maybell. I don't think any of us will be coming back in a hurry.'

But HRH was all lightness and gaiety at dinner and so was Wally.

Poots Butler says she may be forgiven a first offense

164

but someone should have a word with her before she goofs again. Well, it's not going to be me.

Anyway, perhaps princes get sick of people bowing and scraping.

March 14, 1934, Wilton Place
Calls from Anne Belchester and Daphne Frith who had it from Hattie that there'd been an incident at the Fort, with Wally screaming at the Prince of Wales to lick her boots. Hattie says she's only repeating what she heard in the hairdresser's.

March 15, 1934
To the Dorch with Penelope Blythe. She says it's common knowledge in Cadogan Square that Wally was wrongly accused of trampling mud on to a priceless rug and Ernest, incensed, had demanded an apology from the Prince of Wales. How Wally must be enjoying all this.

March 16, 1934
Treated Wally to Claridge's. She says Thelma has a rude shock awaiting her when she returns to London. While crossing the Atlantic she's been accepting bouquets and playing shuffleboard with a certain Prince Aly Khan, and that word has reached HRH.

I said, 'How do you know? They must still be at sea.'

'I'm not at liberty to say,' was all I could get out of her.

March 19, 1934
Penelope Blythe says Aly Khan is a swarthy-skinned prince whom women find irresistible. She says Wally must have the information from HRH himself. She says he probably has spies watching Thelma's every move. Pips agrees, but

she doesn't believe Wally can be party to such sensitive secrets. Also, according to *The Times*, he's in Ayrshire at a Boy Scout jamboree, so even if his snoops are keeping him *au courant* with events in the middle of the Atlantic, Wally has no way of hearing about it.

March 20, 1934

Dinner at Carlton Gardens. The Boddie-Fultons and the Salty Lairds. I happened to have bumped into Fiona Boddie-Fulton only this morning when I was in Cramphorne Doggit with Wally, looking at silver epergnes. She said, 'Did you find something to your liking?'

I said, 'It wasn't for me. It was for my friend.'

Violet said, 'Not Minnehaha? An epergne?'

Hoots of laughter from Elspeth Laird. She said, 'How very ostentatious! Violet, didn't you tell me that this person lives in Paddington?'

I hold no brief to defend Wally Simpson but it seems to me *any* home would be improved by an epergne.

March 23, 1934

Drama at Bryanston Court. Wally and I had just started tea when Thelma Furness was announced and came in looking most distressed. She said she'd seen the Prince three times since her return from America and he'd been noticeably cool toward her and now he won't even say what he's doing for the weekend.

Wally said, 'He's going to Oliver Templemore's.'

Thelma said, 'Then why didn't he say? Has something happened while I've been gone? Has he found someone new?'

If it had been left to me I'd have told her about those

shipboard stories that have reached the Prince's ears, but Wally gave me one of her looks and cut right across me.

She said, 'I'm sure you're imagining things. David's been lost without you. He's been throwing himself more into his work. He's looking into the question of Glaswegian slums at present. I expect he's just distracted.'

Thelma said, 'Slums never distracted him before.'

I heard the telephone ring. Wally chatted on, about the Westminsters' ball, and our Christmas in the Tyrol. No one touched the pastries. It was as if we were all waiting for some next thing to happen.

The new maid came in and Wally tore her off such a strip. She said, 'I told you I wasn't to be disturbed.'

She said, 'I know that's what you said, madam, but it's the Prince of Wales again and he's most insistent.'

Wally didn't say a word. She just got up, left the room, and shut the door behind her. Thelma was leaning back in the chair with her eyes closed.

She said, 'You knew. Wally's stolen him.'

I said, 'That's nonsense. Now, tell me honestly, did you have a little adventure on the voyage home?'

She never did answer that. All she kept saying was, 'I trusted her and she's stolen him.'

I said, 'On the contrary. There are some who think Wally may have worn out her welcome. She's been quite impertinent at times, and she's upset the kitchen staff at the Fort, scrambling eggs for David at all hours.'

She said, 'I didn't know he liked scrambled eggs.'

It was a difficult moment.

I said, 'How was New York?'

'Cold,' she said, 'and full of traitors. Just like here.'

She's no great conversationalist. We sat in silence

waiting for Wally to reappear. I was about to ring for more hot water when the maid came in.

She said, 'Madam makes her apologies. She's had to go out directly.'

I said, 'Where to?'

'Oh, to York House, madam,' she said. 'The Prince sent a car for her and she doesn't expect to be back for dinner. Will I fetch your coats?'

By the time I returned from powdering my nose poor Thelma had gone. I went straight to Halkin Street, but Pips had already left for the constituency and Hattie Erlanger was on her way to a sister in Gloucestershire. Friday afternoon is the worst possible time for sharing a bombshell. I had no choice but to take it to Violet and all she said was, 'Maybell! *Pas devant les enfants!*'

Flora dancing around the drawing room singing, 'I know what that means. I know what that means.'

March 24, 1934
I've gone over and over yesterday's events and can make no sense of them. Called Bryanston Court at nine and was told that Mr and Mrs Simpson had left for Lincolnshire and will be gone till Monday.

March 25, 1933
Benny Thaw called me. Connie has taken Thelma, most distraught, up to Leicestershire. Did I know anything? I told him what I'd heard about Mr Aly Khan and the daily deliveries of roses to Thelma's stateroom. He said he didn't believe a word of it. All I can say is, before a girl starts playing shuffleboard with playboys she had better think of the consequences.

He said, 'Look, Maybell, I have to ask you. Have Wales and Wally become lovers?'

Benny can be such a dope. Thelma getting dropped in favor of scraggy old Wally!

I said, 'The idea's too crazy for words. How can you even suggest it?'

He said, 'Because I remember how Wally operates. I know she's no beauty, but she acts sassy and takes the lead, and I have a feeling Wales is just the type to fall for it.'

He's wrong, I'm sure, and Lightfoot agrees with me, though I thought he went on unnecessarily about Thelma's perfect skin and the dark smolder of her eyes.

I said, 'If you're so taken with her why don't you hie yourself up to Leicestershire. She may be back on the open market.'

'Oh Maybell!' he said. 'Really!'

March 26, 1934

Finally got through to Wally. She said, 'We were at the Perry Brownlows'. I know I told you we were going.'

I said, 'Well?'

'Well what?' she said.

I said, 'Don't play games with me, Wally. Suddenly you're at a prince's beck and call, suddenly you have cars being sent for you.'

She said, 'We're *all* at his beck and call, Maybell. That's what makes him a prince. He just wanted to talk about public housing.'

Public housing! I said, 'Thelma thinks you've betrayed her.'

She said. 'Well, Thelma has to realize men can tire of even the prettiest of faces. There are times when they prefer the company of a woman with a well-formed mind.'

169

She and Ernest are invited to Fort Belvedere again for the weekend, so that's one in the eye for Baba Metcalfe. After the shoe incident she was predicting years of ice-cold exclusion.

Lunched with Pips. She said, 'Well, well! So now the question is, how long has David Wales been playing in Ernest's toy box?'

I said, 'But Ernest always goes with her to the Fort.'

She said, 'So what? Ernest's a ten o'clock man. He'll be too far gone in sleep to hear the boing of royal bed springs.'

It's unthinkable.

March 27, 1934

George Lightfoot spoke with Perry Brownlow who definitely has the impression Wally has moved into a position of special importance to the Prince. As Lightfoot put it, 'She's promoted to Queen Bee and Thelma Furness is reduced to the ranks.' He buys Wally's line about the appeal of a lively mind. He said, 'She's unusual. Not particularly original perhaps, but Brownlow says she remembers useful things and recycles them very cleverly. Wales is always impressed by that kind of thing, having absolutely nothing going on inside his own head.'

Hattie Erlanger says there's nothing unusual about a married woman being asked to act as chatelaine for a public figure who has no consort. She said, 'Thelma was too retiring. I always thought so. But I don't understand why HRH had to choose another colonial. It's just too galling.'

Gladys Trilling is suddenly very warm toward Wally. She's thinking of asking her to be godmother to the unborn child. Judson says we'd all better start being especially

170

nice to Wally. I think I've always been especially nice to Wally.

March 29, 1934
Took Rory and Flora to Fortman's Soda Fountain for ice-cream sundaes. As we walked in Wally was just leaving with an over-rouged little woman in a fox stole. 'Can't stop,' she said. 'Emerald's taking me to meet a new dress-maker.'

Lady Cunard. Flora was open-mouthed. She kept asking, 'But how did she get her hair so jellow?' With the help of a colorblind hairdresser, one can only suppose. Rory was more interested in The Wally, as he calls her, having heard her mocked and slandered in his mother's drawing room. He said, 'Mummy says she's a dangerous person we don't want to know. She doesn't look very dangerous.'

I said, 'She's not. I just don't think Mommy ever liked Wally very much, even when we were girls, and now she's cross because the Prince of Wales goes to Wally's house and he doesn't come to yours.'

He said, 'Oh, but we don't want him too. Ulick says he's jolly unsound.'

March 31, 1934, Hoxney Court, Kent
Apart from the Crosbies a dull group at the Prosper Friths', but I'm not sorry to get away from all that silly London jabbering about Wally. Daphne Frith hasn't even mentioned the subject. Lord and Lady Halifax are here, and Alex and Nellie Hardinge, so we're all seriousness and propriety. Pips says Hoxney Court is a place where men sleep with their wives and all's well with the world, but that may change tonight when Penelope Blythe arrives.

171

April 2, 1934
Now even here the talk is of Wally. Penelope Blythe was the one to break the silence and then Nellie Hardinge couldn't wait to tell us that Ambassador von Hoesch has been placed in an impossible position by this new friendship. HRH had asked for a little dinner at the German Embassy and now he's demanding that Wally be added to the invitation list. I don't see the problem myself. Wally's good value at anyone's table.

Lady Halifax said she'd leave the room if there was any more talk about Wales and his dreadful friends. Daphne Frith covered with embarrassment. She said, 'I'm sure Dorothy didn't mean you.' I don't care if she did. Dorothy Halifax is one of those Englishwomen who says 'dreadful' rather than utter the word 'American'. Edward Halifax has only one hand. I suppose that eliminates golf.

April 3, 1934, Wilton Place
The Crokers have arrived for their season. Lunch with Ethel tomorrow. Pips has chosen a brand-new eatery in Beauchamp Place. Ethel hadn't heard about Wally and HRH. She said, 'Well, she always did know how to get men. Poor Ernest, though.'

April 4, 1934
Ida Coote spotted us before we'd even ordered and hung round our table until Ethel said, 'Why don't you pull up a chair, dear? Take the weight off your pins.'

Pips said, 'Okay, the question before us is, has the P of W bedded Wally Simpson? All those who say "obviously", raise their right hand.'

I was the only one who disagreed, but then, none of them knows Wally as I do.

I said, 'She once told me she never felt inclined to sleep with either of her husbands.'

Pips said, 'No need to get into technicalities. Even if they sit up all night talking soup kitchens, I say it counts.'

Ethel said, 'Me too.'

Ida said, 'And anyway, we're not talking about any old beau. We're talking about a *prince*. *The* Prince, actually. I'd sleep with him in a heartbeat.'

That signifies nothing, though I was friend enough not to say so. Ida Coote would sleep with a corporal of the King's Horse.

Tomorrow to Bryanston Court for dinner. I'll soon get to the bottom of this.

April 5, 1934

A tense evening. Judson and Hattie, the Dimitri Shapaleffs and a tame architect who has ideas about housing for the working classes. Wally's idea of introducing things of particular interest to the Prince.

Most unusually, Ernest wasn't late for his own party and arrived ahead of the Prince, but as soon as HRH did appear *he* began handing around canapés and generally playing the host. Hattie raised an eyebrow.

Wally pushed the conversation along all evening but it felt very brittle. Then Ernest made his excuses after half a cigar, pleading masses of paperwork before he leaves on a trip to Hamburg.

He said, 'I'll leave Wally to take care of you, sir.'

Another eyebrow from Hattie. I don't know. Violet always says it's unforgivable to retire before a royalty.

As HRH was leaving, he said, 'Maybell, come to the Fort this weekend. Wally, have Maybell brought to the Fort.'

'Oh, sir!' she said. 'You make it sound like an arrest!'

Now, do you really call a man 'sir' after he's crossed a certain threshold? I don't think so.

April 6, 1934
Pips had had Hattie on the telephone first thing. She said, 'See! Ernest leaves for Hamburg and Wally sets off for the Fort. It's in the bag. Jeepers, Maybell, you're going to have a ringside seat. Take notes now. I'm relying on you.'

April 7, 1934, Fort Belvedere
The Perry Brownlows are here, plus Judson and Hattie, Oliver Templemore, and Oxer Bettenbrooke. Wally has bedroom No. 1. The Erlangers are in Thelma's old quarters. Hattie invited me in to see. It's like the inside of a chocolate box.

April 8, 1934
Hattie came in at seven, still in her wrap. She said, 'I can't sleep. I'll absolutely burst if I don't tell someone. Judson went down to get a glass of milk at about midnight and he saw the back of HRH trotting along the corridor to Wally's room.'
So it's definite. How thrilling.
Hattie says she isn't convinced Ernest really had to go to Hamburg. She thinks he knows when he's beaten and is probably at Bryanston Court quietly licking his wounds.
She's convening an emergency lunch for Tuesday. As she says, this is pretty momentous stuff.

April 9, 1934, Wilton Place
Pips called first thing. She said, 'Don't even think of coming to lunch without getting the facts from Wally. We

want to know where it started, when he crossed the Mason–Dixon line, and when she's going to meet his folks.'

Wally wasn't playing. She said, 'We've become close, yes, but I can't say more. I'm just running out the door. I'll see you later in the week.'

Violet feigned indifference. She said she was expecting the Yugoslavias any minute.

I said, 'He wants to settle down. He told me himself.'

She said, 'And he will settle down. It's not widely known but Wales is giving very serious consideration to Frederika of Hanover. And Prince George is on the brink too. This could very well turn out to be the year of two royal weddings. Their Majesties would be so happy.'

Flora playing on the backstairs with Pigster wearing a wedding veil.

With George Lightfoot to the Gaiety Theatre to see *Sporting Love*.

April 12, 1934
Dinner at the Belchesters'. Violet and Melhuish, Ambassador von Hoesch, Lady Desborough, and the Marquess of Graham. Mulligatawny soup, sweetbreads, baked apples. Billy Belchester was holding forth about HRH. He said, 'He goes on these tours among the poor and makes sympathetic noises and all it does is whip the working man into a fever of unrealistic hopes. Princes have no business expressing political opinions.'

Ettie Desborough said, 'But the little people feel they can speak to him, and hope costs nothing.'

Jimmy Graham said, 'Wales may be a small, loose cannon when he's leaning over hovel gates patting urchins on the head, but Adolf Hitler looks upon him as a staunch future ally against the Russkis and that's a very important point.'

Dear Leo von Hoesch, always discretion itself, just smiled.

Violet said, 'Anyway, His Majesty is alive and well so what Wales does or doesn't do hardly matters.'

All said looking very squarely at me.

April 13, 1934
Wally's dining at the Italian Embassy tonight. It's something in honour of HRH.

April 14, 1934
Gladys Trilling says Wally's invitation to the Italians wasn't so very great a coup. Whitlow was there and according to him Wally was seated tables away from HRH. Practically in the street, Gladys says.

Invited to the Fort again for the 21st. Me, the Crosbies, Crokers, and the Otto Bismarcks. Pips and Freddie already have something arranged in the constituency, but Wally says they'll have to chuck. You don't say no to the Prince of Wales.

April 21, 1934, Fort Belvedere
HRH was delayed on his return from princing in Wales and barely made it here in time for cockers. He said, 'Sorry, darling. Are you managing to hold the fort?'

She was indeed! She already has the air of lady of the house. There's been a little standoff between her and the butler over the wonderful drinks cart she had delivered. He's refusing to acknowledge its existence. Pips's money is on Wally.

After dinner we played a marvelous new board game

brought along by Boss Croker. It's called Finance. Otto Bismarck couldn't get the hang of it at all. He bought properties that earned peanuts in rent and ended up ruined, Wally bought up all the railroad companies, and HRH spent most of his time in jail, but he seemed to enjoy himself. We didn't finish till two and then he and Wally went downstairs and made us all bacon and eggs. 'What fun!' he kept saying. 'What jolly old fun!'

Ethel said he was like a boy who'd been allowed to stay up late with the grownups.

April 22, 1934

Found myself alone with HRH momentarily after breakfast. He said, 'I hope you're quite comfortable, Maybell.'

I said, 'Sir, this is the most comfortable English house I've been in.'

He said, 'I wish I could be here all the time. I always dread going back to York House. It's nothing more than a place I have to sleep when I'm in town.'

Wally told me it isn't palace-like at all. Just a warren of small rooms quite unsuitable for entertaining. She says the whole place needs gutting.

I said, 'Perhaps you could refurbish it. Wally's good at houses.'

He said, 'To tell you the truth, Maybell, I'm not interested in York House. I know Wally could do wonders with it. She has so much energy. But this is where I feel at home. I'm ready to put down roots and this is where I'd like to do it. I'm going to be forty this year, you know? Hard to believe, but I am.'

I don't find it so hard to believe. His skin is really quite wrinkled. I'd have thought the Palace beauticians could have done something for him.

177

April 26, 1934

Dinner at the Prosper Friths'. Came, the Belchesters, George Lightfoot, the Habberleys, Melhuish and Violet. Belchester said, 'Well, Maybell, your Simpson friend has really shot her bolt this time. Dickie Mountbatten tells me Wales's York House butler has been fired and it's all of her doing.'

Melhuish turned quite purple. He said, 'If it's true then it's a bloody outrage. That butler was given to him when he was first out of the nursery. Been with him for years.'

If that's the case it's time he was pensioned off anyway.

Lightfoot said, 'You know, for the past year everyone's been saying Wally Simpson's a nobody. Extraordinary to think a nobody has that kind of power.'

I said, 'Yes, unless the Prince of Wales has no mind of his own.'

Melhuish said, 'Precisely. And there's the nub of it.'

I can always tell when I've rattled Melhuish. He plays with his earlobe.

April 27, 1934

Wally says the York House butler was obstructive and insubordinate and as old as Methuselah. He refused to put ice in the drinks for one thing. Ernest is back tomorrow. They're driving straight to the Perry Brownlows' for the weekend. HRH is going to Sandringham so Ernest will have Wally all to himself.

To the Fergus Blythes' for two nights, after much begging from Penelope. She says a host of interesting men are coming and she's short of women.

April 29, 1934, Leake Priory

Penelope Blythe's idea of interesting men was Oxer Bettenbrooke and a chinless wonder with a spread in

Somersetshire. Tommy Minskip had also been invited but never replied. Small mercies.

Penelope has squeezed every last drop of juice out of Wally's story. She's cast HRH as the ardent lover and Ernest as the husband who will be expected to absent himself on long tiger shoots. As I explained to her, Ernest's account books keep him obligingly out of the way. There'll be no need for any tigers to pay the price.

I said, 'But time is hardly on Wally's side. HRH is going to be forty. He has to hurry up and settle for one of these princesses. He has to produce an heir.'

She said, 'Of course he must, but that needn't affect Wally's position. I'm sure he'll be very glad of her advice. Just think of it, *our* friend will probably choose the next Queen of England! How exciting!'

Of course, it takes very little to excite Penelope. And I'd hardly describe Wally as *her* friend. Acquaintance would be more accurate.

Raining stair rods.

May 2, 1934, Wilton Place

To Bryanston Court. Wally wearing a new cocktail watch, pink gold accented with brilliants. She said she's had it for years but I know the inside of Wally's jewelry case as well as I know my own. HRH didn't appear at his usual hour and no one else had been invited. Ernest was home by seven.

I said, 'What's this? Did they fire you?' He laughed. He said, 'I made a particular effort, Maybell. I see so little of my wife these days.'

An awkward moment. I said, 'Then why don't I leave you to enjoy your evening together?'

Wally said, 'You'll stay to dinner, Maybell, exactly as we agreed.'

She must have known what was coming. We'd just refreshed our drinks when the maid announced that a car was outside, sent by the Prince. Wally showed no surprise and neither did Ernest. She was on her feet in a trice. She said, 'In that case, you may serve Mr Simpson and Mrs Brumby their dinner on trays,' and she left. I wished myself anywhere else in the world.

We were brought some kind of over-piquant macaroni and a macedoine of fruits. I played with mine but Ernest ate every scrap and didn't say a word until he'd put down his dessert spoon and lit his pipe. Then he said, 'I expect you're wondering why only Wally was sent for?'

I said, 'I know she's been advising him on refurbishments at York House.'

'Yes,' he said. 'And His Royal Highness understands I have a business to attend to. Many evenings I have papers to look through and I can't expect Wally to stay at home on my account. She's a damned vivacious woman, after all.'

He didn't strike me as a man who felt wronged. Just a little lonely, maybe. Perhaps he doesn't mind sharing Wally with HRH. Perhaps he really believes she's just an advisor on royal drapes. He didn't mention the Prince again all evening. He began fetching books from his library so I could admire their bindings. Then he was threatening to introduce me to the delights of Aeschylus, but fortunately he was called to the telephone. Just as well. I was really in no mood for solemn music.

May 4, 1934
Wally was tête-à-tête with Lady Cunard in the Grill Room this afternoon and barely gave me a flutter of her hand. She had better not forget who her friends were when she needed a silver fish slice.

May 8, 1934

Hattie Erlanger says it's all over town that Thelma Furness isn't the only one who's been consigned to history. Thelma's predecessor, Freda Dudley Ward, had still been fondly regarded even though retired with full honors, but as of this week the switchboard at York House has refused to put her calls through.

Hattie said, 'Wally really seems to be the one and only golden girl.'

Wally may be the flavor of the month but she's no *girl*. She tampers with her birth date. Her eyes are a pretty color and she has a retentive mind and that's the best one can say for her. Her hands are very coarse, she laughs like a jackass, and she doesn't have a cent.

George Lightfoot says lack of money won't matter because HRH will take care of her expenses. He predicts Ernest will be offered some kind of ennoblement or be encouraged to live overseas with a tootsie. Or both.

May 10, 1934

Mr Hitler's new special envoy is in town. Mr Joachim Ribbentrop. Freddie met him and came away quite reassured about Germany's rearmament intentions. Pips says the wife looks like an accident in a lace shop. Leo von Hoesch is giving a little dinner on Friday so HRH can meet them. Melhuish and Violet are also invited.

Rory has an exeat this weekend. We may go to the Zoological Gardens.

May 13, 1934

Yesterday to the Gorilla House with Rory, Flora, and Doopie. Flora's pig puppet, formerly Pigster, has been renamed 'Mrs Simpson' but not within earshot of Violet.

Rory said, 'Daddy went to dinner at the Germans and The Wally was there. He said it was a damned disgrace and it's a good thing Mummy has an abscess and couldn't go because it would have been an insult to have to sit at the same table. Why would it?'

I said, 'I have no idea. We were all at school together, you know. Would you cut an old school friend?'

He said, 'Only if he were a complete bounder. But ladies can't be bounders.'

I looked in on Violet when I dropped them off. Her face is still very swollen. Melhuish fussing over her. He kept saying, 'You never get ill, Vee. I don't ever remember you getting ill.'

He said he's not sure about Mr Ribbentrop. 'Bit of a second-rater,' he said. 'A bit of a buffoon, if I'm not mistaken.'

I said, 'And did Wally shine?'

'Wally!' he said. 'Don't bring up that name. It was a bloody affront and Wales should know better. Dragging his popsie here, there, and everywhere. In fact, I'm thinking of bringing it up with him. I think it's time someone gave him a friendly rocket over a spot of lunch.'

Violet said, 'Don't do that, dear. Why don't I mention it to Elizabeth York? Let it go through the usual channels.'

He said, 'Good idea! You are a clever girl. Even when you're ailing you know the best thing to do.'

I called Wally to warn her. She just laughed. She said, 'What do they imagine they can do? Send me to Australia? They're too late, Maybell. David can't manage without me and there's not a damned thing any of them can do about it.'

May 16, 1934

To Ciro's with Wally, the Crokers, the Erlangers, Whitlow Trilling, and at Wally's suggestion the Ribbentrops, or the *von* Ribbentrops as she now insists. He's fair, pale eyes, sounds more like a Canadian than a German. The wife smiles all the time and talks about her children. Wally says she's the one with the money. Her people are in champagne. He danced Wally off her feet, in the absence of both her husband and her Prince.

Ethel said, 'Look at her! Did you ever see such a flirt? I'm going to keep Boss glued to my side.'

Hattie said, 'Relax, Ethel. I don't think anyone trumps the Prince of Wales. Not Mr Hitler's envoy, and certainly not Boss.'

The Crokers' entire Ascot party is invited to Fort Belvedere for Wally's birthday. Ernest finds he has to be in New York, however.

Ethel said, 'How very obliging of him.'

May 23, 1934

To Carlton Gardens for tea which turned into a lecture.

Violet said, 'I hear Minnehaha is running Wales's Ascot party, with her husband out of the country. Does she have any idea what an affront it is to Their Majesties?'

I said, 'Why don't you ask her?'

She said, 'The opportunity will never arise. I don't associate with kept women and if you have any sense of how to behave you'll distance yourself from her.'

I said, 'Even if I wanted to drop Wally, which I don't, it's not so simple. The Prince counts me as a friend too.'

She said, 'In that case, you'd better use your friendship to discourage him in this folly. You, of all people, know

Wally's background. Tell him. Remind him about her husbands. The Empire will thank you for it someday.'

Flora was processing up and down the nursery corridor draped in a counterpane, playing Queen Simpson. She seems to have regained her good spirits.

Doopie was out to a matinee with George Lightfoot. *The Chocolate Soldier*. They might have asked me.

May 26, 1934

To Trent Park for lunch. Seated between Lord Birkenhead and Lord Duveen. Crab flown up from Lympne, truffled noodles, warm apricots.

Philip took me to one side. He said, 'Your naughty friend is causing r-r-ructions, I suppose you know? Syb says her name r-r-reverberates at Buck House.'

Wally will be thrilled.

May 29, 1934

Lunch with Ida. She's met a man who knew her thousands of years ago. They were walled up alive together in Babylon apparently. How small the world is.

June 1, 1934

Saw Benny Thaw on my way into the Savoy. He cut me. It made me very sad. We used to have such gay times, all of us. These things don't seem to bother Wally. She and Ernest are going to a dinner for the Ribbentrops given by Lady Cunard. The *von* Ribbentrops. Wally says omitting the *von* is a gross discourtesy.

June 4, 1934

Lunch with George Lightfoot. He was at the Cunard dinner. He said, '*Von* Ribbentrop, my eye! The man's a complete phony. He bought his title. He married his money. And I'm not even sure he's so very bright. I think he's only here because he speaks English. He's Hitler's fake Englishman.'

George heard from Nellie Hardinge that the King has ordered HRH to look very seriously into marrying Frederike of Hanover. He said, 'I don't think he'll do it without a big fight. She's young enough to be his daughter. But frankly he's brought it on himself. This Wally business is just the final straw for Their Majesties.'

I asked him why he'd taken my idiot sister to a matinee. He said, 'Because they're less crowded than the evenings.'

I said, 'You know what I mean. If you pay her attention she'll develop a crush on you and what a mess that'll be. You know she's not normal.'

He said, 'That hadn't occurred to me.'

Precisely. People just don't think.

June 7, 1934

Hurried off the telephone by my own sister. She said, 'The Nicholases of Greece are here and I have a thousand things to do. Call me after Ascot.'

All I wanted to do was to deliver a little sisterly advice on the subject of Doopie and verify Lightfoot's rumor about the German child bride.

June 8, 1934

Anne Belchester's charity auction. Violet was in attendance with Elizabeth York. She was about to present me to Princess Nicholas Greece and her girls when she suddenly froze. She said, 'A certain friend of yours has just walked through the door. Have the goodness to keep her away from Their Royal Highnesses.' Spoken through clenched teeth.

As though Wally, whose bedside rug has been trodden by princely carpet slippers, could give a hoot about Duchess Bertie York and her poor Greek relations.

I bid for a very pretty musical box but let it go to Daphne Frith.

Ernest has sailed for New York. HRH has arranged for Wally to watch Trooping the Color from a window in the Admiralty Building. Wait till the Salty Lairds hear about that!

June 11, 1934
Wally's apartment is awash with flowers. Calla lilies and black irises from HRH. Red carnations from Mr von Ribbentrop. With his wife in town too. How blatant.

I said, 'Why didn't you send them back?'

She said, 'Why go to the trouble? They're only flowers. And anyway, he's all right. One never knows when a tame German may be useful.'

I said, 'Has the Prince seen them? Won't he be jealous?'

She said, 'He doesn't come here anymore. I go to him. But anyway, a little jealousy in a man is never a bad thing.'

I said, 'Are you in love with him?'

She said, 'Surely the question is, is he in love with me?'

Always joking, always avoiding the point.

I said, 'George Lightfoot heard they might have found a princess for him. Frederike of Hanover.'

She laughed. She said, 'Frederike! That news is so old people have it laid underneath their rugs. David won't marry her. You can take it from me. They're going to have to come up with something better than that.'

I said, 'Well, everyone's saying he'd better hurry along

186

and make up his mind before all the princesses are taken. He is obliged to marry, after all. And then where will that leave you?'

She said, 'It'll leave me precisely where I am now. Even a prince is entitled to private happiness, and his marrying or not marrying doesn't come into the case.'

Hattie Erlanger says Wally's not entirely wrong about this. She says, the longer HRH delays in choosing a wife the greater the risk of having an absolute horror foisted upon him, which would strengthen Wally's position as special friend and provider of extramural pleasures.

June 15, 1934

Red carnations continue to arrive at Bryanston Court. From Ribbensnob, as George Lightfoot calls him. Wally swears she's done nothing to encourage him but still. I said, 'Just remember what happened to Thelma. An innocent shipboard friendship and she was done for.'

'Maybell,' she said, 'Thelma was finished before she even set foot on that ship. And don't presume to tell me my business. I'm no Thelma Furness. No one has ever meant what I do to David.'

Of course, men *say* things like that. She's sleepless wondering what he's going to give her for her birthday. She's going to be so disappointed if it isn't the black pearl bracelet she keeps visiting and viewing and sighing over at Van Cleef. Well, what are birthdays for if not surprises?

I think I may give her scented drawer liners. They are always useful. It's much harder to know what to give the heir to the throne for his birthday. He must have vaults full of cuff links and tiepins. I'm thinking of a cigar cutter. Wally is getting him a silver frame for her new photograph.

June 16, 1934

Lunch with Penelope Blythe. She says the Ribbentrops will never amount to anything in London. According to Fergus he doesn't even have a portfolio. Perhaps Wally should think of getting him one next time we're in Asprey.

June 18, 1934, Sunninghills

To the Crokers' with Pips and Freddie and Judson and Hattie. Charlie and Fern Bedaux are also here. The azaleas are a picture. Wally's at the Fort with the Fruity Metcalfes and the Perry Brownlows. HRH has to go up to the Castle each day for the landau procession.

Ethel has a girl coming up from the town to do our hair and nails before we go to the track tomorrow. We'll show those English frights.

June 19, 1934

Ladies' Day. Wore my cerise. Violet was in the third carriage in a disaster of lime silk and marabou. She springs for new gowns so rarely, if only she'd come to me for guidance when she does.

Dinner at the Fort. HRH is giving Wally a dog for her birthday but it's too young yet to leave the kennels so she has a photograph of it for the time being. I thought it fell rather flat until he brought out a delicious little package from Cartier. A brooch. A cairn terrier in white gold with yellow sapphire eyes. A stopgap until the real terrier is of an age to come home and begin the ruination of her rugs. 'Oh, sir!' she said. 'You spoil me!'

He said, 'Wally darling, I consider it my duty to spoil you.'

Violet would have had a fit.

Champagne by the swimming pool. Shrimp appetizers,

veal scallopine, and a kumquat parfait. After dinner HRH played 'Happy Birthday' on his ukulele, then we danced till late. We're all invited back for his birthday on Saturday.

Wally's showed the kitchens how to make Southern fried chicken and peaches in bourbon. The housekeeper is reportedly fit to be tied, but Wally knows what the Prince likes and they'll do well to listen to her recommendations.

June 24, 1934

HRH adored the cigar cutter I gave him and added it to his watch chain immediately. Wally was in high spirits all day. She gave him her new photograph framed in silver and a rubber duck for his bathtub. Evidently some kind of private joke because they spent a great deal of the evening replying to one another with quacking noises.

HRH has taken a villa in Biarritz for the month of August and particularly asked me along. He said, 'For einums meinums,' he said. 'A special holiday. She's worked tirelessly, reorganizing things for me at York House. She deserves a real rest. But Ernest finds he can't be spared from business so she'll need a companion. If you could join us, Maybell, I'd count it the greatest favor.'

We leave on August 1 which means barely six weeks for the purchase of villa wear.

Freddie says 'einums meinums' is Walesian German for 'one's own most precious little chickywickywoo'.

June 26, 1934

HRH has asked the Crosbies and the Erlangers to Biarritz too. Of course, he asked me first.

July 3, 1934
Bathing suits, kimono wraps, open-toe sandals, all picked up at bargain prices because the woolen suits are about to come in. The sales clerk said the time to buy summer wear is February. Perhaps for people like Violet who know they'll be spending every August of their life in Scotland.

July 6, 1934, Fort Belvedere
Wally, Boss and Ethel Croker, the Humphrey Butlers, Whitlow Trilling and the hugely bloated Gladys. Why she doesn't just stay out of sight until this child has arrived I can't imagine nor why people insist on having a third. Look at what a mistake Doopie was.

July 7, 1934
Prince George drove over to dinner. He taught us a wonderful new dance called the Palais Glide. He learned it from a footman at Buckingham Palace.

Poots Butler says there's a great deal of maneuvering going on between the equerries. No one wants to be the one to go to Biarritz. She said, 'Their Majesties are appalled that Wally's been invited without her husband.'

I said, 'But Ernest can't get away for a whole month. He's in business.'

She said, 'I know. It's frightful. And as far as the King's concerned Ernest's first business should be to keep his wife in check.'

It seems to me whatever he does Ernest is bound to displease one royalty or another.

July 12, 1934, Wilton Place
Rory's thirteenth. Heavy rain, so we went to a cartoon show and then to Ganes's Tea Rooms. He had requested

a place called Ye Little Tea Shoppe in Charing Cross Road. His friend Massingham had been taken there by an uncle during the Easter break, but Melhuish has forbidden Rory to go anywhere near it. He says it's the haunt of theatricals and showgirls. How does Melhuish know, is what I'd have liked to ask but I didn't, for the boy's sake. Actually, not such a boy anymore, although he's still on the short side. I don't think he'll ever make the Grenadier Guards.

He starts at Eton College in September so will have Ulick overshadowing him again, but he doesn't seem concerned. He says he'll be in a different House and they'll practically never see each other.

The Habberleys won't be shooting at Drumcanna this year apparently. He said, 'I think Mummy's still cross about the broken potty.'

July 13, 1934
According to Penelope Blythe, the real reason the Habberleys are missing Drumcanna is that Ralph has become most erratic and has gone off, quite contrary to Jane Habberley's wishes, to Ceylon, to look into tea.

July 15, 1934
Ernest is back from New York. HRH has left on a tour of Scotland. Hattie says they've become like those little weathermen on a barometer. When one's out the other is in.

July 18, 1934
Wally's dog has arrived. It is to be named Mr Loo.

July 20, 1934
To the Kit Kat. Saw no one we knew.

July 24, 1934
Mr Loo makes Ernest sneeze. Wally says it hardly matters because he has to go to Sweden next week.

July 26, 1934
A potluck at Wally's. Just me and the Crosbies. Pips said, 'I'm not going if Ernest and Sir are both going to be there.'

I said, 'They won't be. David's away princing.'

She said, 'I hope you're right. The sight of Ernest being cuckolded at his own drinks trolley would be too gruesome.'

It turned out just a rather dull evening. Even Wally didn't seem able to jolly things along. Ernest was pink and wheezy, brought on by the dog, he says. Wally says he has a summer cold.

Pips said, 'Poor Ernest. I reckon Wally only invited us so she didn't have to spend an evening alone with him.'

July 29, 1934
To the Palm Beach Club with Wally, the Erlangers, and Penelope Blythe. Fergus has already left to fish on Deeside. Wally asked to come and stay with me at Wilton Place till we leave for Biarritz because Mr Loo ate von Ribbentrop's predictable carnations and was so sick she had to get the cleaners in. It would have been just too inconvenient. The house is practically closed up and I'm down to just Kettle, the cook, and one maid. Also Mr Loo has not yet learned to ask for the rest room. She went to the Erlangers' instead. They're as silly as she is about animals.

July 30, 1934
Wally stayed at York House last night. The maid told me when I telephoned. That maid needs training in discretion. I might have been anyone.

August 2, 1934, Biarritz

Caught the afternoon boat train with Wally, the Crosbies, and Hattie Erlanger. Judson, HRH, and Jack Aird who is equerrying, flew to Le Bourget and joined us at the railroad station.

Castel Meretmont is adorable. Pink and white stucco, shady catalpas around the terrace, and matchless ocean views. I can hear the thunder of the surf from my bedroom. I find it perfect, but Wally started making changes the moment we arrived. Chairs moved, the whiskey changed, a large order placed for perfumed roses, the help sent searching for extra vases.

Hattie's already drawing up lists of activities. Today a display of folkloric dancing in Anglet, but Freddie was the only one she could persuade to go with her. He's so good-natured.

She said, 'Let's motor into Spain at the weekend and see a bullfight!'

Let's not! Her infernal busyness reminds me of Violet. Ida Coote says the urge to fill every minute with activity may be a reflection of unresolved turmoil from past lives. Anyway, Wally's not the only one who's had a busy year. I'm here to rest and take beautifying cures.

August 4, 1934

Dinner in town and then baccarat. Several familiar London faces at the casino. Marthe Bibesco, the Dimitri Shapaleffs, Daisy Fellowes.

August 5, 1934

Pips and I have begun our seawater therapies. The Erlangers are only here for two weeks and Judson was hoping to play some golf, but so far HRH won't budge from Wally's side. Jack Aird says Judson should regard this as no great loss because HRH has a weak drive and a tendency to misremember his score.

Wally and HRH are being most unsociable, emerging late, taking long siestas. And when they are by the pool there can be no sustained conversation because he's always fidgeting around, rearranging her pillows or preparing a towel for her while she's taking a dip.

August 7, 1934
Judson still mooning about playing imaginary golf strokes. Jack Aird asked to be released for the day so he could play with him and Wally tore him off such a strip. She said, 'You're not here to take a vacation. You're paid to take care of His Royal Highness.'

Pips said, 'I'll bet he *isn't* paid.'

Boss and Ethel are coming over tomorrow. They're staying with Jessie Woolworth at Saint-Jean-de-Luz.

August 9, 1934
A fabulous poolside party given by Jessie Woolworth's friends, the Bajavidas, who have taken Château La Colline for a month. The gardens floodlit, a team of gleaming kitchen hands turning an ox on a roasting spit, and a gay Cuban band to entertain us. Daisy Fellowes swam in her diamonds.

August 11, 1934
I have taken up watercolors again and have been teaching Hattie and Pips. We motored out to a picturesque harbor for a couple of hours. Hattie's getting the idea but Pips is too fastidious. The secret is simply to splash on the colors. If it turns out not to look like fishermen mending their nets, then call it something else.

Jack Aird is very sour about being kept under house arrest with nothing to do except, as he said, 'Police the functions of Madam's dog and read day-old newspapers.'

August 13, 1934

I don't know that Biarritz is doing Wally much good. She's become very scratchy, threatening to fire the help, snapping at Jack Aird, and sneering at poor Judson at the tables last night. She said, 'Hattie, does your husband have anything going on upstairs? Doesn't he know he should always bet on the bank?' Hattie was livid. She says she's glad they're leaving. Pips says she wants to leave with them, but Freddie says they must stay at least until the Perry Brownlows get here. He said, 'We can't abandon poor Maybell. And anyway, it's absolutely not done to curtail a visit with a royalty, unless there's some kind of emergency.'

Pips said, 'Then, darling, please wire Mussolini and ask him to create one.'

August 14, 1934

Hattie and Judson left this morning. Wally sent her maid down to say she was still busy with her hairdresser and so couldn't come down for goodbyes. She appeared just before luncheon and lay bronzing herself, HRH playing Incey Spider on her arm. 'David,' she said, 'why don't you go and play golf?'

Pips swears she heard Jack Aird whisper, 'Off with her head!'

August 15, 1934

Dinner in town with Marthe Bibesco, the Crokers, and the Dimitri Shapaleffs. Marthe heavily laden with sapphires. Wally and HRH didn't join us. Wally had a sick headache and David refused to leave her.

Ethel said, 'Has she had too much sun?'

Jack Aird said, 'No. Too much heir.'

August 16, 1934

Wally is completely recovered. She came down sporting a pair of fire opal ear clips which appeared on her breakfast tray this morning. HRH silent but attentive. He held her hand all through luncheon. The Perry Brownlows arrived, having motored all the way from Lincolnshire, and went straight on to the tennis court. HRH was called to the telephone twice this afternoon and then again during cockers. Something is going on.

Freddie thinks the King may have ordered David to cut short his vacation. He said, 'The whole thing is pretty blatant, you must admit. Aird's scandalized and he's seen a few things in his time. He's probably fired off a complaint somewhere it was likely to reach the right ears.'

No baccarat tonight. A storm blowing in.

August 17, 1934

A thunderstorm woke me early. I came downstairs for a glass of milk and found HRH busy on his cycling machine. I said, 'The telephone was very lively last night. Not bad news, I hope?'

'Not at all, Maybell,' he said. 'Actually, rather exciting news. I'll let you in on a little secret.'

Yesterday's calls were from Prince George. He's borrowing David's airplane to go and sound out Marina of Greece. If he's favorably received he's going to pop the question. Marina of Greece! She's one of those Plain Janes Elizabeth York brought to Anne Belchester's charity auction. Violet's been promoting her cause for months. I must say I found her rather abrupt. She'll be very lucky to get Prince George. He's such a good dancer.

August 18, 1934
More telephone calls from Prince George. We're not allowed to talk about it in case the help eavesdrop, but one senses that the news is encouraging.

Perry Brownlow says it'll be a great relief to the King and Queen if it comes off because George has gotten himself into so many scrapes. Jazz singers, drug fiends, undesirables who've had to be paid off. Well, I'm sure Marina Greece will soon clip his wings.

August 19, 1934
Pips and Freddie have left for Ireland. Pips said, 'Come with us. Wally doesn't need you.' But I like it here. The villa is a dream, and anyway, I like being at the heart of things. I love doing callisthenics with the future King of England and imagining Nora Sedley Cordle catching flies in her silly open mouth.

August 21, 1934
Marina of Greece has said yes and I was one of the first to know. David and I enjoy an early-morning chat most days since he introduced me to the benefits of callisthenics. He feels Marina is just the girl for George. Steady without being dull, royal without being grand. Kitsie Brownlow appears to know her pedigree by heart. Her father is a Schleswig-Holstein, her mother is a Russian grand duchess, and her sister is married to Paul Yugoslavia. All that said, they're as poor as Job. The royalties have a very strange attitude to money. Many of them don't have any and the

ones who do hold on to it like grim death. Like HRH. All the times I've been with him at Ciro's or the Kit Kat I don't know that I've ever seen him with any jingle in his pocket.

Perry lured him on to the golf course this morning, so Wally has been in a better mood. She's decided to go to Paris at the end of the vacation. According to HRH, Prince George and Marina are likely to get married before Christmas, so Wally's in a hurry to order gowns for the occasion. Kitsie Brownlow said, 'But Wally won't be invited, not even with Ernest at her side. Absolutely not.'

I said, 'But Prince George has eaten at their table many, many times.'

She said, 'Prince George has eaten at countless tables and slid beneath not a few, but that's beside the point. Wally's true position is no secret. She'll never be allowed to set foot anywhere near Their Majesties.'

Time will tell. But nothing is going to persuade her against going to Paris.

August 23, 1934
Prince George's happy news has been announced officially from Balmoral. I expect they're *en fête* at Drumcanna. Violet may even have ordered cream to be served with the oatmeal this morning. Marina Greece's people seem to lead a vagrant existence, considering all the thrones they've occupied. They're now based mainly in Paris and don't keep a London house, so who knows, she may even be married from Carlton Gardens.

Walter Guinness, an old acquaintance of HRH, has turned up at the Hôtel du Palais. He has his yacht here, presently being provisioned before he sets off on another voyage. He's a rugged man with startling green eyes and a strange line in conversation. Eskimos. Solomon Islanders. Prehistoric ferns. Mohammedans. One could feel sorry for the wife, but I suppose his enthusiasms leave her plenty of time for bridge.

August 24, 1934
HRH announced a plan over luncheon. Prince George and Marina are going to be in Cannes briefly before going to London to be feted, so he's going to charter a plane and hop over to see them. He said, 'It'll be great fun and give them such a jolly surprise.'

Wally said, 'Sir, you know I won't fly.'

I saw a flicker from Jack Aird. I suppose because *he* daren't disobey a royalty he doesn't care to see anyone else do it. But I understand Wally and so does the Prince. She saw too many planes fall out of the sky when she was a navy wife. Nothing will get her into the air, not even a Royal Highness.

August 25, 1934
There is now a revised plan. Since Wally won't fly and David won't be parted from her we're going to borrow Walter Guinness's yacht and sail to Cannes. We're inviting the Crokers to join us.

August 26, 1934
Boss Croker is being a spoilsport. He says the *Rosaura* is not so much a yacht as a leaking paddle steamer and he's not yet tired enough of life or Ethel for either of them to sail on it. Also, Walter Guinness is not as grateful as he might be to have the Prince of Wales charter his boat. He says the weather forecasts are worrying, with a strong likelihood of storms. Kitsie Brownlow says she adores

rough seas. HRH said, 'And after the storm, there'll be a delicious calm. We'll be able to swim off the yacht. What heaven!'

I had a horrid dream. Marina Greece was getting married to Melhuish on board a ship and Wally and I were trying to carry her train but the deck kept listing and waves kept breaking over us and ruining our hair. Perhaps I should return to London after all.

August 27, 1934

Wally has begged me not to miss the cruise. She says seasickness is a state of mind. She says she trained herself out of it when she made the crossing to China so I can certainly do the same for a little jaunt around Gibraltar.

She said, 'Anyway, I need you, Maybell. You're my only friend here.'

I said, 'You've got Sir. And the Brownlows.'

She said, 'But you're my only *true* friend here. Aird hates me. Guinness is crazy. And I'm still not sure about the Brownlows. They may be Palace Guard disguised in Prince of Wales suiting.'

We sail tomorrow.

August 28, 1934, the *Rosaura*, at sea

Guinness says we have no chance of reaching Cannes in time to greet Prince George and Marina because the *Rosaura* burns vast quantities of whatever it is that makes ships go and we'll be forced to call at many ports. I hoped we might be allowed to disembark but HRH wasn't at all discouraged by the news. He said, 'If I miss George, I miss him. It was just a fanciful idea anyhow. He'll understand. We'll visit as many ports as you deem necessary, Walter. I'm in no hurry and I'm having an absolutely blissful time.'

200

Our aim now is to reach Marseilles in time to see another brother, Prince Harry. He'll be calling there on his way to Australia to do some princing.

August 29, 1934
I am dying.

August 30, 1934
No mercy.

September 1, 1934
The storm has ended. I ventured far enough from my cabin to ascertain that we are in the hands of the insane. There is a monkey running free, owned by Walter Guinness in the way normal people might keep a cat, also two stewards who are never sober. Perry Brownlow told me dinner began with ice cream last night because the cutlets weren't ready. It matters little to me. I shall never eat again.

September 2, 1934
We have put in at Corunna. Kitsie Brownlow and Jack Aird have gone off with Wally and HRH to visit a cathedral. Perry gallantly stayed behind to protect me from the monkey and the crew. He believes this cruise is the Prince's last fling. He said, 'Next year is Their Majesties' Silver Jubilee and I predict its crowning glory will be David's marriage. This is his final self-indulgence, Maybell. His farewell to boyish pleasures.'

I said, 'But who will he marry?'

'Ah,' he said, 'there you have me. But she's out there.'

Walter Guinness estimates it will take us nine days to reach Cannes, building in a little time for HRH's sightseeing whims.

September 3, 1934

Wally had her first encounter with the press yesterday. Word had leaked out that the Prince of Wales might be putting in to Corunna on an informal visit and a crowd of well-wishers had gathered. A small child presented Wally with a bouquet of flowers and a doll dressed in national costume.

She said, 'I felt rather like a queen.'

HRH said, 'Darling, you are my Queen.'

Jack Aird almost choked on his brandy.

She's given me the doll. It will do nicely for Flora.

September 4, 1934

We are moored off Vigo where we heard the news that Ena Spain has lost a son, only twenty years old. He had a slight bump out motoring with his sister and sustained only a bruise, but Violet once told me none of the Spain children is strong. Kitsie Brownlow says they have a bleeding disease. The boys bleed and the girls pass it on to the next generation. Poor Ena. HRH and I both sent notes of sympathy.

September 5, 1934

We have been abandoned. Wally and HRH went ashore this morning for sightseeing and have just sent word that they've met up with someone Wally knew during her China years and have gone with him to see his house and vineyards. Guinness's instructions are to send Jack Aird and Wally's maid in the tender with enough clothes for four days and then to put to sea. They are going to motor down to meet us at Gibraltar. Perry's furious and was all for getting off and going home, but Kitsie said, 'Dearest, Maybell promised to stay and we can't leave her. No one ever said royalties make easy friends.'

September 8, 1934

According to the Brownlows, Ralph Habberley is not in Ceylon visiting tea plantations but in Kenya with a cigarette girl. Also that Penelope Blythe's name has been linked with George Lightfoot. A lie if ever I heard one.

Kitsie has been pumping me about Wally. She said, 'What are her intentions?'

I said, 'Surely the question is, what are David's intentions?'

She said, 'His Royal Highness isn't at liberty to have any, as I'm sure Wally knows. But she's seems a terribly well-organized person. I'm sure she has a plan. I'm sure she knows exactly what she wants to get out of all this. A good house, I suppose? And a title for Ernest?'

I don't know. Perhaps that is all she wants. She certainly doesn't seem very much in love.

September 9, 1934

We have made Gibraltar in good time and glorious weather. Walter has been showing me his collection of seashells and has given me one for Rory. He has really led a most interesting life.

Wally looked ravishing when she came aboard, especially considering she's been living out of a valise for four days. She was bubbling with excitement about her little Portuguese diplomat, how he was as handsome as ever, what a divine house he has overlooking Viana, how wonderful it had been to reminisce about China, and the more she bubbled the tighter HRH held her hand.

He said, 'I know, let's go to Majorca! I don't want this holiday ever to end.'

September 11, 1934

Majorca is enchanting. Wally, Kitsie, and I spent the morning sampling orange-blossom perfumes. Kitsie can be very forthright. She said, 'Wally, I hope you're not losing your heart to our Prince.'

Wally laughed. She said, 'Not at all. I have no illusions. I'm just here to entertain. I'm the circus before the execution. He doesn't have much to look forward to, does he? Princing. Marriage to some desperate Prussian wallflower. Babies. More princing.'

We spent the afternoon dipping in and out of clear, blue waters. HRH is as frisky as a lamb. Jack Aird is very tense. He says the Prince's dawdling has now caused them to miss two appointments. Prince George and Marina waited in Cannes as long as they could then had to leave for London, and Prince Harry, whom he'd cabled most specifically to arrange a little farewell in Marseilles, has had to sail without seeing him.

The Brownlows are leaving us as soon as we get to Cannes. It'd be nice to see the Cavetts if they're still around, and those nice Rogerses.

September 13, 1934, Cannes

The floors of the Miramar appear to be in constant motion. I've been far too long at sea.

A note from Kath Rogers offering dinner. They have Zita and Bernie staying with them so it's all worked out beautifully, although Wally doesn't agree.

She said, 'You might have asked me before you wired them. The last thing I feel like is trailing up to someone's little villa.'

HRH said, 'I don't know, darling. I rather like the idea.'

She said, 'Well, don't expect much. The Rogerses won't run to your usual level of comfort.'

I said, 'I heard they made you very comfortable when you were in Peking.'

She said, 'Then you heard wrong, Maybell. Kath Rogers knows nothing about food.'

Boss and Ethel's lovely friends the Bedauxs are here. They sent champagne across to our lunch table.

September 14, 1934

The Rogerses' house is entrancing, especially the gardens. Hibiscus, frangipani, night jasmine, and we could look down and see the *Rosaura* at anchor in the bay, hung with lanterns.

HRH said, 'I should like to hear all about your China days. It must have been fascinating.'

Herman said, 'Well, I guess "fascinating" covers it. Kath thought she was in for a quiet life when she married me but China was a tinderbox. Not one war, you understand? Lots of little ones. You never knew where things would erupt next. Amazing really how we managed to carry on with normal things like tennis parties and receptions.'

HRH said, 'And I'll bet Wally sparkled through it all.'

Herman said, 'Indeed. I'm sure she made as great an impact on Peking as Peking made on her.'

Wally snorted. She said, 'I think of my life as having begun when I arrived in London,' and she gave Herman a very long cool stare.

As we were leaving HRH said, 'Your house is adorable. I should love to stay here someday.'

Herman said, 'It's yours for the asking, sir. Anytime.'

After the car door slammed I heard Wally say, 'Anytime after hell freezes.'

September 15, 1934

I am a wreck. Wally and I went straight up and left HRH having a nightcap with Charlie Bedaux. I was asleep when the telephone rang. 'Maybell,' he said, 'it's David. I have to go shopping and I need your help. Meet me in the lobby.'

It was 1 a.m.

I said, 'Sir, everywhere's closed.'

'No,' he said, 'it's all right. I'm having Cartier opened. The night manager is seeing to it now.'

The man from Cartier was very obliging, although I noticed he hadn't combed his hair. He brought out tray after tray. Jack Aird sighing theatrically every few minutes. It was finally narrowed down to a large amethyst pendant or a canary diamond bracelet charm. HRH said, 'You must make the final choice, Maybell. I turn to you in my hour of need.'

Funny how little men understand about jewels, even royal princes. Whatever its size a canary diamond beats an amethyst any day.

'Not a word now,' he said when we were in the elevator. 'I shall present this to her when we're back on board ship.'

Aird groaned. He said, 'Sir, shouldn't we be starting for home?'

David said, 'Don't be such a killjoy. I don't have to be back till the 25th. We still have heaps of time. I'm going to tell Guinness to take us to Italy.'

What a night. Padmore gets more sleep than I do.

September 16, 1934

The Cavetts and the Bedauxs are going join us for our trip to Italy. I'm so happy. Wally's being a crosspatch. She scolded Jack Aird for yawning and HRH for handing out invitations without asking her.

He said, 'But darling, Charlie Bedaux is a terrifically interesting man. He knows all about labor unions and working conditions. And he and Fern have homes everywhere. They might be terribly useful. Also, einums meinums, Fern and Zita will be company for Maybell. I'm afraid she must get very lonely when I'm monopolizing you.'

Wally said, 'Then don't monopolize me. You must go and play golf the very minute we put in to Genoa. I can't be at your side every minute.'

September 17, 1934, the *Rosaura* again

Wally is wearing her canary diamond and a smile. HRH set up a very seductive scene last night and it seems to have paid off. He took Wally up on deck after dessert and Jack Aird motioned to the rest of us to stay put.

He said, 'His Royal Highness has exclusive use of the moonlight for the next hour so I suggest we make ourselves comfortable down here.'

I said, 'Is she getting the diamond?'

He said, 'The diamond, the stars. Perhaps even a bagpipe serenade.'

Fern said, 'How romantic! I don't know about you girls, but I always have to tell Charlie when it's time he went shopping, and what to buy. Really, it's easier if I do it all myself.'

Danforth was the same. He was a busy man. 'Pick yourself out a bauble, Maybell,' he'd say. 'I'll go to five hundred.'

When Aird gave us the all-clear to go on deck the lovebirds had already retired.

What a bump down to earth London is going to seem to Wally. Just boring old Ernest and unlovely George Street.

September 18, 1934, Grand Hôtel des Îles Borromées, Stresa

We have said our final farewells to Walter Guinness and his lunatic crew. We put in to Genoa at eight this morning and were met by cars which have brought us to a hotel on Lake Maggiore. Tomorrow we're going by motor launch to view some recommended gardens. Wally had been threatening to spend a day in Milan buying pocket-books, but that little Cartier diamond has improved her mood no end. Lady Cunard has arranged an appointment for her in Paris on the 21st. A designer called Main Bocher. She says he's fresh and American and will soon be in the vanguard.

Charlie Bedaux says he'd love to take HRH in hand for a year. He said, 'I could really do something with him. There's a lot of potential in the boy and I see it going to waste. I guess his old man's too busy chopping off heads.'

September 19, 1934

To the gardens at Isola Bella. Terraces covered with lemon trees, white peacocks, marble grottoes. Nothing to touch what Philip Sassoon has done at Lympne but still very lovely. Wally made copious jottings. I hadn't realized she was so interested in gardens.

I said, 'Are you and Ernest thinking of getting a place in the country?' She said, 'We already have a place in the country. It's called Fort Belvedere.'

Fern says they have twenty gardeners at their chateau. Wally said, 'Really? I'd like to see it sometime.'

Fern said, 'Then come. We don't stand on ceremony. And bring David.'

Wally said, 'Bring David? Fern, let me save you from future embarrassment. People don't *invite* His Royal Highness. They wait for him to propose himself.'

Fern said, 'Is that right? How quaint. Well, in the meanwhile, if ever you want to bring your husband, I guess that wouldn't be breaking any rules.'

Wally stalked off.

September 20, 1934

Our vacation is at an end, although HRH is dragging it out till Saturday. His usual chirpy chatter has subsided and he's preoccupied with the busy weeks ahead. He said, 'I have to go to Scotland, Maybell, to launch the new Cunarder. I'd give anything to take Wally with me. I'm going to miss her dreadfully.'

I'll be glad to see London. Being surrounded by foreign jabber for weeks on end is very fatiguing. The Bedauxs are off to Germany on business, Bernie and Zita are staying on for another week, and we leave tonight. Mr Mussolini has kindly sent us his private rail car and by tomorrow we will be in Paris.

September 21, 1934, Hôtel Meurice, Paris

Just called in to Ena Spain's suite to condole. She said Gonzalo's death had come as no surprise to them. They'd known since he was a boy that he had the bleeding disease. Another of her boys has it too. Poor dear. She seems so resigned.

Wally had gone out for some last-minute shopping with HRH, so the desk put Ernest's call through to my suite.

He said, 'Where is she, Maybell? I absolutely insist on

209

her being back here by next Wednesday. I have some important clients and I need her to make a dinner for me. Two months is surely vacation enough for anyone.'

They came back with hatboxes. I passed on Ernest's message stripped of its aggrieved tone.

David said, 'But that works out perfectly, darling. I have to be in Clydeside and now you have to feed Ernest's industrialists. Let no one say we don't attend to our duties!'

Wally doesn't feel it works out perfectly at all. She had hoped for at least a week in Paris. Prince George's wedding has been announced for November 29 which, as Wally says, leaves no time at all for undoing fashion mistakes one has been rushed into.

September 22, 1934

David's plane collected him from Le Bourget aerodrome this afternoon. Wally and I went directly to see Mr Main Bocher. He and Wally hit it off immediately. He told her she has the kind of figure that would look fabulous in a paper bag. Of course, Mr Bocher has all the appearances of one of those men who never marry, so his ideas on the womanly form are bound to be bizarre.

He had his people running in and out with bolts of cloth. Wally's chosen a very striking purple lamé for the ball and a soft blue velvet for the Abbey. I'm sure she has no idea how much any of it is going to cost. He said, 'When you come back for your first fitting you must bring with you the mink you're planning to wear and the tiara. I have to see the full picture.'

She loves all that. She said, 'He's a perfectionist, like me. We're going to show those royalties a thing or two about elegance.'

I said, 'What are you going to do about a tiara? Will Ernest be willing to buy one?'

She said, 'He won't need to be. For a royal wedding jewelers are going to be vying with one another to lend me one.'

September 23, 1934

To Le Havre. Wally is in the kind of good humor that follows successful shopping, and quite expansive. She says she never intended for HRH to become so attached but now he has, the advantages outweigh the drawbacks. She said, 'He's sweet, in many ways, but what he really needs is to be properly employed. He has plenty of vim but it needs to be channeled.'

Very much Charlie Bedaux's view of things.

She said, 'No one ever helped him till I came along. He gets into such a state when the King sends for him. His father always gives him a row and his mother sits tight-lipped, disapproving of everything. They sap his confidence. All they ever do is tell him what he *can't* do. Well, I'm fixing all that. I'm building him up, putting some backbone into him. I'm going to turn him into a king no one'll ever forget.'

I said, 'All very well, but what about Ernest? How can you run a prince and a husband?'

She said, 'Ernest understands. He admires the monarchy. He completely sees the value of what I'm doing. And the association is very good for business. Practically the same as a Royal Warrant above the door. Anyway, I'm on my way home to him now. The vacation's over and David has engagements enough to keep him occupied, so I shall be able to give Ernest my undivided attention.'

September 24, 1934, Wilton Place

Just before we docked we received a message that a car would be waiting for Mrs Simpson outside the customs shed. She said, 'If Ernest asks about Paris don't blab about the gowns. I like to deal with these things in my own good time.'

But from the rail there was no sign of Ernest, only Kettle with my car and Ladbrook with HRH's Buick.

Wally said, 'Sir's sent his car for me. See, Maybell? This is what happens when you have a royal connection. Queues disappear, cars become available, doors open.'

And doors certainly did open. There sitting together in the back of the Buick were Ernest and the Prince of Wales. Wally didn't miss a beat.

She said, 'Sir! I thought you were in Scotland launching liners!'

He said, 'I'm leaving directly, but I thought it'd be fun to surprise you and Maybell, and then when we arrived I found Ernest had had the same idea. So here we both are. We've had time for a splendid chat.'

Ernest was in a very affectionate mood, holding Wally's hand. The hand HRH has clung to these last seven weeks.

'Well, dearest,' he said, 'we mustn't delay. I have a car waiting outside and His Royal Highness has a long journey ahead of him.'

A mountain of correspondence waiting for me at Wilton Place. I shall be doing nothing for weeks except opening envelopes.

September 25, 1934

To Carlton Gardens. Violet was expected back from her Sanitarium committee momentarily so I went up to the nursery to wait. Doopie loved her orange-blossom soap and Flora seemed pleased with her Spanish doll, although she removed all its clothes.

She said, 'Uncle Prince George is getting married and I'm going to be a flower baid.'

Doopie is making her dress.

I said, 'Well, you'll certainly have to have your hair combed before you can be a flower maid. And my friend Wally is going to the wedding too. So I shall hear all about it.'

Had a small sherry with Violet. She said, 'You may tell me about places of interest you've visited but I don't want to hear about anyone whose name begins with W.'

Flora then appeared with the naked doll, piping, 'Mummy, Aunt Bayba says the Wally is invited to Uncle Prince George's wedding too. Isn't that a surprise!'

I noticed that funny little twitch Violet always gets in her cheek when something unsettles her.

'Now, Flora,' she said, 'go downstairs and tell Smith we'll be two extra for dinner. Tell her Lady Habberley will have just an omelet.'

Flora said, 'Am I allowed gake?'

Violet said, 'Yes, a small slice. Now kiss Aunt Maybell good night. She's just leaving.'

The moment the door closed she said, 'How could you?! Uttering *that* woman's name to an innocent child. How could you?!'

I said, 'It's not only me she hears it from. Everyone knows Wally is Wales's friend. I'm sure even your boot boy knows.'

She said, 'Knowing about it is one thing, speaking of it is quite another.'

I said, 'Well, pretend all you like, Violet, but London

213

is going to be seeing a great deal more of Wally. She and David are inseparable.'

She said, 'Maybe so, but she certainly won't be invited to George and Marina's wedding, nor to any other occasion where she'll be in the presence of Their Majesties. Wally is a divorced person, and her so-called husband is a divorced person. This is England, Maybell, not a Hollywood movie lot.'

I said, 'You're so old-fashioned. The Prince of Wales doesn't care about people being divorced. Heavens, Wally even soaps him in his bathtub!'

She leapt to the door to check that no maids had been listening. She said, 'I have never wished to quarrel with you, Maybell, but for the sake of my family I must draw a line. Until you disassociate yourself from this scandal you are not to see my children. People talk. Even boys of Rory's age. Imagine if it became known at school that his aunt is that woman's friend.'

I said, 'Are you banishing me? I'm your sister.'

She said, 'The remedy is yours. Walk away from Wally and the rest of Wales's silly set and you'll be as welcome here as ever.'

September 26, 1934
Gladys and Whitlow Trilling have another daughter. I do hope they're not going to keep on till they get a boy.

September 27, 1934
Lunch with George Lightfoot.

He said, 'If it's a choice between patching things up with Violet and sticking by Wally I'd drop Wally. She'd drop you.'

But I don't think she would. She appreciates my

friendship. She knows she can turn to me when she finds herself short or HRH has forgotten his billfold. Anyway, I hate small-mindedness and that's the trouble with people like Violet. They can't see beyond the fence to the Royal Enclosure.

I said, 'What about you? Are you going to "draw a line"?'

He said, 'Of course not. But I'm not in the same position as Violet and Melhuish. I don't have Their Majesties' good opinion to consider. Let's just hope this affair soon burns itself out. You must admit, they make a rather odd couple. The wee Princekin and Mrs Pushy.'

As I thought, the story about him and Penelope Blythe is untrue. He said, 'I think she may have had a bit of a crush on me, but she's started seeing Billy Belchester. He keeps a little service flat on Portman Square.'

Billy Belchester! There's desperation for you. But Penelope's never happy unless she's avoiding someone's wife or waiting by the telephone. I suppose that's why George soon lost his appeal, having no wife to betray and being scrupulously reliable about telephone calls.

He agrees with Violet that Wally's invitation to the wedding is sheer pie in the sky. He said, 'Wales always opens his mouth before thinking. I'll tell you what'll happen. Ernest and Wally's names will appear on the guest list, the Lord Chamberlain will show the list to the King, and Ernest and Wally's names will disappear from the guest list.'

October 1, 1934
Lunch with Hattie and Pips. Hattie says their friends are more fascinated by Wally than scandalized and certainly no one has dropped them.

215

I said, 'Well, I'm banned from Carlton Gardens and Philip Sassoon hasn't returned either of my calls.'

She said, 'Well, I wouldn't lose any sleep over that. The Sassoons are only five minutes out of their desert tents. I'm sure they're completely untrustworthy.'

Pips said, 'Yes. Unlike Wally who'd lay down her life for any one of us.'

October 2, 1934

A letter from Rory. He writes that he won't be able to go to tea and the Planetarium as we'd planned at Long Leave because he's invited to his friend Massingham's house in Gloucestershire. So Violet's gotten at him too.

October 4, 1934

I intercepted Doopie and Flora in St James's Park. Flora spotted me and immediately began whooping, 'Aunt Bayba, Aunt Bayba! We're not allowed to speak to you because of The Wally. But we can do zignals.'

She and Doopie play-acted a little scene. Nurses with bassinets turning to stare at them. I said, 'What did that all mean?'

She said, 'It meaned we'd still like to go to the National Mystery Museum and then for fidge and ships. It meaned we still like you.'

Doopie said, 'Nod vair, Bayba. Nod vair adall. Bud dode worry.' She actually hugged me. What Doopie lacks in intellect she makes up for with simple, honest affection.

October 8, 1934

To Bryanston Court for drinks. Ernest was grumpy because Mr Loo had destroyed his new carpet slippers and Wally kept talking about tiaras. She's off to Paris tomorrow for fittings and I suppose the whole money thing is making him anxious. Twice he said, 'Remember to stay within your budget, Wally. Only a fool spends what he doesn't have.'

HRH's name never cropped up.

I said, 'I wonder when your wedding invitation will arrive?'

Wally said, 'Plenty of time.'

Well, I know for a fact the Belchesters have already received theirs.

October 11, 1934

Lightfoot says the George and Marinas are taking a house in Belgrave Square, just around the corner from the Crosbies. Pips says she expects Marina will be on the doorstep all the time asking to borrow a cup of sugar.

Lightfoot got his invitation too. All this money Wally's spending at Main Bocher. I hope she's not in for a disappointment.

October 16, 1934

To Covent Garden for *Parsifal*. Came, Wally and HRH, the Humphrey Butlers and the Otto Bismarcks. No Ernest, but he is coming to the Fort this weekend. HRH fell asleep during Act I and Wally slapped his hand. Much horrified rolling of eyes by Poots Butler but my sympathies are entirely with the Prince. I'd have nodded off myself if my foundation hadn't become uncomfortably puckered. If someone thought to present an operatic show which dispensed with all the posturing and weeping and simply featured the best tunes I believe they'd have a great success on their hands.

October 17, 1934
Pips says she's lost all sympathy for Ernest if he's willing to crawl back under the Prince's roof. She said, 'To keep up the pretence in public is one thing. You have to give him something for maintaining his dignity. But agreeing to spend a weekend at the love nest! That speaks volumes about Ernest. Basically he's just a ridiculous little snob.'

Pips can be very judgmental.

October 19, 1934, Fort Belvedere
The Fruity Metcalfes are here and the Perry Brownlows. HRH says Wally and Ernest don't need a wedding invitation sent through the mails because he put their names on a list and that's all there is to it.

He and Ernest pruned roses together this morning. I wonder what they talked about. Baba Metcalfe says Marina Greece is shy but adorable and George is deliriously happy, picking out rugs and drapes for their new house. Wally and Ernest are going to give them an inlaid cigarette box. It was given to them by the Benny Thaws and has hardly been used.

October 22, 1934, Wilton Place
Penelope Blythe says Prince George has a love child that was spirited out of the country and is being raised in obscurity. She says everyone knows about it. I'll bet shy but adorable Marina doesn't. She says Billy Belchester is a surprisingly good lover.

October 25, 1934
To Lady Strathnaver's gala for the Not Forgottens. At George Lightfoot's table, as were the Erlangers, the Crosbies, and the Belchesters, putting on a united front.

Wally and Ernest were at the Metcalfes' table. HRH is at Sandringham.

I took care to bump into Violet in the powder room. She was cool but polite so obviously knows nothing of my rendezvous in the park with Flora and Doopie.

November 5, 1934

A brusque call from Hart Casey at First Maryland. He wonders when he may expect a reply to his letter of September 3. He obviously has no idea how much mail a person returns to find after a two-month vacation. I said, 'I don't believe I've even seen your letter yet.'

He said, 'Mrs Brumby, if you had seen it you would remember. Your checking accounts are seriously overextended. We really have to do something about it.'

Damned cheek. I reminded him that Danforth Brumby practically got him into that bank. He said, 'He certainly did. And he always impressed on me the importance of knowing what you've got and where it is. I know he wouldn't want First Maryland to allow your accounts to fall into bad shape.'

I said, 'Well, why don't you just transfer money from accounts that aren't overextended. Do I have to teach you your job?'

He said, 'That's the problem, Mrs Brumby. There isn't really anything to transfer.'

There's obviously been some kind of error.

I said, 'I'll look into it when I have a moment.'

He said, 'And when do you estimate that will be?'

Landsakes, this is a very busy season in London, not to mention I have a friend going to a royal wedding. I'll get Randolph Putnam onto it.

To the Grill Room with Pips.

219

November 7, 1934

Randolph says this is not a good time to sell Brumby stock. Pips says she knows nothing about money. She leaves all that to her trustees.

November 9, 1934

George Lightfoot says he's the worst person to go to for advice. His family have been selling off castles for centuries and they still never make ends meet.

Hattie Erlanger said she has no trouble managing on her allowance. One would never know from the way she dresses.

November 10, 1934

Ida Coote says wealth or poverty are of no importance. What matters is inner contentedness. How annoying friends can be in times of trouble.

November 13, 1934

Saw Doopie and Flora in the park. Gave them an ounce of candy to share. Flora says her flower maid's dress is pretty but her wedding shoes pinch. That's because she's allowed to go barefoot so much.

I wonder how much there is in Doopie's fund? She has absolutely no need of money.

November 14, 1934

To Wally's to see her Paris gowns. They are stunning. And exactly the style for someone who has no natural figure. This regime of lemon juice and hot water she's been following is doing nothing for her neck. After thirty-five a woman needs a little avoirdupois beneath her skin.

November 16, 1934

A voice I wished never to hear again. Junior. He said, 'Greetings, Stepma! I hear you're in difficulties. Now why don't I take Sweet Air off your hands? Free you up some walking-around money.'

Over my dead body. It's thanks to his mismanagement that my dividends are down. Brumby must be spinning in his grave.

November 20, 1934

I have decided to sell Sweet Air to Randolph Putnam. He always admired the place and I've no use for it anymore. He was so thrilled. He said, 'I'll give you a fair price, Maybell. And someday, when you come back where you belong, it can be yours again. My offer of a wedding band still stands.'

I said, 'Don't cloud the issue. If you want the house buy it. And find a nice girl because I won't be coming back.'

He said, 'Okay, Maybell. I hear you.'

A good move all round. I've thwarted Junior and I'll be able to get Hart Casey and First Maryland off my back without ending up as Randoph Putnam's sex slave.

November 21, 1934

London is filling with minor royalties. The Yugoslavias, the Greeces, the Bulgarias, the Denmarks. I asked Wally if she wasn't the tiniest bit nervous about arriving at Buckingham Palace without a board invitation. 'Not a bit,' she said. 'David is taking care of everything.' He certainly seems to have pulled strings at Cartier. They've poked around in their vaults and found an old tiara for her to borrow.

November 22, 1934

To the German Legation. A little reception for the Hohenzollerns. Von Ribbentrop beaming and glad-handing everyone. He said, 'Maybell! Where is our splendid Wally this evening?'

I said, 'I believe she's engaged elsewhere.'

'Ach!' he said. 'I understand! Mummy is the word.'

He was really behaving as though we were guests in *his* house, but Ambassador von Hoesch was far too polite to put him in his place. Violet pecked me on the cheek. Melhuish said, 'I'm glad to see you don't have Wales's peg doll in tow.'

Pips says she's suffering from Royal Wedding Fatigue. She's getting up a lunch for people who want to discuss other subjects.

November 26, 1934

To the Ivy with Pips, Hattie, and Zita Cavett. Hattie couldn't wait to tell us what she'd heard from Poots Butler: that the King noticed Wally and Ernest's names added to the list for the wedding ball, ordered them to be removed, and hauled HRH over the coals about it in front of Humphrey.

November 27, 1934

Pips called first thing. She said, 'Freddie saw Ernest at the Guards' Club last night. He says he looked like the cat that'd been promised a lifetime supply of cream, so what are we to think? Will the Simpsons go to the ball or not? The world holds its breath.'

Wally unreachable of course. First she was resting, not to be disturbed. Then she was with her hairdresser and taking no more calls till tomorrow. I guess that means they're going.

November 28, 1934

Wally and Ernest *did* go to the ball. She called me at ten and said, 'Come over, Maybell. I'll make us French toast and tell you all about it.'

She was in her kimono, sipping milk and very happy to hear everyone is talking about her. Poots Butler was right about their names being removed from the guest list but only temporarily. She said, 'It was a mistake. David had it fixed as soon as he realized and he came down personally to greet us, to make sure we didn't have trouble with anymore mix-ups. It was such a scream. He whisked us through the vestibule, straight past Violet and her gang. You should have seen their faces. And I outshone the lot of them, Maybell. Especially the royalties, all lined up in their prissy pastels, dressed like a herd of milkmaids.'

I said, 'And did you meet the King and Queen?'

'No,' she said. 'The stumbling block there is that Ernest and I have both been divorced. But we may be able to do something about that. I may be able to get Win Spencer annulled. In Ernest's case it might be harder because there was a child, but an annulment isn't out of the question. You just have to know the right people.'

She wanted to hear all the gossip. Who's for her, who's against her, but I told no tales. I said, 'All you need to know is, *I* have always been for you.'

She said, 'I know, Maybell. You've been a treasure and I'll never forget it.'

November 29, 1934

Prince George is now styled the Duke of Kent, which sounds to me like a demotion. Better surely to be a prince than a duke.

The other disappointing news is that Wally and Ernest didn't go to the wedding after all. Hattie says the King probably had Gurkhas posted everywhere to keep them out, but Wally says it was just that Ernest had an emergency at his office and she didn't feel she could face the cold of the Abbey.

Such a shame, after Main Bocher did such beautiful work on her gown.

She said, 'Well, it was only a wedding. When you've seen one you've seen them all.'

To the Whitlow Trillings' for Thanksgiving turkey and fixings. The new child was handed around, very red and howling. They have named it Loelia after the Duchess of Westminster. I hope they got a good gift.

November 30, 1934
Carlton Gardens is still swarming with wedding guests. Trotman showed me into the morning room. The Melhuish sisters were there with Paul Yugoslavia's wife, and Violet looking at me through narrowed eyes, bracing herself for what she knew must come.

She said, 'Were we expecting you?'

I said, 'No, but I happened to be passing and I wanted to hear how you enjoyed the wedding ball.'

She said, 'It was charming.'

I said, 'Yes, Wally thought so too. She had quite a triumph by all accounts.'

She said, 'Is that what you call "a triumph"? Crashing in uninvited, in fact quite expressly *dis*invited. Dancing past Their Majesties dressed like a Christmas tree. A vulgar error is what I'd call it. A grotesque exhibition of bad manners.'

That's Violet all over. She'll never back down.

Flora was on the stairs when I left, in her flower maid's dress and Wellington boots. She was soaping her Spanish doll which she has named 'Damned Wales'. She said, 'Hello, Aunt Bayba. Are you still banquished?'

December 4, 1934
Two full days helping Wally pick out Christmas gifts for HRH's households. So fatiguing. The whole business is too boring for words.

Bernie and Zita Cavett have taken a house near Teddington and want me for the holidays. I don't know. The Crosbies are going to South Africa. Wally and Ernest are going to Devonshire with Ernest's newsagent friends.

December 6, 1934
Lunch with Lightfoot. He said, 'I think you're being treated somewhat shabbily, Maybell. Your only crime seems to be loyalty to a friend and I intend bringing it up with Melhuish. If moves aren't made to welcome you back into the bosom of your family there'll be no pantomime for Flora and Rory this Christmas, gobfather or no. Doopie feels the same way. She's absolutely solid with me on this.' He is a dear.

December 10, 1934
A visit from Violet. Lightfoot obviously issued his ulmitatum.

She said, 'Maybell, don't let's quarrel.'

I said, 'I haven't quarreled.'

She said, 'No, well. It's upsetting Doopie dreadfully. Say you'll come to us for Christmas.'

I said, 'I'm afraid I can't. I already promised the Cavetts.'

She said, 'Who are they? I don't know them.'

I said, 'Bernie and Zita. They're friends of the Prince. Americans. They've taken a house in Middlesex.'

She said, 'Will you-know-who be there?'

I said, 'If you mean Wally, she'll be in the West Country with her husband.'

'Oh good,' she said. 'That's as it should be. Even better if she were to go back to the States. Well, let's hope.'

We embraced when she left. She said, 'You know I only do things for your own good, Maybell. When all's said and done you're still my little sister.'

December 15, 1934, Fort Belvedere

Our last weekend before HRH leaves for Sandringham. The Erlangers are here, also Bernie and Zita, Oliver Templemore, and Fruity Metcalfe. No Baba. She spends a great deal of time with her brother-in-law since her sister Cimmie died. There are young children to be consoled.

Wally had had a tree brought in to the Octagon Room and lit with tiny electric candles. The men all received cigars from HRH and the ladies engraved cigarette lighters, but I know Wally also got a pin with square-cut emeralds. I saw HRH claimed his thank-you kiss while Ernest was playing billiards with Templemore.

December 16, 1934

HRH wants us all to go with him to Kitzbühel in February. The Erlangers and the Cavetts are for it. Ernest doesn't think he can get away.

Wally said, 'Never mind. Maybell will just have to keep me company.'

Fruity says it will fall to Oxer Bettenbrooke to equerry.

I think Fruity and I were the only ones to witness HRH's tears as Wally and Ernest drove away after tea.

'A whole month,' he said. 'A whole beastly month without her.'

Fruity shook his head.

December 21, 1934, Wilton Place

With Hattie to buy skiwear. Wally refuses. She says she's never skied in her life and she doesn't intend starting now. She says she'll just wear furs and take along lots of books.

Hattie said, 'Wally had jolly well better learn to ski. And hunt. And play golf. David's going to get pretty bored with her if all she does is shop.'

It's hard to imagine HRH ever growing bored with Wally.

December 23, 1934

To the compound for hot cider and Christmas carols. Benny Thaw acknowledged me but Connie turned her back. A card from Randolph Putnam. The Sweet Air papers will be ready for signing by the end of January.

December 28, 1934

Zita Cavett thinks Wally should go to Reno, divorce Ernest, and snap up HRH while he's still a free man. I told her, it's a bit more complicated than that. He's the next King.

She said, 'So? If they went off quietly to a little wedding chapel what could anyone do about it?'

Maybe she's right.

December 30, 1934

Wally says she's not interested in marrying HRH. She said, 'Everything's just fine the way it is.'

I said, 'Even for Ernest?'

227

She said, 'Especially for Ernest. He knows which side his bread's buttered.'

January 1, 1935

A new year, a new copybook.

Last night to the Florida Club. George Lightfoot wrapped his silk scarf around his head and looked into his crystal cuff link. His predictions: Ralph Habberley will turn up in Borneo with a lost memory and Jane will forgive all. Whitlow and Gladys will produce another red-faced daughter. The Hohenzollerns will rediscover a princess they had mislaid in a turret room and HRH will become engaged to her on the eve of Their Majesties' Silver Jubilee. Ernest will become Baron Simpson of Bryanston.

January 5, 1935

To the Drury Lane Theatre with Lightfoot, Rory, Doopie and Flora to see *Dick Whittington*.

An impromptu invitation from Philip Sassoon. Park Lane, for tea. I said, 'I thought I'd become a persona ingrata.'

He said, 'What nonsense! I want you to see my new r-r-rococo paneling.'

January 6, 1935

I'm one up on Wally. *I* have been presented to HM Queen.

She suddenly materialized at Philip Sassoon's and asked

Violet to bring me to her. Violet said, 'Just make a short curtsy. It's only four o'clock. And wait for her to speak first.'

She was in gray shot silk sitting on a long blue couch. It struck me she looked rather like one of those round-prowed barges at anchor.

I believe she said, 'They have the very best raspberries at Drumcanna,' but her voice was too quiet for me to be sure. I simply smiled and inclined my head in an attitude of compliance and it all went off very smoothly. Violet was very happy. She said, 'Isn't she marvelous? So gracious. Twenty-five years and she's never made a false step, Maybell. You see how fortunate this country is.'

Philip's new paneling looked very well. It had been brought all the way from Austria, as had the chocolate cake.

January 9, 1935

Gave Wally lunch. Her number-one aim this year is to make a big splash at the Silver Jubilee. We're going to Paris on our way to Kitzbühel so she can order gowns.

I said, 'Can you afford it?'

She said, 'I don't need to afford it. I'm a favored customer, Maybell. No one had heard of Main Bocher till I wore him. Now he's the talk of London. Everything will be on the house.'

Emerald Cunard stopped by our table. She'd just had a vexing morning with her telephone out of order and the Postmaster-General unable to do anything about it because he's shooting at the Perry Brownlows'.

January 11, 1935

Drinks at the Prosper Friths'. According to Daphne, Baba Metcalfe is going to exceptional lengths to comfort Tom

Mosley in his widowhood. She has moved into his bed.

I do hope Baba isn't creating some kind of precedent for sisters-in-law. Melhuish always had a soft spot for me, but it would be too awful if Violet went early to her reward and he expected me to warm his sheets.

January 12, 1935
Randolph Putnam keeps trying to tie me down to a date for the closing, but I have no idea when we'll be back from Kitzbühel.

I said, 'This is a royal skiing party, not a railroad company. We don't go by timetables.'

He said, 'Doesn't Prince Wales have work to do?'

I said, 'Traveling the world and being seen is a prince's work. My lawyer will wire yours as soon as I'm available to sign the papers.'

He said, 'You just better hope Junior doesn't have me murdered while you're gone. That wife of his keeps calling your tenants. If ever she gets her hands on a door key you'll never get the place back, only in a court of law and maybe not even there. Well, it's up to you. Either I buy Sweet Air fair and square or I walk away from it. I can't say more.'

Randolph always did fuss. He lived too long with his mother.

January 18, 1935
HRH is on his way to Austria with Oxer Bettenbrooke. Tomorrow to Paris. The Cavetts are already at Lily Drax-Pfaffenhof's and will meet up with us in Kitzbühel.

January 21, 1935, Hôtel Meurice, Paris
Hattie spent the entire journey from London doom-mongering about Wally's prospects of going to a state ball.

Wally refused to get riled.

She just said, 'Hattie, better to have a gown and no invitation than an invitation and no gown.'

January 24, 1935

Wally has chosen full-skirted silk chiffon, one in silver and one in gold. There were a couple of accounts outstanding, for lingerie and shoes. I've made her a small loan to tide her over.

HRH has telephoned twice urging us to set off before more avalanches prevent the trains from getting through, but Elsie Mendl has invited us to dinner at Trianon and Wally has run into an old Washington friend, Kenny Opdyke, who has a warehouse full of rugs and clocks and other lovely things, all for sale at advantageous prices, so Wednesday really seems to be the soonest we can leave.

January 27, 1935

HRH is so fretful without Wally. He telephones constantly to see whether we're on our way although he knows perfectly well when to expect us.

I said, 'How will he manage when they marry him off?' She laughed. She said, 'He'll probably keep me behind some secret door in a bookcase. No. I'll have been dropped by then. I won't be missed.'

I said, 'Is he going to drop you? He seems more ardent than ever.'

She said, 'That's just absence working its old magic. But of course he'll drop me. He drops everyone eventually. All I need is one more year. Give me another year and I reckon I'll have secured my future.'

After Kitzbühel HRH is going on to Vienna for a few

days. Wally says we should go with him. She's heard the shops there are exquisite.

February 2, 1935, Kitzbühel

We are installed at the Lindenhof and have the use of a commodious lodge with veranda views of the slopes. Lily is here with the Cavetts, the Eugene Rothschilds, and the Milwaukee Gunters, and the embassy has sent HRH a junior attaché to do a little equerrying, as Bettenbrooke speaks no German. Our man from Vienna is Dudley Forwood and Wally has already taken quite a shine to him. She says he plays a very good game of backgammon.

Hattie says the snow here is the very best kind for skiing. I'll take her word for it. Wally, Zita and I sunned ourselves on the veranda all morning and HRH floundered past every so often, flanked by Forwood and a detective, waving his ski poles and shouting, 'Are you watching me, darling? Aren't I doing splendidly?!'

February 3, 1935

We quite took over the Klammer Stube last evening. Hattie, in drink, offered the opinion that skiing isn't the Prince's forte. Wally fairly froze the cherry brandy in her glass. The last thing she wants is for HRH to grow discouraged and start hanging around our veranda all day.

As nice as he is, I don't know why Forwood was sent for. The Prince gabbles away in German to the serving girls as though it were his mother tongue.

Kitty Rothschild says it *is* his mother tongue. I don't think she understands that this is the Prince of Wales we're talking about.

February 5, 1935

Blizzards, but Hattie, Oxer, and HRH refuse to be defeated. They've gone out for a sleigh ride while we hug the fire. Dudley Forwood has been explaining the Austrian situation to us. The Austrians need Hitler's friendship because they're in a bad way financially, but Hitler isn't interested in being just a friendly neighbor. Being an Austrian by birth himself he sees Austria as family and wants Germany to adopt it. Then there's Mr Mussolini. It's all so complicated, especially after a glass of *glühwein*. Wally was taking notes.

February 6, 1935

HRH came in yesterday so enchanted by his sleigh ride Wally has agreed to give it a try. I believe she's slightly uneasy about the amount of time he's been spending in Hattie's company, though I don't know why. I don't think Hattie's apple-cheeked heartiness can hold any attraction for him.

Kitty Rothschild says HRH is like a twelve-year-old in an old man's skin.

February 7, 1935

Wally has decided to make sleigh rides her winter sport. She said, 'Ermine rugs, Maybell. Once you've snuggled beneath ermine rugs nothing else will do. And they lit our path with flares. Such a wonderful racy look. I'm going to see about copying that.'

Not along George Street, I hope.

Tonight dancing to a Schrammel band. The Rothschilds are leaving in the morning, for their Austrian estate. HRH has proposed us for dinner with them while we're in Vienna.

February 8, 1935

Three vigorous polkas with HRH last evening. He was in such a good mood.

February 9, 1935

The Rothschilds left early. There's nothing like the promise of a royal visit to quicken the heartbeat. Forwood has also gone to make sure everything is in order for our arrival in Vienna. HRH and I were the only two down to wave them off. We shared a pot of chocolate and a plate of ham for breakfast.

He seemed rather flat after last night's high spirits. Only one more week then he has to steel himself for a year of more than usually hectic princing. The Silver Jubilee celebrations, state luncheons, levees, tours around the country. It seems no boondock will be left unvisited.

He said, 'What an enviable life Rothschild has. A *schloss* in Austria, a place in Paris, and a spread on Long Island. A little shooting, a little shopping, a little golf. I'd settle very happily for that.'

February 10, 1935, Hotel Bristol, Vienna

My suite has a view of the Ringstrasse but there's no noise. Enormous snowflakes drifting down. I've ordered extra comforters. We sat for ages with the train moving forward in fits and starts as the drifts were cleared and arrived hours late, but the British envoy was there with Forwood at his side, and there were warm cars waiting for us. I think I'm going to like Vienna.

February 11, 1935

HRH was on the road early looking at worker housing but word has circulated that he's in residence. By the time Wally and I had finished breakfast and made hair appointments quite a crowd had gathered outside. There are Socialists down there, who seem to be for him because he's interested in the lot of the working man, but there's another group, Reds, who are against Germany and so are chanting slogans because HRH has a lot of German cousins. Well, no one can help their cousins. One of the Woodhams on Mother's side was fond of naked swimming in public places and Father always said there was a Patterson who was hanged in Dundee, Scotland, but in neither case did it cause us any inconvenience.

Wally is nervous about the rabble at the front door, so the hairdresser will now come to us.

February 12, 1935
All ended well yesterday. HRH braved the crowd outside and engaged them in German chitchat. He charmed them into silence. Most of them, at any rate. Forwood says they'd been standing in the snow long enough for the fire to have gone out of their bellies. By the time we went out to the Wunder-Bar only a few stragglers remained and when they noticed we were wearing red corsages they gave us a hearty cheer. A little tact and imagination goes such a long way. I think diplomacy is a field where I would have excelled, and perhaps still may.

Today shopping, then drinks with George Messersmith, our man in Vienna.

February 13, 1935
At Ambassador Messersmith's insistence Wally and I went to see a horse-riding circus. It was quite interesting but horses smell like horses however well trained they are.

Also bought woolen suiting, winter silks, and embroidered cushions. HRH had a meeting with the Chancellor but we're not supposed to talk about it because it wouldn't be approved of in London. Not that it's any of London's business. They should be grateful to have a prince who takes an interest in international affairs. HRH feels the Austrians have all the right instincts, remaining firm with Germany and at the same time friendly toward Italy. They told him there's even the possibility of bringing back Archduke Otto. Never a bad thing, as he says, for a country to temper the rough-and-tumble of politics with the nobler spirit of royalty.

To the Rascal Club. Men dressed as women, women dressed as men. What a very long way we've come from Baltimore.

February 14, 1935
David has given Wally a valentine pin, a pink beryl heart set in white gold. Tonight we drive up to Schloss Enzesfeld to have dinner with the Eugene Rothschilds. I wonder whether our path will be cleared of ice and lit by burning torches!

Tomorrow HRH flies back to his duties and we begin our long trek home by train. I do wish Wally would take a pill so we could fly too.

February 15, 1935
Wally and HRH chucked the Rothschilds at the last minute so they could dine alone in their suite. I went with just Dudley Forwood and Oxer Bettenbrooke. Kitty R was very gracious about it. She said, 'Never mind. Perhaps we'll have a nicer time. I've always suspected royalties might be bad for the digestion.'

Forwood very wickedly agreed.

Kitty gave us her analysis of the Prince's personality. She said, 'He reminds me of a dog. He sees a lamppost and becomes completely obsessed with it, until someone sticks another one under his nose. Then he forgets the first one.'

Eugene said, 'Darling, you're embarrassing our guests.'

She said, 'Nonsense. They know it's all said most affectionately. Now, the puzzle is Wally. She's very bright, but does she really understand how he ticks? I've noticed how sharp she is with him when he hangs around, getting in her way, but that's not the way to deal with him. It seems to me the crosser she gets with him the more eagerly he wags his tail.'

Well, he certainly wasn't wagging his tail this morning when he had to leave for the airfield. He just hates being separated from her.

February 19, 1935, Wilton Place
Sweet Air, where Danforth Brumby took me as his bride, now belongs to Randolph Putnam. I put a call through to him immediately after I'd signed the papers. I said, 'Well, you finally got what you wanted.'

'No, Maybell,' he said, 'I got part of what I want. The other part is sitting stiff-necked in the office of a London lawyer if I'm not mistaken. Tell me, how's your Prince of Wales?'

I said, 'In love. With Minnehaha Warfield. You'll be reading about it in the *Globe* before long, I'm sure.'

He said, 'Isn't that something! You mean we could have Queen Wally visiting with us at Sweet Air someday?'

That wasn't what I meant at all.

February 21, 1935

Took Violet's Tyrolean tray cloth to Carlton Gardens, and a cuckoo clock for the nursery. Doopie was out, visiting Ena Spain at Kensington Palace.

Violet says Their Majesties are greatly invigorated from their Sandringham break and eager to begin their celebration year. I braced myself but neither of the W words came up.

A brief note from Junior and his wife. May I rot in hell.

February 22, 1935

Aching and feverish. Perhaps Junior has had a curse put on me.

February 23, 1935

Canceled lunch with Pips and Ida. Padmore says I have influenza.

February 24, 1935

A visit from Ida Coote who brought honey and canned spinach. She says we are what we eat. Well, I have eaten nothing since Monday.

Wally's pestering me to go look at a house on Eaton Square. HRH to foot the bill.

I said, 'Will this be for you alone or for you and Ernest?'

She said, 'That's up to Ernest, but it makes perfect sense to keep things the way they are.'

I said, 'Well, count me out. I'm as weak as a kitten.'

March 6, 1935

I feel like a new woman! Lunch with George Lightfoot, who jestingly steered me away from all drain covers lest I slip through in my new svelte condition.

He was in a strange mood. He said, 'Tell me your thoughts on marriage, Maybell. Do you recommend it?'

I said, 'If you marry that Belinda I'll be heartbroken. She has no warmth.'

He said, 'No, I'm not talking about Belinda, though she's much nicer than you say. I'm just asking about marriage in general. I'm thirty-six. A decent age to start thinking about it, don't you think?'

It is indeed.

March 7, 1935

Hattie has been looking at houses with Wally. Chesham Place, Lowndes Street. It's all supposed to be very hush-hush but let Hattie Erlanger in on a secret and it will appear in tomorrow's *Times*.

To the Ham Bone Club. The Crosbies, von Ribbentrop without his smiling hausfrau, Wally without her husband or her Prince, and the Trillings. Gladys's reentry into the world. Her waistline is still looking pretty slack.

Von R danced with Wally all evening. He knew every detail of our trip to Vienna.

March 10, 1935

The Crokers have arrived. They've taken Sunninghills again. Ethel said, 'I hope Wally is going to let us have you for Ascot Week.'

March 14, 1935

Lunch with Ethel and Pips. First thing Ethel said, 'And? Has our Prince popped the question?'

Pips said, 'That'd be a bit premature. There's the little matter of Ernest.'

Anyway, that's not at all the plan. HRH has to marry someone who can be Queen.

Ethel said, 'Okay. So what happens to Wally if he wakes up King tomorrow?'

I said, 'But he's not going to.'

'No,' she said, 'but just say.'

I said, 'Then he'd hurry off and marry one of those Biedermeyer-Bechsteins. Keep her confined to the Palace with a brood of babies and slip away as often as possible to see Wally.'

'God!' she said. 'Long live the King!'

Pips said, 'Apart from anything else, Wally wouldn't be any use as a brood mare. She's too old and she has very irregular insides.'

March 20, 1935

Penelope Blythe has it from Kitsie Brownlow that the King sent for HRH and asked him straight out whether he and Wally are lovers and HRH swore absolutely not. She says it spread like wildfire from the Palace to York House and the Fort and the servants can talk of nothing else because they've seen what they've seen and they know what they know. But the King was apparently satisfied with David's answer and as a show of cordiality he's agreed to turn a blind eye to the fact that both Wally and Ernest have been divorced and allow them to attend one of the Jubilee balls.

Just as well, because Wally's in Paris having fittings and they're hardly the kind of gowns she'd have occasion to wear in Marylebone.

I said, 'What's going to happen when the King finds out the truth?'

Penelope said, 'Oh, he already knows the truth. But having posed the question it wouldn't be done for him to disbelieve Wales's answer. And everyone now feels better for a slight clearing of the air. It's all quite understood.'

Not by me.

March 24, 1935
A call from Ernest. Would I share a simple supper with him tomorrow evening? He said, 'Wally's still in Paris, as you know. But I'd very much like to talk to you, just we two. I'd count it a very great favor, Maybell.'

I'm filled with dread. I do hope he doesn't cry.

March 25, 1935
To Bryanston Court, full of trepidation. A fire lit. Cold cuts and baked potatoes served on trays. I was hardly through the door before Ernest showed me the invitation: A Court Ball on May 14. He said, 'The greatest honor of my life. Something undreamed of.'

Small talk about Vienna while we ate, but then he grew wistful over coffee.

He said, 'Well, Maybell, you see how things are. Thanks to Wally the Prince of Wales has become a close personal friend. The next King of England. He gave me these very cigars. But to get to the point, he's fallen in love with my wife. I have to face facts. I can't keep her to myself.'

He was very calm.

I said, 'I expect this year will be different. David has a very full appointment book, with the Jubilee. Hardly a day off.'

He said, 'Yes. But of course there'll be another long vacation after the celebrations. Another cruise, I dare say. I can't be away from business for weeks on end guarding my wife, and anyway, it's rather gone beyond that. I'd be *de trop*. I suppose you know they're lovers?'

I told him the truth when I said Wally has never admitted to any intimacy.

He said, 'Still, there can be no doubt.'

I said, 'What will you do?'

He said, 'I'm not sure. Wait, I suppose. See what happens. Do you think she wants me to leave her?'

I said, 'Not at all. I think she expects to be dropped as suddenly as she was taken up.'

'Yes,' he said, 'that's what she told me. She expects to be let go with a handsome pension. As though that makes it worthwhile. Are people laughing at me, Maybell?'

Again I spoke the truth when I said they were not. People hardly remember he exists. Ernest is one of those people who's forgotten the moment he leaves the room.

He said, 'I have to go to Germany next week. That's one thing about being in business. It keeps one occupied.'

He was still sucking on his royal cigar but it had quite gone out.

April 4, 1935
George and Marina Kent are back from their honeymoon. She's expecting. Doopie will be thrilled. I'll bet you can't hear yourself think at Carlton Gardens for the clacking of knitting pins.

April 10, 1935
To the Shim Sham with Boss and Ethel, Judson and Hattie, Wally and HRH. Ernest is in Hamburg. Judson now calls him 'The Invisible Man'.

April 12, 1935
A little ladies' luncheon. Soufflé omelets, Florida salad.

HRH has gone to Leicestershire for the weekend but

didn't dare take Wally because Their Majesties are staying nearby. Hattie said, 'I wonder if he'll bump into Thelma,' and Wally snapped, 'Not if he knows what's good for him.'

As Ethel said, one might almost have thought that was a flash of jealousy. She said, 'You don't think she's fallen in love or anything, do you?'

Pips said, 'Not Wally. She's just guarding her nest egg.'

April 15, 1935

Wally is timing her final gown fittings to coincide with Jubilee Day. She says she can't bear to be in London with everyone talking about processions and who wore what. She said, 'All those carriages full of homely princesses, all that waving and nodding. It's nothing to do with the David I know.'

I said, 'Wally Warfield! Are you in love?'

She said, 'No. Well. Maybe it's a kind of love. It's nice to be needed. I suppose that's why some people have babies. I don't think anyone would believe how much David needs me. That's why it's so awful to feel invisible when he's out there princing.'

For a moment she looked quite forlorn.

April 18, 1935

Ambassador von Hoesch has invited me to join Violet and the children at the German Legation to view the procession on Jubilee Day. Melhuish will be riding with the Nicholases of Greece.

Violet says we may expect another royal wedding this year. Prince Harry is engaged to Alice Buccleuch. Her father is an old friend of the King.

With Rory to Oxford Street to see the Jubilee decorations

and then to Selfridges for Welsh rarebit. He's becoming such a young gentleman, always takes my arm when we cross a street and walks on the outside.

He's been learning magic tricks from a boy in his House and wants magician's accessories for his birthday. I said, 'I'll bet there's never been a magician in the Melhuish family.'

He said, 'Well, one can't do it for a living obviously, but it's rather good fun when there are guests. Uncle Prince George greatly enjoyed my rope trick, except Flora told him how it was done. Ulick says conjuring's for the lower classes.'

Pips and Freddie have declined an invitation to the Fort for Easter.

I said, 'You always reckoned it wasn't done to decline.'

Freddie said, 'I've also always thought it's completely not done to call a chap your friend while you're stealing his wife.'

Wally says the Crosbies are no loss to them. The Perry Brownlows are coming, Boss and Ethel, Judson and Hattie.

April 21, 1935, Fort Belvedere
HRH went up to the Castle for Easter church and came bouncing back. 'Duty done!' he said. 'Now I can relax with *my* kind of people.'

He's looking into chartering a yacht for the summer. We'll cruise to Italy and Greece. I can't wait. I shall try out the new sun-kissed look and study the ancients.

April 26, 1934, Wilton Place
Wally believes she's being slandered at the Palace. Nellie Hardinge has been heard to say that she must have been very busy in China for so many people to have known her.

Wally said, 'Someone's been poking about, looking into my past. Well, let them. If I'm still around when David's King I'll make sure the lot of them are fired.'

May 4, 1935
Dinner at the Belchesters'. Came, the Westminsters, the Crosbies, the Prosper Friths. Daphne Frith asked rather slyly after Wally. She said, 'I must say, the Prince of Wales has never looked more handsome.'

Anne Belchester said, 'The whole family is on the crest of a wave. A Silver Jubilee for Their Majesties, the Kents radiant, the Yorks so greatly loved, and now even Harry has found a bride.'

Daphne said, 'Yes, all we need to make it a perfect year is for Wales to name his princess. Maybell, you're on the inside. Anyone in prospect?'

I said, 'No. I don't think he's in any hurry.'

She said, 'Well, he shouldn't delay much longer. He's at that time of life when he'll suddenly lose his looks.'

Pips said, 'Of course, there's always Wally Simpson.'

Billy Belchester said, 'With the current mood of the country Wales could get away with a great deal. Marry a Hottentot, almost. But not the dreadful Mrs S. Never that.'

May 6, 1935
Jubilee Day. I've seen enough processing dignitaries to last me a lifetime. Prime Ministers from distant lands, courtiers in wigs and silk stockings, minor foreign royalties, obscure British royalties unidentifiable to everyone except Violet and Ulick who'd suddenly cry out, 'There's Athlone!' or, 'Is that Tommy Lascelles?' Dear Louis Ferdinand watched with us. His mother was in a carriage with the Denmarks.

There were marching bands, troopers on horseback,

drums, bugles. Finally, we got to the meat of the matter. Prince Harry and the Princess Royal, then the Bertie Yorks, she in eau de Nil. She looks quite pretty in a procession, whatever Wally may say.

Violet was calling, 'Flora, come and wave to Lilibet and Margaret Rose,' but to no avail. She was conducting her own imaginary procession at the back of the room. She's to be tried at a different style of school in September, in a remote backwater of Suffolkshire, but it's not to be mentioned until the day dawns.

After the Yorks came the Kents, she in cream and tan. Then HRH in a landau with two aunts, Toria and Maud Norway. It felt very strange indeed to see him riding in state when I'm accustomed to seeing him on his exercise bicycle. Wally did right not being there to watch. She would have found it unbearable.

More bands, and then the King and Queen, both with very tight little smiles, she in silver and white brocade with her vast bosom covered in pearls. Hattie Erlanger says if you see the King close up his beard is stained with tobacco.

Went back to Carlton Gardens afterwards for a late luncheon. Poached salmon, inevitably, and sherry trifle, and endless cups of tea as people drifted back from the service of thanksgiving. Melhuish reported that the King had been moved to tears by the warmth and gaiety of the crowds. Rory performed a card trick and made a penny appear and disappear, but it began to feel like a wedding breakfast after the bride and groom have left. We were only saved from complete anticlimax by Lightfoot who had the idea of taking Rory and Flora on an omnibus to see the fireworks and the bonfires burning in Hyde Park. Such an adventure. One has to climb a steep stairway to reach the top deck of the bus. Doopie pushing me from behind shouting, 'Ub ya go, Bayba! Ub ya go!'

I had the impression she'd done it before. Goodness knows what she and Flora get up to, filling their empty days.

The park was entrancing. Shooting stars tumbling down over the bonfires, little children writing their names on the sky with magnesium sparklers, bands playing show tunes, booths selling delicious saveloys with fried onions. It was easily the best part of the day. And when Kettle drove me home, well after eleven, Piccadilly was as crowded as if it were the middle of the day. I don't think London is going to sleep tonight.

May 8, 1935

Wally is back from Paris. She's decided to wear the gold gown to Buckingham Palace on the basis that everyone else, lacking imagination, will go to a Silver Jubilee ball dressed in silver. I'm sworn to secrecy about her jewels. HRH has given her a parure of black sapphires. Ernest doesn't know about them yet. She says the last thing she needs is for him to get worked up and develop another carbuncle on the eve of a state ball.

A setback to our summer plans. The King has forbidden HRH to go take his vacation on a yacht because of a grave situation in Abyssinia. It's so ridiculous. All we need do is steer clear of the place. I've never heard of anyone putting in there anyway. Nothing worth buying, I'm sure.

May 15, 1935

Last night to the Embassy Club with the Crokers and the Erlangers to wait for Wally and Ernest to come on from the ball and give us their report. They arrived just after midnight. Wally, followed by HRH, followed by Ernest, very self-conscious in his court dress. Boss actually bowed to Wally. Hattie screamed, 'Boss, what *are* you doing?'

He said, 'I couldn't help myself. Those are some rocks.'

Wally was radiant. She told me in the powder room that the King studied her very closely each time she danced past him. She thinks the next thing will be an informal meeting, rather than the problematical business of being presented. She thinks it'll happen next time she's at the Fort and the Majesties are at Windsor.

May 16, 1935

Violet says HRH caused great offense by dancing the second dance of the ball with Wally. She says after he'd danced with Her Majesty he should have danced with his sister and his sisters-in-law and only then with Wally, if at all.

She said, 'And as for the husband. What a buffoon. I suppose he'd never worn court dress before. It was really rather comical to see him sweating and concentrating so. He treated his sword like a third leg!'

Flora waltzing around the upper stair hall in a car rug and Christmas tree tinsel. What a rude awakening the child has coming to her in September.

Doopie has had her hair bobbed.

May 18, 1935, Belton House

At the Perry Brownlows' with Wally and Ernest. The sunshine continues, but not from Wally. HRH is princing in the West Country and must have telephoned her five times at least. She grew quite exasperated with him. Kitsie B remarked that the 'sapphire dividend' seems to have worn off rather quickly.

May 25, 1935, Wilton Place

There's a story going around that Ralph Habberley has been sighted in Bolivia. I saw Jane H in Derry & Toms only yesterday. We didn't speak.

With Pips and Freddie to a Jubilee garden fete in the constituency. Torrential rain but I won a bottle of egg flip in the prize draw. Bought glass necklaces for Flora and Doopie and marmalade for Violet.

May 27, 1935

Wally invited herself to lunch. She said she couldn't face going to the Dorch and wanted only bread and soup, because of her ulcers. She does look haggard. She says things have grown very tense between herself and Ernest since the Jubilee ball and she's afraid he may make some kind of scene next time he sees HRH.

I said, 'Is it the jewels?'

She said, 'No. He thinks he's being talked about at his club.'

I don't ever remember seeing her so anxious.

She said, 'Things are going so well. It'd be just too awful if he went and ruined everything now. He refuses to come on vacation and he's practically forbidding me to go without him. What am I supposed to do? Sit in London all summer? Trail after him to New York? I need a break, Maybell. And anyway, David's depending on me.'

I said, 'What will you do? If Ernest asks you to choose?'

She was quiet for the longest time.

She said, 'Well, there's nothing to be gained by dramas and divorce, if that's what you mean. Ernest *wants* to be married to me. David *can't* be married to me. So it's idiotic even to talk of choosing. Everyone just needs to keep their head.'

I said, 'But you have taken a lover. Some husbands don't like that.'

She said, 'I'd hardly call David "a lover". And Ernest didn't mind at the beginning. He can't expect me to turn these things on and off like a tap.'

She says she's helping HRH to write an important speech he has to make to British war veterans next month. No wonder she needs a vacation. I thought he had a little man who did all that.

May 28, 1935

Pips says Ernest *is* being talked about at his club. I said, 'Well, she told me David isn't really her lover.'

She said, 'It doesn't matter if they play checkers all night. She sleeps over and Ernest's a laughing stock.'

June 3, 1935

To the Scottish Office to watch Trooping the Color. Melhuish had organized a window for us. Also came, Elspeth Laird, the Otto Bismarcks, Ena Spain, and George Lightfoot. More horses, more bands, then the King rode out on the very stroke of eleven. I suppose if you're the King you can arrange for a clock to strike when you're ready and not before.

Doopie wearing lip rouge and the little necklace I bought for her. Flora looked quite presentable in a blue dress with a white sailor collar but she's in disgrace for trying to make skyrockets out of sugar and pickling salt.

As Doopie said, 'Lide a madge. Boom!'

June 8, 1935

Mr Stanley Baldwin is the new Prime Minister.

George Lightfoot calls him the Dormouse. Mr Attlee, the Socialist, he calls the Slug.

As our lovely cruise has been vetoed, HRH is taking Rock Cholmondeley's villa instead. It's near Cannes and we can have it for the month of August. I can't believe Sybil Cholmondeley knows anything about this. She'd never have agreed to David bringing Wally there, using it as a love nest. Hattie says whatever Syb's opinion Rock will have been in no position to refuse a favor for the Prince of Wales. Rather like Ernest, really.

June 12, 1935
With Wally to Asprey to buy HRH silver hairbrushes for his birthday. I got him a propelling pencil. She has her eye on a gilt fur clasp. A little more than I'd planned on spending for her birthday, but perhaps I'll treat her. She doesn't look well these days.

June 17, 1935
Ernest has fabricated an urgent business trip to Antwerp and refused all Ascot invitations. Our revised summer plans are taking shape. After the Cholmondeley villa we'll be traveling on to Budapest. More worker housing for poor HRH to study, I suppose. Difficult to know what kind of clothes to take.

To the Crokers' for a pre-Ascot dinner.

June 18, 1935, Sunninghills
Boss Croker says Budapest definitely doesn't have a beach, so I'm going to need a whole other wardrobe. He and Ethel believe Ernest may be cracking up. Ethel said, 'The best thing that could happen now is for him to meet a nice girl.'

Best for whom, though?

June 19, 1935
Ladies' Day. Prince Harry's bride-to-be was in today's landau parade. Another little mouse. Elizabeth York wore buttercup, Marina Kent was in café au lait, Violet in the fourth carriage was unusually elegant in delphinium.

HRH drove straight to town after the big race. Tonight is his big speech to the men of the Royal British Legion, as composed by Wally.

June 20, 1935
HRH's speech received a standing ovation, apparently. The gist of it was that it's time to put old enmities behind us and embrace the new Germany. He proposed that the British Legion set an example by sending a friendly delegation to break bread with German veterans.

Poots Butler said, 'Sir! You'll be known as the Prince of Peace.'

Jack Aird stony-faced.

Wally's birthday. She's thrilled with her fur clasp. HRH has given her emeralds to match her Christmas pin. He kissed her in the drawing room.

June 22, 1935, Fort Belvedere
HRH has been summoned to the Castle. Jack Aird has gone with him. Poots thinks he'll be getting a rocket about inviting Mrs Simpson without her Mr, yet again.

June 23, 1935
HRH did get a telling-off from the King but not about Wally. It was about the British Legion speech. Poots got it blow by blow from Humphrey who got it from Jack Aird.

The King told him he had no business making speeches

that contain anything of substance and most particularly not sentiments that are likely to offend Mr Mussolini. He told him his job is to cut ribbons, keep his mouth shut, and find himself a wife.

Well, HM King may not have approved of the speech but Hitler's Mr Goering did. I saw his telegram of congratulations. Fruity Metcalfe says anyway it isn't HRH who's likely to offend Mussolini but Anthony Eden, who campaigns against Italy's ambitions in Africa while conveniently turning a blind eye to Hitler's ambitions in Austria. Just thinking of it makes one tired.

Still, what a birthday present for poor David, rapped over the knuckles and in front of Jack Aird too.

July 4, 1935, Wilton Place

To the compound. The Benny Thaws have gone back to Washington so that chapter has closed. What a relief. Connie never forgave any of us who stayed loyal to Wally. Understandably. Her first loyalty was bound to be to Thelma. I hope Violet would be as staunch for me.

Randolph Putnam telephoned to wish me a Happy Fourth and tell me what he's going to do with my gardens. I said, 'Not *my* gardens, Randolph. They're yours now.'

He never gives up.

July 6, 1935

Dinner at the Prosper Friths. Prosper reckons Anthony Eden is going to flush Mussolini into the arms of Adolf Hitler. Well, I hope he waits until we've all taken our vacations.

July 7, 1935

To Carlton Gardens. Doopie just on her way out to visit Marina Kent. Flora and Ulick fighting because she'd twisted the head off one of his tin Grenadiers.

He said, 'The sooner you're sent to Suffolk the safer for all our property.'

She wasn't meant to know.

I believe Doopie may have started wearing a girdle.

July 12, 1935

Took Rory to Rules for sirloin of beef and Yorkshire pudding. Fourteen years old! A little down on his top lip, his voice no longer what it was but not quite what it will be. He has a new trick with two pieces of string which he performed for me and then for the table next to ours, by popular request.

He said, 'Flora doesn't want to go to her new school. She says she'll run away.'

I said, 'Well, she might take to it. I remember when you didn't like school so much.'

He said, 'Yes. But Flora's different. I thought I might hide a ten-shilling note in her manicure case, so that if she does run away she won't be without funds.'

I said, 'Do you have a ten-shilling note?'

He said, 'Yes. Well, I did have. Uncle George Kent gave it to me and I've got nine shillings and fourpence left. Do you think that would be enough?'

I said, 'I think it's very generous. The trouble is, I very much doubt whether Flora ever opens her manicure case.'

He said, 'Aunt Maybell, can people get married even when they're old?'

I said, 'Even when they're ninety-nine, so you've plenty of time.'

255

He said, 'I'll probably marry Moo Anstruther-Brodie. Lady Anstruther-Brodie thinks it would be a good idea.'

I said, 'I thought you were sweet on Ellen MacNab?'

He said, 'That was when I was young. But her father's only a gillie, you see.'

He says Ulick will go to Sandhurst in two years and eventually marry Lilibet York.

July 22, 1935
Freddie Crosbie is having dinner with Ernest this evening, at Ernest's request.

July 23, 1935
Lunch with Pips, Ethel, and Hattie. The top and bottom of Freddie's dinner with Ernest was that Ernest is coming to the end of his patience and is giving Wally till the new year to decide.

I said, 'To decide what?'

Pips said, 'To tinkle in the pot or get off it.'

Ethel said, 'To decide whether she's going to get a divorce and marry the Prince.'

Ethel's only a visitor here. She doesn't understand how these things work.

I said, 'She can't marry him. David has to marry someone who can be Queen. She has to have the right blood and no previous husbands.'

Hattie said, 'Anyway, what's Ernest doing telling Freddie this? He should be telling Wally.'

Pips says Freddie was there as a sounding board. She said, 'Ernest doesn't really know what he's doing anymore. He was such a fan of the royalties. Like a dog with two tails to have Wales dropping by. He wants to make a stand, tell Wales to back off, but he can't bring himself to do it. It's against everything Ernest ever believed in, poor sap.'

Hattie said, 'Of course, there is another possibility for Wally. If David gave up the succession he could marry her.'

The silliest idea I ever heard.

I said, 'What would he do?'

Hattie said, 'I don't know. Putter around his garden. Take Wally shopping. It's just an idea. He's got three brothers so there'll always be someone who can be King.'

I don't agree. If you took Bertie York and Kent and Harry and put them all together you still couldn't make a king out of them.

I said, 'What I want to know is, why now? Ernest's known about everything for months but he was grateful enough to go to the Jubilee ball.'

Pips says it's a lot of little things. The sapphires, the emeralds, the phone calls at all hours, Mr Loo destroying his Aristophanes.

July 25, 1935

To Bond Street with Wally for last-minute shoes. Ernest left for New York this morning. I said, 'Everything all right?'

She said, 'Perfectly.'

So much for the issuing of deadlines.

I said, 'What would you do if David asked you to marry him?'

She laughed. She said, 'Remind him he's the next King. Remind him things like that only happen in fairy stories.'

I said, 'And what would you do if he turned down the job of King so he could marry you?'

'Run!' she said.

July 28, 1935

Lunch with Lightfoot who hardly spoke a word and allowed his turbot to go cold. I said, 'Are you sick?'

'No,' he said, 'I'm in the pink. I just wanted to say, I'm very fond of you, Maybell.'

He's in love with me.

Tonight the train to Nice. Judson and Hattie, Whitlow and Gladys, Boss and Ethel. Oxer Bettenbrooke is equerrying.

August 4, 1935, Villa Le Roc

Rock Cholmondeley's villa is well equipped but not luxurious. It has tennis courts, a swimming pool, sailboats, two Bugattis. A man's home.

August 5, 1935

Judson and Whitlow have found bicycles and gone off exploring. Boss is swimming laps. HRH is doing needlepoint on the terrace, and leaping up and down to adjust Wally's sunshade. Winston and Clemmie Churchill are staying at the next villa.

August 7, 1935

The Westminsters' yacht put in last night. We're invited to dinner. HRH is for it but Wally never likes to be too much in the company of Loelia. So young, so beautiful, so rich.

August 8, 1935

The Westminsters are setting off toward Sardinia and wanted us to join them, but Gladys says there's a very real danger of getting boarded and raped and plundered by Communist brigands, so we're all quite off the idea.

The Rogerses have invited us to dinner. Wally said, 'Now, Ethel, I don't want you and Herman dragging everyone down your Chinese memory lane. It was all a long time ago and it's very boring.'

Ethel said, 'Nothing much along *my* memory lane, Wally, apart from one dead husband.'

August 14, 1935
Kath Rogers says she sees a great difference in Wally. 'More poise,' she said. 'For one crazy moment I almost curtsied to her.'

August 19, 1935
Daisy Fellowes has arrived with the Bajavidas. There's talk of taking a trip to San Remo to see Lily and the Cavetts. We were meant to have drinks with the Winston Churchills but they've gone back to London because of the crisis over Abyssinia. Wally's strapped for funds. With things as they are she found it hard to ask Ernest for more.

August 23, 1935
A thunderbolt from Drumcanna. A call came through from Lightfoot.

He said, 'I have something to tell you. Doopie and I are going to be married.'

It was a very bad line.

I said, 'She's mentally deficient.'

He said, 'She is not. She's adorable.'

I said, 'Don't do a thing until I get back. You have no idea.'

He said, 'I knew you'd be beastly. We're getting married tomorrow. Before she changes her mind.'

I said, 'Promise me there'll be no children.'

The line went dead. French telephones. Now I don't possibly have time to get to Drumcanna to stop things. Violet is so incompetent.

Hattie says I'm overreacting. She said, 'Doopie's thirty-two and she *is* adorable.'

I said, 'She can't hear.'

Ethel said, 'Well, she seems to have managed to hear a proposal.'

I doubt it. Lightfoot probably got Flora to mime it.

August 24, 1935

Finally got through to Violet. I said, 'Are you going to allow this madness to go ahead?'

She said, 'It's not madness, Maybell. They make a very fine couple.'

They're being married at Crathie this afternoon. Melhuish is giving her away. Then they're going to Skye for the honeymoon. Honeymoon! I'm sure Violet won't have told her what to expect.

Whitlow says probably not a bad thing for one half of a couple to be deaf.

August 25, 1935

To the Rogerses for dinner, though I was in no mood for a party. Bob Boothby was there, also on his way back to London because of the Abyssinian situation. He says if there is a war it will only be a small one. He says the government has done the right thing in demanding sanctions against Italy because there won't actually be any sanctions but Britain has been seen to make a stand and the only damage sustained is to our friendship with the Italians which, knowing the Italians, will soon be regained.

August 26, 1935
Hattie insisted on motoring into Nice to buy a wedding gift for Doopie and Lightfoot. A Russian tea urn. I'm not sure I'll give them anything. Sneaking off like that.

Ethel said, 'I think you were a bit in love with George Lightfoot yourself.'

What stuff! He's too young for me and without a lick of sense, as he's just proved.

August 29, 1935
Wally and HRH are back from San Remo with a wonderful new dance called the rumba. They've proposed themselves to the Bajavidas in Palm Beach for January. Ethel and Boss are going to come with us to Budapest, Hattie and Judson are heading back to London.

August 31, 1935, Hôtel Beau Rivage, Geneva
Tension. HRH and Wally had already left for the train station when Oxer realized nothing had been done about gratuities for Cholmondeley's staff. We raked up enough between us but there was a very frosty moment when we caught up to the advance party and he pointed out the omission.

Wally said, 'Why should we leave them anything? They get wages from Cholmondeley.'

Ethel said, 'But it is usual. They've looked after us very well, and it is usual.'

Wally said, 'Not for royalties, it isn't. Don't you know the Prince of Wales doesn't carry money?'

He does sometimes, though. He bought Wally another wristwatch today.

Bettenbrooke says he won't be sorry to get to Budapest. Jack Aird will be taking over once we get there.

September 3, 1935, The Danube Palace, Budapest
We are very comfortable. HRH has already had a very warm meeting with the Hungarian Regent, proof, if proof were needed, that his British Legion speech has caused no hard feelings at all among Mr Mussolini's friends.

Gorgeous things on sale here. I'm considering a filigree pin with tiny enameled flowerheads that shake as one moves.

Ethel and Boss have found a wonderful place for coffee and walnut cake.

The Hungarians are a handsome people although the standard of dentistry could be higher.

September 4, 1935
An amusing little spat between Jack Aird and Oxer Bettenbrooke. Oxer had his valise packed ready to leave when HRH sent down word he wanted to drive to the Gellért for a steam bath.

Aird said, 'You go. Consider it your final duty.'

Oxer said, 'Not bloody likely. I'm off.'

Aird said, 'Well, I'm not wandering naked among crazy Magyars.'

And he left immediately, with some cockamamie story about having to get a prescription filled. HRH ended up going with Boss Croker and two detectives. Wally says she'd fire Aird in a heartbeat. I really don't see why we need all these equerries anyway. HRH was only going for a steam and a rub down and, as Boss says, the visibility was too poor for an assassination attempt.

Charlie Bedaux is here but not Fern. He's traveling with a scar-faced Frenchman. Ethel believes there are actually several Charlie Bedauxs ready to materialize with a fistful of cigars, anywhere, at any propitious moment.

September 6, 1935

To a cellar bar. Dancing to gypsy violins. Wally and HRH are indefatigable. By 3 a.m. I was ready for bed, but David said, 'You mustn't leave. I'm going to ask for some more czardas.'

Personally I couldn't have eaten another thing. In the end Ethel and I retired and left Boss and Charlie and his friend to see the night through.

September 9, 1935

With Wally and Ethel for a sulfur cure. Then to Lukács for cherry pancakes, to take the nasty taste away.

I've bought the pin with the little flowers. Perhaps I'll give it to Doopie as a wedding gift. Then again, perhaps I won't.

Charlie Bedaux says Hitler is going to purge Germany of Jewish Marxists. Boss says Hitler appears to be spending money he doesn't have so he'd better be careful not to purge any obliging Jewish bankers.

September 12, 1935

To the KrisKros Club. A wonderful floor show. A little pony that can count, tumbling monkeys in romper suits, and a tame black jaguar. Charlie and the scar-faced Mr Gregoire joined us. Wally says he got his scar in a duel years ago and he's now a brilliant lawyer. I think she's rather smitten. Jack Aird says with a shaving shadow like that Gregoire wouldn't even get past the gate porter in Lincoln's Inn.

September 15, 1935

Mr Mussolini has refused to be cowed by the threat of sanctions. Boss thinks there really may be a war and we should all go home. Wally says whatever Mussolini does she's going to Paris first and so is HRH. She says I can please myself.

September 16, 1935
To the Pussy Cat Club. Wore my rainbow voile and my new rhinestone fascinator. The floor show consisted of girls wearing nothing but spangles. HRH giggled helplessly.

Tomorrow my first flight. Ethel says there's nothing to it.

September 19, 1935, Wilton Place
The joy of traveling the modern way! We had touched down at Croydon and I was on my way home when I might still have been lurching and bumping across Germany in a railroad car. Wally really has to overcome her fears.

September 22, 1935
Took the little Hungarian brooch to South Audley Street but Lightfoot and Doopie are apparently still honeymooning on the Isle of Skye. On to Carlton Gardens where Violet was in a black mood. Flora has already been expelled from the school in Suffolkshire for setting fires and was dispatched this morning to Rathgussie to stay with her Aunt Jinty and receive a dose of sharp Scotch discipline. Also Their Majesties are in low spirits and Violet seems incapable of enjoying life if the King and Queen are out of sorts. But low spirits are only to be expected. All this rain, all this gloom about Mussolini, after a summer of sunshine and gay balls and cheering crowds. They're experiencing a natural sense of letdown.

Violet said, 'They allowed Wales to go to Cannes on the understanding that Wally Simpson's husband would be in the party, which I'm sure was never going to be the case. And now he's taken her to Paris, interfering in government business and dragging her everywhere he goes.'

I said, 'I think Wally's only there to order clothes.'

She said, 'Well, Wales isn't ordering clothes. He's meeting high-level people and Wally is a liability of the first order. She's a liar and an impostor.'

Apparently, investigations have been made into the back of the Warfield closet. It's come to light that her mother was unmarried when she was born, *and* Wally was never christened.

I said, 'Well, that can hardly matter now. She's nearly forty.'

Violet said, 'It certainly does matter. It means she had that wedding in Christ Church, Baltimore, under false pretenses. It sums up everything about her.'

I said, 'But if that's the case and her marriage to Win Spencer was irregular then Ernest is actually her *first* husband, not her second, and there's therefore no reason not to allow her into the Royal Enclosure at Ascot next year.'

That silenced her.

September 25, 1935

Lunch with Penelope Blythe. She was in the next chair at Monsieur Jules and seemed at a loose end. She and Fergus have had a reconciliation. Boring, but necessary, she said. It had been a question of jingle. She lamented George Lightfoot's disappearance into the maw of marriage. She said, 'I know she's your sister, but really! That puts him *hors de combat* for at least two years.'

She says Ralph Habberley isn't in Bolivia at all but in Egypt with Ida Coote. He has a cousin there who's in cotton. Jane Habberley apparently believes his behavior was all brought on by a fall he had riding out with the Quorn. She wants him to see a brain man in Wigmore Street.

September 30, 1935
Dinner with Pips and Freddie. Freddie says Violet is right about one thing: HRH had no business going to Paris and discussing British foreign policy.

He said, 'I don't understand the man. He tells people all he wants is Wally at his side and more time for golf and then he steams off to Paris and starts playing the statesman. Eden is at his wits' end and so apparently is the King. Strictly between these four walls, it might not be a bad thing if David and Wally were to take the plunge, go away somewhere. Give Bertie York a year or two to limber up, I believe he could do the job as well if not better.'

October 2, 1935
George and Doopie are back from their honeymoon. Doopie bashful with me, as well she should be. She liked her Hungarian pin. She's very upset about Flora. 'Boor Vora,' she kept saying. 'Boor Vora. See sood gum live wid us.'

George said, 'Darling, we have to respect Violet and Melhuish's decision. But I'm sure they'll let her visit. I can't believe Jinty will be anxious to hold on to her for long.'

They asked me to stay to dinner but I see enough kissing and hand-holding at table when I'm with Wally and her Prince.

October 4, 1935
Mr Mussolini has invaded Abyssinia.

October 7, 1935
Wally is back from Paris. Main Bocher is making her five wool suits and three evening gowns, one in balboa, two in charmeuse. She says it was the best part of the vacation because HRH was kept busy all day brokering peace and she had lots of time for shopping with Elsie Mendl and Kenny Opdyke.

Lady Mendl gave a dinner for them and Gregoire introduced her to everyone worth knowing.

I said, 'And how's Ernest?'

She said, 'I haven't seen him yet. This little Italian war is creating extra work.'

I said, 'And are you going to Prince Harry's wedding?'

She said, 'Prince Harry? Who cares about a minor royal wedding. I'm beyond that.'

October 11, 1935
Marina Kent has given birth to a son.

October 15, 1935
Dinner at the Belchesters'. Came, the Westminsters, the Boddie-Fultons, Violet and Melhuish, Oxer Bettenbrooke. Much talk of the situation in Abyssinia. Percy Boddie-Fulton says there's a killing to be made in mining rights. If Danforth Brumby were still alive he'd be in there already. Anne Belchester has a bee in a bonnet that the League of Nations should be doing something.

Melhuish said, 'You're wrong, Anne. In these little African situations it's almost always best to do nothing.

It's no use baying for sanctions and then finding them left on one's hands, like yesterday's herrings.'

Fiona Boddie-Fulton said, 'What I'd like to know is, what does Wales think he's up to, sticking in his silly oar? Is he trying to send the King to an early grave?'

Violet tried to hush her but the Belchesters' hock was talking.

She said, 'No, Violet, Oxer is a member of the Inner Circle. I think he should explain.'

Oxer said, 'Nothing to do with me. Ask Aird. All I did was pay the bills and oil the wheels from Cannes to Budapest.'

I said, 'That's funny. I thought Boss Croker paid most of the bills and Ladbroke oiled the wheels.'

Much laughter. Belchester said, '*Henry VI, Part 2.* And that's my only word on the subject.'

I said, 'And what does that mean?'

He said, 'York is the worthier. That's what it means. Mark my words.'

October 26, 1935

To Carlton Gardens. Flora is still at Rathgussie.

Ulick said, 'Best place for her. One can't go around setting fires. It's completely not done.'

I said, 'Well, I just hope she doesn't climb out on to any more roofs.'

Ulick said, 'I can't agree. A cold night on the tiles might do her the world of good.'

Took Rory to the Golden Egg.

I said, 'Why didn't you tell me Doopie and Lightfoot were planning to get married?'

Sheepish grin.

He said, 'Well, I only sort of knew. It wasn't definite

until Aunt Doopie said it was. Daddy says it's a lady's privilege to change her mind.'

He has a new trick with steel rings.

November 7, 1935
Prince Harry has married Alice Buccleuch and they've been made the Duke and Duchess of Gloucester. Lightfoot says now the pressure is really on HRH. The one they're looking to for an heir and he's the only one not married.

I said, 'Just because you rushed into things. David has plenty of time. He's young for his age.'

November 16, 1935
Wally and Ernest seem to be over their difficulties. Wally's stayed home every evening this week and now they've gone to the Perry Brownlows' for the weekend.

I, on the other hand, am invited to Fort Belvedere!

November 17, 1935, Fort Belvedere
The Dickie Mountbattens are here. Also the Cavetts and the Erlangers. Took morning tea with HRH after our callisthenics.

He said, 'Do you know what I'd really like to do, Maybell? I'd like to take Wally and run away to my place in Canada. Leave the world behind.'

I don't really see Wally as a rancher's wife. Alberta would be a terribly long way to come for fittings, but I didn't have the heart to say so. I think I'd better warn Wally. Just when things seemed to be settling down.

November 20, 1935, Wilton Place
Lunch with Pips. She too thinks the worst of the storm has now passed. She said, 'All credit to Ernest. He's

sweated it out and now he may well get his wife back. If he really wants her. Talk about used goods!'

Hattie thinks the Palace are about to rustle up a princess and get a ring on her finger immediately.

I said, 'David didn't say anything when I talked to him.'

She said, 'It'll probably be in the bag before he realizes what's going on. Like giving a dog a worm powder.'

November 25, 1935

If Flora continues to keep her slate clean she's to be allowed back to London for Christmas. The Cavetts want me for Christmas night so that all works out rather well. Wally and Ernest have accepted too.

I said, 'All quiet on the home front?'

'Yes,' she said. 'Almost too quiet.'

December 9, 1935

Ernest is in Stockholm. HRH came to Bryanston Court for drinks but couldn't stay to dinner. His Aunt Toria died today so he had to go and condole with Their Majesties. He says she was a hypochondriac and an old shrew but she cheered the King up with her complaining so he's bound to feel her loss greatly, which foreshadows an even gloomier Christmas than usual.

December 12, 1935

My Christmas plans have fallen into place. On Christmas Eve, dinner at the Erlangers'. On Christmas afternoon, tea at Carlton Gardens, then Kettle will drive me to the Cavetts' in Surrey. Wally's joyful at the prospect of my company there. She says my job will be to engage Ernest in gay chitchat if HRH's telephone calls become too frequent. As she says, *she* doesn't particularly welcome all those calls either. They go on forever and never amount to anything. But she's determined to see it out now and hopes Ernest can be soothed into doing the same. Well, if anyone call pull it off it's Wally. Still, I do feel for Ernest. He's not a bad husband by any stretch.

December 21, 1935, Fort Belvedere

Our last royal weekend for a while. Ernest has made himself busy in town. HRH leaves for Sandringham tomorrow afternoon so he and Wally have exchanged Christmas jewels. From her to him, a set of onyx dress links. From him to her, a gold clasp bracelet set with three rubies. I gave him a red Japanese maple. I said, 'To save you going away to Canada, sir.' He laughed. Almost the only time I've heard laughter today.

Poots Butler says Humphrey and Fruity keep trying to have a man-to-man chat with the Prince but so far they haven't managed to separate him from Wally. She said, 'You and I have to take her away for an hour or two tomorrow morning. It has to be done.'

I said, 'Wally's not the problem. I'm sure she'd love to go into town. The problem is getting David to let her out of his sight. He's not going to see her for three weeks.'

She said, 'Well, Humphrey's determined to have this out with him. The King won't stand for anymore half-truths and gossip about Wally. He's in an absolutely thundering mood. David has to be made to understand. The party's over.'

December 22, 1935

Wally came to church with me, Poots, and Baba. It was quite charming and took only forty-five minutes. HRH tried to talk her out of it but she insisted that he see Fruity and Humphrey. She said, 'They're only courtiers, darling. Don't be scared of them. You're the Prince of Wales.'

When we got back Humphrey and Fruity were fuming over very early whiskeys and HRH was bubbling away, talking about taking Wally to Palm Beach in the new year.

Baba said, 'No joy?'

Fruity said, 'It went in one ear and out the other.'

Baba said, 'Not surprising. There's very little in between to stop it.'

December 27, 1935, chez Cavett, Teddington

Flora was back from Rathgussie in time for Christmas. A little thinner. She sat between me and Doopie at Carlton Gardens and hardly said a word. Violet was very much on edge, checking all the time that the help hadn't left matches lying around, whispering to Lightfoot not to flaunt his cigarette lighter. He said, 'I think you're worrying unnecessarily, Vee. She's tried her hand at fires and all it bought her was a long stretch at Rathgussie. I don't believe it'll happen again. She may try other types of mayhem but I think we're safe from being roasted.'

Rory thinks it might be better if they didn't send her to anymore schools for awhile. He said, 'She just likes playing with her dolls. My friend Massingham's sister only likes riding her pony. Girls can get away with that kind of thing because they'll never have to go into Parliament or the Colonial Service or anything.'

Lightfoot said, 'I don't know. Lady Astor's in the Commons, never forget.'

Ulick said, 'And that surely strengthens the argument against educating girls.'

Much talk too about the divinely handsome Mr Eden who is the new Foreign Secretary. Melhuish doesn't care for him. He says Eden seems determined to make an example of Mussolini.

He said, 'Why not let him have Abyssinia? No one else wants it except a few spear carriers and that strange cove Selassie.'

Rory put on a little display of conjuring for us after tea and asked Flora to be his assistant. He said it was safer than allowing her to sit in the audience shouting out all his magic secrets.

I gave her a compendium of board games. It will give her an interest, wherever she ends up. She said, 'I expect I'll be going to live with Doopie and Uncle Lightfoot.'

The poor deluded child.

Bernie and Zita have the Milwaukee Gunters staying, which is a further diversion for Ernest. The Gunters are Ernest's kind of people and Bernie and Zita are very gay hosts. There's never a quiet moment. HRH called three times and then Wally went out for a drive with Zita, leaving me to speak to him if he called again, which of course he did.

He sounded so disappointed. He said, 'Ask her to call me the moment she returns, no matter how late. You can't imagine how time drags without her.'

January 2, 1936, Wilton Place
We toasted the New Year at the Embassy Club, then went on to the Berkeley in the hope that a change of scene would make us feel peppier, but somehow the evening never took off. Came, the Erlangers, the Cavetts, Daisy Fellowes, Wally and her friend Kenny Opdyke who's in town from Paris. The Crosbies didn't show. Pips says Freddie's in a depression because there'll probably be another war. Judson says it's more likely because he's going to be forty.

Hattie was scandalized by the way Wally was flirting with Kenny Opdyke.

January 3, 1936
Lunch with Pips and Hattie. Hattie still talking about Kenny Opdyke. She said, 'I think she's trying to hurry David along. Make him a little insecure so he settles some serious money on her.'

Pips said, 'More likely she's just plain bored. I never thought I'd feel sorry for Wally but just look at her. She's trapped between Boy David and Deadly Ernest and neither of them will give her an inch to move. It must be a nightmare.'

January 6, 1936
Shopping for Palm Beach. A pretty pleated chiffon dance gown and a cotton print playsuit. Wally got two skirted bathing suits and a pair of grosgrain sandals. She says the Bajavidas keep an indoor staff of thirty. She says Kenny Opdyke is an old, old friend and a fruit.

January 9, 1936
Violet and Melhuish have agreed Flora can stay with Doopie and Lightfoot instead of returning to Rathgussie but only on condition that she behaves nicely to the tutor they're going to find her and works hard at her lessons. Violet says she seems very happy and already has her dolls packed and ready for the move.

She said, 'Now, this jaunt to Florida, Maybell? Can't you talk Wally out of it? Their Majesties are so distressed about it.'

I said, 'It's a private vacation, Violet, which a prince is certainly entitled to. And as for Wally, this situation is hardly of her creation. If anything she's the one who tries to get him to spend more time with his family. But he won't be thrown off. Even if we don't go to Palm Beach, he won't be thrown off.'

January 10, 1936
HRH has had to cancel our weekend at the Fort. The King has a heavy cold and has deputed him to take over his appointments for the next week. I'm not sorry. I still have a million and one things to do before we sail. How much easier it is for men. A good valet will see to everything.

Wally says the Bajavidas eat everything off gold plate, even hamburger!

January 13, 1936
The King's cold is worse. He should take Dr Collis Browne's linctus.

January 14, 1936
Called briefly at South Audley Street. Doopie and Lightfoot have engaged a young woman as a day governess for Flora and they're getting along very well. She allows the dolls into the schoolroom, including Damned Wales who I notice is back dressed in her flamenco gown. I never saw Flora so happy. Lightfoot says she's fairly ripping through geography and history.

January 15, 1936
Drinks at Bryanston Court. The Prince left before Ernest arrived home and so did I. HRH has two engagements to perform for the King tomorrow morning. If he's still too sick to go out after that, Bertie York and George Kent will have to manage things while we're away.

He wants Wally to go with him to the Fort for the weekend, but I saw her hesitate. She's already had a scene from Ernest about our trip and the very least he expects is for her to stay at home for a few days and do wifely things. How difficult. A prince who behaves like a husband and a husband who's starting to behave like a prince. No wonder she has ulcers.

January 16, 1936
Wally called just before five. We have a crisis on our hands. The King's condition has suddenly worsened and HRH has hurried back to Sandringham. I wonder how bad things really are. It could just be a ploy to prevent him taking a vacation in Florida. I suppose the rest of us

could still go. The Bajavidas will be so disappointed if we cancel.

January 17, 1936
Snow overnight. A scratch lunch with Wally who was pensive. HRH telephoned twice. The King is comfortable but very weak. I said, 'What will happen if he dies?'

She said, 'He's not going to die. He has a cold.'

I said, 'But he's an old man. Just say he did die, where would that leave you?'

She said, 'It would leave me very nicely, thank you. If David were King he could see who the hell he liked and do whatever he damn well pleased and he'd be kept a lot busier.'

I think she is just a little bit anxious though. All the newspaper placards say is: THE KING.

January 18, 1936
The King's condition has deteriorated. The George Kents and the Princess Royal have gone to Sandringham, but HRH told Wally his father is so confused he hardly knows any of them. He and Bertie York are driving down to see the Prime Minister, but this is not to be generally broadcast. Hattie Erlanger says this undoubtedly means that the King is dying and funeral plans have to be discussed. Padmore is certainly wearing a funereal face and my breakfast tray was late because everyone below stairs keeps stopping to listen to the wireless bulletins.

Another heavy fall of snow.

January 19, 1936
Wally has invited herself to luncheon. David has been calling her at least once an hour and she feels it would

be tactful to leave Ernest to enjoy his Sunday nap in peace. She says HRH is desperate over his father's condition. Panic-stricken, in fact. She said, 'I don't understand it, Maybell. He's had forty years to get used to the idea of being King, so why the flap now?'

January 20, 1936

This evening we should have sailed away to a month of sunshine but the King is dead and everything is changed.

Wally and I were in a movie theater, in retreat from the jangling telephone, when things started to happen last night. They broke into the Fredric March feature to post a news bulletin on the screen. *The King's life is drawing peacefully to a close.*

Wally was on her feet immediately. I said, 'We may as well see the end of the movie. David will be at the bedside. He won't be calling you.'

She said, 'Possibly. But if anything happens and he can't get me he'll go to pieces.'

We went back to Bryanston Court. Ernest was listening to the wireless, very affectionate with Wally, his usual old self with me. Perhaps he feels he'll soon have Wally to himself again.

The call came almost on the stroke of midnight. I suppose we were among the first people to know. All we heard Wally say was, 'Your mother must need consoling, sir. And I'm sure you must have a lot of people waiting to speak to you. But I'll sleep by the telephone. I'll be here.'

They played 'God Save the King' on the wireless and Ernest stood to attention throughout. Then he went to bed.

Wally said HRH was almost hysterical. He told her

they'd all been at the bedside when the end came. He's not HRH anymore though. He's HM King.

She was talking to him again as I left, soothing him like he was a fretful baby. 'There's nothing to fear,' I heard her say. 'Einums meinums will still take care of her boy.' She was very tender with him.

Everything today has seemed muffled by fatigue and snow and a dead king. They fired cannons before it was daylight. Pips says Freddie was in the Commons by seven ready to swear his oath to the new monarch. He's to be King Edward VIII, but I shall never be able to think of him as any such thing. To me he'll always be yellow-haired David.

January 21, 1936

Dinner with Pips and Freddie. Freddie said, 'What's Wally up to? Melting down the Crown jewels?' I don't know about that, but she's certainly at St James's Palace taking care of her King.

HRH – except now I must get into the habit of calling him HM – HM and Bertie York flew down this afternoon ready for tomorrow's proclamation, which is not the same thing as a coronation, apparently. That will come later, perhaps not till next year. He's the first King of England ever to travel by airplane. Advance warning to all those wheezing old courtiers that a new era has dawned.

Violet called to see if I wanted to go with her to hear him proclamated. I said, 'I've already made arrangements. I'll be watching with Wally and His Majesty.'

She said, 'I think you've been misinformed, Maybell. A king doesn't watch his own proclamation. And as for Wally, she might take her cue and fade into oblivion.'

Violet never misses an opportunity.

January 22, 1936

I always thought St James's was rather a toytown-looking palace and Friary Court made a very dull setting for a proclamation. Oxer Bettenbrooke found us a window to watch from just as the heralds' carriages began arriving. The trumpeters came out on to a balcony, all scarlet and gold, and played a fanfare, and then a twenty-five-gun salute began on Horse Guards Parade, so we couldn't hear the words that were being read.

Anyway, Violet was wrong because HM *did* watch with us, the first sovereign ever to do so. Another sign that he's going to do things in his own modern way. Edward Albert Christian George Andrew Patrick David, King of the United Kingdom of Great Britain and Ireland and Emperor of India.

He had Ladbroke drop us off at Bryanston Court on his way back to Sandringham. The King of England dropped us off! We laughed and laughed about that.

I said, 'Now what?'

She said, 'Well, I can hardly leave him at a time like this.'

January 23, 1936

HM has been dealt a terrible blow. His father's will was read last evening and he's been left nothing. Wally called me first thing.

I said, 'Well, he can't be penniless. He's the King.'

She said, 'He has income from his duchies, but that's not the point. The brothers and sister get all that money when David's the one who'll have the much greater expenses. It's sheer vindictiveness. He's always said his father preferred all the others, and there it is.'

Dinner with Lightfoot and Doopie. Lightfoot said, 'But

he ought to be able to live perfectly well on what he has, provided he eases up on the purchase of sparklers for Wally.'

I said, 'I'd have thought the need for the woman in his life to outsparkle all others is greater than ever.'

He said, 'That depends on what one means by "the woman in his life". When he chooses his Queen she'll have all the *richesse* of the family jewels at her disposal, not to mention the Crown regalia. But that won't be Wally. So Wally's sparkle will have to be bought out of income.'

Doopie said, 'He good sell Buggingham Balass.'

They brought the old King back to London today for the lying-in-state. They say there are already long lines to view the coffin, but Wally says we won't have to queue. The funeral is at Windsor on Tuesday.

January 24, 1936
Penelope Blythe forced herself on me for lunch. She says when the gun carriage was bringing the coffin to Westminster Hall the jeweled cross on the top of the imperial crown fell off and rolled along the street. She says it's an omen. Penelope is one of the silliest people I know.

To Selfridges for black stockings.

January 25, 1936
To Westminster Hall with Wally and Pips. We were ushered in through the Private Members' entrance. The coffin is covered with a purple cloth. There's the crown, back in one piece, and one small family wreath. There's an officer of one of the Household brigades guarding each corner of the catafalque. I never felt such cold. When we came out there was a car waiting to take Wally to St James's Palace.

Pips said, 'She's going to find it very hard to give up the Waiting Car treatment.'

I don't know that she is going to give it up.

Tea at Carlton Gardens. Anne Belchester was there and Ena Spain, come for the funeral. According to Melhuish it was a Grenadier sergeant major who saw the cross fall off the crown and scooped it out of the gutter, without even breaking step.

Anne Belchester asked after Wally. She said, 'I suppose she'll retire to the country now.'

Ena Spain said, 'I don't see why. As long as she behaves in a seemly way. Kings always have mistresses.'

Anne said, 'But one would expect her to withdraw, at least while he's choosing a queen.'

Violet said, 'And anyway, Ena, you're wrong. Kings don't always have mistresses. His father never did.'

Ena said, 'Then he was the exception. I should know.'

Poor Ena.

January 26, 1936

Ernest has had to go to Hamburg on business. Freddie saw him at his club and he told him that he believes everything will now be resolved. He said, 'A king is a very different person than a prince, Freddie. His Majesty will now move far away from our humble orbit.'

Loelia Westminster's mother is making one of her windows available to me and Wally for the funeral procession. They have to take the coffin from Westminster Hall to Paddington station for the journey to Windsor. Imagine having to go to a railroad station even in death!

January 28, 1936

Another gray, bitter morning and Pall Mall was lined with gray, silent people. The only sounds were the muffled drums and the boots of the Foot Guards. The coffin was borne on a gun carriage with HM walking behind. He looked up at our window. He knew exactly where Wally would be. I thought how small he seemed in his greatcoat and that funny old bicorn hat. Bertie York, George Kent, and Harry Gloucester walked behind him. Then, as they turned into St James's Street, the Queen's carriage came into view. She sat very stately in a black cloth coat and a fox capelet.

All the shops were closed for the day, so we rustled up Pips and Hattie and went to the Savoy for an early lunch. Wally says she's going to get Elsie Mendl's boys in to redo Buckingham Palace. She says it needs a clean sweep and not only the décor. She says there are courtiers who are practically mummified they've been around so long. Perry Brownlow's going to be Lord-in-Waiting, which will be a very good thing. But Rock Cholmondeley is the new Lord Great Chamberlain, which may not be such good news, with Sybil thick as thieves with the Bertie Yorks and the old Queen.

Hattie said, 'Well, you can't sack the Lord Great Chamberlain, Wally. It's hereditary.'

Wally said, '*Has* been hereditary. Don't forget, Hattie, you're under new management now.'

Alex Hardinge is to stay on as Private Secretary. Wally said, 'We'll see about that.' She won't even consider rebooking our passage and going to the Bajavidas'. She says the King can't go, and if he can't, she can't.

February 1, 1936
With Pips to buy a christening gift for some distant Crosbie infant. When we got back to Halkin Street we found Freddie in the drawing room struggling to find the right thing to say to a clearly overwrought Ernest. Freddie must

have been praying for our return. As soon as Ernest saw me he erupted. He said, 'She's at Windsor, Maybell. Did you know she was going? Windsor! And the old King barely cold in his grave.'

I can honestly say I didn't know. I'd rather assumed our weekends would go the same way as Palm Beach house parties, for awhile. Violet gives the impression that we're all supposed to sit around dabbing our eyes with black-edged handkerchiefs for six months. We're even excused going to the opera.

Ernest said, 'I may not have as much pep as His Majesty, but I think I know how to behave. Well, the King obviously takes court mourning rather lightly, so I see no reason to hold back. I'm going to speak to him. The time has come.'

Pips said, 'Better not to go to the Castle, Ernest. You could get arrested.'

He said, 'Don't worry. I shall simply wait for him to turn up for cocktails. I'm sure I shan't have long to wait. He seems so very attached to my drinks cart.'

He went off very pink and puffed up, his goodbyes rather formal. He said, 'I bear you no ill will, Maybell. I know Wally inspires great loyalty and I'm glad she has yours. She's sailing into uncharted waters. She's going to need her friends more than ever.'

Pips said, 'Poor sap. The sooner he leaves London the better.'

Freddie says the straw that finally broke poor Ernest's back was the blocking of his application to become a Freemason. Freddie said, 'It's because his wife is known to "associate" with another member of the lodge. In short, HM King. But I promised I'd have a word with Prosper Frith. He might be willing to propose Ernest for his lodge.'

February 2, 1936
Ernest has moved out to his club. Wally's looking very strained.

February 6, 1936
A chilling scene at Bryanston Court this afternoon. We'd just sat down to tea when Ernest arrived to collect more of his things. I made to leave but he asked me to stay. He said, 'I'd like you to hear this, Maybell, in case Wally fails to understand me. Our marriage is at an end. I'll have my books collected later in the week.'

Wally said, 'You can see I'm not well. Why are you making a scene now?'

He said, 'Because an hour ago His Majesty informed me he intends to marry you and be crowned with you at his side.'

Wally said, 'This is sheer fantasy. You know it can't happen. Tell him, Maybell. We all know it's out of the question.'

Ernest said, 'So we're all told, but I've begun to see that nothing's impossible for a king. He tells me he's already settled £300,000 on you, as a token of his sincerity. I wonder, Wally, you never thought to mention it to me.'

I wonder she never thought to mention it to me.

She said, 'I didn't say anything because the papers haven't been signed, and as I recall it's only £100,000. It's in recognition of the expense we've been put to by our friendship with him.'

Ernest said, 'I never counted the cost of having the Prince of Wales at my table. Not till now.'

Well, that's not strictly true. He's always gone through the housekeeping books, querying every little item of expenditure. But still, it was too awful a moment. A man

285

should never walk out on his wife while they have company.

She cried after he left, but I think they were tears of exasperation not sorrow.

Later on she said, 'He'll change his mind when he realizes what a vulnerable position he's putting me in. Once he's calmed down.'

But I think he was horribly calm throughout. I think between them Ernest and HM King have outmaneuvered her.

February 9, 1936, Fort Belvedere
No change of heart from Ernest. He's having his books packed while Wally's out of the house.

Went up to the Castle to watch *King Kong*. The place is an unmanageable pile. If HM has any sense he'll keep the Fort on for weekends and only use the Castle for big state affairs. Wally had some fun with those poker-faced footmen. She made them serve refreshments on their knees so as not to cast shadows on the screen and ruin the movie.

February 10, 1936, Wilton Place
Wally stayed on at the Fort this morning, to talk to HM about 'The Situation'.

A message from Ernest when I returned home. Would I be kind enough to see him? He came at four, very composed, dapper as ever.

He said, 'I owe you an apology. My behavior last week was unpardonable. I allowed passion to overrule good manners.'

I said, 'The most important thing is, you mustn't leave Wally. She's devastated.'

He said, 'Only devastated that things haven't gone

according to her plan. I don't think anyone can accuse me of being hotheaded. I've been more patient than most. She's made her bed, Maybell, and now she must lie in it.'

I said, 'It's just that all those times when David used to send for her you never seemed to mind.'

He said, 'I did mind, but there was the honor of a royal friendship to consider. I minded very much more when all of London began laughing behind my back. And now with money settled on her, and talk of marriage, well, there's nothing left for me but to go.'

I said, 'So, are you divorcing her?'

He said, 'I believe the procedure is for her to divorce me. Don't worry. I'm not going to make a fuss. I'll co-operate.'

He kissed me on both cheeks when he left. He said, 'Take care of her for me, Maybell.'

I called Pips and we went directly to Wally's. She was sitting in her coat and hat, drinking brandy. She'd just come from the Fort.

She said, 'David has lost his mind. He doesn't seem to realize, we can't allow Ernest to leave me. It's going to ruin everything and achieve nothing.'

Pips said, 'Well, what about if *you* leave David? Wouldn't that settle it, if you want to keep Ernest?'

Wally said, 'One doesn't just *leave* the King. Especially not David. Anything might happen. God, I'm so tired.'

Red carnations everywhere. I said, 'And what about von Ribbentrop? I see he's still pursuing you. No wonder you're tired.'

She said, 'Those flowers aren't for me. They're for *us*. Me and David. And they're not from Ribbentrop. They're from Adolf Hitler. He's invited us to visit with him in the summer.'

Pips said, 'Well then. I won't waste anymore time commiserating with you. Seems to me you have everything under control.'

February 14, 1936
HM has given Wally a gold sweetheart locket set with aquamarines. He also seems to have persuaded her that becoming Queen isn't impossible after all. Apparently, he's gone into it with a brilliant lawyer and there's a very simple way out of this muddle. Wally can have both her marriages annulled on the grounds that to all intents and purposes she's a virgin.

I said, 'Are you?'

She said, 'To all intents and purposes, yes.'

Extraordinary.

I said, 'But if you become Queen won't you have to have a baby?'

'Not at all,' she said. 'The Yorks are next in line after David and they have those two girls. One of them can succeed.'

Judson Erlanger says if Wally's a virgin he's the King of Siam, but Freddie says HM's lawyer is Walter Monckton and if anyone can achieve miracles Monckton can.

Penelope Blythe says Wally might want to think twice about seeking annulments. She says doctors could be brought in to give evidence, not to mention two discarded husbands.

February 19, 1936
A little lunch party at Bryanston Court for Lily Drax-Pfaffenhof. She's encouraging Wally to explore every possible way for HM to marry her and Wally certainly seems to be changing her tune. Yesterday she said,

'There's no such thing as the impossible. Read the history books.'

Today she said, 'I have my detractors of course, but all I need is a little time. The public just needs to get to know me. I could be very popular. I'm hardworking. I've pulled myself up by my own boot straps. And they'll love my clothes.'

Lily said, 'And when you're Queen I wonder who you'll choose as your lady of the bedchamber?'

'Yes,' she said. 'I wonder who!'

The Socialists got elected in Spain. I don't imagine poor Ena would want to go back now even if they asked her.

February 20, 1936
Wally is looking into having her family tree tidied up. She's tired of HM's old courtiers looking down their noses at her. As she says, it's no fault of hers that her parents weren't married until after her birth. Her father was a consumptive and forbidden to marry. And the only reason her mother sometimes had to charge her guests rent was the sheer meanness of the Warfields. Her Uncle Sol Warfield had plenty of money. He just never missed an opportunity to remind Wally's mother she was a charity case.

February 24, 1936
Tea at Carlton Gardens. Violet says HM is making a fool of himself talking about a throne for Wally. She said, 'All the annulments in the world won't make her suitable to be Queen, so she may as well hang on to the husband she has.'

Doopie looked in with Flora, very nicely dressed in a tartan skirt and a cardigan set. I was just thinking there was hope yet of making a lady of her when she said, 'Aunt Bayba, does Damned Wales still give The Wally lots of gisses? Ulick says he's asking for a bloody thrashing.'

Violet busied herself with the teacups.

Sunday, to Paris. Wally has a very long shopping list. Now HM is free of his killjoy father he intends taking a villa near Cannes and vacationing with whomsoever he pleases.

March 3, 1936, Hôtel Meurice, Paris

To Elsie Mendl's *pied-à-terre* for a working luncheon. Every one of HM's homes is going to require complete refurbishment and Wally's going to make sure Johnnie MacMullen does everything.

To the Eugene Rothschilds' for drinks. Tomorrow, to Paquin for light woolen wraps and to Hermès for clutch purses.

March 5, 1936

Wally has ordered Chinese side-buttoned evening sheaths in coral, lime, and hyacinth. Tomorrow, daywear, shoes, lingerie.

March 7, 1936

We've decided on candy-colored ginghams from Schiaparelli, to be worn with canvas pumps and flowered barrettes. A very youthful, carefree look.

Mr Hitler has entered the Rhineland.

March 8, 1936

Not a good day. One sales clerk wouldn't allow Wally to take a little musical box on approval and another, at

Geneviève, was very offhand about the delay with Wally's camisoles. I don't think these people realize quite who she is. Then at Chez Raphael they served her omelet too *baveuse*.

She said, 'I don't know about the Rhineland. I hope Hitler invades you, and soon.'

March 13, 1936, Wilton Place
HM's brother-in-law Earl Harewood has made a speech to the British Legion condemning Hitler and entirely contradicting everything HM said in his speech about the avoidance of future wars. Wally's dictated a note for HM to send to Harewood telling him to keep his warmongering opinions to himself.

March 14, 1936
Dinner at the Belchesters'. Came, the Crosbies, the Metcalfes and the Humphrey Butlers. Belchester said Wally might as well be crowned next week because she's obviously running everything already.

Fruity says the amazing thing is, HM now seems to be enjoying his new role, after all that talk of not being cut out to be King. He said, 'Say what you like, I think it has to be down to Wally. She invigorates him.'

Anne Belchester said, 'But come on, Fruity, she can never be a serious contender as a wife.'

Fruity said, 'If you'd asked me a month ago I'd have agreed, but I'm beginning to think she's essential. If Monckton can fix it for her, the country will get a much more effective King.'

Belchester said, 'Never heard anything like it in my life. Invigorates him! He needs a dose of salts.'

March 21, 1936, Fort Belvedere
Just me, Wally, and the Erlangers. Ernest has gone to a country hotel to have breakfast in bed with a floozie and get his moral turpitude certified.

I said, 'How long till you'll be free to marry David?'

She said, 'Don't say that. Don't ever say that. You never know who may be listening. I'm not divorcing Ernest so I can marry David. I'm divorcing him because he abandoned me and he's about to become an adulterer. Be clear about that, Maybell. I am the innocent party.'

Such a charade.

March 25, 1936, Wilton Place
To the Westminsters'. A dinner for the von Ribbentrops. Came, Violet and Melhuish, Jimmy Graham, Ava Ribblesdale, Jack Aird, and the Crosbies. Everyone is agreed that it was only a matter of time till the Germans were permitted back into the Rhineland, so all Hitler has done is to anticipate the inevitable, and there won't be any retaliation from the French who are shivering in their shoes. So we can all carry on as before. Aird says HM is making economies right and left and the staff at Sandringham fear for their positions.

Melhuish said, 'That's Wales all over. Sack a few gardeners so he can buy another bangle for his tootsie. And I hear he's had the clocks changed too, so there goes another tradition. Sandringham Time has always been half an hour ahead, and Balmoral Time, for as long as I remember, and my father before me. I suppose the next thing, he'll decide he's going to be crowned wearing a check suit. We'll be seeing our monarch reviewing his troops in golf knickers. Mark my words.'

Violet darting anxious looks in my direction, trying to

hush him with light remarks about their new terrier, but he was enjoying the sound of his own voice. It's finally dawning on her. They're going to live the rest of their days under a king who doesn't like them anymore than they like him. The old Queen's going to be retired to a little palace somewhere, Wally will be declared a virgin, and Violet and Melhuish will be outcasts for evermore.

Pips says Ribbentrop makes her think of a commercial salesman.

March 29, 1936, Fort Belvedere
HM in good spirits this morning in spite of a telling-off from Wally last evening because he stood his nightcap glass on top of some official papers and left a ring mark. Wally says Hardinge is a complete martinet over Cabinet papers and has a fit if he thinks HM has been perusing them in the drawing room. It's about confidentiality. But our weekend parties are small while court mourning prevails, just the inner circle and I'm sure we're all to be trusted with any government secrets we happen upon. And Wally sees absolutely everything anyway. Otherwise how could she advise the King?

April 3, 1936, Sunninghills
At the Crokers' for their first weekend party of the season. Ethel says all their American friends are lining up to come to Merrie England and meet the King.

She's wondering whether they'll be invited to the coronation. I was able to put her mind at rest. All HM's *true* friends will be invited. It's people like the Devonshires and the Melhuishes who may as well put their court costumes in mothballs.

The postage-stamp people have gone ahead without

permission and made a design showing HM in right profile. Wally says it'll have to be changed. He looks so much more kingly from the left. Alex Hardinge says King George was pictured from the left and it's the tradition to alternate, but he has to understand, David isn't going to be that kind of King. If something needs changing he won't be afraid to change it. As Lightfoot says, Wally is throwing wide the windows and HM is enjoying the breeze that's blowing between his ears.

April 8, 1936, Wilton Place
With Violet to a charitable sale of work. Bought raffia bread baskets but omitted to bring them home. The person selling them was worryingly vague as to whether they had been made *by* lepers or in *aid* of lepers. Jane Habberley was manning the tea urn. Marina Greece looked in and bought a sponge cake. Ettie Desborough won a bottle of sherry wine. I must say, the lepers seem to know everyone.

April 10, 1936
Good Friday. Tonight with Pips and Freddie to the Fergus and Penelope Blythes'.

April 13, 1936
The Halifaxes were at Leake Priory and some of Penelope's people came to Sunday lunch. She's one of the Staffordshire Ewells.

Halifax says HM is receiving bad advice from Walter Monckton if it's persuading him he can ever marry Wally. He said, 'The kindest thing would be for their friends to deprive the idea of oxygen and allow it to die.'

Pips said, 'That's you, Maybell. Can't you take Wally away somewhere?'

I said, 'Wally's hardly the problem. It isn't her fault if they can't come up with a single tempting princess. Marriage wasn't her idea.'

Halifax said, 'Indeed. From what I hear of Mrs Simpson, she doesn't seem terribly suited to the condition.'

He has the perfect face for running a funeral parlor.

Wally got diamond and filigree ear clips from David for Easter.

April 15, 1936
Leo von Hoesch is dead. I only saw him on Monday. He waved to me as Kettle turned into Carlton Terrace. Fifty-five. They say it was a heart attack.

Wally said, 'It doesn't make a lot of difference. He was about to be recalled anyway.' She gets to hear everything now she helps HM with his boxes. She says Leo was shaky on a number of key points. She never did like him. I suppose she's rooting for Ribbensnob.

April 17, 1936
With Violet and Melhuish to pay our last respects to Leo von Hoesch. The Grenadier Guards provided an escort for his coffin as far as Victoria railroad station.

He gave such wonderful parties.

April 20, 1936
HM is taking Wally to Royal Lodge to have tea with the Yorks. She's going to wear a polka-dot silk and matinee pearls.

April 21, 1936
Wally says yesterday was an ordeal not to be repeated. Bertie York hardly spoke a word and the wife didn't have

a serious thought in her head. Apparently, she just twittered to HM about his bagpipe compositions and didn't ask Wally anything about herself. But then, what could she have asked? There's so much about Wally one no longer dare mention, and anyway, I'm sure Elizabeth York has it all unabridged from Violet.

Wally said, 'I suppose I daunted her. She's like a little pink marshmallow.'

April 26, 1936
Luncheon at South Audley Street. Lightfoot believes Leo von Hoesch was bumped off on orders from Berlin. Doopie shaking her head and saying, 'Dordie, nod in vront a Vora.'

Flora's reading is coming on very well with this new tutor, and they do singing too. She couldn't carry a tune in a bucket but she's very enthusiastic.

May 4, 1936
To the Crosbies'. Freddie says HM and Wally went together to Walter Monckton's chambers this morning. He said, 'What can David have been thinking? If he insists on Wally using his lawyer, which is a bad idea, he certainly mustn't be seen to attend their conferences. It makes it look as though he's a party to the case.'

Pips said, 'Oh please! It's only the difference between a barefaced lie and a polite pretence.'

Freddie says that's a very important difference. He's suggested I have a word with Wally. He says when the case is called, if the judge has any doubts about Wally being an innocent party she just won't get her divorce, King's lawyer or no.

May 5, 1936
Wally says HM went with her to see Monckton purely as a friend.

I said, 'If you needed support, surely I was the one to ask?'

She said, 'Well, yes, but David insisted. Frankly, I'd rather have had you there, Maybell. You don't fuss.'

I told her what Freddie said. She said, 'Oh, but I'm not using Monckton. I just went to him for a recommendation. I'm going to see a man called Goddard. He's supposed to be very good.'

May 7, 1936
Marina Kent is expecting again. Wally has hired Theodore Goddard.

May 10, 1936
I'm invited to a little reception at the compound on Tuesday, to meet the Charles Lindberghs. They've come to Europe to get over that sad business with their baby. Wally ruffled not to have been invited. I called Judson immediately and pointed out the oversight. This is no time to be making an enemy of the future Queen of England.

May 11, 1936
The date for HM's coronation has been announced. It will take place one year from tomorrow. Freddie says if he's determined to marry Wally it would make sense to wait until after he's been crowned, but we all know he wants Wally crowned beside him.

Wally's pretending to be bored with the subject and refuses to comment. Her invitation to the Lindbergh reception arrived by special messenger. Her ulcers have flared up again.

May 12, 1936
Colonel Lindbergh is very good-looking. 'Just plain gorgeous,' was Wally's appraisal. She didn't rate the wife but she's going to have them to dinner at York House anyway.

Hattie Erlanger has heard a whisper about HM and a Danish princess.

May 14, 1936
Violet says Princess Alexandrine of Denmark is indeed a strong possibility. She's only twenty-one, but I guess he's missed the boat with the older ones.

So perhaps everything can be resolved after all. Wally will get to keep the money HM has settled on her and she'll be free of Ernest. She could do what Elsie Mendl did and marry a titled pansy. Leave Princess Alexandrine to supply the nation with royal babies. It sounds perfect to me, but Wally reacted rather sourly.

She said, 'Alexandrine! Not that silly story! I don't suppose Violet mentioned that they tried to marry him off to her mother twenty-five years ago. That's how desperate they are. Well, I'd say he's given them chance enough to find someone acceptable. Now they'll just have to let him please himself.'

May 15, 1936, Fort Belvedere
The Stanley Baldwins are dining tomorrow evening. HM wants them to see Wally in action and understand what a wonderful Queen she'd make. Meanwhile, there's been a ruckus because HM has to receive some Arabs on

Monday and quite naturally wants Wally to assist him, but the Foreign Office say they won't allow it. The Foreign Office, dictating to the King! How can they prevent it? That's what I'd like to know. If HM wants a chimpanzee to assist him, what business is it of pen-pushers in Whitehall? Apart from any other consideration, HM is a better man with Wally at his side. Everyone says so.

May 17, 1936
The Baldwins were so lacking in fire and sparkle. Quite out of their depth. I heard Mrs Baldwin talking to HM about the folk dances of Worcestershire!

Alice Gloucester has been rustled up to help meet the Arabs tomorrow. Wally says she couldn't care less.

May 20, 1936, Wilton Place
To *The Pearl Fishers* with the Crosbies, the Belchesters, Lightfoot and Doopie. Philip Sassoon was in Lady Cunard's box. Blew me a kiss but he didn't come round in the intermission.

HM has taken a villa for August. Château de l'Horizon. He's stayed there before and says it's a wonderful place, with a marble chute one can slide down, straight from the sun terrace into the sea. He wants Wally to get complete rest before she faces the divorce ordeal. How his eyes shine when he talks about her! I don't think Princess Alexandrine ever stood a chance.

May 28, 1936
Wally's dinner for the Lindberghs was stunning. Artichokes with a mousse of foie gras, tarragon chicken, blueberry ice cream. Edwina Mountbatten tried to draw out Mrs L with questions about her flying adventures but Wally was

determined to keep the Colonel in the spotlight. 'What a waste,' she said. 'A great man like that puttering around in exile, and all because of a baby-crazy wife.'

I hope she isn't planning another seduction. Freddie Crosbie says he hopes she is. He thinks that may be the kind of cold shower to wake up HM to realities. Freddie is a typical English worrier.

June 5, 1936
The Communists have been voted in in France. Boss Croker thinks we should cancel the villa but HM says the Reds have no quarrel with him. He's always been for the working man. Wally says look what happened in Russia. We could be murdered in our beds. HM said, 'Darling, we'll see how things develop. I'd never take you anywhere you'd be in danger.'

June 7, 1936
Our villa has been canceled. HM spoke with Herman Rogers who said the red flag flies over the Côte d'Azur and he and Kath are away for the summer. They're thinking of Portofino. HM has instructed Jack Aird to find us a yacht.

Lunch with Penelope Blythe. She said she's bored to distraction and needs a summer affair. Just something to get her through August. She says Templemore talks about salmon rods in bed.

June 8, 1936
Wally has asked me to help her out on Friday. They have the King of Egypt coming to call and he's only a boy. She said, 'You're used to children, Maybell.'

300

June 12, 1936

To York House. Wally has done wonders already. Masses of white flowers, needlepoint cushions, well-placed mirrors. There was far too much furniture in there before and no light. King Farouk is a very jolly boy. He arrived laden with shopping bags and unpacked all the toy cars he'd bought at Hamleys. He loved the angel food cake.

June 13, 1936

Wally says a silver snuffbox has disappeared from a side table since little King Farouk's visit. She says it's not at all the way things are done. She says if a royalty sees something they'd like to have they simply let it be known that it would make an acceptable gift. Queen Mary got half her stuff that way.

June 15, 1936, Fort Belvedere

With Wally to Garrard to collect engraved claret jugs for HM's birthday, then Kettle drove us here. HM was in Hampshire all day visiting army camps and inaugurating a new firehouse, but he was back in time for dinner. The Erlangers and the Crokers are here. Humphrey and Poots Butler are driving down tomorrow, in time for lunch before the racing. Oxer Bettenbrooke is equerrying.

June 17, 1936

Another Ladies' Day. Now we'll start to see a few changes. Already Melhuish has been relegated to the fourth carriage with Ena Spain and the Gloucesters, and Violet only made it to the fifth. By next year she'll be watching from the sidelines and *I'll* be the one riding in the parade. Elizabeth York was in azure, Marina Kent in pigeon, Alice Gloucester in peach.

HM escaped at the first opportunity and we had a gay evening, with Wally's fried chicken and dancing to gramophone records.

June 20, 1936
Wally's birthday. I gave her a snakeskin roll for her costume jewelry. HM has given her a Buick, an exact replica of his own. It comes with an advanced driver, approved by Scotland Yard, in case anyone tries to attack her. Though who would? Outside of fashionable London no one knows who she is.

June 21, 1936
Poots Butler says I'd be surprised at how many people know exactly who Wally is and would love to see her Buick run off the road. Lady Astor for one, who had always understood that royalties only mixed with Americans from good families.

HM is in great form. He said, 'Things are going awfully well, you know, Maybell? I never thought I'd enjoy kinging, but I've really rather taken to it. Wally makes all the difference, of course. I don't think I'd enjoy it one little bit without Wally to come home to.'

Jack Aird may have found us a yacht for August. We'll be able to keep clear water between us and the Communists.

July 1, 1936
Our yacht is chartered. She has eight staterooms and a crew of fifty and Jack Aird promises there'll be no mad cooks and no monkeys running wild. We'll travel to Venice by train and then sail to Greece. Lily Drax-Pfaffenhof has confirmed. Herman and Kath Rogers may join us too.

July 4, 1936, Wilton Place
A call from Randolph Putnam. He said, 'I'm amazed to find you at home. I thought maybe you'd moved to Buckingham Palace.'

I said, 'By this time next year I may well have done. Wally is getting a divorce from Ernest and His Majesty is set on marrying her.'

He said, 'I know. We see her picture in the papers all the time.'

Very odd. She's not in the papers here.

He said, 'I'll see you for the coronation, if not before.'

I said, 'You won't be able to get a seat, you know. It's not like a ballgame. It's strictly by invitation.'

He said, 'Won't bother me. I'll stand in the street like everyone else. Can't miss a historic moment like that though. An American Queen! And from Baltimore.'

July 12, 1936
Rory's fifteenth. Gave him a set of magic nesting glasses and a trick cigarette pack. For his treat he chose *Storm in a Tea Cup* at the Garrick. Lightfoot, Flora, and Doopie came too. Afterwards to the Cosy Corner for a mixed grill. Flora had memorized all the tunes in the show. She has no natural shyness about her and sang away all through high tea.

She said, 'Let's talk about The Wally. She's going to be Queen.'

Rory said, 'No she's not, Flora. Absolutely not.'

Lightfoot said, 'She'd have to change her name for one thing. Wally isn't a very queenly name.'

I said, 'Well, her real name is Bessie Wallis and Bessie is certainly a queenly name. Good Queen Bess!'

Rory said, 'But she's the wrong kind of person. It's obvious.'

Doopie said, 'Bud Ging loves her, Roar.'

Rory said, 'But it's not suitable. Daddy says so.'

Doopie said, 'Ging loves her a lod. Vunny. See loogs lige a nudgragger.'

She did a very good impersonation of Wally, with that hard jaw of hers snapping open and closed and her eyes never still.

July 13, 1936

Dinner at Carlton Gardens. Family only. Ulick and Rory were allowed to join us for drinks. Melhuish said, 'Maybell, I heard the King may be going to Italy. Is it true?'

I said, 'Yes, it's all arranged.'

Ulick said, 'One would have thought he'd go quietly to Balmoral, this year of all years.'

Violet said, 'He never liked Deeside. I don't suppose we'll ever see him up there now. It'll be all cruises on floating gin palaces.'

Melhuish said, 'Perhaps he'll bugger off on a permanent cruise, Vee. Leave the Yorks to take over.'

Lightfoot said, 'Take care now, old boy. If Maybell repeats this over their morning callisthenics you could find yourself in the Tower.'

Doopie said, 'You'll be vor the chob, Melsh. You'll have your head tugged udderneath your arb.'

Ulick asked if I still keep my diary. He said, 'What kind of things do you record in it? Appointments at the beauty salon?'

I said, 'No. I jot down the things people say to me.'

He said, 'I hope you ask their permission first.'

July 17, 1936
A madman has tried to murder the King. HM and Bertie York were on horseback on their way from a military parade in Hyde Park yesterday when a Communist pulled out a gun and would have shot him had a police horse not frisked into him and knocked the gun from his hand. Jack Aird was a few paces behind and saw the whole thing.

I must say, Wally seems very unconcerned about it. A heat wave is forecast for the weekend.

July 19, 1936, Fort Belvedere
Wally threw an impromptu poolside party this afternoon. The Kents and the Louis Mountbattens looked in but kept their distance from the inner circle. I remember when George Kent was more than happy to eat Wally's crab claws and dance a tango. I think marriage to Marina Greece has made him very stuffy. HM and Jack Aird retold Thursday's drama. HM says he saw something go flying through the air and found himself wondering very calmly if it was a bomb. Aird says he would have dismounted and kicked the gun into the middle of Constitution Hill but his uniform is so tight these days he was worried about getting back on his horse.

July 20, 1936, Wilton Place
It looks like all-out war in Spain. Lightfoot says he'd like to go and fight. I can't think why, unless marriage is palling already.

July 24, 1936
To the Shim Sham with the Erlangers, the Crokers, Kenny Opdyke and Wally. Home just ahead of the milk cart.

HM had to dine with his mother. Judson may be posted to the Low Countries. Hattie says they speak English there.

July 28, 1936
We're having to make fresh arrangements for our cruise. The Foreign Office found out our plans to start from Italy and have told HM it will cause the country great embarrassment if he sets foot there given the current international situation. Wally says Anthony Eden is full of bluster and we should go anyway, but HM doesn't want to make unnecessary trouble when he'll need the government's cooperation if he's to marry Wally. Our boat will now pick us up somewhere on the coast of Yugoslavia which means HM will have to make a courtesy call on the Crown Prince Pauls. Bolsheviks in Cannes. Situations in Italy. War in Spain. Travel is becoming impossible.

July 31, 1936, Sunninghills
Boss and Ethel's final English party for this year. A clambake in Surrey! They had sand laid around their pool and a top chef brought in to cook the lobsters. We had the greatest fun in spite of the rain. Boss told me he saw Ernest last week, in the Aldwych, and he seemed very well. He said, 'Between you and me, Maybell, I don't know that he's so heartbroken over Wally. I think he's decided it's all worked out for the best.'

Monday, to Paris, to await HM who's kinging till Friday. Just the Erlangers, the Humphrey Butlers, and the Crokers for the first leg. Jack Aird to equerry.

August 6, 1936, Hôtel Meurice, Paris
Shopping for peignoirs with Ethel, Poots, and Hattie. Wally has hardly left the side of Kenny Opdyke. She says

306

he knows everything there is to know about Paris. Poots says he's completely harmless but I don't think HM would at all like the way he whispers in Wally's ear and makes her laugh. HM never makes her laugh.

August 10, 1936, somewhere in Austria

We finally got away on Saturday evening. HM finished his duties and just hopped across the Channel in a little airplane. I do wish Wally could be persuaded to fly. It may be frightening but the ordeal is over faster. Our rail car is well appointed but still a rail car. Pips says she feels carefree and adventurous when she travels by train. I find the swaying doubles the time for my toilette.

Lily Drax-Pfaffenhof joined us at Salzburg. They say we should reach Yugoslavia by this evening.

August 11, 1936, somewhere in Yugoslavia

The landscape grows wilder. Jack Aird says these mountains are full of cut-throats. Wally is already a nervous wreck. She and HM had to go to tea with the Crown Prince Pauls yesterday afternoon and she says their driver fairly threw the car around blind bends, in case any brigands lay in wait. The wife wasn't at all friendly toward her either. Well, she's Marina Kent's sister. Ice maidens both, I'm sure.

August 13, 1936, the *Nahlin*, off Šibenik

At last, the sea and our spandy white yacht. She's called the *Nahlin*. There were crowds of well-wishers lining our route from the railroad station to the harbor, all dressed in their gay peasant costumes. HM said, 'Come along, darling. Give them a wave. You're going to have to get used to this.'

I caught Humphrey and Aird exchanging looks.

We have two dear little destroyers escorting us, so I now feel completely safe.

August 14, 1936
The staterooms are rather smaller than they first appear and completely airless. HM and Wally have nabbed the best suite in the bow. The only thing to do is stay on the sundeck as much as possible. HM and Boss and Hattie have been larking around in the sea. They say the water is warm. I'll take their word for it. Humphrey sits all day with an atlas on his lap trying to identify islands. A fool's errand. They're just white rocks. Why would they have names?

Tomorrow, Dubrovnik. Lily says it's an enchanting town with lots of inexpensive little things to buy.

August 16, 1936, at sea
The press were waiting for us when we moored yesterday. Jack Aird suggested we leave immediately, without going ashore. HM said, 'Why?'

Jack said, 'Might we have a word in private, sir?'

I'd never seen HM angry before. He said, 'Absolutely not. Explain yourself here.'

Humphrey said, 'Jack's worried about photographs, sir, and so am I. With Wally as the innocent party in a divorce case one needs to be cautious. About her being seen in the company of a man, if you see what I mean?'

Wally said nothing. She'd be desperate if anything scuppered her divorce. But HM said, 'Nonsense. The British press promised me complete privacy during my vacation. These Johnnies are all foreigners and English judges don't read foreign newspapers.'

Wally made all the girls wear sunglasses and headscarves for going ashore, to confuse any mischievous hacks. 'HM's harem', Hattie called us.

Aird stayed on board and stewed. He's not much of a shopper anyway.

August 19, 1936, still at sea
Wally's being a very strict taskmaster with HM. He'd asked for the dinghy to be put out this morning so he and Judson could fish for octopus but Wally countermanded his order and said he had to do his boxes first. Even on vacation a king has official papers to read and sign. Humphrey said, 'You know, Wally is starting to look like a very promising queen. She takes it all jolly seriously.'

Aird said, 'Perhaps I should just get her to do the boxes and leave His Majesty to play in peace.'

HM did his duty in record time and then was allowed the dinghy. As Hattie said, from a distance, paddling around in his bathing trunks, he looks like a boy. A very happy boy.

August 20, 1936
Humphrey and Poots are going to leave us when we get to Athens. Bernie and Zita Cavett will take over their stateroom. First, we have to call on another royal cousin. George of the Hellenes. HM is reluctant but Wally says he must. Actually, she's rather keen to meet him because he's a king *and* divorced *and* he has a divorced sweetheart. She's interested to find out how the Greeks manage these things.

August 21, 1936, Corfu
HM and Wally have gone ashore to have dinner with King George. HM dragged his feet and they were very late

309

setting off. Jack Aird says Greece will be the next place to have a revolution. I can quite see that by next year the only place left for us will be Palm Beach.

August 22, 1936

Having tried to wriggle out of dining with George Greece last evening, HM has now invited him to come aboard for luncheon before we sail. He said, 'To tell you the truth, Maybell, it's not that I especially like him but I do feel sorry for him. They've brought him back here to be King but he really has nothing to do. He's just hanging round waiting for them to put a bomb under his car or send him back to London. He's quite miserable.'

Wally says the girlfriend has good bone structure but no pizzazz. She's also furious with HM for talking to her too avidly and omitting to turn between courses.

Poots said, 'That's pretty rich, Wally, considering you and Kenny Opdyke are always sniggering at private jokes and neglecting the rest of us.'

August 24, 1936, Athens

Bernie and Zita Cavett have come aboard. Zita isn't happy with their accommodation but she might spare a thought for those of us who've sweated and suffered thus far. Big crowds waiting for us as we nosed into Piraeus. Jack Aird got a tongue-lashing from Wally for suggesting HM might want to put on a shirt before getting within range of the press cameras. She said, 'If His Majesty needs your advice he'll tell you.'

Aird is returning to his regiment after the cruise and not before time. With Wally in charge his days must be numbered anyway.

Humphrey said, 'Poor Jack. Cruising isn't his kind of

thing at all. I think he's worried he'll be required to wear espadrilles to the next investiture.'

Tonight we dine on dry land in a picturesque tavern. I pray the revolution Jack Aird is predicting holds off till tomorrow at least.

Lovely cloisonné belt buckles to be had here, and all kinds of darling amulets and crosses for knockdown prices.

September 1, 1936
A heavy swell. Next summer I shall vacation on dry land.

September 2, 1936
Smaller seas, but I've returned to my room. Wally is snapping at everything HM says and it makes for such a tense atmosphere. Tomorrow we're to visit the Dardanelles. Jack Aird speaks of them as though I should know them, but I really don't recall them. One meets so many people.

September 3, 1936
HM went ashore with Bernie, Boss, and Aird. We girls stayed aboard and had massages and pedicures while they visited a battlefield. Padmore and Wally's *lingère* went too. They both lost brothers there.

Tonight we sail for the fabled city of Istanbul but there is a terrible row brewing. The British Ambassador says HM absolutely must meet the President of Turkey. HM says he's on vacation and has no intention of meeting anymore people. We're only going to Istanbul so he can play a round of golf. Now the ever-interfering Foreign Office has entered the affair and Wally is adding her two cents. She says it would be rude to call in and not at least say hello to Mr Atatürk. Jack Aird agrees. He says in the event of any future troubles we want the Turks firmly on our side, not running off to the League of Nations, and there's no better person to convey the message than the King of England.

September 4, 1936, Istanbul
The diplomats had their way. HM went ashore to be received and he got along so well with President Atatürk that he brought him back for drinks. *Very* good-looking and quite charming. He gave Wally a choker of hammered gold and turquoise, a very pretty rug, and an invitation to dinner.

September 5, 1936
It was midnight before HM and Wally came back from being feted and they had an escort of thousands. Little boats strung with lanterns milling round them. Jack Aird says it was a nightmare for the detectives. This morning HM is in a black mood. It turns out there's nowhere for him to play golf and Wally has done nothing but talk about Mr Atatürk's lovely eyes. She says he's the kind of man who could make a girl melt.

To the bazaar with Ethel, Zita, and Lily. Bought bangles and sheepskin rugs. Our last night on the *Nahlin*.

September 6, 1936, another train
Mr Atatürk put on a wonderful farewell firework display for us and has loaned us his train for the first part of our homeward journey. When we get to Bulgaria King Boris is going to meet us with *his* train, which he actually drives himself. What hard times some of these little kings have fallen upon.

HM seems very depressed. When we get back he has to go to Balmoral. He doesn't like it but it's expected of him. Also, just as Aird and Butler warned him, his lawyer has told him that if he doesn't behave more discreetly there's a real risk that he'll endanger Wally's divorce. Monckton recommends that he simply not see her at all until the case has been heard, but he'll never agree to that.

September 8, 1936
The air is crackling between HM and Wally. The Pauls of Yugoslavia have sent their train for the next leg of our journey, so Wally says the very least we must do is have them to dinner. HM says he's tired of all these relations who litter his path wherever he goes.

September 9, 1936
Wally won the day and the Yugoslavias came to dinner. HM said, 'Well, don't expect me to talk to them. It's only a month since I had tea with them. I've done my whack.'

And he was as good as his word. He sat right through dinner and hardly spoke.

After the Yugoslav suite had left we could all hear Wally telling him what a naughty king he'd been. Hattie said, 'Lord, listen to her! If they ever crown her she should carry a cane instead of a scepter.'

September 12, 1936, approaching Paris
HM left us at Zurich. There was a plane waiting to take him to London. He has a dinner engagement with his mother. Wally gave him a most affectionate send-off. A great relief because nerves have been frayed this last week. I'd begun to wonder whether the shine hasn't gone off the affair but this morning they were as devoted as ever.

Wally says she believes HM has the makings of a great king if only these so-called advisors would stop interfering and leave her to handle him when he becomes difficult. She says he's just not accustomed to applying himself, but she has a knack with him, a little discipline, a little reward, like training a dog. Funny, that's pretty much what Kitty Rothschild said when she saw them together.

As soon as we get back to London she's going to resume house-hunting. She says it's not only a question of security but also fittingness. She said, 'It was one thing for the Prince of Wales to come to Bryanston Court. But not the King.'

Lily said, 'So are you going to marry him?'

She said, 'I'm not free to marry him. But if I get my divorce and if it can be managed, yes, I'll marry him.'

Ethel said, 'But can it be managed? That's the point.'

Wally said, 'If His Majesty says it can, it can.'

If it comes off her title will be Queen Consort. And I'll be the Queen Consort's Best Friend. Let Nora Sedley Cordle put *that* in her teapot and brew it.

September 15, 1936, Wilton Place

To South Audley Street to give Flora her sheepskin rug and Doopie her bangles. Lightfoot says HM dropped an enormous clanger by not inviting the Prime Minister to Balmoral. He says it's something that's written in stone. The Prime Minister always goes, and the Archbishop of Canterbury, who hasn't received his usual invitation either. I'd have thought they'd both be grateful for the change.

September 16, 1936

House-viewing with Wally. We've seen properties in Mount Street, St James's Square, and Beauchamp Place. More tomorrow.

To Carlton Gardens with Violet's Turkish jam spoons.

She said, 'Ah, so you're back. Well, I hope you realize you people are breaking Her Majesty's heart.'

A fine greeting.

I said, 'What people?'

She said, 'You know. Truck tycoons. Johnny-come-latelies. Swanning round the Mediterranean. Don't imagine we didn't get to hear about it at Drumcanna.'

I said, 'David is a grown man. He can surely choose how to spend his vacations.'

She said, 'He is a grown man, and a king too, though you'd never think it to see pictures of him cavorting half naked with gangsters.'

Boss Croker is no gangster, and they weren't cavorting. They were shrimping.

She never mentioned Wally and neither did I. Let her hear it from the Yugoslavias next time they come to call.

September 18, 1936

Penelope Blythe says she saw newspaper photographs of HM on his cruise but Wally wasn't in any of them. Very strange, because he was never more than two inches from her side. They must have removed her. I wonder how one does that. Wally is taking a house in Cumberland Terrace. Its furnishings are rather overbearing but it has good views across Regent's Park, and anyway, she's not likely to be there for long. I have a feeling she'll have yet another address by the time the year turns. The lawyer Goddard says she'll need an advocate to represent her in court. He's recommended someone called Birkett.

To the Crosbies' for dinner.

September 19, 1936

Freddie says Penelope Blythe is absolutely right. Wally was removed from the photographs before they appeared in the British newspapers. He also said Wally's divorce is being discussed in Whitehall, the principal question being, can HM be allowed to marry a divorced commoner? Pips said, 'Cut to the chase, darling. We already know the answer to that. The real question is, when Parliament tells him he can't marry her, what will he do?'

No one knows. And there don't seem to be anymore princesses in prospect, not even from the bargain basement.

September 21, 1936

The lawyer Goddard says there are so many divorces waiting to be heard in London this fall Wally might have to wait as long as a year for her case to be called. HM says the delay is completely unacceptable. He wants Wally free to marry him before the coronation on May 12. Supper with Wally at Bryanston Court, just we two. HM telephoned three times. She's as jumpy as a flea. She said, 'It's all too hurried, Maybell. There's too much to be worked out and if we rush things it could all go wrong.'

If only they'd nursed the old King more carefully. He might have had another year or two in him.

September 22, 1936

Mr Goddard has come up with a suggestion: Wally's divorce could be heard in a little country court where there aren't such long lists. It would have the dual advantage of speeding things along and removing the case from the spotlight of London. HM and Wally are both in favor.

September 24, 1936

Wally's divorce has been transferred to a town called Ipswich. We have to go there. She has to be in residence for three weeks before the case is called. She said, 'Please come with me, Maybell. I can't face it without you.'

She isn't sure where Ipswich is but HM has Oxer Bettenbrooke finding us a house.

She's gone off to the Perry Brownlows' for the weekend.

September 25, 1936

To Ciro's with the Crosbies, the Erlangers, and the Cavetts. Hattie says Ipswich is no distance from London. She's offered to drive out and keep us company from time to time. Pips says she'll do the same.

Zita said, 'I'm muddled. Everyone says David can't marry Wally, but what will they do if he just goes ahead and does it? They can't fire the King. And who are "they", anyhow?'

Freddie says the marrying couldn't take place because there'd be no one willing to perform it. Well, I'm sure someone could be persuaded. A crisp bank note left between the pages of a prayer book to whet the appetite. There's always *someone*.

Freddie said, 'The greater danger is that David will do something hotheaded. Run away to Canada, for instance. I know he's spoken of it. You may be crucial in this, Maybell. Remind Wally what the risks are. Ask her to think of stopping her divorce until after the coronation at least. I think he'll be less likely to bolt after he's been anointed.'

Zita said, 'Yeah. I guess those ermine robes'd slow him down some.'

Zita may have famous legs but she's not terribly bright.

317

September 29, 1936

Wally couldn't be clearer. She absolutely will not marry HM if the throne is at risk. She said, 'Of course not. You know as well as I do what happens to those exes, trailing round the world, hocking their jewels to pay their hotel bills. That's not for me, Maybell. I've tried poor, remember? It just doesn't suit my constitution. So if they make things impossible for us it's me he'll have to give up.'

I said, 'But where will that leave you?'

She said, 'I'll be just fine. I'll look around and find someone else. I'll have the pick of London.'

She seemed pretty breezy for a person who's already tried the throne for size. Then there's HM. I can't imagine him letting her go, and they'll get no proper kinging out of him if he doesn't have Wally cracking her whip. It would be a disaster.

Von Ribbentrop is the new German Ambassador.

'See?' she said. 'Didn't I tell you?'

October 1, 1936

Wally has her going-away-to-get-divorced gifts from HM. A black fox capelet to keep her warm while they're apart and a river pearl sautoir to remind her she's his Queen. Bettenbrooke has found us a house in a town called Felixstowe. His says it's quiet but handy for Ipswich. Wally's things will be moved into Cumberland Terrace while we're gone. I have drunk my last martini at Bryanston Court.

October 2, 1936

To Harrold's for candy. Saw Philip Sassoon.

He said, 'Maybell! Have you left any pr-r-ralines for the rest of us?'

I said, 'I'm going to Felixstowe for three weeks and I'm sure they never heard of Floris there.'

He said, 'Give me your address. I shall have cr-r-rystalized quince sent to you from Lympne. But why Felixstowe? Why, why?'

I felt him cool as soon as I spoke Wally's name.

'Oh dear,' he said, 'the tigress's cage is about to be opened wide. Do take care, Maybell.'

Lightfoot says London is quietly assembling into two camps. Those who are for HM, Wally, and True Love, and those who don't want anything to upset the old Queen.

I said, 'I know where Violet and Melhuish stand but what about you and Doopie?'

He said, 'You know we're both romantics at heart, but frankly I think there are more important battles on the horizon.'

He's still talking about going to Spain and fighting the Fascists. Crazy. George Lightfoot couldn't fight his way out of a paper bag.

October 5, 1936
Penelope Blythe says Ernest is seeing someone. No names. All she's heard is that it's an old acquaintance he looked up when he was in the States and he's very smitten. If Wally knows she's not letting on.

October 7, 1936, Felixstowe
We are installed in a cold, cramped house at the ends of the earth. I don't believe Bettenbrooke even looked the place over before he took it. HM would be furious if he knew Wally was living in such grim conditions. The sea is gray, the sky is gray, Wally's mood is black. Pips is coming down on Friday, thank heavens.

A pause in the rain this afternoon, but our detective has warned us against venturing into town. He said the place is crawling with American press. So much for getting out of the spotlight of London. Wally says there's nothing worth seeing in Felixstowe anyway.

October 10, 1936

Pips arrived with extra blankets, more vermouth, and a checkerboard. She also confirmed the story about Ernest. Not only is he seeing someone, the someone is Mary Kirk. He met up with her in New York in August, cried on her shoulder, no doubt, and now she's planning to leave her husband and follow him to London. All this delivered in whispers after Wally had retired. I think she should be told. Wally hates not knowing things. And little Mary Kirk! Who'd have thought she'd keep popping up in Wally's life like this? Bridesmaid when she married Win Spencer, matchmaker between Wally and Ernest, and now 'the other woman'. What a busy bee. Perhaps I'll wait till after the weekend before I bring it up with Wally. Pips also says Walter Monckton just came back from overseas and is letting it be known that he thinks the divorce case is being badly handled. He says Goddard shouldn't have had it moved out of London and he shouldn't have hired a big-gun advocate like Birkett.

I said, 'Well, Monckton recommended Goddard.'

Pips said, 'I know, but you can see his reasoning. Instead of treating it like any ordinary little divorce, it's drawing attention to the fact that there's something big at stake. It could look like a put-up job.'

But it *is* a put-up job. And it's too late to change everything now. We just have to stay in the house with the drapes closed and hope for the best.

October 13, 1936

Wally says she already knew about Ernest and Mary.

I said, 'Then why did he have to go to a hotel with a floozie?'

She said, 'Because he doesn't want her name dragged in. You know Ernest. Ever the gentleman. But it's only happened because he's on the rebound. If I called off the divorce he'd drop her like that.'

October 16, 1936

Hattie and Judson are visiting. They brought magazines and smoked salmon and new rumba records. One week to go.

October 17, 1936

An unexpected guest. HM drove through the dark and arrived in time to take in Wally's breakfast tray. Cries of surprise and joy. Judson said, 'Is this advisable, sir? Isn't Wally supposed to be in purdah until after the divorce?'

HM said a) no one need ever know he was here, and b) if they do, what could be more natural than one friend visiting another when they're in the throes of a divorce?

He's given Wally a bracelet of channel-set rubies. It has 'Hold Tight' engraved on the clasp. He's staying the night. Bernie and Zita are going to motor up for the day tomorrow.

October 18, 1936

A telephone call just as we were finishing luncheon. Fort Belvedere trying to track down HM. The Prime Minister wants a meeting at his earliest convenience and is willing to go Sandringham if necessary, where he'd been given to understand HM was hosting a shooting party. But

Sandringham were under the impression HM was already back at the Fort.

Hattie said, 'Alex Hardinge must be having kittens. He's mislaid the King!'

HM was very relaxed. He said, 'It's Sunday. Let the buggers wait.'

Wally was beside herself. She said, 'Sir, please don't antagonize Baldwin. And please don't risk being discovered here. I haven't endured two weeks in this hellhole to have my divorce thrown out of court.'

HM made a leisurely departure after dark. Kings don't jump for the likes of Mr Baldwin.

October 19, 1936

Wally on the telephone for hours with HM. I ate dinner alone. He granted the Prime Minister an audience, Baldwin asked a number of personal questions relating to Wally, and HM put him firmly in his place. Reduced Baldwin to tears, effectively. She seemed reassured but went to bed without eating. She's looking as thin as a pencil.

October 20, 1936

A different version of the Baldwin meeting from Pips, courtesy of Freddie who had it from Fruity Metcalfe who had it from Alex Hardinge.

Baldwin wants Wally's divorce case dropped and for her to leave the country, so there can be an end to speculation that HM intends to marry her as soon as she's free. Well, if Stanley Baldwin wants to get to the heart of the matter he should apply to me. I could tell him everything he needs to know. Wally won't leave the country. She's made London her home and she likes it there. And as for the marrying, it will only happen if there are no obstacles to her becoming Queen Consort. Wally has always been firm on that point. If there's opposition to her being crowned she'll retire quietly to Cumberland Terrace with her nest egg. If they won't have Wally as Queen they'll just have to dig deeper and find HM another candle-end princess.

Wind rattling the windows. More rain. Three days to go.

October 21, 1936
Ernest telephoned. He isn't coming to Ipswich for the hearing. His lawyer will represent him. Wally seemed unsettled by his call. She said, 'We weren't unhappy, you know? If David hadn't come along I suppose we'd still be getting along perfectly well.'

October 23, 1936
Tomorrow is Wally's hearing. She's decided on a navy wool coat and a felt hat. No jewels except for a platinum bangle. She said, 'My one and only appearance as a Baptist missionary.' The first laugh we've had in weeks.

October 24, 1936
The worst thing. This morning we were told Wally's case had been postponed because the judge's calendar was too full. The earliest it can now be heard is Tuesday and we are prisoners here. The town is full of American newspapermen so we daren't even peek outside and the lawyers have absolutely forbidden any further contact with HM. Easier said than done. His telephone messages are so tearful and anxious I wouldn't put it past him to turn up here tonight. I feel like a switchboard girl and Wally is like a caged animal.

October 25, 1936

I made warm milk for Wally last night and it seemed to help her to sleep. This morning she was in a much brighter mood. She said, 'David isn't worrying so why should I? He says everything will fall into place once I'm divorced, so let's look on the bright side. Let's make plans.'

I said, 'You mean wedding plans?'

She said, 'Wedding plans. Honeymoon plans. Coronation plans. We should go to Paris as soon as this is over, to start choosing my trousseau.'

She says they'll keep on the Fort even after she's had Windsor refurbished because it's a place where they've been happy. She intends getting rid of Sandringham House and I agree with her. Let someone who enjoys freezing flatlands have it. Then there's his ranch in Calgary. All very well when he was an adventurous young man, but he's King now, and not so young. He needs homes appropriate to his position, in sunny climes where she can help him to relax after his kingly duties. Wally favors Majorca.

She's thinking of Brussels lace over ice-blue satin for her wedding gown. It will probably be an April wedding. And for the coronation she's thinking of using the coronet David had for his investiture as Prince of Wales. It's an adorable little circlet set with pearls and amethysts and, as she says, will be far less ruinous to the hair than one of those dreadful old crowns. She's full of modern ideas.

I feel very excited. We've been jogging along at a steady pace but suddenly we're on a runaway train. Little Minnehaha is going to be Queen of England and I'm her right-hand woman.

October 26, 1936

Rain again, and Wally is sitting on thorns. She says the old King's dying has plunged her life into unsought chaos. I said, 'Are you telling me you don't really want to be Queen?'

'No,' she said, 'I don't mind being Queen, but they're all going to make it so tricky for us. His mother's against me, the Yorks are against me, that little pig-farmer Baldwin is against me. What if David caves in to them now? He's quite easy to push around, you know? Where will that leave me?'

I said, 'But David adores you. He'll always take care of you.'

She said, 'I imagine Thelma Furness believed that.'

I said, 'It's just the waiting that's getting on your nerves. But it's almost over. Why throw it all away now?'

She said, 'I don't know. My head's spinning. Half of London has been waiting for me to fail. I'd hate them to think they'd scored some kind of victory over me. It might all be easier if Ernest and I just go away together. South Africa sounds interesting.'

I think Mary Kirk might have something to say about that. She's left her husband to be with Ernest, after all. Fortunately, just at the moment of Wally's greatest wobble, a courier arrived with a diamond pin and a note from HM. He says he cannot and will not live without her.

Pips has often said she doesn't think HM is very bright but he seems to me to have an astute understanding of Wally. Tomorrow is the big day.

October 27, 1936, Wilton Place

Our exile is over. Mr Birkett met us at court and told Wally to breathe deeply, speak up, and simply answer any

325

questions the judge put to her. I'm told he's one of the highest paid advocates in the country. If that's so I wonder he doesn't smarten up. He was wearing the most moth-eaten old rug on his head. The judge was extremely disagreeable, interrupting Wally when she was speaking, sneezing and coughing into a handkerchief, and there was one awful moment when he just sat in silence, glowering at Birkett. I thought he might be going to throw the case out. And then all of a sudden it was over. He awarded her a divorce decree nisi, which means she will be free to marry David in April. We were in and out in twenty minutes, and the press were prevented from leaving the courtroom until we were all safely out of the building and into our cars.

We went directly to Cumberland Terrace. It's in a messy state, half of Wally's things not unpacked and more boxes have arrived from Buckingham Palace, things David wants her to have. It all seems rather silly to me. In six months' time it will have to be packed up and sent back there. Wally said, 'I don't live my life that way, Maybell. Making do. I pay attention to every detail every moment of every day. Why would I use a creamer from Heal's when I can have one that's been used by monarchs?'

She'd told her cook we'd have Spanish omelets at eight, but at seven HM appeared with chilled champagne and pheasant sandwiches and an emerald ring. Wally said, 'Maybell was just leaving.'

Pips gave me dinner. Freddie was at the January Club. Pips says Wally had better not start flashing a royal engagement ring around the day after her divorce hearing or she could find herself hauled back before the judge.

October 29, 1936

To Carlton Gardens for tea. The boys are home on Long Leave.

Violet said, 'You can wipe that silly smile off your face. It doesn't matter what sordid lengths she goes to, Wally Warfield will never be Queen.'

Violet was a bad loser when we used to play crazy eights and she's never grown up.

I said, 'So far you've been wrong in everything you've predicted. You said she'd never get as far as royal circles. She did it within months. You said she'd never go to the Kents' wedding ball or the Jubilee ball and she went to both.'

She said, 'It's a pity you clutter your mind with such trivia.'

I said, 'There's nothing cluttered about my mind. I have it all written down in my diaries. Every step in Wally's climb to the throne, and the names of all those swankpots and sneerers who've scoffed at her.'

Rory said, 'Gosh. I'd like to read those.' Violet sent him out to walk the spaniels.

Ulick said, 'I hope none of *our* names appear.'

Violet said, 'Do our names appear, Maybell?'

I said, 'Yes, they do. You'll be comforted to know that every objection you've raised has been carefully recorded. No one will ever be able to accuse the Melhuishes of sitting on the fence.'

Ulick said, 'This is insufferable. I shall speak to Father.'

That boy is old before his time.

Friday to the Fort. Pips and Freddie are coming. Also the Crokers and the Erlangers. 'Little America', Violet calls it. Sour grapes of course.

November 1, 1936, Fort Belvedere
The men played golf yesterday afternoon. Freddie says he's never seen HM play so well nor be in such good spirits and I had the same impression at breakfast this morning. HM said, 'Things are going our way at last, Maybell.'

Oxer Bettenbrooke says the British people are one hundred percent behind him.

Ethel said, 'I thought the British people didn't know about Wally.'

He said, 'It's not widely reported, true. But if they knew they'd support him. All those factory workers he's taken the time to visit, all those Tommies who remember how gallantly he fought in the Great War; if it comes to a confrontation over the Wally Issue, *theirs* are the voices that will be heard.'

HM said, 'Oxer's right. A little thing like this isn't going to bother them.'

Ethel said, 'I know Wally keeps a slim line, sir, but I'd never call her "a little thing".'

He laughed.

November 2, 1936, Wilton Place
Dinner at South Audley Street. Violet and Melhuish came but no guests. Figs and ham, oxtail ragout, pear tart. If a halfwit like Doopie can produce a decent dinner why can't Violet?

I was there to be pumped for information. Melhuish said, 'What's your pal up to this week, Maybell? It sounds like the Great Terror at Buck House. Wigram's gone. Halsey's been sacked. Trotter's been allowed to resign. It's a bloody disgrace.'

I happen to know that Brigadier Trotter had continued to fraternize with Thelma Furness, so the man has only himself to blame. He was as old as the hills anyway.

Flora said, 'Skinner says they have gartoon shows now at Uncle King David's house. And bath salts.'

This is the kind of thing kitchen help chatter about. Violet tutting.

I said, 'Bath salts! Well, that's a hanging offense.'

She said, 'And heaven only knows what he's spending on coal. Marina Kent says he has the furnaces roaring.'

Lightfoot said, 'We mustn't criticize that, Vee. Think of the miners. I'm sure he's doing it for the sake of the Principality.'

Doopie said, 'Or burnin old wood. Drow anudder gortier onna vire, Wally! Wades nod, wand nod!'

Thank goodness someone in the family has kept their sense of humor.

November 3, 1936
Today HM opened Parliament and Wally and I watched him from the Distinguished Strangers' Gallery. The next time he does it Wally will be beside him in that gilded coach. She watched everything very closely and made notes.

November 5, 1936
Randolph Putnam telephoned to tell me Roosevelt has been reelected. I can't say he ever did a damned thing for me except steal my gold. Randolph said he'd seen Junior and his awful wife at Nora Sedley Cordle's museum gala and they were very curious to know how close I am to Wally Simpson. *Le tout* Baltimore is talking about her, apparently. They should be talking about me too. Last night I wore my chocolate silk and danced across a glass floor with the King of England.

November 6, 1936

To the opera. The Cunard box for *Götterdammerung*. Wally, Emerald C, Lily Drax-Pfaffenhof, and the Erlangers. Philip Sassoon sought me out during the intermission. He said, 'Maybell, I note there are two dazzling emeralds in your box this evening and one of them is on Br-r-r-unnhilde's finger. Is she betr-r-rothed? I think we should be told.'

It's too late for him to try and humor me now. He never invites me to Trent anymore for fear of Sybil.

Sunday, to Paris.

November 9, 1936, Hôtel Meurice, Paris

Bought nightgowns at Cadolle and ordered day dresses from Patou, simple crepes. Wally's not short these days but she doesn't seem in any hurry to settle her bills. We've gone our separate ways for the evening. I'm dining with Ena Spain, Wally's going dancing with Kenny Opdyke.

November 11, 1936

Ena is very troubled about HM and Wally. She says the old Queen is desperate and the Yorks are furious. She said, 'It's the unseemliness of it, Maybell. The weekends, the niteries. That cruise. He's tarnishing the crown before it's even properly on his head.'

I said, 'Well, David's his own man.'

She said, 'Oh, I don't think he is. I think we both know that's not the case.'

Ena should have someone ease the seams on her bodices. I'm sure she wouldn't perspire so if she accepted that we all grow a little rounder with the passing years.

To Schiaparelli for evening gowns, then the boat train to London. HM is inspecting the Fleet. We rendezvous at the Fort for the weekend. The Brownlows and the Erlangers are joining us.

November 13, 1936, Fort Belvedere
An unsettling evening. We were at drinks when a letter arrived for HM. He read it then asked Perry B to go with him to his study. He didn't even show the letter to Wally. He and Perry were closeted for the longest time, then Alex Hardinge arrived. Raised voices. Dinner was delayed until ten-thirty and was then hurried through without any attempt at gaiety, even on Wally's part. HM was drained of all color. Wally went straight to bed after the savory. Hattie's gone up to see Kitsie B, to see if she knows what's going on, and Judson's downstairs playing solitaire, hoping to glean some information.

November 14, 1936
Four a.m. and Wally just went back to her room. The letter that blighted our evening was from Hardinge, warning HM that the British newspapers are about to reveal all about the love affair. I said, 'But isn't that good? If you're getting married in April surely you need to reveal all before too long?'

She said, 'Not by newspaper reports. They'll get everything wrong, and anyway, there are procedures to be observed. The government has to give its agreement and so far it hasn't even been asked. And apart from anything else, this might cost me my divorce. If this is splashed all over the papers that old beak might refuse to make my decree final. Birkett said there was a very sticky moment in court when he thought the judge was going to throw out the chambermaid evidence against Ernest. Something like this could finish it.

David's been too damned impetuous. I told him to be more careful.'

She said the letter was signed by Alex Hardinge, but she's sure the old Queen and the Yorks had a hand in the composing of it, threatening him with the government resigning, trying to spook HM into giving her up.

She feels the only thing to do is to go away until it's all blown over. Paris, probably. She said, 'We'll go today. Have your maid start packing now. Leave early, before David is up. I'll make your excuses. Then meet me at Cumberland Terrace.'

I said, 'I have commitments. I'm running the tombola at Anne Belchester's Epileptics benefit on Wednesday. I can't just run away.'

She said, 'We're not running away. *I'm* defusing a delicate situation and *you're* keeping me company.'

November 15, 1936, Wilton Place

Padmore is unpacking. We're not going to Paris after all. I waited for Wally at Cumberland Terrace all afternoon yesterday and heard nothing till 6 p.m. Then she telephoned to say HM had persuaded her to stay at least while various avenues are explored. She said, 'I'm sorry, Maybell. He won't hear of my going away at present.'

All very well but Anne Belchester has now given the tombola to Daphne Frith.

Pips and Freddie gave me dinner. Freddie said Wally's name has been mentioned in Parliament. She'll be thrilled. He thinks HM is hoping to talk his mother round to accepting Wally. If the old Queen relents something might be managed. Pips thinks he's already decided to give up the throne. He'll be wasting his time if he does. Wally's not interested in ex-kings.

November 16, 1936

Violet was shown into my morning room at the ungodly hour of nine-thirty. I received her in my wrap. She said, 'I can't be long. I have my Pit Ponies at ten. Is it true you're going away with Wally Warfield?'

If you want news spread in London just allow a boot boy to overhear it. It'll travel from Belgravia to St James's via Mayfair faster than a hackney cab.

I said, 'We'd thought of going to Paris for awhile but now we may not.'

She said, 'I very much hope she does go to Paris, or somewhere more distant. It may be the only way to shock His Majesty into sanity. But you mustn't go with her, Maybell. She's going to be remembered evermore as the hussy who almost ruined a king and you'll be remembered as her friend.'

I remarked that even a hussy is entitled to a friend. Violet said, 'Well, let it not be you. Let it be that silly Hattie Erlanger, or one of those gangsters' wives, but not you. You'll be ruined.'

I said, 'Well, we're not going. David won't allow it. He's talking to the Prime Minister and the old Queen. It's all going to be worked out.'

She said, 'Worked out? Worked out! This isn't a quarrel over a grouse moor. There isn't anything to work out except how far away that woman can be sent and how fast. David Wales is going to be anointed and crowned six months from now and he has to start behaving correctly. Wally must go. There is no place for her in the royal family.'

I said, 'Don't you feel sorry for him? All he wants is to marry her.'

She said, 'Yes, I do. But sympathy doesn't come into it. Kings have to put duty first.'

I said, 'Pips thinks if he can't have Wally he'll walk away from the job.'

She said, 'A very good example of the silliness surrounding His Majesty. Anyone who understands anything about this country knows that kings don't walk away. He needs stiffening, Maybell, not tempting with idiotic fantasies. Well, until you come to your senses and distance yourself from the affair please stay away from Carlton Gardens. I have Melhuish to think of and my boys.'

And out she blazed.

Treated Ida Coote to the Dorch. She now eats only vegetables and nuts. Daphne Frith cut me.

November 17, 1936

Freddie Crosbie has come up with an idea and has asked to see HM tomorrow. He thinks the answer is simply to take a more leisurely approach. To silence all talk of marrying until after the coronation, giving Wally time to set out her stall. Do some volunteer work. Make carefully selected public appearances. Let the British public get to know her and take her into their hearts.

HM is dining with his mother this evening, then leaving first thing on a tour of shipyards.

November 18, 1936, Cumberland Terrace

Wally has asked me to move in for a few nights. Her ulcers have flared up and she's finding it hard to sleep. We're supposed to have an armed guard outside the house around the clock but all we seem to have is two dopes in a car and a bobby who bicycles past once an hour.

HM's dinner with the old Queen didn't go well. All he got was a sermon on the subject of duty. When he gets back from Wales he's going to see George Kent and Harry Gloucester to try and get them on side. Also Mr Beaverbrook. If he were to come out in favor of Wally in his newspapers it would make an enormous difference.

Freddie's proposal fell on deaf ears. HM says he doesn't want Wally laboring away at charity galas and consigned to the tail-end landau. He wants her at his side.

November 19, 1936
The newspaperman Harmsworth has asked Wally to have lunch on Thursday. He says he'd like to help.

To the Rialto with Lightfoot and Doopie to see *Showboat*. The newsreels showed HM surrounded by cheerful welders. I'm sure simple folk like that would be perfectly happy for him to marry Wally. It's all so silly.

It turns out that Mr Beaverbrook is on his way to Arizona for his asthma but he's been told to sail right back. His King needs him.

November 20, 1936
Wally to Claridge's with Harmsworth. I to the Ritz with Penelope Blythe. Fergus dined with Humphrey Butler last night and Humphrey told him that the Kents and the Gloucesters are lukewarm about Wally but on the whole would prefer having her to losing HM. For one thing, if HM goes Bertie York will have to be King and the rest of them will all have to do a lot more princing. The Yorks absolutely won't accept her but they don't want the throne either. They seem to want everything their own way. Poor HM.

November 21, 1936

Wally is in much better spirits. Esmond Harmsworth has come up with a very clever idea and has offered to take it to Mr Baldwin on Monday morning. It's called a morganatic or 'left-handed' marriage and they were apparently once popular with the Prussians. Even the old Queen's grandfather did it that way. It would mean Wally agreeing not to receive and never to seek the title 'Queen'. She says she'd be quite contented to settle for Royal Duchess. Also, any children of the marriage wouldn't be eligible to succeed, but as Wally says, there aren't going to be any children. The simple beauty of it is that HM could marry her and still remain King. I don't see how anyone could object to it. Not even Violet.

To the Fort.

November 22, 1936

HM doesn't like Harmsworth's left-handed idea. He said, 'Darling, I won't have you shortchanged. I want you to be my Queen, not the Duchess of Lancaster. And anyway, Baldwin and the whole bally lot of them would still have to approve it. I don't see why we should make all these concessions. It smacks of groveling.'

Wally's asking Fruity Metcalfe to try and make HM see the beauty of the morganatic solution.

The Crokers and the Cavetts are coming to dinner and Wally's ordered a gypsy band from the Hungaria. We have to do something to lighten the mood.

HM said, 'I had the most marvelous welcome in the Rhondda this week, Maybell. They sang "Men of Harlech" for me. Everywhere I went they lit their Davy lamps and cheered me. I'm still their Prince of Wales, you see, even though I'm King.'

November 23, 1936

Fruity played golf with HM and persuaded him to look again at Esmond Harmsworth's proposal. They took beer and sandwiches into the study and came out an hour later with HM all in favor and wanting it put to the Prime Minister immediately. Walter Monckton's been sent for.

Wally said, 'David's so alone with all this. If only he had a few wise heads to advise him.'

Fruity said, 'He had plenty of wise heads. Somebody sacked them.'

Dinner with the Crosbies. Freddie said, 'The morganatic idea will never succeed but at least it may buy us some time. At least while Baldwin's looking at it HM isn't likely to do anything rash. Between us three, things are far worse than he understands. It's not just the divorce. There's a whole dossier on Wally. Family, husbands, various goings-on in China. And then there's the von Ribbentrop business. Did you know she gave him a signed photograph for Hitler?'

I thought Mr Hitler preferred blondes.

November 24, 1936

To South Audley Street. I may be banished from Violet's hearth but at least I'm still welcome there.

Lightfoot says there's a growing body of opinion that HM should go, even though the Bertie Yorks are reluctant to be King. Melhuish told him confidentially that the old King always hoped HM would neglect to marry so the succession would pass to Bertie York and then his girls.

I told him about the morganatic idea. He said, 'It might have worked if Wally was a pious, virginal Citizen Jane, but as things stand there's too much against her. Two husbands too many. Not to mention her gatecrashing the Kents' wedding ball and all those courtiers she trampled over to get to the bridge of the *Edward VIII*. No, I really don't see the Archbishop of Canterbury buying it.'

He agrees with Freddie that whatever else happens the coronation should come first. Doopie busy with some item she's crocheting for Marina Kent's baby. Flora reading *The Fortunes of Philippa*, following the words with her finger.

Lightfoot said, 'Of course, Archduke Franz Ferdinand made a morganatic marriage, and we all know what happened to him.'

Flora asked what I dared not. Apparently the Franz Ferdinands were shot. What an unhappy thought.

November 25, 1936

HM has sent for Mr Baldwin. The man has had Esmond Harmsworth's proposal on his desk for almost two days and seems to lack any sense of urgency. Wally afraid we're all being spied on by Alex Hardinge. She wishes she'd gotten rid of him while she had the chance. She has gowns waiting to be fitted in Paris but HM won't let her go. He's afraid she won't come back.

November 26, 1936

Mr Baldwin is not being helpful. He told HM the morganatic idea would have to be put to Parliament, where he had every reason to believe it would be rejected, and that it would also have to be put to the Dominions, whoever they are, and they would certainly reject it.

Boss and Ethel are getting up a crowd to go to the Paradise Club, but neither Wally nor I are in the mood. Freddie Crosbie talked to the lawyer Monckton. Monckton says HM isn't willing to wait to get married till after his coronation because it would mean swearing the oath with a lie in his heart.

Wally thinks David should go on the wireless and speak to the nation. She says if the ordinary people knew how unfairly he was being treated there'd be riots in the streets and Stanley Baldwin's head on a pike. Beaverbrook's boat docks in the morning. He's going straight to the Fort to meet with HM.

November 27, 1936

Beaverbrook's advice is to withdraw the morganatic proposal immediately. He says Baldwin is holding a very strong hand and the most sensible course is for Wally to go away, for the coronation to take place, and then in the fullness of time for the nation and Commonwealth to become properly acquainted with Wally through her charitable works and occasional, decorous appearances. He says if it's put to the Dominions Eire will vote against anything involving a divorcée and so, in all likelihood, will Australia and New Zealand because they have Roman Catholic Prime Ministers.

I often think politics would be more agreeable in the hands of women. What could be a more sensible arrangement than a happy king and a Wally satisfied to be a royal duchess? Pips says Wally's satisfaction may be one of the problems.

She said, 'She might agree to "Duchess of Lancaster" now, but she'd soon start wheedling for more. You know Wally.'

Hattie said, 'And what if a baby were to come along? It's not out of the question. Jane Habberley's sister had a child when she was forty-six.'

What a very unsettling piece of information.

339

Wally is now cooling on the morganatic option herself. At dinner she said, 'Have your bags packed, Maybell. I'm reconsidering plan A.'

November 28, 1936

Cross words between Wally and HM this morning. I heard her say, 'It's a goddamned fiasco! What does Monckton say? Why don't you listen to him?' She was blazing when she came off the telephone. It transpires it's actually too late to withdraw the morganatic idea because it's already been put before the Dominions. That little man Baldwin certainly moves fast when it suits him. She sat for a minute then she said, 'There's nothing left but to disappear.'

I said, 'But Sir will never allow it.'

She said, 'He should have thought of that before he bungled this business with Baldwin. Well, now he'll have to manage without me. We'll go tomorrow, early. But whatever you do don't tell anyone. Not Pips, not Ethel, not anyone.'

She had a headache so went back to bed. I took a turn toward the new rose gardens but soon turned back. There's no place more chilling than a London park in November.

My luncheon soup had just been served when HM arrived. He ran straight up to Wally's bedroom and didn't say a word to me. It was almost two when they came down together, Wally still pale but sporting a new star sapphire pin on her lapel, HM fussing about whether the coast was clear out in the street. He might have thought of that before he left his Daimler standing there for an hour. All Wally said was, 'Maybell, I'm going to the Fort. I'll send for you.'

I said, 'Is it still plan A?' From the way she hushed me I think it is.

David said, 'Hurry along, darling. I want to get you to a place of safety.'

The maids went in Wally's car. Now there's nothing to do but wait.

November 29, 1936

I was woken just after midnight by the sound of breaking glass. The footman found a brick end thrown through the dining-room window. The kitchen maid had hysterics and went home to her people in Hackney still in her nightdress.

Lightfoot drove round immediately to collect me. He believes there's a plot to murder Wally and that I may get blown up by mistake.

November 30, 1936, Wilton Place

The news from the Fort is that Wally is prostrate with sickness of the nerves and is not to be disturbed. HM has had three doctors to see her and they all agree the only thing is for her to rest in a darkened room, so it seems unlikely we'll be traveling for awhile. I've given in to Pips's pleading and am moving to Halkin Street this evening before *I* need three doctors.

Freddie thinks it's all up for Wally, even though Mr Beaverbrook appears to be championing HM and trying to find a solution. He said, 'Beaverbrook's only in it to bait Baldwin. He doesn't give a damn about the King. Well, only in the way one might feel a pang for a cat squashed on the roadside. What Beaverbrook wants is for Baldwin to bungle this and have to resign.'

It's all such a horrid muddle and I must say, some of the blame must rest with Ernest. If he'd kept the situation under control and not allowed Wally to get in too deep, we'd all be able to sleep safe in our beds.

December 1, 1936, Halkin Street

Great excitement last night. The Crystal Palace Pleasure Gardens burned to the ground. The sky was quite red as we went to dinner. They say every hook and ladder was called out, so just as well I hadn't stayed on at Cumberland Terrace waiting to be firebombed on behalf of Wally.

I mentioned to Freddie Wally's idea that HM should speak to the nation by wireless. President Roosevelt's fireside chats have proved very popular and something similar would remind the British public that the King is a man just like themselves. However, Freddie says the King can't just sit in front of a microphone when the urge seizes him. He'd need the Prime Minister's agreement and the Cabinet would want to check in advance that they approved of what he intended saying. Very puzzling. What's the point of the King having a government if he has to go to it, cap in hand, every time he wishes to open his mouth? And I suppose the same would apply to Wally, which leads me to think she might not be so suited to be Queen after all. She'd just come right out with it.

December 2, 1936

Further alarums. Beaverbrook says the British press is about to break their silence on the Wally situation. He says it's already started in the provinces. A North Country cleric made a speech yesterday, questioning whether HM is approaching the coronation with the correct sense of duty, and the local papers reported it. This morning the *Manchester Guardian* has picked up on it and asked if the British public are really willing to accept a divorced American as their Queen?

Well, it had to come out before long and now is as good a time as any. HM has never been more popular.

I'm sure all those dusty little miners will scrape together their farthings to send him a wedding gift. King Edward VIII and the Duchess of Lancaster will be loved and remembered when Stanley Baldwin and the Bishop of Bradford are long forgotten.

Tried to do a little Christmas shopping but it was hard to concentrate and then I found myself having a dizzy spell among the neckties. Wally isn't the only one feeling the strain. One can't be braced for action day after day without the body eventually breaking down. And as sweet as Pips is I think I need to go home, unpack my bags, and sleep in my own bed. We'll look back on this in a few years and laugh at all the fuss and drama.

December 4, 1936, somewhere in France

Yesterday was the longest most extraordinary day.

Hattie Erlanger woke me early to tell me every newspaper had front-page photographs of our cruise on the *Nahlin*, photographs in which Wally had magically appeared. Then Lightfoot called to tell me the Bertie Yorks had cut short their visit to Scotland and were on their way back to London in an absolute fury with HM. He said, 'The fat's well and truly in the fire now, Maybell. It's decision time for HM.'

I no sooner got him off the line when Wally called.

She said, 'It's all over. We'll leave after dark this evening. Bring no more than two valises. A car will collect you at four.'

I said, 'Where are we going?'

'Abroad,' she said. 'You're not to tell anyone, particularly not Violet. This morning I need you to go to Cartier and collect everything of mine they've had for cleaning or remounting, ready or not. Ask for Phillips. He's expecting you.'

343

Pips was very sweet. She promised not to tell anyone else, at least until we were clear away. She said, 'Ignore what Wally said about luggage. Two valises sounds pretty mean to me. She's sure to have at least forty.'

I dropped by the Grosvenor Chapel on my way to see Lightfoot and Doopie. Just sat there awhile. I don't know why. They had all the newspapers at South Audley Street. Lightfoot said Beaverbrook and Harmsworth had written up HM in a very complimentary vein but Wally is going to be harder to sell. He thinks she looks too angular and polished. He said, 'We British like our royalties to have womanly hair and a generous prow, to carry off the regalia. While you're away see if you can't fatten her up a little.'

I said, 'Do you think she'll be coming back to wear the regalia?'

He said, 'Actually, no, I don't.'

Doopie said, 'Where you going, Bayba? Wan Dordie da gum with you?'

Flora was allowed down from her schoolroom but we didn't tell her I was going away. She said, 'Hurrah! Are we going to a Gorner House?'

Doopie said, 'Negs dime, Vora. Negs dime.'

I wish I could have seen Rory too. If we have to stay away until after Wally's divorce we'll miss our pantomime. Passed Gladys Trilling as we turned out of Curzon Street but she didn't see me. All the newspaper placards said the same thing. THE KING AND MRS SIMPSON.

The fog was rolling in by the time I got to the Fort. Wally was very pale and quiet and hardly greeted me. HM was bustling about, full of light chitchat. Perry Brownlow was there. The plan, to catch a ferry boat to France and then drive south to stay with Herman and Kath Rogers. They expect us by Sunday or Monday. Two cars. One for

344

me, the luggage, and Wally's maid. The other for Wally with Perry Brownlow and a Scotland Yard detective named Jimmy. Tea was brought in at five but no one touched it. Wally had her sable on already, anxious to be gone. It was HM who was reluctant to let us leave.

When she went out to the car he said, 'She's everything to me, Maybell. Take care of her. Make sure she eats properly.'

We left the dog behind. HM lifted it up and waved its paw as we pulled away. He looked so lost. He reminded me of how Rory used to look when it was time to go back to school.

I didn't get another opportunity to speak with Wally till we reached our cabin. We were on the ten o'clock sailing from Newhaven. She said all she felt was relief. She's felt in constant danger these past few weeks, from the Palace plotters, from any crazy who got it into his head to remove her from the scene. Even from David. She said, 'He's a weak man ordinarily but he's had such a strong grip lately. They say that about drowning men, don't they? That they can pull a stronger person under.'

Just as well the maid wasn't there to hear that unfortunate comparison. She told me in the car that she's a nervous sailor. She lost a brother at Jutland and her stomach has never been right since Walter Guinness sailed us through that hurricane off Biarritz.

We docked just after midnight and drove to this hotel, God knows where.

Perry B decreed that the drivers had to get a few hours' sleep and Wally seemed happy for him to take charge. She's tired, I suppose. We all are.

Perry says my job is to paint a bright picture of the future and not allow her to dwell on thoughts of HM.

345

But I don't think she is. I think she's completely resigned. HM is the one who's obsessed.

Perry says HM told Wally he'd soon be at her side, but he won't be going anywhere. He's going to be kept busy in England, safe from acts of romantic folly until he's safely crowned. He said, 'If Wally understands that, good. But she may waver, especially if he sends her letters full of wild promises. So you must help me keep her steady. Plan trips. Chat to her about gowns. Encourage her to notice eligible men.'

The sheets are coarse and the pillows are like rocks but Wally is fast asleep.

December 6, 1936, Villa Lou Viei, Cannes

Arrived at the Rogerses' last night after battling with snow-storms and roads without signposts and uncooperative French peasantry. Where Wally and Brownlow are, we have no idea. The decision to travel separately instead of in convoy was taken by Perry when he realized the press were on to us.

That was Wally's fault. She's grown so accustomed to giving orders she's lost all idea of how to be a discreet presence. If she hadn't started complaining the minute she walked through the door I don't suppose the *patron* would have paid us any attention. I don't like to see stale flowers in a hotel lobby myself, but we were only there for the briefest stay *and* we were trying to travel incognito. But Wally started up, a phone call was made, and reporters began to arrive. They set up camp in the parking lot to prevent our slipping away, so Perry decided we had to create a diversion. Wally's maid and I to leave by the front door and take the Buick, while he and Wally slipped out through the kitchens and into our station wagon. I said, 'No one's going to mistake me for Wally, you realize.'

He said, 'Paint on a beauty spot. Wear a headscarf. We have darkness on our side.'

How little men understand of what it is that makes every woman uniquely herself. No cosmetician in the world could turn me into Wally, I'm glad to say. But the press, being simple-minded men, saw me dash for Wally's car and fell for the ruse. They gave chase, and it was only when we had to stop for gas and they saw me with my hair prettily ruffled and the beauty spot wiped away that they realized their error. It was a rather amusing moment.

The weather worsened the farther south we drove. Ladbroke telephoned to the Rogerses' that we shouldn't arrive before midnight and Herman told him the reporters were here too, watching for Wally, so someone has blabbed. It's a pity Wally made enemies of so many of HM's staff. People like that are quick to turn. What Herman had described as 'a small press presence' was at least a hundred, and more have arrived since. I can see them from my window. There are gendarmes down there too, keeping the photographers from mobbing every vehicle that tries to get through to the house.

Herman and Kath have made me as comfortable as they're able considering they're in the middle of refurbishments. Herman says it was the most astonishing phone call he's ever received, HM begging him to take in Wally at short notice. Kath keeps saying, 'It won't suit her. I know Wally. There's brick dust everywhere.' Herman says they had no choice. It was tantamount to a royal command.

HM has been telephoning at all hours, checking to see if Wally has arrived.

Herman said, 'The next thing we know *he'll* be on his way here.'

I said, 'That's not the plan. They're going to keep him in London until he's gotten over her.'

He said, 'Well, I suppose if there's anyone resolute enough to deliver the death blow it's Wally, but I can't imagine anything she could say to him at the moment that would do the trick. The man seems to be out of his mind.'

I hope we're not going to spend the rest of our lives on the run from HM King.

December 7, 1936
Wally and Brownlow arrived last night. By the time they got here there were so many reporters and police outside the gates it looked like an army camp down there, but they didn't get the photograph they'd been waiting for. When the car pulled up outside the house there was no sign of Wally. She was on the floor beside Brownlow's feet, covered in a tartan rug. She thought the whole thing was a great lark and was in very good spirits, until Herman told her HM had been telephoning all day and was likely to ring again at any minute.

She said, 'I'm not speaking to him. Put Maybell on. Maybell, tell him I'm not here yet. Tell him spies are listening in.'

I refused. Kath and I have discussed this and are agreed, Wally is far too free with her orders and now that she's withdrawn from royal circles she'd better accustom herself to behaving like a mere mortal again. So she was left with no choice but to speak with HM and I believe there were tears, at both ends of the line, especially when he put the dog on to say good night.

Kath had put me in the dressing room adjoining Wally's

room. She thought Wally would be glad of my company after the terrors of the journey, but Wally has insisted that Brownlow have the dressing room *and* that he keep the door open. She said, 'I'll sleep better with a man nearby.'

Her last words before she retired were, 'Tell Herman to turn up the furnace. Kath keeps this house so damned cold. And has she got my special soap?'

Herman joked that someone had better warn Kitsie Brownlow about the sleeping arrangements because if Wally's back on the loose Perry's virtue may not be safe. But Wally's not going to be interested in a minor courtier. As a matter of fact, I think she's altogether bored with love.

The news from London is unsettled. Before he turned in, Brownlow spoke to Fruity Metcalfe. The Stock Exchange is jittery and public sympathy seems to be moving away from HM. Fruity says the Socialists are certainly against him. Well, that's no surprise. They're always against everything. Then the Conservatives are against him because of the way he keeps visiting paupers and raising their hopes, and the court wives have let it be known they have no intention of curtsying to a woman who grew up in a boarding house. Which, as Perry says, leaves only the true romantics and perhaps those chafed by the chains of their own imprudent marriage who may be hoping Wally is going to make divorce the latest thing.

December 8, 1936
Wally emerged just before luncheon. She slept through all the ringing of telephones. HM, desperate to talk to her. Fruity, desperate for her *not* to talk to HM. The secretary of the lawyer Goddard, to say he's on his way here. Freddie Crosbie, with bulletins. Also, Daisy Fellowes sent a wire.

She'll be arriving off Cannes tomorrow and has offered to keep her yacht steamed up and ready to whisk Wally away at a moment's notice. I'll bet Hattie put her up to that.

Perry said, 'Let's keep that one up our sleeve. It might provide a useful emergency exit, but we don't want Wally going anywhere else until she's made it clear to the King that they're finished.'

The puzzle is, why is Goddard coming? Wally can offer no explanation.

Herman said, 'You didn't slip any Crown jewels in your bag, did you, Wally? We don't want to get arrested as accessories.'

HM telephoned throughout the afternoon. Wally says she wishes they'd find some extra boxes to keep him occupied.

At dinner Perry floated a new suggestion. He said, 'Wally, if you were to withdraw your divorce action now, wouldn't it send the clearest possible signal to HM that marriage is out of the question?'

She said, 'It should. But it's David. I don't think he'd take any notice. Nothing is going to stop him now.'

It seems to me it's worth a try, if she really wants to disengage herself. But that's the crux of it. I'm not sure she does want to. I never saw her dither like this before. She's said she'll sleep on it. She went to bed as soon as dinner was over, with orders that she wasn't to be disturbed, but she heard the telephone when Fruity called just before midnight and came out in her wrap to find out if there was any news, which there certainly was. HM has begun negotiating for a title and an income in the event of his abdication.

Kath gave her a brandy and soda but she didn't drink it. She just sat twisting the glass round and round.

350

She said, 'You see? This is what I was afraid of. He's only saying these things because I've gone away and left him. Talk to him, Perry. Tell him to stay calm. Tell him I'll wait quietly until after the coronation and so must he.' She started to go back to bed, then she said, 'Tell him I have no interest in being the Queen of Nowhere.'

I stayed down and had a nightcap with Kath. She said, 'She has an escape route staring her in the face. All she has to do is stop the divorce. Why is she hesitating, Maybell? Can it be she actually loves him?'

I think perhaps she does, just a little. And she could still be the Duchess of Lancaster. It surely has to be better than being Mrs Simpson.

December 9, 1936

The lawyer Goddard has arrived, and not alone. He's brought a physician with him because HM is worried Wally's health is breaking down under all this strain. Perry B is livid. He said, 'Just what we need! Five hundred hacks outside the gate watching every move we make and we get a house call from a royal doctor. You realize what everyone's going to think?'

He deputed me and Kath to find out from Wally if she's carrying HM's child. She shrieked with laughter. She said, 'I've got ulcers and palpitations and my hair's falling out, but not that, thankfully. Never that. David isn't heir-conditioned.'

The doctor has prescribed rest and plain food. I think I could have been a doctor.

The purpose of Goddard's visit is rather serious. On Monday afternoon a person in London swore an affidavit that he can show good cause why Wally and Ernest's divorce shouldn't be finalized. He's called a Common

Informer, with the emphasis on 'common', I'm sure. It's just some elderly clerk who has obviously been paid to do it, but Goddard says it places HM in a very dangerous position, the allegation being that Ernest's infidelity was a charade performed to oblige the King.

Herman said, 'Of course, this Common Informer is only saying what everyone has known all along.'

Goddard said, 'He most certainly is not. When His Majesty asked me to advise Mrs Simpson in the matter of a divorce I had absolutely no idea he had in mind to marry her.'

Herman said, 'I see. And would you be uncovering your legal ass too much to advise Mrs Simpson what she should do now?'

Goddard said, 'She could withdraw her application. Or not.'

Wally said, 'It's obvious. I have to call the whole thing off. I'll tell David.'

Perry went with her to the dining room to wait for her call to be put through and we all sat in nerve-stretching tension, but it turned out HM wasn't available and he still wasn't available by the time dinner was over. Wally said, 'I'll do it in the morning. If I tell him at this time of night he'll get drunk.'

Kath said, 'I don't believe I've ever seen David drunk.'

Perry said, 'There was a time when we all drank too much. When we were young.'

Goddard is leaving in the morning with Wally's new instructions. The question now is, how Ernest will take the news. I don't imagine he'll want Wally back when he has Mary Kirk waiting in the wings. In fact, he may absolutely insist on being discovered in adultery and divorced.

Wally said, 'In the morning, Maybell, I want you to go into Nice and buy us tickets to somewhere. China. Anywhere.'

Herman said, 'Do you want to go to China, Maybell?'

I'm not at all sure I do.

Wally was very sharp with him. She said, 'China was the first place that came into my head. We can go anywhere. Maybell knows what to do. And the detective can go with her. He's supposed to have a brain.'

Rain lashing against the windows. I haven't been outside for two whole days.

Letters have begun to arrive. How puzzling people are, to take out their pens and write pages of abuse to a total stranger. We read a few and when the tone of them became clear Herman told his head gardener to take all mail addressed to Wally directly to the incinerator.

December 10, 1936

Everything is falling apart. When Wally finally got through to HM and told him she was stopping her divorce, he said it would make no difference because the papers for his abdication have been drawn up and he intends to follow her to the ends of the earth. 'To the moon!' she said. 'I don't know whether to laugh or cry. He says he'll follow me to the moon if necessary. He's really quite lost his mind.'

Herman and I drove in to Nice and purchased tickets for the overnight train to Brindisi on Saturday. There are plenty of sailings to faraway places from there. There's a boat sailing for Ceylon on Sunday which Herman thinks may fit the bill. Wally took a pill after lunch and slept. News came from London in fits and starts. Sometimes the telephone rang but the line was so bad we couldn't hear anything. It seems the lawyers are arranging the transfer of Balmoral and Sandringham to the Yorks.

HM has agreed to leave Britain for at least two years and in exchange may be allowed to keep Fort Belvedere, except for the lawn-mowing machine, which Bertie York always coveted. Kath said it sounds more like a fire sale than the end of a reign.

HM's new title will be His Royal Highness Prince Edward Duke of Windsor. Herman said, 'So Wally still has the chance to become a Royal Highness. I say, Maybell, if I were you I'd hold off ordering your tropical gear. Ceylon may be off.' As far as I'm concerned it was never really on. Wherever Ceylon is, I'm sure it's inconvenient.

Ernest called, but Wally was still in a drugged sleep so Herman asked me to speak to him. He was very civil.

He said, 'I heard from my lawyer. Will you please tell Wally, I'll do whatever seems best but in the long run I'd still like a divorce. I'm with Mary Kirk now, you know, and I want to be free to marry her. But if it helps Wally to delay things a little, till all this has calmed down, she has my word.'

I said, 'There's talk of going to Ceylon.'

'Is there?' he said. 'Well, I'm sure she'll be a great hit wherever she goes.'

Then Fruity got through to say that the abdication papers had been signed and Baldwin was making a statement to Parliament. Perry sat with his head in his hands after taking that call. He said, 'His Majesty is to make a farewell broadcast to the nation tomorrow evening.'

Except I suppose he won't be HM anymore.

Apparently, he's giving a little dinner tonight. The Erlangers, the Crokers, Fruity and Baba. The old faithfuls. 'The Last Supper,' Perry said.

Wally came down, still groggy from her pill, and took a call from HM. We heard her say, 'But where will you go? You can't come here.'

She put Perry on. She said, 'You talk to him. He says he's going to a hotel in Zurich. He can't go to a hotel. The man is clueless.'

She paced round while Perry was on the phone. He suggested the Westminsters' place in Normandy, or Schloss Pfaffenhof. I heard him say, 'Sir, a private house would be much more suitable.'

It was Herman who thought of the Eugene Rothschilds.

Wally was shouting, 'Tell him the Rothschilds'll have him. Tell him Herman's going to wire them and arrange it. Tell him he absolutely must not come here. And tell him I've gone back to bed.'

Perry looks quite gray. Kath said, 'Does anyone else have the feeling they've slipped through the looking glass? Is this really happening?'

I said, 'It's a pity a sweet little king like David can't be allowed to marry the woman he loves.'

Kath said, 'If you ask me the real pity is that he doesn't love a better woman.'

Herman spoke with Kitty Rothschild. Eugene is away in Paris but she's happy to put Schloss Enzesfeld at HM's disposal, if he doesn't mind sharing it with her. More calls to and from the Fort. It seems there's nothing left to be done. David has given away his throne so he can have Wally but Wally doesn't really want him without his throne.

Herman answered a final call just as I was preparing to come upstairs. He said, 'If you look in on Wally, please tell her Rex Quondam says "sweet dreams".'

I found her on the bed still in her clothes and sobbing

quite pitifully. Such tears. I've never, never known Wally go to bed without putting on a fresh nightgown and having Burke take everything away for brushing and hanging. 'He's ruined everything,' was all she'd say. 'The goddamned fool has ruined everything.'

She was so distressed, I didn't even mention Mr Quondam. Perhaps he'd be willing to go with her to Ceylon. Whoever he is.

December 11, 1936
This has been the saddest day. HM, or HRH as we must now revert to calling him, left Fort Belvedere this afternoon. He went up to Windsor Castle to dine with his mother and his brothers and then made his wireless broadcast from a room in the Augusta Tower. We heard it in Herman's library, relayed by French radio. He said that he had felt unable to do the job of King without the help and support of the woman he loved and so he had been succeeded by his brother, the Duke of York. He didn't actually say Wally's name. He called her 'the other person most nearly concerned'. He said the decision to abdicate was his and his alone and that she had tried to dissuade him from it. Then they played 'God Save the King'. It was all over in five minutes.

I cried and so did Perry and Kath. Wally remained very composed, but I guess she's already done her crying.

Pips called us later. She said everything seemed muffled in London, like after a fall of snow. She said there were crowds outside Buckingham Palace but all very orderly, just standing there, trying to take in the news. Freddie thinks once everyone is over the shock they'll take quite happily to the new management, especially with them having those two little girls. They'll be able to trot them out in pretty little dresses and the newspapers will adore them. This could be a big opportunity for Flora if only she'd stop wearing Rory's old sweaters and learn to get along nicely with the York girls. There must be great excitement at Carlton Gardens today. Violet will be getting her coronet out of storage.

Bertie York is going to be known as King George VI. I wonder what they'll do with all those coronation items they've already had manufactured? They'll have to start over now with new pictures.

The telephone has now fallen silent. I guess HRH must be on his way to the Rothschilds'.

December 12, 1936

The Brindisi train, for which we held tickets, left without us. All the pep seems to have gone out of Wally. She said, 'Maybe I'll go to the Argentine. I know people there. I think I'll talk to David. See what provision has been made for him. I think he'd rather like it there. He likes ranches, and they have good golf there too.'

Herman says she's been doing her math. Wally minus David equals middle-aged outcast living off her capital. Wally plus David equals a title and an income for life. He said, 'I think, Maybell, you may soon be off the hook, Kath and I will be left in peace, and Perry will be able to go home.'

I don't know that it's going to be so simple.

Walter Monckton called this afternoon with a progress report on HRH. He drove with him as far as Portsmouth, saw him aboard the destroyer that was taking him to France, then said goodbye. David is traveling with just one valet, a detective, Joey Legh as equerry, and Wally's dog. Monckton said the final moments were quite heartbreaking.

The royal party, such as it is, should be at Enzesfeld some-time tomorrow.

'Twenty-four hours without pointless phone calls,' was Wally's only comment.

I still can't believe it's over. We all know about revo-lutions and the havoc Communists can wreak but I'd never realized a king can just stop being king.

December 14, 1936

HRH – just when I'd grown accustomed to calling him HM – is now installed at the Rothschilds', but there's already a problem because neither Joey Legh nor the detec-tive nor the valet speak German and Kitty R hasn't trained her servants to understand English. If I married a Rothschild, even a minor one like Eugene, the first thing I'd do is import a smart American staff.

Wally is in a softer mood. Now the throne is well and truly gone I think she's preparing herself to become the Duchess of Windsor. She's certainly told Goddard to go ahead with the application for her divorce to be finalized.

She said, 'I'll take my chances with this Common Informer. I didn't go through the hell of Felixstowe to have some hired monkey deprive me of my divorce. I want it, Ernest wants it, and anyway what can they do to David now? Send a constable to Austria to arrest him?'

Perry B is leaving for Enzesfeld in the morning. Herman drove me and Wally into town to shop for David's Christmas presents. Cigars from me, cashmere sweaters and a possum leather coat with a fur lining from Wally.

More rain. The press are packing up and leaving.

December 18, 1936

A difficult day. Wally is down in the dumps. She says she's committed no crime and yet she's been sentenced to life. She says she felt in constant danger yesterday while we were in town, as though at any moment some mad person might shoot her or throw acid in her face. Of course, if she'd just dress 'down' a little no one would even notice her. So many jewels before luncheon is guaranteed to draw attention.

I said, 'People will soon forget.' Even that was the wrong thing to say.

She said, 'I'm not the kind of woman people forget. Those Yorks are probably planning to have me assassinated.'

Herman said, 'Wally, dearest, if that's what they wanted they'd have had it done while you were handy. I don't think the Yorks would go to the expense of sending an assassin to Cannes.'

She said, 'None of you has any idea. I'm stuck here in this freezing house, weeks and weeks of it stretching before me and at the end of it nothing but uncertainty. It's all very well for you. You can come and go as you please. You can go back to your old lives. But I've given up everything. I'm a prisoner here, and I'm going through absolute hell.'

She slammed the door and went to lie down. Herman slammed another door and went to burn some more of her hate letters. As Kath says, we seem doomed to pay for each of Wally's gayer moments with ten of Lady Macbeth. She said, 'I don't know how you put up with her, Maybell.'

Well, we go back a long way. I'm the sister she never had, and she appreciates me a good deal more than Violet

Melhuish does. And Wally may be going to be the Duchess of Windsor but I still see that desperate little girl from Biddle Street.

Kath says she should look for a house in the new year. She said, 'She needs her own establishment. She's driving all our help to distraction and it's going to be months before she can join David, if that's her plan.'

I said, 'I know. I'll suggest it. Are you worried about a repetition of what happened in Peking?'

She said, 'Nothing happened in Peking. Not that it wasn't offered and not that Herman mightn't have been tempted by a beautiful woman, but Wally had far too much mileage on the clock even then. She was really known as quite an old drab, you know? And that voice! Of course, she's toned it down since she moved to England, but it still reminds me of a buzz saw.'

December 20, 1936

Perry Brownlow is in Enzesfeld and reports that HRH is very happy and optimistic. 'Demob fever', Perry called. That nice young attaché, Forwood, has agreed to act as German-speaking equerry. Wally's happy about the appointment. Perry was supposed to go home directly from Enzesfeld, but he's agreed to make a detour to come back here and deliver Wally's Christmas gifts. Wally tried to winkle out of him what he's bringing but he wouldn't even give her a hint.

December 24, 1936

Perry B got here late last night with a mink cape and a choker of baroque pearls. Wally says the cape is of a rather old-fashioned cut but she'll probably be able to have it remodeled once she gets to Paris.

She gave Perry quite a grilling on the state of negotiations over HRH's money and was far from satisfied with his answers. He said, 'These are complicated affairs, and without precedent, so we must just be patient. His Royal Highness is hardly on the breadline, Wally.'

She said, 'Don't you Wally me. You'll call me "ma'am" from now on.'

We were all speechless. He left for the aerodrome immediately, anxious about getting home for Christmas.

Kath gave her a piece of her mind. She said, 'How could you speak to him like that? Perry's been a tireless friend to you and the most loyal of servants to David.'

Wally said, 'I know that, and he knows I know. But he still better get used to calling me ma'am.'

Kath said, 'Don't you think that's a bit premature? Don't you think you ought to count your friends and your blessings while you're still Wally Simpson?'

Herman said, 'And Perry's borne heaven knows what expenses out of his own pocket.'

Wally said, 'He can afford it. It's only for the time being. David will take care of things when his money comes through.'

I don't know. David doesn't usually take care of anyone except himself and einums meinums.

I hope they'll have patched things up by dinnertime. We're meant to be going to the Palm Beach Casino. Daisy Fellowes is giving a party and the Cavetts will be there.

December 25, 1936

All the church bells were ringing as we drove to the casino last night. It was wonderfully picturesque. I gave Wally a set of silk lingerie bags which are going to be embroidered with her monogram. As she says, whether she becomes the Duchess of Windsor or reverts to Wally Warfield, a W will see her through the rest of her life. She gave me Vetiver cologne and the Rogerses a little silver card tray. I think I remember it from Fort Belvedere, but I'm sure Herman and Kath are thrilled to have it, wherever it came from.

I put a call through to South Audley Street and spoke to Lightfoot. He said things are so calm in London you would never believe how people felt only two weeks ago. He said, 'It's all going to turn out for the best. Bertie York didn't want the job but now he's got it he'll settle down to it.'

He and Flora were about to leave for luncheon at Carlton Gardens. Doopie was with Marina Kent who is expected to give birth today.

He's still talking about volunteering for Spain. I said, 'What about Doopie? You can't get married and then go off fighting other people's wars.'

He said, 'Perhaps she'll volunteer too. I think she'd make rather an angelic nurse, don't you?'

Wally was on the telephone with HRH for more than an hour. The tone seemed to be intimate. Herman says a pearl choker is a well-known aphrodisiac. Tonight to Cap-Ferrat for dinner with a neighbor of the Rogerses who writes books. Mr Maugham. Wally insists that I've heard of him. Apparently, he used to be married to Syrie Maugham but now lives in an unnatural alliance with a secretary from California. Poor Syrie. She was the one who did Pips and Freddie's sitting room in bone and buttermilk. It was considered the height of fashion for about five minutes.

December 26, 1936
Wally says she enjoyed last evening, but I found Willie Maugham rather rude. I asked him all the questions one

knows to ask a writer. Are they at work on their next tome? Where do they find their inspiration? I even offered him some of my own ideas but he didn't thank me for them. And Wally may think he found her very witty but I think his tone was rather mocking. Also the secretary kept interrupting dinner with abrupt entrances and exits and silly remarks to no one in particular. I believe he may have been tight. Not surprising, because the martinis were stiff ones, but still, a secretary should be kept busy at his typewriter. He should have no occasion to go anywhere near the drinks tray.

December 31, 1936
The sun tried its best to break through this morning but Wally's mood is somber. I suppose whether she looks back or ahead she sees nothing but regrets. When I wrote my first entry for this year how little I suspected.

Kath has invited people in for this evening. Her idea is to nip in the bud any talk of going to a casino.

January 1, 1937

Herman and Kath did their very best to keep things gay last evening. Came, Daisy Fellowes, the Bajavidas, the Cavetts, and the Genoas who'd motored in from Menton. But the telephone was brought to Wally during dinner and one couldn't help but hear poor HRH sobbing in faraway Enzesfeld. It was a tricky moment but Wally remained very calm. 'Tomorrow's a new year, darling,' she said, 'and we can attack all these problems with new vigor.'

When the call ended she said, 'He's had too much brandy. No one will have thought to warn Forwood about solitary drinking. I seem to be the only person who takes proper care of him.'

Pips and Freddie are proposing to visit on their way to Chamonix. Kath and Herman say they may take advantage of Wally having new distractions and go away for a few days themselves.

January 4, 1937

Dudley Forwood reports that HRH is suffering from earache. Wally told him to get a doctor sent out from Harley Street but Forwood says that a very good ear doctor from Vienna had made a house call and Kitty Rothschild is personally supervising the treatment he recommended.

Wally said, 'Is she indeed? Well, she'd better not be getting any ideas.'

Kath said, 'What can you mean? Kitty is a happily married woman.'

Wally said, 'Happily married for the *third* time. Who's to say she's not on the lookout for number four? Especially a king.'

Kath said, 'Wally! Aren't you planning to marry for the third time? Anyhow, David's not King anymore and Kitty must be fifty-five if she's a day.'

'All the more dangerous then,' Wally snapped right back. 'The desperate age.'

January 5, 1937

Every time Wally speaks to HRH she questions him about Kitty Rothschild. I had no idea she could be so jealous. She denies it, of course.

She said, 'I'm not jealous. But David's hopelessly weak. Look how he allowed Baldwin to bully him. Look how he allows the Bertie Yorks to dictate to him. Keeping him out of his money. Forbidding the brothers to visit. If Kitty Rothschild decided to seduce him he'd just cave in.'

HRH had been hoping that George Kent or Harry Gloucester might fly over for a weekend, to keep him company, but apparently this has been vetoed from above.

January 8, 1937

Pips and Freddie have arrived like a breath of fresh air. Pips says anyone known still to be a friend of HRH or Wally has been dropped. Daphne Frith cut her in the Army & Navy. Melhuish walked into the Guards' Club, saw Freddie, and walked right out again. And the Perry Brownlows sound to be absolutely finished. I feel so sorry for them, especially her. She didn't do anything. She didn't even know Perry was escorting Wally to France until after we'd set off, but his actions have damned them both. Pips says they may just as well pack up and go to the South Pole.

Wally's been pumping for stories about Elizabeth York. Who's going to be her couturier now she's Queen? Does she still talk about fishing? Will she get her teeth fixed before the coronation?

Pips says she doesn't like to disappoint Wally, but all the signs are that the Yorks are going to be very popular. She said, 'All that talk about David modernizing things. I think the country's relieved. The British don't like modernity. They like squashy old armchairs covered in the same style of chintz their mothers had, and that's exactly the kind of monarchy they're going to get with Elizabeth and Bertie York.'

January 9, 1937

The Rogerses have left for a short holiday at Schloss Pfaffenhof. Kath said, 'Wally's talking about taking a house till her divorce is final. Will you go back to London?'

I said, 'I will if someone spells me as her companion. I promised David I'd look after her.'

Pips said, 'Don't look at me. And I wouldn't oversell yourself as *companion*, Maybell. Frankly, I think she uses you.'

Once upon a time, maybe, but not anymore. I'm her closest friend. People talk about her vivacity, but she's lonely too. She needs someone to confide in. And we do have some laughs. Not recently perhaps, but we will again.

January 10, 1937

Instead of going to Chamonix, Pips is going to stay on here a little longer and Freddie's going to join Fruity Metcalfe's skiing party at Kitzbühel. We girls are going to shop and have a jolly time together. We're going to put this shocking last month behind us.

Dudley Forwood says Kitty Rothschild is going to Paris at the beginning of February and then on to New York, leaving them with sole occupancy of Enzesfeld. Wally won't have to worry about guarding HRH's honor for much longer.

Freddie says he's not surprised to hear the Rothschilds intend spending more time in Paris because Eugene R is a Jew and if Adolf Hitler takes over Austria people of that persuasion can expect the same treatment as their German cousins. Apparently, they're not allowed to sit on park benches and can have their schlosses taken from them at the drop of a hat. I had no idea.

January 13, 1937

Wally is being disagreeable to the Rogerses' staff. She says she's just attempting to bring them up to standard and it's true they are not as efficient as the staff she's been accustomed to in London, but France is a backward country and I'm sure Kath has done the best she can. Anyway, I don't think it's at all right that Wally's having furniture moved and *objets* stored away. It's not as though we've taken a lease here.

Pips said, 'Wally, you have no class. How would you feel if I came for the weekend and started bundling all your horrible embroidered cushions into a closet?'

Wally said, 'I'll never invite you for a weekend. And *I'd* never ask anyone to live with all this oak and pewter. At least my cushions are witty.'

Pips said, 'Well, let's change the drapes while we're about it. And how about knocking down a few walls?'

Wally said, 'Don't think I wouldn't if I had to stay here much longer.'

The main butt of her crossness is HRH. She goes through lists of complaints whenever they talk and she never seems satisfied with the answers. She's made several marks on the dining-room table where she keeps banging with her gold pencil.

This morning we could hear her blessing him out. 'Tell them you'll go back if they don't pay you every cent you're owed. Go anyway. Take the damned crown back. You're such a milksop. Why did you let them push you out? Why didn't you go the people? Those little miners would have defended you. They still would.' She was white with fury when she came off the telephone.

Pips said, 'You're not serious about David going back? That would amount to a revolution.'

Wally said, 'What if it did? We Americans had one and it didn't do us any harm.'

But she isn't truly serious about it, because she's going to marry him and she already told me she has no intention of living in England again. She said, 'They could have had me as Queen. They could have had me as the King's special friend. But nobody gets a second chance with me.'

Pips said, 'Then be careful what you say to him or he may just go and do it.'

Wally said, 'No he won't. He can't organize a tea party without me, let alone a coup. I only say these things to try and put a little fire in his belly. He's up there in that goddamned *schloss*, practicing his putting while the Yorks are taking the bread from his mouth. And he doesn't have anyone there to keep him on track. Legh's a yes man and Forwood doesn't have the confidence. Brownlow might have been more useful but he's gone scurrying back to wifey at the first opportunity. So it falls to me. If I don't nag he's going to end up with nothing.'

As Pips says, 'Oh boy!'

Only a few newspaper stragglers left outside the gates now. The world has forgotten about Wally already, just as I predicted.

January 15, 1937

Drove into Monaco to meet Hattie Erlanger who's in town with Daisy Fellowes. Also came, the Genoas and a little maharaja they have staying with them. Modest losses at roulette. Wally and the Maharaja played chemin de fer. She says she made enough to buy herself a little something. Hattie says the Belchesters have dropped her and Judson and are now sucking up to the New Bunch.

January 18, 1937

Wally spent her casino winnings on a python purse. The Crokers may come for a few days next week. Every little helps.

We drove up into the hills this afternoon and bought honeysuckle scent for a song.

January 20, 1937

Fruity Metcalfe has offered to go up to Enzesfeld when his ski party leaves Kitzbühel and relieve Joey Legh as equerry. HRH is thrilled, which has put Wally's nose out of joint for some odd reason. I heard her say, 'Day after day I try to comfort you and all I hear is what a wretched time you're having of it, but as soon as Metcalfe deigns to pay you a visit you become bright and cheerful. It's pretty insulting.'

January 25, 1937
Pips left this morning just as Boss and Ethel were arriving. As Ethel says, it's like a relay race and Wally is the baton that must not be dropped.

To the Ladybird Club. The Bajavidas are giving a party.

January 26, 1937
Who should turn up with the Bajavidas last night but Fern and Charlie Bedaux. Charlie says his money was still on David for King. He said, 'He'll make a comeback. You'll see.'

Wally said, 'He doesn't want to. He's glad to be out of it. And the New Bunch don't even like him telephoning to offer advice, so to hell with them. He can be the King across the water and have more time for his golf.'

January 27, 1937
Fern Bedaux telephoned this morning. She said, 'I know there are rules about the way these things are broached, but I'm not even sure if David's "royal" anymore. Charlie and I would like to offer Château Candé. Wally can stay there till her divorce is through and then, if they want to, she and David can be married there. Kath and Herman are sweeties but I really don't think you can perch there for months. Will you put it to Wally, or David, or whoever? I can have Candé ready in two weeks.'

Wally accepted immediately. Once she's settled at Candé I think I'll go back to London for awhile. See whether there's anything of my life to pick up.

January 28, 1937

Dudley Forwood has warned HRH against accepting offers from Charlie Bedaux. He says certain adverse reports exist in which Charlie's name appears. Adverse reports! The British hate a self-made man, of course. They don't want to know you unless you have a bed King Charles slept in and a family tree that goes back to the year dot. Anyhow, Wally has already accepted, and I don't see it's anyone else's business.

January 29, 1937

Shopping. Wally bought a silver-fox coat and a gray crepe day dress with little mirror buttons. Blue skies and sunshine. We sat out on the *quai*, had champagne and shrimp, and talked about the great turnaround of the past year.

I said, 'You know, there was a time when I thought you didn't want to marry David.'

She said, 'I never looked for it. I never meant for all this to happen, but then the King went and died on us. I blame myself in many ways. I should have realized David's judgment wasn't to be relied on. But what's done is done. Now I'm going to make lovely homes for him and take care of him. He's not difficult to manage after all, and quite presentable. I think we'll do very well.'

I said, 'I thought I might go back to London. See a few people. You'll have Fern for company at Candé.'

She said, 'Yes, why don't you. You've been a brick, Maybell. A true friend. But don't be gone for long. We're going to have a royal wedding to organize!'

February 2, 1937

A call from Dudley Forwood, who asked for me. He said, 'It's rather delicate, Mrs Brumby. Baroness Rothschild left for Paris yesterday and I'm afraid His Royal Highness has caused her great offense. First of all, he didn't get out of bed to say goodbye to her. But what concerns me more, he didn't tip any of her departing staff and they'd looked after him exceptionally well. I wondered if Mrs Simpson could bring her influence to bear? Perhaps get His Royal Highness to write the Baroness a little note? I wondered if you could mention it? Also, there's the question of ongoing expenses. The Baron and Baroness have been very generous, but they're not *that* kind of Rothschild, you understand? The telephone bills alone are terrifying. I think a word from the right quarter might encourage more consideration.'

I said, 'Why don't you speak to Mrs Simpson yourself?'

He said, 'I very much doubt she'd listen as patiently as you have.'

Wally said, 'How petty. Telephone bills! Well, I'm not bothering David with a thing like that. He has quite enough to do battling with the New Bunch for his dues. Let Metcalfe deal with it, and the tipping. Let him earn his keep.'

Hattie has arrived.

February 4, 1937
HRH's sister, the Princess Royal, is going to Enzesfeld to visit him this weekend. Wally says this may be a positive sign. It may mean that Baldwin has at last loosened the purse strings and agreed an allowance. She says Bertie York is too stiff-necked to let George Kent or Harry Gloucester bring David the good news but probably feels it's all right to allow the sister.

Hattie said, 'David must be so happy. He adores his sister.'

I said, 'I met her once, at Violet's.'

Wally said, 'Well, I never met her and never wanted to.'

February 6, 1937

HRH is in the doghouse. He went into Vienna to meet his sister and her husband and discovered that instead of bringing good news they brought bad. He's to receive no monies from the Civil List. Not a dime. This means that all he'll have is a pittance from the sale of Sandringham and Balmoral, out of which he'll have to pay pensions to old retainers who will, as Wally says, all live to be a hundred. So effectively, he's going to be living on his meager capital. Poor HRH, literally. And poor Wally. This is not at all what she'd been led to expect.

She said, 'He's taking it lying down of course. No spine. And as if that's not bad enough, he's offered to give them a day of his time and show them around the Schonbrunn while they're in town. I told him, he'd better charge them. He'd better tell them that's what he has to do for a living now those ingrates have cut him off without a penny. A king giving guided tours! What a shabby outfit England has become. *And* he treated them to lunch at the Bristol.'

Hattie says she doubts HRH has ever treated anyone to lunch in his life. She predicts that Fruity will have had to put his hand in his pocket.

It's all a gruesome mess. At this rate I can quite see the wedding not coming off.

February 9, 1937

Georgie Kent is now going to visit Enzesfeld after all, but without his wife. She's only just out of childbed. Wally's hoping it means Baldwin has had second thoughts about HRH's money. Hattie says there's been a rumor circulating ever since the abdication that HRH walked off with some very particular emeralds, formerly the property of his grandmother, so it could be Kent is being sent to retrieve them.

Wally said, 'David took no jewels. He left in the clothes he stood up in. I wish he had taken them. They'd look a damned sight better on me than on that little Scotch dumpling they have for a queen now.'

February 12, 1937, Château Candé, Tours
Fern and Charlie's chateau is exquisite. We arrived just after a shower of rain and the pines along the driveway smelled wonderfully refreshing. There is a first-rate American furnace keeping the place warm and an army of properly trained staff. The crystal and plate are all of the highest quality, the flowers are perfectly arranged, and Fern Bedaux has even given up her own room, so Wally is happy at last.

Hattie and I can leave her without a backward glance.

February 15, 1937, Wilton Place
It feels unreal to be here. Every pillow and powder bowl exactly as I left it, when so much else has changed. Two letters from Randolph Putnam, the first written while HM was still HM, the second wondering whether 'the strawberry-blonde companion of the exiled King's moll' could possibly be me!

No one at home at South Audley Street or at Carlton Gardens. Bumped into Penelope Blythe in Piccadilly and she suggested lunch, but at some little hole in the wall in Chelsea. She said she had a portrait sitting at two so it would be more convenient, but I guess she didn't want to risk anyone connected with the New Bunch seeing us together. She even insisted on going Dutch for lunch, drawing a certain line between us, I suppose.

She said, 'I do feel sorry for you, Maybell. After all, anyone can back the wrong horse.'

I said, 'It all depends whether you think it was a fairly run race, and I don't. I feel HRH is being treated very badly.'

She said, 'But he was the one who started it. This is England, you know. In this country when a king takes on Parliament, Parliament wins, thank God. Well, now he's ruined. Wally Simpson's best plan would be to go to Australia and hope to meet someone with money.'

I was never especially fond of Penelope.

February 16, 1937

Violet appeared just as I was about to go up for my bath. She said, 'So? Back with your tail between your legs?'

I said, 'No. I'm here to see my London friends, but not for long. I'll be going back to France, to help Wally plan her wedding.'

'Ah,' she said, 'the blushing bride. Again. Just as well you're not staying long. I must ask you not to come to the house. Melhuish has been rocked by recent events. I won't have him upset.'

I said, 'But he always reckoned Bertie York would make a better King. Surely he's happy the way things have turned out?'

She said, 'You misremember, Maybell. He never reckoned any such thing. Melhuish was always loyalty itself to Wales. He'll never forgive him for what he's done. Queen Mary is heartbroken. And the poor Yorks. Their lives will never be the same.'

I said, 'Well, HRH isn't having such a wonderful time of it. He's stuck on a mountainside in Austria and having to count every cent.'

She said, 'He gets no sympathy from me. Nothing has happened to him that he didn't bring on himself. I've come only to tell you that Doopie and Flora are at Carlton Gardens. You'll find no one at South Audley Street. Lightfoot has gone to Paris to volunteer for Spain.'

We must have passed each other in transit.

I said, 'So how am I supposed to see my sister and my niece if I'm not allowed across your threshold?'

She said, 'You should have thought of that before you threw in your lot with that woman. I rue the day you ever took up with her again.'

February 17, 1937
Intercepted Doopie and Flora at Duck Island. Flora was so excited to see me. She said, 'Aunt Bayba! You've been even badder than me! Ulick says we're not obliged to know you anymore but Rory and I still love you.'

Doopie smiled. She said, 'Done worry. Zoon be vagodden.'

I said, 'And what does Lightfoot think he's doing, volunteering for wars? Why did you let him go?'

Flora said, 'But it's exciting. I wish we could go.'

Doopie said, 'Baps we will, iv it's a log war.'

If Violet heard that kind of talk Flora would be back at St Audrey's under lock and key. But she won't hear it from me.

To the Crosbies' for dinner. I said, 'Shall I wear a wig and come to the tradesmen's entrance? I don't want to ruin your standing in London.'

Pips said, 'You can come in a grass skirt for all the

difference it'd make to us. We don't have any standing. Never did have.'

February 18, 1937
Pips has started wearing pants. *Très* chic. Of course, she has no BTM.

Freddie says Fort Belvedere is closed up and HRH's things have been taken to Frogmore for storing. All he took with him to Enzesfeld were twenty-six suits and his photographs of Wally. Perry Brownlow continues to be treated disgracefully. He's been sacked as Lord-in-Waiting to the new King for no reason except he was loyal and obedient to the last one. Damned if he did, damned if he didn't.

Lunch today with Ida Coote. She at least is willing to be seen with me at the Dorch if there's a free meal on offer. She says London is changed. She went to Ciro's the other night and didn't see anyone she knew. She's thinking of volunteering for Spain like Lightfoot. She has no nursing experience but believes there may be a need for concert parties. Everyone seems to have Spain fever.

I've decided to pay a visit to Eton College on Sunday. Violet may have banned me from Carlton Gardens but I don't believe she said anything about visiting Rory at his school.

February 19, 1937
Rory's Housemaster was charming when I telephoned. He said Melhuish Minor would be delighted to see me after chapel on Sunday. He said, 'Unfortunately, Melhuish Major will be in Snowdonia for Cadet Force exercises.'

Good. An unsought bonus. To a wonderful little shop

behind the Strand for a ghost tube and a selection of magician's silks.

February 21, 1937

The familiar road to Windsor and yet it seemed like a lifetime ago. I had Kettle drive me up to the Fort before we continued on to Eton. It was as Freddie said. Everything closed up, and the gardens looked so sad and wintery. There'll be no more gay chicken fries there I'm sure.

Rory tells me he is now five feet eight and a half inches tall. He said, 'It was pretty plucky your coming here. Ulick says we should have nothing more to do with you. Ulick thinks kings who abdicate should be strapped across a gun carriage and flogged and their friends should be sent to Coventry.'

I said, 'And what do you think?'

He said, 'I don't agree. Not if it's an aunt, because family is family. And not if it's a lady, because ladies should never be blamed for their errors.'

We went to the Nook Tea Rooms for cream buns and he tried out the ghost tube. He said it was highly excellent. He asked in a whisper about Wally.

I said, 'She's going to marry the King.'

He said, 'You mean the Duke of Windsor. We've got a new king now.'

He says he likes school except for the canings. I said, 'But why do they cane you? Have you been a naughty boy?'

He said, 'Not naughty exactly. I forgot to light my fagmaster's fire. I forgot twice actually, but he let me off for my first offense.'

I said, 'Does your mother know you're being beaten?'

'Of course,' he said. 'Melhuishes have always taken

their beatings. And I expect in the future I'll be grateful for it.'

He tried his trick cigarette pack on the people at the next table. People fall for it every time.

February 22, 1937

Such a horrid day. First Elspeth Laird accosted me as I was leaving Derry & Toms. 'People like you,' she said, 'are a stain on decent society. That woman has as good as killed Queen Mary, and you, you! You're shortening my brother's life with your scandalous associations.'

Completely unfair. If anything is shortening Melhuish's life it's all the Stilton cheese he eats.

Then Gladys Trilling was ushered to the chair next to me at Monsieur Jules while I was being curled, and asked very loudly to be seated elsewhere. When I think of the hospitality HRH lavished on them. I hope Whitlow Trilling gets posted to Mumbo Jumbo Land and Gladys's one and only evening gown grows mildew.

Then when I got home Violet was waiting here, pacing the floor. She didn't even wait for me to take off my hat. How dare I sneak off to see Rory expressly against Melhuish's wishes, how dare I discuss That Woman with an innocent boy, how dare I taint the Melhuish name with my infamous connection.

I said, 'You only forbade me to come to your house. You never mentioned school. And Rory was delighted to see me.'

She said, 'Rory isn't there to be delighted. He's there to make the right kind of friends, although heaven knows what harm your turning up has done him. And the consequences are even worse for Ulick.'

I said, 'I didn't even see Ulick.'

She said, 'That's not the point. One of the Belchester boys saw you. It's all over the school that Mrs Simpson's best friend visited Rory Melhuish. Ulick's hoping for Sandhurst next year and this is the kind of thing that will follow him around. You're so selfish, Maybell. You expect to swan about with Wales and his crowd without paying a price. You and Wally thought it great fun to run away and topple a crown and leave others to pick it up and try to repair the damage. And now you walk back into our lives as though nothing happened. Well, no more. I forbid you to have any contact with any of my children anywhere. And don't get tricky with me. I'm having Duck Island watched.'

So. Penelope Blythe will only meet me incognito in Chelsea, Gladys Trilling refuses to be dried in the chair next to mine, Elspeth Laird believes I'm killing the Queen, and I'm cut off from my kith and kin. Pips says I should think of it as liberation. She said, 'Melhuish and Violet will mellow. In the meanwhile, think of the gains. No more of Gladys's baby pictures to admire. No more of Violet's poached salmon.'

But it's easy for her to say. She has Freddie. They're very jolly together in their own impecunious way. I'm alone. I think I may return to France. There's not much reason to stay in London.

February 28, 1937

Spoke with Randolph Putnam. He said, 'Why don't you give that place up? Seems to me it's a waste of good money. I've called you every week since Thanksgiving and you're never there.'

He said someone has bought the house the Warfields had on Biddle Street, planning to open it as a museum and charge people to see Wally's old bedroom. He rather wishes he'd thought of it himself.

March 2, 1937
An excited phone call from Wally. The Common Informer has withdrawn his allegations. She has no more idea why he stopped the action than she does why he started it but whoever put him up to it has clearly had second thoughts.

She said, 'It doesn't matter. I'm in a forgiving mood. In six weeks I'll be a free woman and then David and I are going to be married. I need you here, Maybell. There are a thousand and one things to do.'

Pips very caustic at lunch. She said, 'A thousand and one things to pay for, more likely.'

I said, 'Well, call me a softie, but when I hear the sound of wedding bells . . .'

'Wedding bells!' she said. 'I hear the ringing of cash registers. Be careful you don't end up paying for the whole bang shoot, Maybell. You're such a softie.'

I don't care. What am I supposed to do? Go back to Baltimore to be gloated over by Nora Sedley Cordle? Stay in London to be pilloried outside Derry & Toms? I may as well go where my money and I are appreciated. Besides, I'm not rushing back the instant Wally snaps her fingers. First, I'm going to Paris to visit with Ena Spain. I leave on tomorrow's lunchtime sailing from Newhaven.

March 6, 1937, Hôtel Meurice, Paris
Ena Spain is good company. Unlike Wally she doesn't race from shop to shop and skip lunch. Of course, she was raised the old-fashioned way. In the morning she writes letters, in the afternoon we go out for a little fresh air, whatever the weather, then take tea. Ena thinks the

positions people are taking up in London are so much hypocrisy. She says the old King used to tell anyone who'd listen that he hoped Bertie York would get the throne. She says he never liked David. She says actually he didn't really like any of his children except the girl, who could do no wrong.

The Yorks' coronation is somewhat on her mind at present. She'll have to be in her seat by nine o'clock and then have to sit for hours without being able to powder her nose. It's all right for the men. They can secrete comfort bottles under their robes, but the women just have to suffer. It's amazing to think that an establishment like Westminster Abbey doesn't have restrooms. That's something Wally would have had corrected before any coronation of hers.

March 9, 1937

Ena and I have had an adventure. We rode on the Métropolitain underground railway from rue de Rivoli to the Tuileries Gardens and back again. You purchase a ticket and climb aboard and you have no way of knowing who you may find sitting next to you. Rattling along beneath the streets in the company of total strangers! Ena has done it several times before. She says once you have lost a child nothing holds any fears for you.

Tea in the Winter Garden. I sometimes think I could happily give up luncheons and dinners and live on tea and cake.

Friday, to Candé.

March 13, 1937, Château Candé

The chateau is an absolute spring picture. Miniature jonquils, crocuses, the last of the snowdrops. Wally is looking much more relaxed. I believe she's gained a few pounds. She's decided she doesn't want a May wedding because May is unlucky and also the attention of the world will be on the coronation. It looks like June 3.

Fern's worried she's tempting fate by making plans before the divorce is definite but Wally says it's a risk she has to take, otherwise there isn't a hope of her trousseau being ready in time. She's already talked to Main Bocher about her gown. On Tuesday a *vendeuse* is coming from Schiaparelli and on Wednesday a little woman from Reboux to talk about hats. Wally's already filled several notebooks with lists. She says she's going to make a perfect wedding for David.

Dudley Forwood is leaving the diplomatic corps to become a full-time equerry to HRH. Wally says he'll do nicely once she's trained him.

March 16, 1937

A most productive day. Wally is never more decisive than when she's buying clothes. She's ordered five of the nip-waisted wool day dresses, one in each color, some good basic knitwear, edge-to-edge cardigans, evening sweaters decorated with fringing and marquises, and then some wittier outfits. A sealskin suit with a matching Tyrolean hat, a Rhodophane evening coat, and a wonderful scarlet cocktail gown with tiny buttons like little holly berries. Main Bocher is bringing his wedding dress drawings on Friday and staying overnight.

There's a flap on though, because Wally has mislaid her birth certificate. She's sent a wire to her Aunt Bessie Merryman in Baltimore, but I don't suppose there's anything she can do about it.

March 17, 1937
Pips called. She said, 'Lost her birth certificate my eye. I'll bet she's lied to HRH about her age.'

March 21, 1937
Wally has chosen gray blue for her wedding outfit, ankle-length bias-cut satin crepe with a little box-shouldered jacket, pin-tucked to show off her tiny waist. Main Bocher is delirious about being chosen to make the wedding gown of the year. He flitted around with fabric samples, lavishing compliments on Wally's bony line. For me he's proposed orchid silk with butterfly-wing sleeves. Perfect for a chateau garden in June.

HRH is leaving Enzesfeld at the end of the week. Without the Rothschild staff the *schloss* has become very inconvenient to manage, so Forwood has found a secluded guesthouse in St Wolfgang. I suggested Wally organize a little gift for Kitty R, to say thank you and goodbye, but she didn't respond.

Perhaps Fruity will think to organize something.

March 22, 1937
Wally now has a very positive attitude to the future. She said, 'I know I'm not beautiful and David's not the sharpest item in the knife box, but we make a good team. The world had better watch out. Especially those Yorks. They may have the throne but once David and I are established we'll give them a run for their money. *We'll* be the ones people talk about.'

She's bought some colored pencils and begun sketching designs for their servants' livery. They'll have a house in Paris and then a place in the country or maybe something near Cannes, a place to relax away from the pressures of being the Windsors. Fern Bedaux has her people looking out for suitable properties.

Wally says HRH is like a lost puppy without her. Wally always had a strange fondness for little dogs. She's so fastidious in every other respect but it amuses her when they tinkle on the rugs and leave their teeth marks on the chair legs.

A courier just arrived from Enzesfeld with this week's love token. A corsage of knotted gold chains. The note says, *Darling, this is a double half hitch. A knot that holds fast however great the storm.*

March 26, 1937
A miracle. Wally's Aunt Bessie has managed to track down the doctor who attended at Wally's birth and he's agreed to swear an affidavit. It should serve in place of the lost birth certificate. HRH is now installed at St Wolfgang and Dickie Mountbatten is traveling there tomorrow to pay him a visit. We're hoping he's taking with him better news about money.

March 28, 1937
Mountbatten arrived at St Wolfgang empty-handed. A social call, he said. He wanted to offer himself as HRH's best man, but apparently a royal bridegroom doesn't have a best man. Wally said, 'Princes have supporters, as Dickie Mountbatten well knows, and David intends to follow tradition.'

We don't expect the Yorks to attend. They'd only sour the happy occasion, so let them stand on their dignity and stay away. But we do hope George Kent and Harry Gloucester will come, and perhaps the sister. There's even room here for them to land their airplane.

Dudley Forwood is still nagging about us using Candé for the wedding. He says Charlie Bedaux has dubious friends and fingers in suspicious pies. He's only been a proper equerry for five minutes but he's already getting above himself. Anyway, the wedding has to be here now. Wally's chosen the color of her gown to tone with the silk on the walls in the salon. She's blooming. Like a true bride.

Sunday to the Rogerses' for two nights. We have houses to view. Possible future residences for the Duke and Duchess of Windsor!

April 5, 1937, Villa Lou Viei
We've looked at properties from Théoule all the way to Nice and my head is spinning. The favorite so far is Château La Croe in Cap d'Antibes. Herman thinks it looks like a beached ocean liner. Wally says if she takes it, it'll not only *look* like a liner, it'll be run like one, with constant hot water, and staff who know how to mix martinis. Herman said, 'Ah! You mean unlike our poor, leaking ship of fools.'

La Croe's situation is very lovely, though I'm not sure I'd want Willie Maugham as a neighbor. He's rude and difficult and as he's had to turn to scribbling one presumes he wasn't a good doctor. Struck off, probably.

April 8, 1937, Château Candé
Wally's little terrier is dead. We got back here this afternoon, he went gamboling into long grass and was bitten by a snake. She's inconsolable.

I feel badly now that I complained about him so.

April 9, 1937
A letter from Pips. Freddie says HRH is in for an almighty shock if he thinks he can have a royal wedding. He predicts

the only royal thing about it will be the frosting on the cake. *What cleric is going to be willing to do the marrying for them?* she writes.

Well, we haven't gotten around to things like that, but the one thing the world will never be short of is priests. Anyway, now is certainly not the time to ask. Wally's visited Mr Loo's grave three times today.

April 12, 1937
Wally has picked up her wedding lists again, even though, as she says, the principal guest is dead. She says they don't need a clergyman. She says the local mayor will do everything.

April 13, 1937
HRH says he very much wishes to have a church wedding. He's getting Forwood to organize the English vicar from Vienna. Wally says if it makes HRH happy she has no objections. The only question is, if there are to be two ceremonies should there be two wedding gowns? Fern has a pretty little painted cabinet in the drawing room which turns out to contain a harmonium, so we'll even be able to have the Wedding March!

Wally's still hesitating about La Croe. It does need improvements and HRH's budget is still far from clear.

April 14, 1937
Wally has *two* new doggies. One from HRH, bought in St Wolfgang, and another from Fern, which is to be named Pookie. Poopie, more like. Wally hasn't let it out of her sight all day and screams at anyone who leaves an outer door open.

Some good news. The New Bunch have at last agreed

to pay HRH a pension. I should think so too, after everything he's done for that country. Fighting in its army. Smiling and nodding his way around those endless factories. Wally says she can now get to work creating a suitably royal ambience for their life together.

April 18, 1937
The Archbishop of Canterbury has forbidden the vicar of Vienna to marry any divorced person. I question why the Archbishop was even consulted on the matter. Everyone knows he's an avowed enemy of Wally and David. Well, it's the Vienna man's loss, not theirs. There must be plenty of vicars in England who'd give anything for a free jaunt to France and the honor of marrying the former King.

HRH has toothache. Gown fittings on Tuesday.

Particulars keep arriving of Paris houses but so far nothing seems suitable. Wally says she has to consider appropriateness as well as security. She said, 'Royal Highnesses can't live in a walk-up. They can't have an address on any grubby little street.'

They can always keep a suite at the Meurice until the right house turns up. There's a lot to be said for a good hotel. I'm thinking I may take Randolph Putnam's advice and let Wilton Place go. Claridge's has always taken good care of me.

April 20, 1937
My gown is looking wonderful. Still undecided between raspberry straw or moss green for my pillbox.

Wally said, 'Don't fuss so. The cameras are going to be on me, not you.'

Perhaps so, but that doesn't mean I should attend her wedding dressed in a feed sack.

Herman and Kath have invited me to go with them to Italy after the wedding. I'd been thinking of going back to London, packing up Wilton Place, but Kath has persuaded me. She said, 'Italy first, then chores. We all need to remind ourselves there's such a thing as Life After Wally's Wedding.'

April 27, 1937
We are almost through our ordeal. Wally's lawyer expects her case to be considered on either Friday or Monday. In anticipation, HRH has chosen the first stop on their honeymoon, an Austrian schloss. It's called Wasserleonburg and is owned by Count Munster. He used to be a friend of Melhuish and the Yorks, but he now seems to be nailing Windsor colors very prominently to his mast. The schloss has a swimming pool and a golf course nearby and Munster has even offered to have the tennis courts resurfaced.

April 30, 1937
Lily Drax-Pfaffenhof knows Wasserleonburg.
She said, 'Wally, it's on the top of a mountain. You'll never get down to do any shopping. Tell him you want to go to Capri.'
Wally says it wouldn't have been her destination of choice but she's going to let David have his way. It's his first honeymoon after all.

May 1, 1937
Charlie Bedaux is home. He said, 'Can't have His Highness arriving without a proper welcome from his host.'
Wally slightly miffed. I believe she's grown to consider Château Candé as her own. She was looking forward to

playing the grand chatelaine, with Fern discreetly in the background, but Charlie doesn't know the meaning of 'background'.

May 2, 1937

Charlie gave me a golfing lesson. He says my style is 'wristy', which sounds like a very desirable quality.

Charlie says the New Bunch at Buckingham Palace show no interest in using HRH's talents and experience so he intends stepping into the breach. 'Like a dad,' he said. 'Or a big brother. That's what the kid needs.'

I said, 'Hardly a kid. He's forty-two.'

He said, 'Maybe so but he still seems like a kid to me. And I'm going to give him a bit of fatherly direction. Foreign visits. I'm gonna send him to Germany. Sweden. The States. People love a royal visit. I tell you something, Maybell. He may be an ex-king but he's far from finished. And Wally's a real asset. She's got the right instincts and I've got the useful contacts. Between us we're going to get him back into the swing.'

May 3, 1937

Wally's divorce was made final this morning and HRH is already on his way here. Fruity is returning to London till the wedding so there'll just be Forwood, a valet, and a detective. Their train should get to Verneuil by early tomorrow. Wally's sending the Buick and a station wagon to meet him.

I said, 'You're sending a car? Don't you want to meet him yourself?'

She said, 'No. After all we've been through, I don't want to meet him at some hayseed railroad station.'

She's nervous, I think. After all, in a separation of five

months all kinds of changes can occur. I'd say Wally is certainly more in love than she was in December. I just hope HRH is as ardent as ever.

May 5, 1937
HRH *is* as ardent as ever. I watched from an upstairs window as he emerged from the car. He fairly sprinted up the steps to embrace Wally. It was rather a shy embrace considering he gave up a throne for it, but I like to see physical reticence in a man. Philip Sassoon may be a turncoat but I will say this much for him: he never pressed for anything more than a kiss on the hand and even then was restrained enough not to make contact.

Quite a crowd had gathered outside the gates to see HRH arrive and several of the maids were watching from a landing window, till the major-domo hauled them back downstairs to be on parade. Charlie greeted David American-style, Fern curtsied, and by the time they all trooped through the front hall Wally had already gained a bouquet of edelweiss and a gold bangle. HRH was delighted to see me. He's thinner.

May 6, 1937
The wedding date is now firmly fixed for June 3 and Planning Headquarters have been set up in Charlie's den. Fern and I expected to spend the day sending out invitations but only Wally's Aunt Bessie is to get anything in writing. HRH says we can circulate the date by word of mouth and then it's up to people to propose themselves as guests. I suppose this is another of those royal wedding customs.

Wally has a new engagement ring and is radiant. She

always felt the emerald had been selected with undue haste and is much better pleased with this sapphire.

HRH has asked to see me privately tomorrow morning. I expect he's eager to settle Wally's expenses over these many months. I think, too, I may be offered an official position in the new household. Lady-in-waiting, perhaps. He's presented the Bedauxs with a cuckoo clock, as thanks for the use of the chateau. I wonder whether Kitty R ever got anything for her trouble.

A new wireless was delivered today, to ensure good reception of a certain event in London next Wednesday, an event I'd have thought we'd all be happy to ignore.

May 7, 1937

I was fully an hour with HRH who is completely recovered from his long journey and bouncing with energy. He said he was fully cognizant of the debt of gratitude he owed me, for remaining staunchly at Wally's side while others ratted on her, right and left. He presented me with a set of painted wooden spoons which are apparently a very popular item in Tyrolean kitchens. He wanted to know whether London is still talking about him.

I said, 'Sir, London will never forget you.'

He said, 'I'm jolly glad to hear it. Not that I miss it one iota. Now on to business. I notice you're not yet in the habit of curtsying to Wally. Well, in less than a month she will be a royal duchess, so I must insist that you accustom yourself to correct behavior without delay. Others who aren't certain of protocol will be watching you and following your lead. You have an important role to play.'

It's going to feel very odd, curtsying to a girl from Biddle

Street. I shall have to ease myself into it. Heavens, even Ena Spain doesn't expect curtsies from me anymore.

I asked whether I'd have any other role. He said, 'Yes. I want you to continue as before, doing those little things that relieve einums meinums of at least some of her worries. And you know, Maybell, you will always be welcome in our homes.' So, effectively, lady-in-waiting!

It seemed an opportune moment to bring up the subject of some accounts that are overdue.

He said, 'These dressmakers won't expect to be paid. They only send in their bills to satisfy their accountants. Don't give it another thought. Dressing Wally is a huge honor for these Johnnies, and of course, in the long run they're going to benefit enormously from the connection. In fact, it seems to me that if any money is to change hands it should be them paying us.'

He said he had planned to wear his Welsh Guards uniform on his wedding day but it transpires he's no longer their colonel-in-chief. The small print of abdications!

May 11, 1937
The wedding date has been announced to the press. Tomorrow is coronation day. How far away London seems. Tried to put a call through for news of Lightfoot but couldn't get a connection.

May 12, 1937
The Yorks were crowned this morning. King George VI and Queen Elizabeth. We listened to Bertie York's coronation broadcast on Charlie's new wireless. A very labored affair. He isn't a natural speaker. Heavy rain here and in London too according to Pips, who called this evening. She said everyone at the Abbey sparkled, even Violet,

whom she'd spotted sitting between Ettie Desborough and Anne Belchester, but Loelia Westminster had stolen the show with her rubies. She said everything ran like clockwork until after the royalties had processed out. Then it developed into a robed free-for-all and Tommy Minskip complained that Baron Hulver had pushed his way out to the conveniences ahead of all the viscounts. I expect he was in a hurry to get back to Yorkshire for the Battle of Waterloo.

She said Freddie hopes to be offered a peerage before the next coronation because you get a better seat.

HRH is knitting a sweater for Wally, 'to match her beautiful eyes,' he says.

May 14, 1937

I was worried that the arrival of the British newspapers might cast a pall, but Wally has greatly enjoyed the coronation photographs. She's gone over them and over them. She describes Bertie York as looking like a rabbit caught in someone's headlights and his wife like a little roly-poly cook. Bunny and Cook!

She said, 'I'm glad it's done. Now all that's out of the way *we're* going to show the world how these things should really be done.'

Only three weeks to go and Forwood still hasn't managed to find a clergyman. They all seem to be yes men to the Archbishop of Canterbury, all too frightened of hazarding future preferments.

May 17, 1937

A letter from Ernest in today's post, wishing Wally all the very best in her new life and informing her that he and Mary Kirk hope to marry before the end of the year too.

Funny the way things turn out. We all made our debut the same year, me, Wally, Pips, Violet, Mary. Now Wally's going to a Royal Highness and Mary gets Ernest as a consolation prize.

He wrote that he deplored the way she'd been made the target of so much ill feeling in Britain and hoped she'd found the happiness she deserved with 'her princely Peter Pan'. I thought it was rather sweet, but HRH was fuming when he read it. I think it was the Peter Pan bit he didn't like. He's asked me to retrieve the letter from Wally's room and destroy it. Wally says she's torn it up already but I'm not sure I believe her.

The Dickie Mountbattens will not be coming to the wedding. Neither will the Princess Royal.

May 19, 1937
Not a single member of HRH's family will be at the wedding. At the very least they might have sent Harry Gloucester. Wally says she couldn't care less. 'Bunny and Cook got at them,' she said. 'And there's not one of them with enough spunk to defy them.'

Then we heard that the mayor expects Wally and David to go down to the town hall, like ordinary people. HRH got on to the British Ambassador immediately. He's insisting on a house call. They can't possibly be expected to trail down there and get jostled and gawked at and photographed by all and sundry. Mr Cecil Beaton is coming to do the wedding portraits and absolutely no one else.

May 20, 1937
A breakthrough. A vicar has written offering to officiate at the wedding, for the usual fee plus travel expenses. Dudley Forwood is investigating his bona fides.

The Crosbies and Lily Drax-Pfaffenhof have proposed themselves but the Perry Brownlows find themselves already engaged for June 3. Pips says it isn't to be wondered. They've taken such punishment from the coterie around the New Bunch. All the more reason, I'd have thought, to remain firmly in HRH's camp. Fruity Metcalfe will be HRH's supporter. I'm to be matron of honour.

May 24, 1937
The plucky Reverend Jardine has been hired to perform the wedding ceremony. He told Forwood he thinks it's a scandal the way HRH has been treated and he doesn't care a damn about the Archbishop of Canterbury, in fact he's been thinking of emigrating to America anyway. The wife is insisting on coming too. Wally objected but soon gave in. It's too late in the day to start quibbling over extra little expenses.

Wally and HRH in such high spirits, opening wedding gifts, throwing sticks for the dogs, dancing to gramophone records till long after midnight last night.

May 30, 1937
The Crosbies have arrived, and the Erlangers and Walter Monckton who, as lawyers so often do, brought with him a black cloud. The King has issued a decree that Wally will not become a Royal Highness. She's to be styled Her Grace, the Duchess of Windsor. It's to be gazetted in London tomorrow, so it will be general knowledge and a great triumph for Wally's enemies. A charming wedding present.

There was the most blistering row between Wally and HRH after Monckton broke the news. We could hear her throwing things. Then we heard David crying outside her door, begging to be let in. It was pitiful.

Freddie says either HRH didn't pay proper attention to the terms that he agreed or the lawyers have dropped a tremendous clanger. Monckton says there was nothing in the abdication settlement about Wally's future title. This is an afterthought and one that can be challenged. He says Elizabeth York was a commoner but there was never any question of denying her an HRH.

Pips thinks Wally will call off the wedding. She said, 'I can't see Wally settling for this. As well ask her to be called Mrs Windsor.'

Neither Wally nor HRH came down to dinner.

I went in to her late and she was wide awake, wearing eyeshades. She said, 'Another insult from Bunny and Cook. And not the last, I'm sure. They're little people with little minds.'

Hattie says Emerald Cunard cut her in the Ritz Grill. Of course, it's possible Emerald simply didn't remember her. Hattie has one of those faces. She says the news from Spain isn't good. There's been fierce fighting and someone Penelope Blythe knows has arrived home without any legs. I do hope Lightfoot has come to his senses and returned to London.

May 31, 1937

HRH summoned us all to the apricot drawing room and told us that yesterday's announcement is to be ignored. He said, 'My wife will be addressed as Her Royal Highness and will be curtsied to. Kindly inform your staffs.'

Wally is calm after yesterday's storm. She said, 'They'll be shamed into giving it to me someday, and in the meanwhile the world is going to find out I'm a thousand times more regal than Queen Cotton Candy.'

Main Bocher and his people have arrived, and so has the *chapelier*, and clothes always cheer her up. Tomorrow Mr Beaton arrives to take the official photographs. Dudley Forwood has set off for Cherbourg to meet Wally's Aunt Bessie and bring her here. The secretaries can hardly keep pace with the gifts. Mr Mussolini has sent a clock. Mr Hitler a gold candy box.

June 1, 1937

Baba and Fruity Metcalfe are here and the Rogerses are driving up today. All we need now is the vicar and the party is complete. Aunt Bessie is a game old bird, dashing around the chateau with her sleeves rolled up looking for things to do. Plain-spoken too. She said, 'Wally had better make this one work. Three husbands is enough for anyone. And why aren't there more guests? Where are their friends? I disapprove of hole-in-the-wall weddings. It's not a good way to start.'

I think everyone found this 'propose yourself' idea very confusing.

Mrs Spry has arrived to do the flowers. I'm giving her a wide berth. In spite of there being a Mr Spry she is apparently of the same persuasion as Nada Milford Haven and I'm in no mood to find myself cornered in some turret of the chateau by an invert with a pair of secateurs.

Mr Cecil Beaton is buzzing around downstairs making all kinds of demands. Aunt Bessie doesn't approve of the wedding clothes being worn before the event. She says it brings bad luck. Better though than having Mr Beaton here on the wedding day moving vases.

June 2, 1937

As Mr Beaton left, the Reverend Jardine arrived. A blustering, red-faced man, but he wears a dog collar and seems to be the genuine article. He and Charlie are ordering people around, trying to create a more chapel-like ambience. I came upon them huffing and puffing and ransacking a linen press for something suitable as an altar cloth. They're like a pair of removal men from Maples.

Telegrams have come from the old Queen and from the Yorks, but no eleventh-hour appearance by any family member. George Kent could have hopped over in an airplane in no time. It would mean everything to HRH. The Crokers are expected any minute.

Burke has everything laid out ready in Wally's dressing room and it all looks magnificent, except for the hat, which I always did think was a mistake. To me it looks like something one might use to decorate a cake stand. I much prefer my own little confection. HRH's wedding gift to her is a tiara of diamonds. I just hope she's going to find opportunities to wear it.

No sign of nerves in Wally. Well, it is the third time. She said, 'Thank you for everything, Maybell. I couldn't have got this far without you.'

I said, 'All the years I've known you, I finally get to your wedding.'

She said, 'And this is the wedding that matters.'

I said, 'Did you know, the first time you met David? Did it cross your mind?'

'No,' she said. 'It didn't. To tell you the truth, he didn't impress me. But it all seems perfectly obvious now. We're a good fit.'

We took one last turn around the house before dinner,

checking everything is in order. Mrs Spry has really done a very fine job. There can't be a peony left standing in France tonight. Wally had the help move a gilt mirror behind the altar, to give an even more sparkling effect when the candles are lit. The weather forecast is good.

June 3, 1937

The deed is done. Little Bessie Wallis Warfield is now the Duchess of Windsor and whatever Buckingham Palace may have said about it, *everyone* here curtsied to her when we went in to lunch. The convoy with the honeymoon luggage left at breakfast time, then Herman went down to the gates to brief the newspaper people. They've promised to leave Wally and David in peace at Wasserleonburg. Lily says that's because they've seen where it is!

The mayor came just before noon, swathed in an enormous red, white, and blue ribbon, in honor of the British groom and the American bride, I suppose. A nice gesture, although the red argued a little with the pink of some of the flowers. He did the French part of the marrying in the drawing room. It was over in no time at all, then we processed to the salon for the Reverend Jardine to do his part. Herman gave Wally away.

David actually wept a little, which led to a slight fluffing of his lines, but Wally was word-perfect and she was so right about having that mirror placed where it could reflect the candlelight. Her sapphires and diamonds were dazzling.

More tears from HRH when they were pronounced man and wife so Wally postponed the traditional kiss so as not to muss up her makeup. I saw a look pass between Baba Metcalfe and Walter Monckton. I don't think they'll ever forgive Wally her American polish.

I've also heard a few sniggers about the statue Fern and Charlie have given as a wedding present, because it's *new*. The British hate anything new. I suppose certain parties think one of Mr Elgar's armless old marbles would have been more appropriate.

Lunch was lobster, strawberries, and champagne. The newlyweds plus dogs left at three, with motorcycle outriders and cars full of detectives and staff fore and aft. David all smiles, Wally looking a little tense, I thought.

Tonight, dinner for the survivors, as Herman calls us.

June 4, 1937

I had Fruity on my right last evening. He's *very* charming. I can't imagine why Wally doesn't like him. He said it was the most melancholy wedding he'd ever attended. 'All perfectly staged,' he said, 'and pretty as a picture, but not fitting for a man born to be king.'

I said, 'Well, that's all over. Now he's starting a new life.'

He said, 'He was greatly loved, you know, till this. There were men who would have laid down their lives for him. I still would. But we're a diminishing band.'

I believe it was the champagne talking.

He said, 'Wally had better be good to him. He's sacrificed everything to be with her.'

I said, 'He's not the only one who's made sacrifices.'

Aunt Bessie said, 'Yes, let's not forget poor Ernest.'

Fern said, 'And Wally. Her life is never going to be the same again. She's setting out with David into the unknown. That's love for you.'

Baba Metcalfe said, 'Well, she doesn't behave as though she loves him. I didn't see a single loving gesture from her today. Not one.'

Of course, Baba is famously generous with *her* loving gestures.

Herman told Freddie that some of the press photographers down at the gate described Wally as 'having a tang of the dockyard' about her.

I said, 'What can they mean?'

Pips said, 'Darned if I know. Apart from her big beefy hands and that hyena laugh she's a picture of femininity.'

Dudley Forwood has asked to see me before we leave for Italy. He has something for me from His Royal Highness and Her Grace, the Duchess. I think I can guess what it is. HRH knows I've always admired the silver rose bowl that used to stand in the Octagon Room at Fort Belvedere, and now Daisy Fellowes has sent an almost identical one as a wedding gift, so I believe I may be the lucky beneficiary of the original.

June 5, 1937

Forwood handed me a bundle, an *absolute bundle*, of accounts this morning. I told him, now the royal monies have been agreed Wally has no need of me to keep her creditors happy. He said, 'I see. Her Grace gave me the impression . . .'

I said, 'I never mind picking up a few things here and there. I was raised to be open-handed. But these are major expenses.'

He said, 'Yes. Of course, if it's a question of timing I'm sure some of these people would be prepared to wait.'

Freddie says Forwood is about to discover the real cost of being David's equerry.

Pips said, 'And what about the honeymoon expenses? I wonder what they're doing for jingle up on that mountaintop?'

I said, 'Wally told me the blockage in the tube had been cleared and David's funds are now flowing freely.'

Hattie said, 'Dribbling, Maybell. Not flowing. Dribbling. David doesn't have enough a year to cover Wally's gowns, let alone anything else.'

No rose bowl either. But Forwood has put the bills back in the letter tray. He's off to Austria, as Honeymoon Equerry. And I refuse to be in a bad mood. Tomorrow Italy!

June 10, 1937, Portofino
We are at the Splendido Mare. Wally would be so jealous if she knew. Dozens of people are in town. Tonight the Genoas are giving a party.

June 15, 1937
Walked as far as the lighthouse with Kath and Herman. Portofino is such a pretty town. I could settle here in a moment. Rent one of these adorable pink houses and hire a handsome Italian driver. The Gandolfis are throwing a cocktail by the saltwater pool. Afterwards to the Regina di Liguria for dinner with friends of Lily Drax-Pfaffenhof.

June 17, 1937
Boss and Ethel's yacht put in this morning. They have the Bajavidas on board, and two other couples from Palm Beach, the Dekuypers and the Orly-Guzmans. They saw Bernie and Zita Cavett in Monaco. Ethel says Zita's still in a huff about missing the wedding. They sent a very good tea service, apparently.

June 20, 1937
Boss Croker says HRH may live to regret allowing Charlie Bedaux to arrange his foreign tours, especially

to America. He says Charlie may be known over here for his generosity but in the States he's known for taking on the trade unions and squeezing the life blood out of the working man. Lily says she doesn't know anything about that but Charlie's the perfect man to arrange something in Germany. He knows everyone worth knowing and with HRH speaking German so well it's bound to be a profitable partnership.

On Thursday we move on to Como and on Tuesday to Sirmione. Bought some smart new luggage and a selection of lace dressing-table mats. The Crokers and their party are continuing on to Capri.

June 25, 1937, Mistral Blu, Sirmione

Our rooms here are meant to have lake views but the rain has so far prevented us from judging them. There doesn't seem to be anyone of consequence in town. Lily may be taking us to meet her friend Mr D'Annunzio who has a place nearby. I believe he's an old beau of hers.

July 2, 1937

The visit with Mr D'Annunzio finally took place. He has lovely grounds but very cluttered interiors and such a strutting, bombastic manner. As Pips says, like a crazy old rooster. Lily leaves us tomorrow to prepare for house-guests and we'll probably head down to Venice on Tuesday or Wednesday. Pips is already thumbing through her Baedeker, earmarking paintings she wants to gaze at yet again.

July 4, 1937

No celebrations. The Italians appear not to know about the Fourth. This is the first year since I became a cosmopolite

404

that I've evaded a sentimental phone call from Randolph Putnam. One of the bonuses of keeping on the move.

July 8, 1937, The Excelsior, Venice Lido
Received such a warm welcome. *All* the staff remember me.

Kath has heard that Wally's old Peking flame, Ciano, is in town. We're going to try and see him. He's now married to Mr Mussolini's daughter, apparently.

July 10, 1937
With Pips and Herman to a tiny mosquito-ridden island to see mosaics. No shops.

This evening to Freddie's old college friend, Bobo Farinacci. He has a palazzo, but not an important one.

July 12, 1937
It's a small world. At Bobo Farinacci's we met friends of the Bajavidas, Ludo and Fancie Fannulloni. Fancie Fannulloni is from Savannah and was at school with Breeze Bajavida. Also came, little Barbara Hutton, no longer married to that Russian and minus her new husband. She was being squired by a Woolworth cousin.

Rory's sixteenth birthday.

July 13, 1937
To lunch with the Fannullonis. They're sending their boat.

July 18, 1937
I have met Wally's Count Gian Galeazzo Ciano! Devilishly handsome. I can see why she fell for him. He and his wife were lunching at Herman's favorite fish restaurant and we were invited to join them. I felt Herman was rather

showing off his Italian, ordering platters of this and vats of that, most of it ugly little creatures that ought to have been thrown back into the ocean. How hard it is to find a good broiled steak in this town.

Ciano believes democracy will soon be a thing of the past.

July 23, 1937
Pips and Freddie are leaving on August 1. I may go with them. So many things to do, and there'll be no one left in London to snub me.

July 27, 1937
The honeymooners are here.

We realized something was about to happen this morning because the lobby was suddenly buzzing with pressmen. Then a concierge told Pips that the Duke and Duchess of Windsor were on their way from the railroad station in a motor launch. Wally pretended to be surprised when she saw us but I'll bet she's had every hotel in Italy telephoned, trying to track us down.

Herman said, 'What's this, Wally? Is the honeymoon over?'

'No,' she said, 'this is Part Two. The schloss was all right, but once I'd reorganized the furniture there wasn't really anything to do up there. There comes a time when a girl needs to see civilization.'

We're all having dinner tonight. I grabbed a moment with her when she went up to bathe.

I said, 'Well? How has it been?'

She said, 'Maybell! I'm hardly a child bride. It's been fine. Boring, but fine.'

I said, 'You'll never guess. Count Ciano's here.'

Not a flicker.

She said, 'Is he? Well, I suppose a lot of people are. Venice is that kind of town.'

July 28, 1937

HRH has gone to Alberoni to play golf with Judson. Wally joined us by the pool. She's desperately looking for volunteers to tag along when she and David move on to their next destination, another of Charlie Bedaux's residences. Borsodivanka. She thinks it's in Czechoslovakia but it may possibly be in Hungary.

Kath said, 'I always thought honeymooners wanted to get away from people.'

Wally said, 'We've already had six weeks of *that* kind of honeymooning. Now David needs diversions, otherwise he just pads around behind me. I can't even go to the bathroom without him missing me. So far the only time he's left my side was when I got Forwood to suggest a hike, and even then he kept signaling me with a damned pocket mirror so I'd know how far they'd progressed.'

Complaints already, as Kath says, but all very lighthearted. I think she loves being a duchess. The staff here are meticulous about bows and curtsies.

We took a launch into town after lunch.

Pips said, 'Hold on to your purse, Maybell.'

But those days are over. Wally picked out dozens of table linens at Asta's and she signed her own chits without hesitation. I knew Forwood was mistaken about those wedding bills.

Babs Hutton is giving a party tomorrow night at the Grand.

July 30, 1937
The Hutton party was well attended. Came, among many, Ludo and Fancie Fannulloni, Bobo Farinacci, Tori and Paola Nasibruni, Clarice Sfogginomi, and the Count Galeazzo Cianos.

Kath and I waited with baited breath to see how Wally handled meeting the Count again but she was as cool as a cucumber. He might have been no more than a nodding acquaintance from long, long ago. HRH chatted with him too. There was apparently one sticky moment when Ciano demanded to know why Mr Selassie, the ex of Abyssinia, had been invited to the coronation. He said it was an insult to Italy. HRH said, 'Nothing to do with me. It wasn't *my* coronation.'

Peals of laughter.

With Wally to Nardi to help her pick out a pair of blackamoor ear clips. Venice is the most inconvenient of cities. One trudges over bridge after bridge and none of the streets is wide enough for a limousine so it's impossible to have a driver waiting. If they only filled in the waterways the locals would notice an immediate improvement in efficiency. They should send someone to Baltimore, to see how a modern city should be run.

August 2, 1937
The Crosbies left this morning, but not before Pips brought up the subject of money with Wally. She said, 'You know Forwood gave Maybell a load of your bills to settle, and she would have done too, if the rest of us hadn't stopped her. She won't bring it up herself but I think it's time you were clear about money. Tell her you don't need her picking up your checks anymore.'

Wally said, 'It was a misunderstanding, Maybell knows

that. Fortunately, she doesn't worry about such things, but for *your* peace of mind, Pips, I can promise you Borsodivanka isn't going to cost her a cent. Charlie Bedaux is paying for everything.'

I do wish Pips wouldn't interfere. Now I feel cheap.

August 9, 1937, Borsodivanka Castle
Like Candé but smaller and wilder. Lots of dark wood and boars' heads. The footmen wear baggy trousers tucked into high leather boots and are rather fiercely good-looking. Fern is in Paris, Charlie comes and goes, always busy, busy, busy, sending wires, making calls. Lily Drax-Pfaffenhof has driven over with the Cavetts and some jolly Austrians in national costume.

August 14, 1937
Wally has been so disagreeable, picking on HRH all through dinner. She's bored and seems to have spent the afternoon brooding over the events of last December, especially Esmond Harmsworth's morganatic proposal which she now regards as a major mistake.

She said, 'You should never have given Baldwin an excuse to go to the Dominions for an opinion. It was obvious they'd raise objections. You never stop to think.'

He said, 'But darling, you seemed so keen on the idea.'

She said, 'Don't blame me. All those advisors you had on the payroll. What were they thinking of? You as good as handed the Yorks your crown on a plate. You should just have gone ahead with the coronation, to hell with the goddamned Dominions, to hell with marrying. We could still have seen each other. We could have worked something out. But no. You're such a fool.'

It was a very unhappy moment. Herman tried to change

the topic and so did I, but she wouldn't be stopped and poor HRH just chewed the inside of his cheek.

August 15, 1937
Kath says it's time to go home. She says the whole thing is too Gothic, sitting here with the rain lashing against the glass, playing checkers and listening to Wally lambasting David. Today's bugbear is Walter Monckton. She wants to know what he'd been doing allowing Bunny and Cook to cheat her out of her rightful title. She said, 'He knew the New Bunch would be looking for ways to spite me. It was a fundamental point and he should have been watching out for their dirty tricks. Calls himself a lawyer! Well, I hope he hasn't been paid because he doesn't deserve a penny.'

Forwood said Monckton quite definitely hasn't been paid.

It's all very well to talk of leaving but we're not even sure what country we're in. Zita says it doesn't matter, as long as our drivers know where we are. I suppose.

August 20, 1937
The Rogerses left this morning. Herman said, fond as he is of Fern he too is beginning to have second thoughts about Charlie's German connections. He says Mr Ley, whom Charlie talks of all the time and who features so prominently in plans for our tour of Germany, is nothing but a thug in a suit. Forwood agrees. He said, 'His Royal Highness has had a year of bad press. He should be thinking about ways to repair his reputation, not make matters worse. In my opinion he needs to be very careful about where he goes and who he's seen with.'

Of course, scratch Forwood and you'll find a Foreign

Office clerk. A belt-and-suspenders man. He doesn't understand Charlie's grand plan at all. Or Wally's flair for putting on a good show.

August 22, 1937
Callisthenics with HRH this morning. Quite like the good old days at the Fort. HRH asked me how I think Wally seems. Very irritable is how she seems, but I didn't really feel I could say so.

I said, 'She's a little strained. It's been a big year.'

He said, 'It has. She's suffered terribly. And she's being so unfairly treated by certain parties. That's why the German trip is so very important. She'll receive a very warm welcome from the Germans. Bedaux's doing a marvelous job. It'll be as good as a state visit, and that's what Wally deserves. She's going to be so awfully good at this.'

Charlie has left for New York. He's going to prepare the way for a November tour of the United States. Oliver Templemore and Oxer Bettenbrooke are coming here for the chamois hunting. Also the Humphrey Butlers.

It seems a very social time considering it's a honeymoon. Brumby and I had a few days at Marshalls Creek, just the two of us and a stock market ticker-tape machine, but Wally and David seem to thrive on company.

August 27, 1937
We hear that the Reverend Jardine has surfaced in America. He's announced his intention of writing his memoirs and opening a wedding chapel, something exclusive, suitable for Hollywood stars.

Wally said, 'Bumptious little chancer. He'd better not include us in any memoirs.'

Hardly fair. After all, he did travel a long way at short notice and defied his bishop and destroyed his chances of preferment. No one else volunteered and if he hadn't come along when he did Wally and David would have had to make do with being married by a Frenchman draped in a flag.

Zita said, 'If you don't want to get memoired you'd better have a word with Maybell. She writes us all up in her diary.'

Wally said, 'Do you still do that, Maybell? Did you ask His Royal Highness's permission?'

I said, 'Hardly. They're just my own little musings. Current affairs. Family things.'

'Oh,' she said, 'how dreary. If people must keep diaries they should make them worth reading.'

Zita said, 'Yes. When I went into show business my ma said, "Keep a diary, Zita. Someday it may keep you." But I never did.'

September 2, 1937

The Humphrey Butlers have arrived. Walter Monckton has also asked to make a flying visit. Wally said, 'He'd better come with an apology from the Yorks and my rightful title.'

I made noises about returning to London but Wally won't hear of it. She said, 'We have to go to Paris, Maybell. I don't have a thing to wear. And then I'm going to need you in Germany. You're my lady-in-waiting.'

Poots Butler says only royalties have ladies-in-waiting.

September 4, 1937

Monckton has brought neither an apology nor a title for Wally. He's come to try and talk HRH out of going to

Germany. He says Charlie Bedaux's German friends are all Nazis and the trip will be a great embarrassment to the British government.

Wally said, 'He's been sent by the New Bunch, I'll bet you dollars to donuts. They're nervous about David getting back in the public eye. Serve them right. It's their own damned fault for sending him to the scrapheap. Well, we're going to Germany, whatever anyone says.'

We head for Paris next weekend. Poots says she discerns a pattern with Wally. Two happy days followed by twenty-four hours of snapping and paranoia.

I don't think she's paranoid at all. I think she's being treated very unkindly indeed.

September 5, 1937
Today's subject has been HRH's banishment. Wally says much as she adores Paris, England is where they really belong. She said, 'It's a terrible waste of a king. David knows everything there is to know about running the country. He was trained for it, unlike Bertie York. He should be asked back and given something useful to do.'

Humphrey Butler said, 'The problem with that, Wally, is that no new king wants to have an ex-king watching over his shoulder.'

Wally said, 'Well, he'll have to be given something to do. I can't have him under my feet for the next thirty years.'

September 6, 1937
HRH says he won't go back to England until and unless Wally gets her due rank and is properly received by the two Queens. Walter Monckton told him he sees no

reason why this can't be achieved given time, patience, and tact.

Wally said, 'Patience and tact, fiddlesticks! Go and phone your brother and tell him you have to have a job. And this time don't allow him to fob you off.'

September 7, 1937

So far the King hasn't been available to come to the telephone and speak with David. Wally said, 'Of course he's available. He just daren't contradict orders from the Scotch Cook. She's the one who wears the pants. You wouldn't think it, to look at those dimpled cheeks, but she does. And she's the one who has it in for me.'

We sensed another rant coming on but Poots headed it off by asking Wally's advice on hemlines.

HRH is acting so forlorn about us going to Paris. He keeps saying, 'Must you go, darling? After what we went through last winter I don't ever want us to be separated again.'

It's so silly because Wally's organized a lovely shooting party to see him through her absence. And his night table is covered with photographs of her.

September 10, 1937

Charlie now has everything in place for our first two tours. Forwood is preparing a bulletin for the press. We go to Germany on October 11, for two weeks, then back to Paris just long enough for the maids to turn everything around and repack before we sail for New York on the *Bremen* on November 6.

September 12, 1937, Hôtel Meurice, Paris

Wally is lunching with Elsie Mendl and has left me with lists to go through with her *lingère*. I'm sure I'm efficient enough to manage lingerie lists *and* go to Trianon for lunch. Ena Spain is still in Scotland.

Bought stockings.

September 13, 1937
No sign yet of Wally. Her maid says she didn't come in till 2 a.m. If HRH was trying to get through to her for his goodnight kiss he'll be frantic.

Appointments at Chanel and Main Bocher. Tomorrow, lunch with Kitty Rothschild. Instead of Prunier we're going to go to a real Parisian market, to buy ingredients, bring them to the house, and cook them ourselves. What unusual lives people lead in Paris!

September 14, 1937
The Rothschilds have a very modest apartment. They are staying liquid until they see what Germany's intentions are. Kitty says if Hitler takes Austria they stand to lose Enzesfeld. It's the Jewish question. She says we're going to be very shocked by what we see on our trip. Thuggery in the streets. Shops that are barred to Jews. She made it plain she doesn't approve of HRH's visit, but he's only going to study labor conditions and housing and all those things he's keen on. I see no harm in it. And what can we do if German shopkeepers choose not to serve Jews? Anyway, it's all arranged.

She said, 'I only hope Charlie Bedaux doesn't turn the Windsors into a pair of performing pooches. That man never does anything for nothing.'

Lunch was exhausting. First we went all the way to St-Germain with Kitty's friend Winnie Gulliver, battling through the crowds to buy mushrooms and salad greens and cheeses, then we carried them home by taxicab and made our own omelets. Thank goodness she had the help clear away. Playing house is good fun but it takes up so much time.

Winnie Gulliver says she cooks for herself all the time, but she's English and quite down on her luck by all accounts. Rather like Ida Coote, except Winnie does afford a daily.

Wally was at the Bricktop last night with Kenny Opdyke and his crowd. She says there were naked black girls in the floor show.

She's having new buttons put on her dark blue coat-dress. She evidently plans to meet Mr Hitler dressed like a Bible-class teacher.

September 18, 1937
Called Pips but got Freddie. He said, 'This German jaunt is a wholly bad idea. It's going to send completely the wrong message to Hitler.'

I said, 'It's a private visit. A few folkloric pageants and luncheons with dignitaries. It's going to have no more significance than if we motored down to Menton for a weekend.'

He said, 'Private visit! That's not how it's going to look and David knows it.'

Lightfoot has been heard from, apparently, and is alive and well, or at least, alive. Doopie volunteered too, for nursing duties, but is still at Carlton Gardens. Well, I'm sure they won't take her. She can't even say 'bandage' properly.

A valet has arrived with the dogs. HRH will be here tomorrow. That will put a stop to late nights at the Bricktop.

September 21, 1937
HRH says he received a letter from Prosper Frith asking him, for the sake of Great Britain, not to break bread with Adolf Hitler. Prosper Frith! He's got some nerve, after the way that wife of his switched camps. Anyway, we're not *breaking bread* with Mr Hitler. We're having afternoon tea.

Ena Spain is back.

September 25, 1937
Fruity Metcalfe has now joined the throng telling us to cancel our trip. Wally says he's just disappointed not to have been asked to equerry. Well, Forwood suits us better. He has the language and he doesn't presume upon an old friendship.

Ena Spain is terribly depressed about the war. She says the godless are fighting the godless and it's the poor little people who are being squeezed between the two. I wonder if Lightfoot realizes he's in the ranks of the godless. He was always pretty keen on churchgoing at Easter and lowly mangers on his Christmas cards.

We have received our program for the United States. Charlie Bedaux has been very busy. HRH will start by visiting industrialists in Rochester, Schenectady, Wilmington, and Bayonne. Wally and I will have our own activities in New York. Then we'll all make a brief stop in Washington to see Wally's Aunt Bessie, and Baltimore, for old times' sake. This is going to give Nora Sedley Cordle and Brumby Junior something to think about. If they make any approach, hoping to use me as a conduit to the royalties, I shall snub them. As far as I'm concerned the only friend I have in Baltimore is Randolph Putnam.

The tour will then resume with HRH going to Detroit,

but Wally and I may go directly to San Diego and then meet up with him again in Honolulu.

Charlie says he can arrange further fact-finding tours for next spring too. There's interest from Sweden and the Argentine. What wayfarers we're becoming!

October 3, 1937

It seems that no one wants us to go to Germany except the Germans. The newspaperman Beaverbrook is trying to dissuade us. He says it's too controversial a thing to do so soon after the abdication and that having clashed head-on with Stanley Baldwin the last thing HRH should do is set a collision course with Neville Chamberlain, especially if he still hopes for an early end to his exile.

Now Forwood tells us that the British Embassy in Berlin has been instructed to offer us nothing more than powder rooms and a cup of tea. Wally says it'll be the doing of Bunny and Cook.

She said, 'They know we're going to be a big success. They're terrified David's going to stage a comeback.'

I said, 'And is he?'

'That,' she said, 'remains to be seen.'

I wish they'd make up their minds. The last I heard she had Elsie Mendl's people combing Paris for a suitable townhouse.

The maids and valets start off with the luggage in the morning.

October 8, 1937

A little farewell dinner at the Tour d'Argent. Came, the Ambassador Bullitts, the Marquess of Graham, Fern Bedaux, and Elsie Mendl. The Eugene Rothschilds sent regrets. Jimmy Graham says Adolf Hitler doesn't have any policies, as such, only random thoughts, some of which are followed through but many of which are not. According to Elsie the man to watch is Dr Goebbels.

October 11, 1937, Kaiserhof Hotel, Berlin

Charlie Bedaux has been as good as his word. Everything got off to a wonderful start. We were met at the railroad station by a very smart contingent of top Germans. By contrast, the British Embassy sent only a Third Secretary, the Ambassador and most of his suite having chosen today of all days to leave town. So mean-spirited. But Charlie's friend Mr Ley had organized sparkling Mercedes limousines to take us to our hotel, with brass bands and an escort of storm troopers and hundreds of smiling Germans lining the route. I can't say I noticed any of those anti-Jewish shop signs Kitty Rothschild talked about.

Tonight, dinner with the Otto Bismarcks at the Eden.

October 12, 1937

Wally and I shopped while HRH visited a ball-bearing plant. He was most impressed by what he saw. He says the workers are given a free meal that provides them with all their daily nourishment, and they have glee clubs and inoculations and beautiful flower beds all around the factory. I wonder what Brumby would have thought of that! We had mines and smelters all over the world and they were perfectly productive without us going to the trouble of flower beds.

Wally bought two dozen Meissen plates and three pairs of branched candlesticks. She says she finds Mr Ley over-familiar, but he'd arranged private visits to the most exclusive shops, and really, nothing seems to be too much trouble for him. Tomorrow HRH has to go to Potsdam to inspect a flap-valve factory. He was keen for us to go with him, but we have hair appointments and Mr Ley has more shopkeepers expecting us. We can hardly disappoint them.

October 13, 1937
To the Kranzler coffee house for ice cream. Wally has let it be known she's seen two pieces of Biedermeier that would be very acceptable as late wedding gifts, should anyone ask: a walnut secretary and a four-drawer commode with some very pretty marquetry. Tonight to Mr Ley's home for drinks. It's a pity he picks his teeth.

October 14, 1937
Everyone who's anyone in Germany was at Mr Ley's last evening. Very few of the wives though, which suited Wally. She always prefers a room full of men. She quite monop-olized Mr Speer, but I made a great hit with Colonel Jodl who offered me the use of his hunting lodge. What I'd do there I can't imagine.

Champagne in abundance, mountains of caviar and pretzels, and a Tyrolean band playing HRH's favorite music. A gay evening which ended with scowling faces and HRH pulling out of the luncheon he's supposed to attend tomorrow. Dudley Forwood says it's to do with a newspaperman called Streicher, who's on the guest list for the luncheon. Apparently, Mr Streicher just published a story stating that Wally has Jewish blood. Too ridiculous for words. We didn't have Jews at Oldfields. Hattie Erlanger once hinted that Ernest was slightly Jewish, but even that's nothing to do with anything anymore. Ernest Simpson is history and Mr Streicher should check his facts.

Tonight to the opera.

October 15, 1937

A difficult evening. HRH still simmering about Mr Streicher's slur and dragging his feet over *Lohengrin*, and then when we arrived at the Opera House Mrs Goebbels was wearing a white taffeta identical to Wally's. Wally carried hers better and her diamonds outshone all the Germans put together, but still, it quite ruined our entrance and was an unforgivable gaffe on the part of the *vendeuse*. HRH felt that Mrs Goebbels should have withdrawn, but of course she didn't have the wit to do it. She's just a milch cow with her head full of feeding schedules and baby ailments. They say Dr Goebbels can send for any movie actress who takes his fancy. Extraordinary. To me he looks like a little goblin in a surgical boot, but Wally talked to him and she says he has a brilliant mind and a voice like black velvet. She'd better not share that observation with HRH.

The opera went on for hours and as guests of honour we felt obliged to stay to the end, though one act is surely enough for anyone.

Today we visited with the Air Marshal Hermann Goerings. They say he used to cut a dashing figure but he now wears his trousers hoisted far too high. Emmy Goering is very vivacious and a former movie star. I wonder whether Dr Goebbels had her? She's just learned that she's expecting a child and so Hermann was like a dog with two tails. He said, 'When my son is born one thousand planes will fly overhead in salute.' A German tradition I suppose, but I wonder people don't just send flowers. So much quieter.

Hermann and HRH played with a magnificent electric train set while Emmy gave us tea and a tour of the garden.

October 17, 1937

While HRH has been descending into coal mines and inspecting new highways Wally and I have visited two kindergartens, three hospitals, and an institute for old soldiers with no legs. It's so hard to know what to say to such people. We were also subjected to an overly detailed demonstration of the manufacture of synthetic rubber which made us so late returning to the hotel the manicurist had to rush and I went to the Saxe-Coburg dinner with a smudged left hand. If this relentless busyness is a taste of what Wally has let herself in for, I pity her. At least I can get Hattie or someone to take over as lady-in-waiting, but for Wally there'll be no such escape. No one can stand in for the Duchess of Windsor. I begin to understand her flashes of bitterness.

If David had hung on to his throne and kept her quietly in the wings she would have had none of these tiresome duties; smiling at cripples, admiring fat babies, showing an interest in welding processes. That side of the business could have been left to Elizabeth York and Marina Kent. I'm sure it's the kind of thing they enjoy.

October 18, 1937

A display of flag-twirling by the League of German Maidens. Tomorrow, dinner with dear Prince Louis Ferdinand and his mother, then on Friday we visit with President Hitler. Wally is still set on wearing the dark blue coatdress and a little felt hat. I can't think why. If all these cheerful flags and banners flying along Unter Den Linden are any indication, Mr Hitler is rather fond of red. I'm going to wear my scarlet twill.

We went a different route to avoid traffic and saw some of those shops with Jewish star placards in the window.

Mr Ley says they are public information notices, to save Jewish people wandering into stores that sell things like blood sausage, forbidden to them by their religion. Not at all the impression Kitty Rothschild gave.

October 19, 1937, Cecilienhof, Potsdam

Crown Princess Cecilie may be a Romanov and a Mecklenberg and a great many other unpronounceable things, but her house is of a comfortably manageable size and quite reminded me of houses I've seen in Surrey.

Louis Ferdinand as adorable as ever. He thinks he's found a wife, one of his Russian cousins. He says she's not only extremely suitable but also good and beautiful. Still, I always rather hoped he'd marry a nice American girl. He's working in an airplane factory now and quite enjoying it. Hudson's choice, I suppose. There's no work for royalties in Germany at present.

While Wally was freshening up, Cecilie told me that Hitler is rumored to have moving pictures of her, taken when we were on the *Nahlin*. She said, 'They say he plays them all the time. He must have quite a crush on her!'

I'm afraid the Führer may be in for a disappointment. Emaciated women may photograph well, but in the flesh they lack the bloom of natural good health. There's a happy medium between the stoutness of German women and Wally's sharp angles and there's no better example than myself.

Louis F says von Ribbentrop is on the outs and Mr Hess and Mr Speer are the darlings of the moment.

Tomorrow, Munich. A demonstration of butter-churning and a youth concert.

October 20, 1937, Bayerischer Hof, Munich

Forwood says Friday's meeting will be strictly between HRH and the Führer and that Wally and I will just be shown around the gardens. Forwood obviously hasn't heard what Crown Princess Cecilie has!

October 22, 1937, Goldene Ente, Salzburg

Today we visited with President Hitler. We were given a trout luncheon at a wayside hostelry then driven up to the Berghof in time for tea. As our car approached the house Forwood let out a great whoop of laughter. He said, 'Good grief, it looks like something a builder just put up in Middlesex.'

Forwood has a certain side to him. I thought it was a charming house, and with matchless mountain views. Also, it's in a very select neighborhood. The Albert Speers have built nearby, and the Martin Bormanns are just a little farther up the road, so everyone knows everyone, rather like West Palm Beach.

As Wally got out of the car, Mr Hitler came trotting down the steps to greet her. He has a pasty face and is rather short in the leg. He was wearing patent leather evening shoes and an ugly brown jacket, but was all smiles and not at all overwrought as he always appears to be in the newsreels. He and HRH spoke in German and then the three of them set off up the steps. Forwood and I were rounded up by two aides and taken in by a different door to meet the fiancée. Miss Eva Brown.

Well, Eva may *style* herself 'fiancée' but she wears no ring. She's a natural blonde, average figure, very young. She calls the President 'Uncle Führer'. We went to her sad little sitting room. Cheap chintzes, animal pictures torn from magazines, a small shelf of novelettes. Tea and éclairs were served and she showed us her collection of glass animals. She'd been kept strictly offstage during our arrival and so was eager for information about Wally's clothes. She chattered away so inanely Forwood had difficulty keeping up as our interpreter.

Does the Duchess wear a foundation garment? What's her favorite scent? Had Uncle Führer presented her with flowers? What are her dogs' names? Has she seen the new Nelson Eddy and Jeanette MacDonald movie?

There's no date fixed for a wedding. She said the Führer is too busy at present. She said she'd so wanted to meet Wally and His Royal Highness but protocol prevents it until she becomes Mrs Hitler. I don't see why. HRH always presented Wally to everyone, even when she was still married to Ernest. The Germans are such sticklers.

She clung to my arm when we got the word that HRH and Wally were ready to leave, doing everything she could think of to delay our departure, but she didn't come out with us to our car. Not allowed, I suppose.

Once Wally and HRH had climbed into their motor I seized my opportunity. I caught the Führer's eye. I told Forwood to tell him how glorious his zinnia beds were and that I hoped he and Eva would have a lovely wedding. Soon.

I received a very cordial bow. I wish I could have had more time to talk with him though. For one thing, I should have liked to recommend Dr Prilstein's Tonic Iron Pastilles. I'm sure he'd benefit from them.

Forwood said, 'Don't be disappointed. I don't think ladies-in-waiting usually get to speak. You and I are just spear carriers, after all.'

Spear carriers! I said, 'Speak for yourself. If it weren't

425

for me the Duchess of Windsor would still be having her gowns made by a little woman on Cromwell Road.'

HRH is full of their visit. He said, 'We hit it off immediately. He's a thoroughly agreeable sort and only wants a fair deal for his country. Who can fault a man for that? All this scaremongering by men like Eden is so much nonsense. I told him, as far as I'm concerned there must be no more wars between Britain and Germany and he agreed with me. We're all of the same blood, after all. Go back far enough and we're all Huns.'

Well, *I'm* not. Father's people were from Richmond, Virginia, and Mother was one of the Washington Woodhams.

Wally also very smitten. The Führer told her she'd have made a very fine queen and that her day will yet come. He'd showed her the view from his panoramic window, clear across into Austria. She says he has artistic hands and eyes as blue as a mountain lake. I must say he put me in mind of a ventriloquist's doll.

Tomorrow we turn for home.

October 28, 1937, Hôtel Meurice, Paris

Two more secretaries started today but we're still working against the clock, to finish the letters of thanks for the wedding gifts *and* finalize our US engagements. I'd have thought it was enough to have a letter that says *Thank you for the gift* and just run off however many copies, but Wally insists that we personalize each one by filling in the blank. *Thank you for the most useful shooting stick. Thank you for the thoughtful lobster hammers.* So tiresome.

Tea with Ena Spain.

November 2, 1937

Our luggage was dispatched to Cherbourg this morning but there is a small cloud on the horizon. Since the newspapers reported Wally and David's tea party with Mr Hitler, the Jewish lobby in America has been putting people under pressure to cancel our engagements. They say no one who is a friend of Germany can be a friend of Jews, which is not at all fair. The Eugene Rothschilds are Jews and HRH stayed with them for months. Also, it's not Germans in general who dislike Jews, nor even the Führer. It's Mr Streicher who's the problem and, as Wally says, he's of minor importance in the coming Germany. She laughed off his slurs and the Anti-Defamation League might learn to do the same.

November 4, 1937

Our trip to America now hangs in the balance. The New York longshoremen have said they won't unload the *Bremen* if it has bedfellows of the German National Socialists on board. Hardly *bedfellows*. All we did was pay a few visits, exchange gifts and pleasantries, and oil the wheels of international goodwill, something these Communists don't understand. I think we should just quietly change to a different sailing, but Freddie Crosbie says it makes no difference whether HRH deliberately climbed into bed with Hitler or got there by sleepwalking, the damage is done. He says David and Wally are now labeled as Nazi sympathizers and don't have a snowball in hell's chance of slipping unnoticed into the United States.

HRH is going to speak to the press tomorrow morning, to clear up the whole misunderstanding.

November 5, 1937
America is off. Charlie Bedaux wired this afternoon that he could no longer guarantee the success of the tour, because of adverse union propaganda. Also, that at the request of the British Ambassador, the State Department would not be according Wally royal status. That was what decided HRH. He canceled immediately.

It's such a waste. All our wonderful new gowns, all those people who are going to be disappointed. Pips was on the telephone the very moment she heard. She said, 'Well, Freddie did try to warn you.'

I said, 'Freddie didn't see what a huge success Germany was. We had no problems there with trade unions and people refusing to curtsy.'

She said, 'Maybell, you're spending too much time with that pair. You're losing touch with reality.'

I think Pips may be a touch envious of my position.

Wally's blaming the New Bunch. She said, 'Bunny and his Cook again! They have wall-to-wall advisors on foreign affairs and could easily have spared one to pop over here and explain the political nuances to HRH, instead of allowing him to go ahead and get into this scrape.'

I don't know. I'm not sure he's disposed to listen to people from Westminster anymore. Still, let's hope sanity prevails and I shall still get my chance to spurn Nora Sedley Cordle.

November 7, 1937
The *Bremen* sailed without us, our luggage is sitting in some quayside shed, and Charlie Bedaux has checked out of the New York Plaza, destination unknown. The whole business has been a disaster.

Elsie Mendl is giving us a consolatory dinner.

November 13, 1937
A wonderful evening at Elsie Mendl's. Her help all wore stars and stripes and she had hirèd an all-girl saxophone band to play for us after dinner. Came, the old Queen of Egypt, the Dimitri Shapaleffs, the Piston-LeRupins, Lucky Patrice, and Count Maximilian Finto. Nazli Egypt wore a Molyneux gown and a rivière of brilliants and cognac diamonds. I'd rather expected her to be shrouded in black.

November 15, 1937
Flowers from Maxi Finto. I think I have an admirer.

November 17, 1937
Ernest Simpson and Mary Kirk are to be married tomorrow in Fairfield, Connecticut. Wally says he still carries an enormous torch for her but I think she was just having a bad day. This damned rain has kept David off the golf course for a week now.

More flowers from the Count. He wants dinner. Elsie Mendl says he has a spread somewhere in South America. When he's in Europe he just stays with people.

November 20, 1937
Herman and Kath Rogers are going to the States for Christmas and have offered Wally and David their house. Tonight I dine with my Count Maxi! He sent an orchid.

November 21, 1937
Confined to bed with the repercussions of sauerkraut *garni*. Maxi said he thought a brasserie would be more fun than going to Grand Vefour yet again. He's a fascinating man. Mother was Irish, father Italian, born in the Argentine. He used to raise cattle until he had a bad polo

accident. Now he does this and that. Green eyes and still a fine head of black hair. My wrap still smells of his cologne. Funny, it's made me quite nostalgic for Brumby. Well, anyway, Maxi leaves for a trip on Tuesday. Paraguay.

Wally's invited Lily Drax-Pfaffenhof and the Bernie Cavetts to Cannes for Christmas.

I said, 'Does that mean you can spare me?'

She said, 'As long as you're back by the middle of January. We have to get down to house-hunting.'

She's going to show La Croe to David while they're down there at Christmas, and then decide on a Paris house in the new year. The Meurice is delightful but with a hotel there's always the problem of security. She says she lies awake listening for assassins.

HRH has no idea where he wants to live. 'Whatever you think, my darling,' he says. She could propose moving to Greenland and he'd go along with it.

November 23, 1937
Pips wants me for Christmas. She's promised there'll be no lectures from Freddie about the German situation. Actually, *I* may give Freddie a lecture. *I've* met the Führer, after all. And I have this feeling that someday people like Freddie are going to view Adolf Hitler in a very different light.

I fly, *fly*, to Croydon aerodrome on November 30. Wally thinks I'm crazy.

November 25, 1937
Dear Ena Spain has taken up my cause with Violet. She told her it made no sense to keep the drawbridge raised when the battle is over and the troops have all gone home. David and Wally are leading a new life far from Carlton

Gardens and the New Bunch are apparently making a decent job of things, so there's no longer any reason for a family to be divided. Violet told Ena that if I choose to call when I'm next in London I won't find the door barred.

I said, 'Hardly a warm invitation.'

Ena said, 'Now, Maybell, Violet always *means* well. Just go and see her. Life is short.'

November 29, 1937
A last doggy walk with HRH.

He said, 'Remember me to dear old London, Maybell. I do miss it all.'

I said, 'Well, sir, you've already served nearly a year of your exile. Time flies.'

He said, 'It does, but sometimes I think we'll never be able to go back. I want you to take soundings while you're there. When you come back I shall want to hear about the mood of my nation.'

We reminisced about that gay weekend we had at the Fort, when Wally cooked campfire sausages and Bernie Cavett played the accordion. Then for one awful moment I thought he might be going to cry. He's plagued with toothache and smoking far too much.

Freezing fog. I wonder how my airplane pilot will know which way to go.

December 1, 1937, Claridge's Hotel, London
A corsage waiting for me at Le Bourget, from Count Maxi.

Pips looks well. They have a new crimson dining room.

December 3, 1937
A year ago this night, Wally and I were hurtling through the dark to Newhaven. Perhaps I'll call Perry Brownlow.

Doopie is back at South Audley Street, hoping to be sent to Spain. She said, 'Dordie wone gum home dill a job's done.'

Flora is growing a bosom but she still carts around that Spanish doll given to Wally at Corunna.

She said, 'Are we speaking to you? Are you allowed to take us to Lyons for gake?'

I guess I am. Tea with Violet tomorrow.

December 4, 1937
Violet's first words were, 'Are you back to stay?'

I said, 'No. Just for Christmas. I'm letting Wilton Place go.'

She said, 'Are you going back to Baltimore? Is it Randolph?'

I said, 'No. I have a suite at the Meurice. I'm a European now.'

'Oh dear,' she said.

Rory will be home on the 10th.

She said, 'Of course, he may not want to see you. I make no promises. He's all too aware of recent events.'

Her hair is whiter, Melhuish's gout is apparently worse, and there's a scorch mark on the stair-hall runner where Flora set a fire while she and Doopie were back in residence. It seems to have been brought on by Elspeth Laird suggesting it was time they tried her at another school.

We embraced. Violet's still rather stiff with me but at least the ice has been broken. I believe I smelled poached salmon as I was leaving.

Spoke with Perry Brownlow.

I said, 'I hear you've been well and truly pilloried.'

'Ah,' he said, 'an anniversary call! One veteran to another.'

He said, 'It can only be a matter of time till we're back in fashion. The silliness of London will always outweigh its viciousness.'

He asked after Wally and HRH. He said he never hears *from* them, only *about* them.

He said, 'I did everything I could to keep him from abdicating, you know? But now the dust has settled I think it's all turned out for the best, don't you?'

I do.

December 16, 1937
To the Erlangers'. Hattie says no one's talking about Wally anymore. Freddie says that's because they know they may soon have a war to worry about.

December 10, 1937
Rory and Flora are very impressed to have an aunt who flies in airplanes. Flora kept asking, 'But how do they stay in the sky?' A very good question.

Rory says it's due to aerodymanics.

We went to Madame Tussaud's Museum to see a wax likeness of Wally. Rory was spellbound but of course he's never actually seen her in the flesh. In my opinion they haven't really captured her. She's in a red gown glaring across at the Archbishop of Canterbury, so they're on the right track and yet they don't quite have her.

Afterwards to the Marble Arch Lyons. Flora announcing very loudly that she now wears a bust bodice. 'Thirty-four inches,' she bellowed. She forgets we're not all like Doopie.

How grown up they both are all of a sudden. I'd so love them to visit with me in Paris.

Flora said, 'Let's go now.'

Rory said, 'You have to learn French first, you noodle.'
Such nonsense. I live there and I don't speak a word.

They chose their own presents; a nest of wands and a rather alarming set of magic handcuffs for Rory. Next year I shall go to Truefitt & Hill and get him a shaving brush. Flora got *The Secret of the Border Castle* and a flashlight. She picked out a woolen scarf for Ulick. Harrold's will always change it if he finds it too colorful.

December 13, 1937
Anne Belchester called to invite me to her Spanish Field Hospital benefit. Doopie will be selling prize-draw tickets and is sure to be glad of help. I believe I'm in the process of being rehabilitated. If I'm not very careful Gladys Trilling will start speaking to me again.

December 17, 1937
Lunch with Penelope Blythe and at the Dorch! I must truly be on my way back. And so much news. Ralph Habberley has sunk without trace, Jane Habberley has turned to God, Percy Boddie-Fulton was arrested for drunken driving, in Battersea inexplicably, Ida Coote is working on a telephone switchboard and Tommy Minskip has taken to shooting at people who approach his front door. Not that there can be many of those. Penelope says if Maxi Finto played polo Fergus may remember him and if he doesn't Rock Cholmondeley certainly will.

She says the new Queen is blossoming, the old Queen is nesting at Marlborough House, and Fergus predicts HRH will eventually be asked to go to Australia as Governor General. I don't think Australia is what Wally has in mind.

December 19, 1937

Spoke with Zita Cavett. They have rain in Cannes. Wally was resting and HRH was in town picking up her Christmas necklace. Zita says they've received Christmas greetings from President Hitler, Mr Mussolini, and the New Bunch.

To the Legation for Christmas carols.

December 23, 1937

Penelope telephoned all the way from Leake Priory to say Fergus has never heard of Maxi Finto. And a Merry Christmas to you too, Penelope.

January 2, 1938
To the Savoy with the Erlangers and the Crosbies. We learned a riotous new dance called the Lambeth Walk.

January 5, 1938
Encountered Daphne Frith in Church's trying on ankle boots. She said, 'I hope we can let bygones be bygones, Maybell. I do hope we'll see you at Hoxney Court this year.'

I should be so desperate.

I said, 'I live in Paris now, Daphne.'

'Yes,' she said, 'I heard. No distance from Kent at all. I should so love to see Paris again sometime.'

January 7, 1938
Gladys Trilling made straight for the seat next to mine at Monsieur Jules.

She said, 'It's too bloody, everything that's happened. How are poor Wally and David?'

I said, 'Never better. They adore living in France. We all do.'

'Still,' she said, 'it must be small comfort after everything they've lost. Stripped of rank. Reduced to penury. Although, of course, Wally was always terribly clever about making a little go a long way.'

Damned cheek from a woman who takes soap from hotel powder rooms.

Judson says Whitlow is being posted to Jakarta. There is a God.

January 9, 1938
To tea at Kensington Palace with Ena Spain. She's visiting her mother. Ena is convinced Anthony Eden is going to drag us into a war. She said, 'I'm going to move to Switzerland, Maybell, and you should think of doing the same. When it comes, as it will, I don't want to see or hear anything about it. I'm too old for more heartache.'

Poor Ena lost a brother in the Somme. Old Princess Baby didn't come down. She's in a bad way with rheumatics but doesn't seem to know how to die.

Wally wants me back posthaste. She's found a house near Versailles.

I said, 'I thought you wanted to be in town.'

She said, 'I do. But if we take this, David can garden.'

There's a flight on Thursday.

January 15, 1938, Hôtel Meurice, Paris
Wally signed a six-month lease in a fit of frustration but now she's having second thoughts. She said, 'It's not quite right. I'm going to get us out of it. I don't see why we should make do with the first thing that comes along, like a pair of refugees.'

HRH roamed in and out till she told him off. There's been too much weather for him to be able to play golf. His face fell when he saw her gathering up her things to go out. He said, 'I rather hoped we'd have lunch.'

She was running out to meet Kenny Opdyke.

He said, 'Shall I come with you?'

'No,' she said. 'Kenny's found me a nice little console table, but I'm going to have to beat the dealer down. I don't want you there confusing things.'

I stayed behind and shared his plate of sandwiches. He said, 'I don't believe Hitler wants a war, but if it should come to it I shall go back into uniform. I know war is a terrible, terrible thing, but I must say I remember it as the happiest time of my life. Except for now, of course.'

He asked a thousand questions about London. I think he pictures it just as it was when he left it, frozen, waiting for him to return. It would break his heart to know no one talks about him anymore.

Charlie Bedaux is back in town. He and Fern are dining with us next week. The America fiasco is not to be mentioned. Wally says what happened was completely beyond Charlie's control, and anyway, he's still a very useful and understanding friend.

January 25, 1938
Came last evening, Charlie and Fern, Princess Grimaldi, the Lazslo Melchiors, and a movie star called Maurice Chevalier. Charlie says we should all be in armaments. I must talk to Randolph Putnam.

Walter Monckton has proposed himself for next weekend. HRH is very buoyed up. He thinks it signals that the New Bunch are ready to welcome him back.

January 26, 1938
Randolph Putnam says I'm already in armaments.

Walter Monckton brought no news at all. He says he came simply to see how HRH was faring. Wally says he came for a jaunt, more like. She's now talking about going back to the States instead of settling in France, but Monckton advises against it. He says if they go to America they'll get squeezed for taxes, whereas the French are proving to be very considerate about David's particular financial circumstances.

Monckton's also concerned that HRH doesn't get political briefings anymore.

I said, 'He gets lectures from Freddie Crosbie.'

He said, 'Well, it's not enough. It's no wonder he seems so lost. The man needs to be kept *au courant*.'

I said, 'Wally sees to that.'

He said, 'I don't mean *au courant* with hat fashions and Paris niteries.'

He underestimates Wally. She reads the newspapers cover to cover every day.

Anyway, Monckton says he's going to try and impress upon London the importance of HRH continuing to receive little notes and visits, to help keep him informed of British policies. 'Otherwise,' he said, 'I very much fear the Germans will gain his ear and he may go off at dangerous tangents.'

February 3, 1938
Wally is busy with fittings. HRH is in a depression. I walked the dogs with him this morning. He said, 'My brother Bertie used to do whatever I told him, but since he's become King he gets quite testy if I telephone him with advice.'

I've suggested watercolors. When time hung heavy at Drumcanna I found it a very useful way of getting through the day.

Hattie Erlanger is coming for the weekend.

February 6, 1938

With Wally, Hattie, and Kenny Opdyke to a flea market. Hattie says Wally looked like an old rag-and-bone man the way she picked over everything. She can be very cruel.

HRH has decided to write his memoirs. Wally said he should find out how much a publisher is willing to pay for them before he wastes any time on them but he's already filled five and a half pages.

She's going down to Cannes with Kenny Opdyke and Johnnie MacMullen to make a final appraisal of La Croe. I think she's already decided to take it.

February 15, 1938

Wally has signed a ten-year lease on La Croe and is on her way back to claim her valentine. There have been heavy hints about an unset canary diamond.

February 16, 1938

Wally got a bracelet of cat's-eye rubies and a suite full of long-stemmed roses. HRH was pipped at the post in the bidding for the canary diamond by Mrs Standard Oil.

To La Huchette with Wally and HRH, the Lazslo Melchiors, and the Piston-LeRupins. Maxi Finto arrived around midnight with the Grimaldi woman, but he came over the instant he saw me. He's just back from his travels. Such a pleasure to be in the arms of a natural dancer again. I believe I feel the sap rising.

The Crosbies are going to try and come down to Cannes at Easter, international tensions permitting. Pips says there's a big row brewing in Parliament over the Italy question. The general feeling is that some kind of accommodation should be reached with Mr Mussolini, but

Anthony Eden is digging in his heels. Freddie is behind Eden. He would be.

February 22, 1938
Wrecked. Went with Maxi Finto to a *caveau* near St-Lazare to hear a rough little chanteuse he's discovered. The show didn't finish till three. Wally barked at me, said she doesn't want a yawner-in-waiting, but she's keen to come along next time we go. She does like to keep up with trends.

Anthony Eden has resigned, so perhaps we'll be spared from going to war with Italy.

February 26, 1938
A red-letter day! *Look!* magazine has named Wally as one of the ten best-dressed women in the world. She's deliriously happy and says now she's on the list she intends not only to remain on it but to achieve Number One position. Designers are going to be queuing up to dress her now. There'll be no more overdue accounts hanging around like last week's fish.

March 1, 1938
Sunshine at last. HRH has laid aside his memoirs and gone to play golf with Ambassador Bullitt. Maxi gave me lunch in a droll little bistro near St-Severin. He has to go back to Paraguay and has put a very interesting investment opportunity my way. Oilseed. It's top secret to prevent too many people getting in early and ruining our prospects.

March 4, 1938
To Elsie Mendl's last evening. Came, the Ambassador von Welczeks, Henri and Alix Piston-LeRupin, Sylvie Vieille-

Soiffarde, and Lucien Ecornifleur. I taught them the Lambeth Walk. They very much regard me as their eyes and ears in London. A sort of cultural attaché.

Wally's in a whirl of color charts and fabric samples for La Croe. Everything from the Fort is being fetched out of storage ready for shipping. She said, 'They may have taken away his palaces, Maybell, but he's still a prince of the blood and I intend to give him what he's due. I'm going to give him a truly royal home.'

They're very affectionate at present. Lots of golf seems to be beneficial.

Pips says now Anthony Eden's gone homburgs are absolutely out. She's making Freddie get a bowler.

March 9, 1938

It's been announced that King Bertie York and his Queen will make a state visit to France in July. The whole world at their disposal and they have to choose France! Wally says we're not going to wait around to be ignored while Bunny and Cook get the red carpet treatment. We shall leave the country. HRH has Forwood looking into yachts.

Johnnie MacMullen has made a brisk start on La Croe. Blue and white for the drawing rooms, with accents of yellow, peach for Wally's suite, royal scarlet for HRH, toile de Jouy for the guest rooms, Wedgwood blue for mine.

March 12, 1938

Hitler has sent his troops into Austria. Everyone is walking around with shocked expressions, but Kitty Rothschild has been predicting it for weeks. They all speak the same language so it simply amounts to a revision of frontiers, and as HRH says, there were many who argued for this very arrangement at the end of the war and the case may be stronger now because the Führer is himself Austrian and so has a natural care and affection for the place.

Tomorrow to Cannes. We're staying at the Cap-Argent until La Croe is habitable.

March 15, 1938, Cap-Argent, Cannes

The Crosbies are still dithering. Freddie says now Austria has fallen Czechoslovakia will be next. I don't see that that need upset our plans. Adolf Hitler is hardly going to send his tanks to the Côte d'Azur.

Boss and Ethel are going to motor over from Menton with Lily and the Bajavidas, so things may liven up. Herman and Kath are sweet but they don't keep late hours and they have Monckton and his wife staying. Hardly the life and soul of the party. The Moncktons are the kind of people who sit for hours studying books with no illustrations.

March 22, 1938

Motored to Monaco to meet the Crokers. Played a little roulette but Lady Luck deserted me. The Moncktons stayed home with the Rogerses and played bridge. Lily says Eugene Rothschild's brother has been arrested in Vienna. HRH wants to propose himself to go and parley with the Nazis but Wally won't hear of it. She says he could easily be taken hostage and the New Bunch wouldn't lift a finger to rescue him. Also, his furniture from Fort Belvedere arrives next week and she needs him here to decide which pieces he wants in his rooms. Still, what a worry for Eugene and Kitty.

March 29, 1938

The King of Albania is to marry a stenographer called Geraldine. Her mother was a Stewart from Richmond, Virginia. Married a Hungarian who ran through her money, and there's not much left, by all accounts. As suitable royal brides go, this girl makes Wally look like a Crown Princess.

The first of the furniture wagons are expected tomorrow. Wally is praying the good weather holds. She's going to have everything unloaded on to the lawns and inspected so as not to waste time carrying into the house pieces that have no place there. The carpenters are on standby with their chisels. The housemaids are at the ready with beeswax and cloths.

April 3, 1938

HRH has spent the day running around in golfing knickers reclaiming forgotten treasures. 'Oh look, my drum table!' I heard him cry. 'And remember this, darling? My tapestry footstool!'

Wally's creating a special room for him on the top floor. She's on great form. I think she's quietly rather pleased with what she's found in the crates. None of the silver is missing, the linens have survived the trip, and there are lots of decent paintings HRH had in storage, things she's never seen before. There's going to be enough for here and for Paris.

Fruity and Baba are going to come for Easter.

April 10, 1938, Château La Croe

Our first night in residence. Wally and David seem more like honeymooners today than ever they did last June.

HRH waylaid me as I was going up for my bath. He

said, 'Maybell, I haven't shown you my new realm. Come up and visit the Admiral of the Fleet.'

This is Wally's special gift to him. You go through his dressing room and then up in a tiny elevator to the penthouse. MacMullen has fitted it out like a boy's dream. It has a desk for his typewriter and baize on the floor so he can practice his putting. He has his bagpipes up there, and his ukulele, and a telescope on the little terrace, so when he goes out for a cigarette he can survey the horizon for battleships. He's named it 'The Bridge'.

I said, 'Sir, you'll be able to alert us when Daisy Fellowes hoves into view.'

He said, 'I will indeed. Isn't it all wonderful? Wally's so, so clever. I've never had a room like this before.'

Tomorrow, a celebratory luncheon for the Erlangers, the Metcalfes, and the Rogerses.

April 12, 1938

La Croe made a glorious debut. Wally had the terrace doors thrown open so that when people arrived they had an uninterrupted view through the hall, across the lawns, and down to the sea. Herman murmured, 'Good old Wally, ever the stage manager. Even the sun remembered its cue.'

The entrance hall was filled with sprays of white lilac. No paintings. Just David's old Garter banner hanging from the stair gallery. Very dramatic.

Wally kept trying to herd us out to the terrace for drinks but HRH was bounding around, overexcited like the dogs, pointing out little features and *objets*. It was such a good-humored lunch. Piquant chicken livers, eggplant baked with tomatoes, custard ice with crème de cassis.

Fruity says he's relieved to find HRH looking so well. From what Monckton had reported after his last visit,

445

he'd expected to find David smoking like a chimney and generally going to pieces.

I said, 'Wally won't allow that. She finds little chores for him to do, but it's all such a strain on her. It'd be far better if someone else gave him things to do. Papers to sign or something light like that, just for the mornings.'

He said, 'I know. Chamberlain will bring it up again with His Majesty. It's a question of timing. What about his memoirs? Monckton had high hopes of that, but he doesn't appear to have made much progress.'

I'm not sure. I think his pen ran out of ink one morning, and then Dimitri Shapaleff called up and suggested golf and somehow he just didn't get back to it.

I said, 'All I know is, it seems crazy that he's hanging around, opening and shutting snuffboxes and checking the time every few minutes, when Wally and I are up to our necks in menus. Surely there's something the New Bunch would be grateful to offload?'

He said, 'It's a problem, Maybell. It's a family thing. Tricky. Her Majesty's worried that if David becomes active again the country might rally to him, that there might be some kind of attempted return. Of course, she's remembering him when he was full of vim. If she'd seen him after those months at Enzesfeld she'd know that much of the fire has gone out of him. Actually, I'd say he's entirely harmless and could be a useful extra pair of hands, but Her Majesty's very protective of the King, you see? Every bit as fierce as Wally, when it comes to looking after her husband.'

April 18, 1938
Fruity and HRH have been up and down to the Bridge all day. Roars of laughter and the reek of tobacco.

446

Wally's all gaiety and confidence. She even volunteered to keep Baba company when she drove over to see the Rogerses this afternoon and she's never really been fond of Baba.

Hattie is trying to persuade me to go back to London. She says the monarchy has been saved, HRH has his Treasury elves cranking out ready money, and Wally is in her element, so there'll be no further excitement. She says I should leave them to live happily ever after.

I said, 'I'm lady-in-waiting.'

She said, 'Wally doesn't need anyone-in-waiting. She doesn't have state occasions to attend.'

Hattie didn't see us in Germany. Besides, what would I do in England? Put up bottled plums? Weekend at Leake Priory and play whist in gloves? How can I return to that after Paris? I need a colorful arena. I need food for my lively mind.

April 19, 1938
HRH wore his Lord of the Isles kilt at dinner and played one of his own bagpipe compositions, 'The Belle of Baltimore'. Afterwards to the casino. Saw Nazli Egypt and Lucien Ecornifleur at the chemin de fer tables.

Back to Paris on Friday. Fern Bedaux's people have found a house that sounds promising. Boulevard Suchet.

April 26, 1938, Hôtel Meurice, Paris
Wally has snapped up the house. It's on a very busy street but once you're inside the noise doesn't penetrate and the interior has great potential. There's an important staircase, an enfilade of salons, and a pretty view over the Bois de Boulogne. It needs bringing up to scratch from A to Z but Johnnie MacMullen says he can make a start on it as

soon as he's finished the Lazslo Melchiors' house at Le Touquet.

Randolph Putnam says I shouldn't have put anything into Maxi Finto's oilseed factory until I'd had him look into it. He treats me like a child.

To the Piston-LeRupins. Just carafe wine and Saltines and far too many people. Wally says it was their way of discharging a whole year's worth of social debts.

Afterwards to the ABC to hear Johnny Hess. Kenny Opdyke said Sylvie Vieille-Soiffarde had been planning to oust me as lady-in-waiting until she discovered all the job paid was a dress allowance and accommodations. Dress allowance! If only!

I said, 'Excuse me, Kenny! All it pays is a suite at La Croe and an interesting life.'

May 10, 1938

Lord Halifax is coming for tea with HRH. Part of Walter Monckton's campaign to keep him in the swim.

Dudley Forwood has found us a yacht for July. She's called the *Gulzar*. We're going to take her down to Portofino, pick up the Nasibrunis and Clarice Sfogginomi, and continue on to Capri. As Wally says, best to give the Bertie Yorks a wide berth while they're kinging in Paris, and with Queen Dumpling that means a very wide berth indeed.

To Didi Grimaldi's scavenger hunt last evening. Rather a put-up job, I thought, because Winnie Gulliver must be the only woman in Paris with access to a size 13 evening sandal. Still, I was the only contestant who managed to produce a four-leaf clover. Cloisonné, admittedly, but I was still the only one.

Didi has also gone into oilseed with Maxi. So much for it being hush-hush.

Tomorrow, back to La Croe. Boss and Ethel are coming for Wally and David's anniversary. Possibly the Cavetts too.

June 1, 1938, La Croe
The Hermann Goerings have a baby girl. What a blessing. Only five hundred airplanes in the fly-past. Anniversary cards and letters and presents are arriving by the dozen, many of them addressed simply to 'The Duke and Duchess of Windsor, France'. All offering affectionate good wishes. The difference a year makes.

We're going to mark Friday with a small lunch party.

June 3, 1938
HRH and Wally posed for photos on the lawn before lunch. Fern came without Charlie who is away on some secret mission. Lily believes it's not unconnected with the bailing out of that poor Rothschild who's still incarcerated in Vienna.

Great hilarity over the quantity of baby bootees among the anniversary gifts.

Boss said, 'Well, Wally, what about it? It'd be cute to see a little David gamboling on the lawn.'

Ethel said, 'She already has a little David who gambols on the lawn.'

Wally said, 'I have an even better idea. Let's pack up the bootees and send them to Emmy Goering.'

David gave her a platinum eternity band.

Ethel said, 'I take my hat off to her. She's taken a disaster and turned it into a happy ending.'

Well, Wally was never deterred by unpromising material. Even at Biddle Street she made her mother use their few bits of good china every day.

Lily has offered a little birthday dinner for Wally in Nice.

June 20, 1938
We took over Le Cirque last night. Lily had offered to pay for twelve but to my certain knowledge Wally invited twenty, and then people like Lucky Patrice, whom we actually hardly know, brought extras with them. Wally says Lily can afford it.

HRH gave her a jet and diamond leopard pin.

June 30, 1938
The Cavetts and the Erlangers have arrived. We board the *Gulzar* tomorrow in time for dinner. First stop, Rapallo.

July 5, 1938, off Rapallo
Wally and HRH have gone ashore to see the Victor Emmanuels. Their youngest daughter just got engaged to a Bourbon-Parma. Tori and Paola Nasibruni came aboard last evening. We're picking up Clarice Sfogginomi off Sperlonga.

July 12, 1938, off Anzio
All day being dragged around Roman ruins by Hattie. Tomorrow Judson can go with her. I'm going to the Tiberio spa to relax and put aside all busyness. Wally says the facials alone make the whole trip worthwhile.

Rory is seventeen today. How he'd love the *Gulzar*. Better than any of those little canoes he gets to sail with old Salty Laird. He'd be beating to windward and splicing the yardarm and having such fun. Perhaps next year. And Flora too. Violet can't expect them to spend every summer of their lives at Drumcanna.

July 19, 1938, Pensione Bon Sol
We've put in to Sestri Levante for our last few days and who should we find sitting on the veranda of our pensione but Maxi Finto. He's been chasing up and down the coast of Italy for the past three weeks trying to find me. The oilseed business is about to take off in a very big way so this is a golden opportunity to increase the size of my investment. Wait till Randolph Putnam hears about this!

Tonight, dinner *à deux*. Zita says she can smell love in the air. I don't know. Maxi is a dream, but we're business partners now. We can't afford to let sentiment cloud our decisions.

July 23, 1938
Wally offered Maxi a ride back with us to Cannes, but he's staying on to look into cork. Well, Brumby was a great believer in diversification. And Randolph Putnam isn't going to hear about my oilseed killing yet either. Maxi says financial advisors are well known for scaring people off good prospects so they can mop them up for themselves.

August 1, 1938, La Croe
We got back here late last evening and the help were all lined up outside the front door, crisp summer liveries and nice straight backs. Wally's done such a good job on them.

Pips and Freddie were here ahead of us. Freddie says General Franco looks like winning in Spain which will mean Lightfoot is on the wrong side. What a fool.

Pips says La Croe makes Fort Belvedere look like a flophouse.

August 11, 1938

The Neville Chamberlains are at Balmoral. Monckton says HRH's future is definitely on the agenda.

August 15, 1938

No news from Balmoral.

August 21, 1938

We closed Boîte Noire at five and went on to Chez Zazzi for pancakes and coffee.

Still nothing from Balmoral.

August 24, 1938

We're going back to Paris. Monckton wants to see HRH but is too pressed for time to come down to La Croe. Maybe this means good news. Wally says Monckton will never bring good news, from Balmoral or anywhere else. She says the man is a Jonah.

Freddie said, 'Well, this is hardly the time to be pestering the King about David's future. I'm sure his mind is on the Sudetenland.'

There's always something. One thing about the United States. There aren't all these little local disputes going on.

Wally said, 'If they don't hurry up and do something for David, maybe we'll give him something else to worry about. We could, you know. We could go back and set up there and create a fearful row. They're completely foul of the law, keeping me out of my title.'

She's always like this toward the end of a vacation. Nagging and picking and revisiting old wrongs.

September 3, 1938, Hôtel Meurice, Paris

Wally and Freddie were both right. Monckton says Balmoral simply wasn't the moment for Chamberlain to bring up HRH. He says there are worrying rumblings from the direction of Czechoslovakia which monopolized everyone's thoughts.

Wally said, 'Another opportunity missed. Another winter on the way with David unemployed.'

Monckton said, 'Strictly off the record, Halifax thinks the Czechs are bound to have to cede something to Hitler, so it may be settled pretty quickly.'

Wally said, 'And then there'll be something else. Everything gets settled except *our* affairs.'

To Gerny's to hear the delicious Charles Trenet.

September 7, 1938

The Ambassador von Welczeks to dinner. Also came, Bendor Westminster, the Lazslo Melchiors, and Elsie Mendl. I now understand all about the Sudetenland. Everyone who lives there is German anyway, so it makes no sense at all for the Czechs to hold on to it. Common sense must surely prevail.

September 12, 1938

They say German troops are massing on the Czech frontier.

September 14, 1938

Mr Chamberlain is flying to Germany tomorrow to see President Hitler and ascertain his intentions. A perfect example of a job they could have given to HRH. As Wally says, Neville Chamberlain must have a hundred calls on his time, whereas HRH has spent the morning whistling through his teeth and watching the rain beat down.

September 15, 1938

HRH's cousin Arthur Connaught has died, but as he still has three months of his exile to serve he's not allowed to go to England for the funeral. It was cancer, apparently. I met the wife once, at Carlton Gardens. She's very keen on hospitals and sits on various committees with Violet.

Hitler told Chamberlain that the Sudetenland is a private German matter and nothing to do with the League of Nations. France says if so much as one German boot enters Czechoslovakia it will take steps.

Forwood says what France means is, it will issue a statement deploring Germany's actions. He says they can't possibly think of going to war because they'll find themselves marching alone. Britain is by no means ready for any military adventures and America isn't interested. It's all so unsettling. Perhaps Ena Spain has the right idea. Move to Switzerland and stop listening to the wireless.

September 18, 1938

Lunch with Kitty Rothschild and Winnie Gulliver. They think Hitler is playing with Neville Chamberlain as a cat plays with a mouse. Kitty says after Czechoslovakia it will be Poland, then Yugoslavia, then Romania, and so on, until the German flag flies all over Europe. Even France.

Eugene is in New York overseeing work on their Long Island property because they foresee it becoming their only safe haven.

Wally says the Rothschilds are one case, we're quite another. She says we'd have nothing to fear in the unlikely event of Germany invading France.

She said, 'Don't forget, David's as much German as he is British so it'd make no difference to us. In fact, it might be to our advantage. Adolf Hitler would certainly give him a job.'

September 29, 1938

Neville Chamberlain is flying to Germany again for more discussions with the Führer, and this time Mr Mussolini will also attend. Everyone is very tense. After great difficulties I got a call through to Carlton Gardens, but neither Violet nor Melhuish were home. Left a message.

Managed to speak to Pips who says they're digging trenches in Hyde Park and the War Office is recruiting women for the home defenses. Cooks, drivers, typists. She's going to volunteer.

I said, 'You're too old.' She said, 'I'm not a bit too old.'

I'll bet she is. She hasn't looked into it properly. She doesn't even know what the uniforms are like.

She was at the House of Commons yesterday to hear Chamberlain speak before he left for Munich. She says there were extraordinary scenes, everyone very emotional and braced for the worst. She said the House was packed. Even the old Queen was there.

September 30, 1938

Violet returned my call. They heard yesterday that Lightfoot has been injured in Spain, but not seriously, and is being sent home. No other information except that it happened as long ago as August so Doopie may find him on the doorstep at any moment. What a relief. I hope this has cured him of wars.

Fruity Metcalfe is here. He wants to discuss war plans with HRH, but I don't think we have any.

October 1, 1938

The warmongers have been routed! With the help of Mr Mussolini's diplomatic efforts Neville Chamberlain has achieved a concord with Hitler. He's to be allowed to have the Sudetenland provided he promises to leave the rest of Czechoslovakia in peace. Exactly as Halifax predicted. It sounds to me as though Mr Mussolini has earned that little piece of Africa that's been such a bone of contention.

Everyone is happy except Fruity. He says it's like telling a burglar you won't call the police if he puts back the diamonds and just steals the teaspoons. Of course, Fruity is itching to get back into uniform.

October 7, 1938

Penelope Blythe has pitched up for a long weekend. She says she'd been looking forward to having Leake Priory requisitioned and being able to do some kind of daring war work, but everything has now gone off the boil. She's seeking new excitements.

Took her to lunch at Wally's who was at her most gruesome, nagging HRH to go to Boulevard Suchet and throw some royal weight around with the laggard electricians. The suite was full of red carnations, never Wally's choice.

'Just cordial wishes from the Führer,' she said. 'But no prizes for guessing the name of the delivery boy!'

They're dining with the Ambassador von Welczeks tonight and the von Ribbentrops will be there. Penelope and I to Maxim's and then on to the Revue Negre with Sylvie Vieille-Soiffarde's crowd.

October 9, 1938

Ena Spain has lost another son. He was in a car accident in Miami. I haven't been able to speak with her. Anyway, what can one say? Her life has been nothing but tragedy. And still Princess Baby hangs on.

Penelope says Lucien Ecornifleur squeezed her thigh last evening. I said, 'Start to worry when he squeezes your purse.'

October 15, 1938

Joey Legh is over to play some golf with HRH. Wally's relieved to have him entertained. He's become very peevish lately about her lunches with Kenny Opdyke. She said, 'David, I married you for better or for worse, but not for lunch.'

The Communists are threatening strikes.

October 17, 1938

A letter from Pips. Lightfoot is home and in a much worse condition than they'd been led to expect, having lost an arm. He's in St Thomas's Hospital being seen to.

October 20, 1938

A brief conversation with Violet. George Lightfoot has lost his right forearm. It could have been worse. Just as well, though, that he settled for Doopie because his chances with anyone else would now be reduced. One saw a lot of it after the war, men with an empty sleeve pinned across their chest. I never found it in the least dashing.

Violet said, 'I do wish you'd come home, Maybell.'

I said, 'I am home.'

But I may visit. November is out of the question because we have fittings for our spring gowns and several important parties. Also, we're also threatened with the Harry Gloucesters who may call in on their way home from princing in Africa. Perhaps I'll go in December, when Rory is home from school.

November 4, 1938

Lily Drax-Pfaffenhof for the weekend. She says the Munich accord was a simple case of common sense because no one in Germany wants a war, not even Hitler. As for the way the Jewish folk are being bullied, she wonders whether the Führer knows the half of what's going on.

Charlie Bedaux says I should buy francs while they're such good value.

November 7, 1938

Maxi Finto is back. He says our oilseeds will be in profit by the summer and he's found the very cork grove for me. I'd forgotten I was even looking for one! He reminds me of Brumby in some ways. Always dreaming up business schemes, even on the threshold of the boudoir. Always alert to opportunities. Of course, Brumby never used brilliantine, and he was an early riser whereas Maxi goes to bed with the lark.

Tonight to Pigalle.

November 11, 1938

The Harry Gloucesters. They toyed with their sweetbreads, she whispering to me that they prefer simple food. What a mixed bag these royalties are. King Bertie York and Gloucester and the sister are so dull and HRH and Kent are so vivacious, or at least they used to be. The only sign of animation in Gloucester came when HRH told him he'd sold off his Canadian livestock.

'Oh no!' he said. 'Not the shorthorns! What a tragedy! Damned fine herd! How much did you get for them?'

I just hope he carries the story back to the New Bunch. It's high time they realized homes fit for a royal duke cost a great deal more money than they've allowed him and sacrifices have had to be made.

After lunch we showed them Boulevard Suchet which smells of fresh paint but is almost ready for the drapes to be hung, then HRH went with them to the airfield to see them off.

November 12, 1938
Mr Atatürk died yesterday. We had such an agreeable time with him in Istanbul. Wally is wearing her Turkish choker in remembrance.

November 23, 1938
The Neville Chamberlains are dining here tomorrow. HRH hopes they're bringing news of a thaw at Buckingham Palace. Wally says one might as well look for a thaw at the North Pole.

I'm taking a rain check on cork groves but have plunged a little deeper into oilseeds. Maxi leaves for Paraguay on Sunday.

November 25, 1938
If Mrs Chamberlain possesses any good jewelry she elected not to wear it last evening and her gown was *le dernier cri*. She was caught between the glitter of my diamonds and the flash of Wally's sapphires and looked like a dazed woodland creature. Still, at least she bobbed a curtsy.

Despite our best efforts, conversation was like a slow game of handball, and when the men joined us after their brandy HRH looked ominously deflated. Apparently, Chamberlain's talk had been of nothing but international tensions and his only word on the subject of David's exile had been that 'now didn't seem quite the moment'.

Wally said, 'It'll never be "quite the moment", David. Why don't you face facts? We're never going back.'

HRH says he found Chamberlain very sound on the important points. 1. War against Germany is unthinkable because the French are in no state of readiness and we can't start hostilities without them. And 2. We should anyway be addressing the more urgent question of how best to deal with the Soviet bear.

We just heard that his Aunt Maud has died. They're taking her back to Norway, so strictly speaking he could attend the funeral without breaking any promises, but he's decided not to. He doesn't want to travel without Wally and even if Wally could be persuaded to climb aboard an airplane he knows when they got there none of the royalties would speak to her.

He said, 'I burn with shame, Maybell, every time I think of the wrong they're doing her. Her only offense has been to be loved by me.'

Of course, there's more to it than that. They hate her because she's American. They hate her because she won't be fenced in by their silly old rules. But none of it matters anymore. Anyway, he wasn't close to Maud Norway.

Claridge's have reserved me a nice junior suite. Wally's shopping list grows longer. Marmalade, dog treats, ink, Mrs Spry special flower-arrangement wire, magnesia tablets.

I'm going to try to coax Violet and Melhuish out of their rut and give them dinner. I'll bet they haven't been to a restaurant in years.

December 6, 1938, Claridge's Hotel, London
Dear Lightfoot is in a very bad way. He's thinner than ever and racked with pain from the arm he no longer has.

Still full of jocularity though, in spite of it. He said, 'I suppose I should change my name to Light*hand*.'

He's quite unrepentant about going to Spain. He said, 'My only regret is that the British Battalion didn't stay until the job was done.'

I said, 'Well, please promise you'll stay at home from now on.'

He said, 'No choice. If it comes to another war the army won't have any use for me now. Can't even push a bloody pen.'

Doopie loved the scent I took her.

December 8, 1938

Violet may still be a little starchy with me but I seem to have reestablished full diplomatic relations with Melhuish. He actually kissed me as they were leaving. A roast partridge can work wonders.

He asked after HRH. I said, 'He's fit and well but under-occupied. Why doesn't the King give him a job?'

He said, 'I'm sure he will. As an opening arises.'

Violet said, 'Can't France use him? What about worker housing and pithead baths? Has he lost interest?'

As I reminded her, when he made a study of such things he got nothing but criticism.

Melhuish is all for Chamberlain. He says British politics can always be relied upon to produce the right man for the moment.

He said, 'Baldwin managed the abdication satisfactorily but only Chamberlain could have pulled off Munich.'

Rory is home tomorrow. He has his heart set on going to Dartmouth next year as a cadet officer and Melhuish is resigned to him choosing the navy instead of the army. He said, 'Could be worse. At least he's not going to end

461

up in the corps de bloody ballet!' A sly dig at the Belchesters' middle boy.

December 13, 1938
Rory and Flora came to tea looking quite the young lady and gentleman.

Flora said, 'I wish Aunt Doopie and Uncle Lightfoot would have a baby. I like babies.'

Rory said, 'They can't have babies now, you noddle-head. Uncle Lightfoot only has one arm.'

So adorable. He gave me a fake camellia that squirts water.

Tomorrow, home.

December 16, 1938, Hôtel Meurice, Paris
The station wagons leave for La Croe in the morning with the luggage. Johnnie MacMullen is going ahead too, to supervise the dressing of the tree. The Crokers are coming and the Erlangers. Herman and Kath will motor over on Christmas Day.

December 22, 1938, La Croe
Arrived just before dark. MacMullen had had the shutters left open and every window glowed with light. Pine cones dipped in colored wax burning in the drawing-room fireplace, the foyer tree dressed with snowberries and white velvet bows, glasses of eggnog waiting for us. Just as everything looked set for a perfect holiday, Kath Rogers telephoned bearing the glad tidings that Thelma Furness and sister Gloria are spending Christmas at La Belle Garoupe, not half a mile away. Wally completely unperturbed. She said, 'Half a mile *geographically*, Kath, but light years in every other respect.'

I think the news has slightly unsettled HRH though. He's asked me to go with him to Cartier tomorrow, to help him pick out a few extra little *douceurs* for Wally, just in case there are any 'tricky encounters'.

December 26, 1938
Wally got a blue diamond pin. She gave HRH a pair of ship's decanters for the Bridge and me a set of ivory elephants that are supposed to bring good luck. I believe I remember them from Bryanston Court.

A strained moment after dinner last evening when Hattie suggested a game of charades and HRH clapped his hands for joy. He said, 'Oh yes! I haven't done that in years.'

Wally said, 'We are *not* playing charades. This is La Croe, not Sandringham. We're going to the casino.'

Fortunately, that little Maharaja friend of the Bajavidas was there and staked her very generously.

January 2, 1939
New Year's Eve at Willie Maugham's. A bad start when a spiteful little cluster of guests stood in Wally's path and absolutely would not curtsy. HRH went right up to Isabel Carteret and asked her if she'd forgotten her manners. He was in a fury and so was she. She said, 'No, sir. In our family we only curtsy to Royal Highnesses.'

HRH is still simmering over it but Wally hasn't said a word. Hattie says the Carterets don't give a damn. Their people have been around since 1066 so they don't feel the Windsors have anything to teach them.

January 6, 1939
Johnnie MacMullen has gone back to Paris to make sure everything is perfect for the move to Boulevard Suchet. He says Wally's the most exacting person he's ever done a house for and he always feels he's only one misplaced pillow away from appearing in her Grumble Book. I'd say it's unavoidable. One needs four paws and an annoying little yappy bark to be spared that fate.

January 10, 1939, Hôtel Meurice, Paris
Boulevard Suchet is truly fit for a king. The livery looks especially magnificent. Black and scarlet for daywear,

scarlet trimmed with gold for formals. The buttons have a coronet and a W intertwined with an E which the valet seems to think stands for Edward Windsor but Wally says it stands for Wallis and Edward. HRH insists it simply spells 'we'.

'Einums meinums and her boy,' he keeps saying, 'against the rest of the world.'

I do wish he wouldn't. And I wish he wouldn't kiss her in the drawing room. It's so juvenile and I know Wally hates it, because of smudges.

January 12, 1939
Wally and I now have a routine. We meet every morning in her little Louis Quinze sitting room, as soon as she's given the secretaries the letters for the day. We make telephone calls, find out who's doing what, decide on clothes, juggle guest lists. We lunch, usually with Didi Grimaldi or Fern Bedaux or, if Wally's having a shopping lunch with Kenny Opdyke, I see Kitty Rothschild or Winnie Gulliver. The hairdresser comes at five. If people are invited I come back to the Meurice to change. Otherwise I just have a sundowner with HRH, while Wally's dressing and then leave them to dine alone.

The Charles Lindberghs are going to be in town at the end of the month and Wally's determined to get them for dinner. I believe she may still have a crush on him.

February 5, 1939
Dinner at Boulevard Suchet last evening in honor of the Charles Lindberghs. Also came, the Ambassador Bullitts, Charlie and Fern, Lucien Ecornifleur, and the Lazslo Melchiors. I don't know what Wally sees in Lindbergh. All the man talks about is inventions. I don't believe

he notices women at all. I had the impression he couldn't wait to escape from the table and go home and calculate velocities or whatever it is he does. Mrs L must welcome the opportunity to be in company. I find her rather sweet but Wally doesn't see any point to her.

King Bertie York and his Queen are to visit the United States and Canada in the spring. I'll bet they're only going to rub David and Wally's noses in Charlie Bedaux's fiasco.

Freddie Crosbie has decided there isn't going to be a war after all so he and Pips are venturing to Paris for a weekend. They make it sound like trekking through darkest Africa. Pips has lost all her pluck. Whatever happened to the Pips who flew her drawers from the Oldfields flagpole on Founders Day?

February 12, 1939
Pips has a new short haircut. She got it in anticipation of wartime austerity and has decided to keep it. Freddie says a war grows less likely by the day because Hitler is very unpopular with the German military and so can't depend on them at all. Meanwhile, Britain is rearming at such a clip Germany must think twice before embarking on any future adventures.

Wally told Pips off for slouching. Pips said, 'Better a relaxed womanly posture than looking like someone put a broom handle up your gown.'

Nervous laughter from HRH. Wally is fierce about deportment. Always has been.

Freddie thinks Maxi Finto sounds like a big fake. He says I should have gotten something on paper.

February 15, 1939
Freddie went with HRH to the English church. Wally was cross. She says he'd meet much better people at the Madeleine.

March 1, 1939
The Lazslo Melchiors are giving a costume party to welcome the spring. We all have to dress as rustics.

March 2, 1939
Wally says she's not dressing as a rustic for anyone. She may ask Main Bocher to make her a little muslin milk-maid gown and just add seed pearls. It's at times like this it would be so handy to have Doopie around the corner.

March 8, 1939
I've written to Violet suggesting Rory and Flora visit me as soon as Rory is released from school in July. That would give us three clear weeks for jaunts and much needed shopping. Flora seems to own nothing but ragged woolens suitable for Drumcanna. She has practically nothing smart for town. What fun we'll have.

March 16, 1939
After all those promises he made at Munich, Hitler has upped and marched into Czechoslovakia. People are saying Poland will be next. It's becoming very hard to keep a good opinion of Adolf Hitler. HRH says the average German is a jolly, sociable chap and the last thing he wants is a war. He says the only conclusion he can reach is that Hitler now has a screw loose.

Tonight to the Lazslo Melchiors'. Kenny Opdyke has it

from a reliable source that Lucien Ecornifleur intends wearing nothing but a vine leaf.

March 18, 1939
A fabulous party. The Dimitri Shapaleffs came as vulgar boatmen, Sylvie Vieille-Soiffarde came as Circe with Johnnie MacMullen as an enchanted swine, and the Piston-LeRupins came as themselves, but the scene was stolen by the Esterhazys who arrived on hired donkeys. Wally carried a wooden pail and HRH wore his old gardening hat and carried a trug of nosegays.

April 2, 1939
Mr Chamberlain has put his foot down. If Hitler makes the slightest move, Britain will go to Poland's aid. All very well but if, as people like Winnie Gulliver believe, he has his eye on half a dozen other territories too, then what? One can't rush around the world helping every little country out of difficulties.

Wally has had the idea of HRH making a broadcast to the American people. As she says, if Britain gets into another war, before too long she'll be looking to America for assistance, so the American public must be made to stop and think. They are the ones who'll be asked to pay the price, after all. And who better to make them think than a British prince with an American wife. HRH is very keen and has Dudley Forwood looking into it.

April 8, 1939
The world has gone mad. Italy has now invaded Albania and poor Queen Geraldine has had to get out of her childbed and flee. If she has any sense she'll get herself straight to a good American hospital.

April 9, 1939
A letter from Violet. She says July is out of the question
for Flora and Rory to come to Paris. She's convinced we'll
be at war by then. Of course, what she doesn't know is
HRH is going to broadcast to America and pull us all
back from the brink. Forwood is discovering great enthusiasm for the project. Replied by return. I said then let
them come sooner. Rory's Long Leave in June would be
perfect. I know Elsie Mendl would adore to throw a little
party for them.

I might make a start on jewelry for Flora too. Another
year or two and she'll be out and apart from a very dull
tiara and an ugly cameo brooch I don't believe she stands
to inherit anything from the Melhuish side.

April 15, 1939
HRH's peacekeeping message to America is to be broadcast in early May from the town of Verdun. Wally will
accompany him.

April 17, 1939
Freddie Crosbie got wind of HRH's broadcast. He said,
'Tell him, Maybell, when you're out walking those bloody
pooches, he's not going to help himself or world peace by
asking America to wink at Germany's ambitions. He's
going to come across as Hitler's friend which, I may say,
a lot of people already believe him to be.'

I'm not going to tell him any such thing. He's so enjoying
preparing his speech.

April 19, 1939
Humphrey Butler wants to know if HRH has cleared his
speech with the New Bunch. Wally told him to mind his

own business. I agree with her. You can't throw someone out of house and home and then expect to be kept informed of their every movement.

Lunch with Winnie Gulliver. She said she hoped I didn't give Maxi Finto a lot of money. I wonder what she means by 'a lot'.

April 25, 1939

Beaverbrook has now added his voice to the dissenters. He says he's concerned about the timing of the broadcast because it will coincide with the New Bunch visiting with the Roosevelts and there may be confusion as to who speaks for Great Britain, the new and untested King or the seasoned older brother?

When one looks at it that way, perhaps he has a point. I think David should speak before Bertie York has time to open his mouth, but Forwood says the dates can't be changed.

May 7, 1939

Walter Monckton called to try and persuade HRH to postpone his speech but he and Wally had already left for Verdun. Anyway, their minds were quite made up. As Wally said, this could be a turning point, the moment when the world wakes up to David's value as a statesman. And it's a very fine speech. I've heard him practicing it.

I speak as a soldier who served in the Great War, all too conscious here in Verdun of the presence of that great company of the dead. It is my earnest prayer that such cruel and destructive madness shall never again overtake mankind.

And so it goes on. Who could possibly object?

May 10, 1939
Forwood says HRH's broadcast appears to have sunk without trace in England.

Elsie Mendl is going to give a birthday party for Wally at Trianon. Wally has given me the job of pointing HRH in the direction of a diamond pendant she's seen at Cartier. It would do for her birthday or for their anniversary.

May 12, 1939
Violet continues to be obstructive. She claims Rory has to go to Felicity Massingham's ball during June leave and Flora has three teeth to be filled. Just because *she's* never been to Paris is really no reason to prevent her children broadening their horizons.

May 18, 1939
Sacks of mail have started arriving for HRH, applauding his Verdun speech. Letter after letter makes the same point. No one wants another war. HRH has spoken to the ordinary little people of America and the Dominions and struck a chord, and if they're not prepared to fight there can't be a war. QDE, as Danforth Brumby used to say.

May 23, 1939
Wally and HRH are going to Candé for their second anniversary. Returning, as Forwood puts it, to the scene of the crime.

June 4, 1939
Such sad news from London. Philip Sassoon is dead. Violet telephoned to tell me. He had an infected throat and instead of taking his doctor's advice and resting

in bed he went out in the rain and developed pneumonia. She says Sybil is devastated. Violet seemed in low spirits herself. They're calling up all twenty-year-olds for military training. She says Ulick is raring to go but now it comes to it she begins to wish she'd had all daughters.

I said, 'But Melhuish knows so many useful people in the Guards. If it should come to anything serious, I'm sure it could be arranged that the boy doesn't get sent into anything too dangerous.'

She said, 'Melhuish would never ask any such thing. Melhuishes do their duty.'

I was only trying to cheer her up. Anyway, Ulick's very handy with a gun.

June 6, 1939

Wally and HRH are back from Candé. She got a gold cobra bangle with sapphire eyes, so now she's fretting as to whether she'll get the desired diamond for her birthday. I said, 'Well, I delivered the suggestion. I can do no more. I have more serious things on my mind.'

'Such as?' she said.

I said, 'Such as the death of an old friend and before his time.'

She said, 'I don't recall Sassoon being all that much of a friend. He dropped you soon enough. You should follow my rule, Maybell. Never forgive, never forget.'

Well, *I* have some very happy memories of Philip.

June 7, 1939

Kitty Rothschild says it's not done to send flowers when Jews die. Too late. I already sent them.

June 10, 1939
HRH says it doesn't seem appropriate to splash out on diamonds when the world is so full of uncertainty. He's bought Wally a pair of tourmaline ear clips for her birthday. Very pretty, but a long, long way from a diamond.

June 19, 1939
Wally is forty-three again. Gave her an antique crystal scent spray filled with Joy.

She wasn't wearing her tourmaline ear clips. She said, 'Some messenger you turned out to be. Well, no matter. I'll buy that pendant myself.'

Precisely. That's always the best way with husbands and jewels.

Tonight to Trianon.

June 20, 1939
Elsie had had the whole garden lit. A sprung dance floor installed and two champagne fountains. There were tumbling dwarves and fire-eaters and a darling baby elephant pulling a cart with Wally's birthday cake. Elsie's people seem to be able to get their hands on anything.

June 24, 1939
Fruity Metcalfe is going to come down to Cannes in August but without Baba. She doesn't want to leave her family. He says London is all on edge about Germany and Italy and the Russians. He says the best thing would be if we make an alliance with the Russians while we can. He says that might cool Germany's Polish ambitions.

Wednesday to La Croe. The Crokers are worried about remaining in Europe and the Cavetts have canceled. Hattie may come but without Judson. He can't get away. As for

Adolf Hitler, I'll bet he's sitting up in the Berghof, eating cookies and laughing at all these nervous nellies. I'll bet *he's* taking a vacation.

July 1, 1939, La Croe
So many villas seem to be empty. I think it's going to be a very dull summer. Daisy Fellowes is undeterred, however. Her yacht should be off Cannes in time for our July 4th chicken fry. She has the Fannullonis and Clarice Sfogginomi on board. Lily is motoring over with the Milwaukee Gunters, so there should at least be a golf partner for HRH.

Kath Rogers is stockpiling canned goods.

July 6, 1939
Our chicken fry was better attended than we'd feared. Daisy and party, Lily and party. Afterwards to the casino where Jessie Woolworth appeared with Ecornifleur on one arm and Maxi Finto on the other. He said oilseed business is flat because of uncertainties in Europe. Sweat on his top lip.

The Piston-LeRupins are just down the road. The season is so dead here, they've managed to rent La Belle Garoupe for a knockdown price.

July 12, 1939
Rory's eighteenth birthday. Got a telephone connection with no trouble at all but he wasn't at home. He was attending a tennis party at the Boddie-Fultons'. Poor boy. He hates ballgames. Violet says he can't wait to get started at Dartmouth. Of all the times to be joining the military. Lightfoot is apparently still in a depression. Ulick is going to Drumcanna with him ahead of everyone else. They're going to try and rig up some way of him managing in the

474

butts. I'm sure there's something safer than shooting he could do with only one arm. Netting butterflies, perhaps.

Boss and Ethel have braved it to La Croe. Ethel says if the world is going to end let it happen while she's sunning herself beneath a blue Mediterranean sky. Hear! Hear!

Alix Piston-LeRupin says she thought there was some kind of prohibition against Maxi Finto going into business again after the cocoa bean scandal.

July 18, 1939
Dudley Forwood has been told to report to his regiment. Wally said, 'You can't leave until Fruity gets here to take over.'

Forwood said, 'I don't think you understand. I have to follow orders.'

She said, 'You certainly do. Our orders. You're to stay here until His Royal Highness releases you.'

I said, 'Wally, you're putting Dudley in a very difficult position.'

She said, 'Do you think so? Then let me reconsider. Yes, on second thoughts, Forwood, pack your bags and go. You were never much use anyway.'

I didn't mean to make things worse. Forwood says I didn't.

'Merely clarified things,' he said. 'Thank you, Maybell.'

July 19, 1939
Forwood was gone by the time we got up this morning. Faces like thunder but neither HRH nor Wally has said a word.

July 25, 1939
Fruity has arrived and not a moment too soon because now David's valet has been called for military service.

Fruity says it's likely to get worse. He says von Ribbentrop is in Moscow, dancing with the Russians. Well, he is a very good dancer.

August 3, 1939
The Rogerses' gardeners have been called up. Kath says the same thing will happen to everyone, but Wally says we're a special case.

Wally and Hattie had words. One of the terriers chewed Hattie's tennis bat.

August 10, 1939
Call-up papers for two of our footmen and three of our gardeners. Wally told HRH to make some telephone calls, but he doesn't seem to have made any headway.

Charlie Bedaux has a Hawaiian nut plantation they may buy.

I said, 'Does this mean we'll be moving to Hawaii?'

She said, 'If that's where we have to go for staff we can call our own, yes.'

Hattie said, 'What nonsense. Come back to London with me, Maybell. Wally seems to be losing her grip on reality.'

I don't know. They say Hawaii has a very agreeable climate. Hattie says she wouldn't buy a bicycle pump from Charlie Bedaux.

Herman says we should all keep locked canisters of gasoline in our garages, in case of shortages.

August 13, 1939
Fruity says the Commons may be recalled early. If Germany moves against Poland, it's war.

August 18, 1939
A letter from Violet. Ena Spain hasn't risked the trip to
Drumcanna this year. Rory is crewing for Salty Laird
off Dorsetshire. Lightfoot is crazed with pain and threw
a bottle of Scotch at Ulick. Flora has entered woman-
hood. Well, now her troubles begin. I do hope Violet
has told her about boys. The child is still so natural and
spontaneous.

August 23, 1939
The wily Russians have made an accord with Germany.
Herman says this means Poland is done for. HRH has sent
a wire to Hitler reminding him of the lovely tea they
enjoyed together and their agreement that there was only
one enemy to be vanquished: Communism.
    Boss and Ethel are leaving tomorrow. Also Fruity. He
says the writing is on the wall.

August 24, 1939
Fruity is gone. He leaves behind a large void. When Wally
and I came back from shopping HRH was in the morning
room trying to pluck a tune on his ukulele.

August 26, 1939
HRH received a telegram of reply from Hitler. It said
Germany had never wished to quarrel with England but
if, as it appears, England now chooses to pick a war with
Germany he'll have no choice but to respond. The house-
keeper says there's already a run on blackout material.

September 1, 1939
This morning, while Wally and I were having our nails done
and HRH was up on the Bridge scanning for battleships,

Germany invaded Poland. Also, an anti-aircraft battery arrived and proceeded to dig latrines upwind of our bathing pavilion without so much as a by-your-leave. When war approaches courtesy flies out the window.

September 3, 1939

War. It has finally come to it. Freddie got a call through to us last evening to say things were coming to a head and the House of Commons would be meeting this morning, the first time in all its history it has sat on a Sunday. He said the only question still being debated was how long Germany should be given to withdraw from Poland. The French were suggesting a week, Neville Chamberlain thought a day or two, but his Cabinet wanted an immediate end to it. So Hitler was given until eleven o'clock this morning, twelve noon here. We went up to HRH's Bridge to listen on his wireless.

Chamberlain said he'd asked Mr Hitler to undertake to withdraw his forces from Polish territory, but no such assurances had been received; indeed, German tanks had moved deeper into Poland, so Great Britain was now at war with Germany.

HRH has been trying to get through to Bertie York all afternoon. He's going to offer to return to England immediately, at the service of King and Country. Wally says we can't leave until the best things have been wrapped and stored.

September 4, 1939

We woke to the news that France has fallen into line with Britain, so we're at war here too. HRH is suddenly full of pep. He thinks it'll be a short war but long enough for him to make his mark again. He spoke to King Bertie late last night and will be meeting with Walter Monckton in Paris, to discuss war jobs.

Tried to get through to Carlton Gardens, without success, but did speak with Flora at South Audley Street. She said, 'We're at war, Aunt Bayba! Isn't it exciting! The sirens sounded yesterday but we didn't get bobbed yet.'

She says Lightfoot is having his Burgundies reorganized so as to make room for an air-raid shelter and that he's gone to offer his services as a recruiting officer. Who knows, perhaps this new war will force him to buck up.

We got cut off before I could ask about Rory.

The silver and the smaller paintings have been taken down to a bank vault in town. Wally and I expect to be in Paris by Thursday at the latest.

September 5, 1939
Kath and Herman came over to say goodbye. They may go back to the States, unless it's all over before they've had time to get a passage.

September 6, 1939, Hôtel Meurice, Paris
Paris doesn't look any different. The Pigalle is still open. The Communists are still picketing the factories up in Sentier. The front desk seems a little busier with people checking out, but that's about all.

To La Samaritaine. Wally says we must stock up on face powder.

September 7, 1939
We're all going to England. Monckton came to Boulevard Suchet this morning with the good news. There are several possible war jobs lined up for HRH and they're sending a boat for us early next week.

Wally said, 'Good. There are things I need to buy in London.'

Monckton said, 'Oh, I don't think they visualize this as an opportunity for shopping, ma'am.'

She said, 'They? Who are *they*?'

He said, 'Well, the navy, I suppose. And Their Majesties. If you were to accompany the Duke, I'm afraid you won't be received.'

HRH said, 'If that's the case, darling, you must stay here with Maybell. You know my feelings on this.'

She said, 'No, David, my place is at your side. This is war.'

I'm not sure whether she meant the Germans or the New Bunch.

September 8, 1939

Not only will Wally not be received, no provision has been made for accommodations while we're in England. We can't even use Fort Belvedere. But Freddie and Pips have offered us rooms at Halkin Street and the Metcalfes have offered us their place in the country. You find out who your friends are.

Dickie Mountbatten is picking us up from Cherbourg on Tuesday.

September 13, 1939, Halkin Street

We docked just after eleven last night. Everything was blacked out but HRH knew exactly where he was. He said, 'This is where I said goodbye to England. This is the jetty I sailed from, on my way to Enzesfeld.'

There was a small guard of honor and a band played 'God Save the King', but there was no welcome party. Just Baba Metcalfe with two cars. She'd made reservations at the best hotel Portsmouth can offer, but just before we disembarked a signal had come through that Admiralty accommodation was being made available for HRH and Wally for one night. So Baba and I were the beneficiaries. We took the pick of the rooms she'd booked and poor Wally had to sleep in a navy cot!

Baba grows on me. She's never concealed that HRH has been a disappointment to her and that she finds Wally common, but she's still doing everything she can to ease their homecoming, which is more than can be said for some. They didn't even bother to send them a car. She drove me up to town this morning and was fuming about the war work being offered HRH. There's something in civil defense, in Wales, or a desk job at GHQ in France. He's leaning toward Wales.

Baba said, 'But he must get back into uniform. He got an MC in the last lot, for heaven's sake.'

Pips is glad to have me stay. Freddie's practically sleeping at the Commons. HRH is seeing the King today. Wally's been advised to stay down in Sussex and rock no boats.

September 14, 1939

Freddie says HRH should take the civil defense job. He said, 'They'll be able to live here and Wally can be seen to take part in the war effort. By the time it's over she'll have won the good opinion of even her greatest enemies.'

Baba's been trying to rustle up people to go down to Sussex and keep Wally entertained. Hattie went down for lunch today, but a lot of people won't go anywhere, worried about gasoline shortages. We're supposed to carry gas masks but they really don't look right with anything except a uniform.

Everything seems calm at Carlton Gardens. Dear Rory

was home on twenty-four-hour furlough from Dartmouth, very smart in his midshipman's uniform. Melhuish is running an Air-Raid Precaution post until such time as he's called from the Guards' Reserve, but he thinks the danger of raids by German bombers is greatly overrated. He says the Germans are far too busy with the Russians, dividing up Poland like a sponge cake, to bother flattening St James's. I agree. Sounding those sirens unnecessarily only makes the servants hysterical.

Ulick is training artillery recruits, whereabouts unknown, and Violet has offered herself to the navy. Her age is against her but she has top brass like Sybil Cholmondely and Salty Laird rooting for her so she's bound to get something. I must say, it does have the best uniform. A good-quality doeskin skirt and a very stylish tricorn hat. I wonder if they'll make her cut her hair?

We parted more affectionately than I ever remember. War does so improve people.

Rory said, 'Transport alongside, ma'am!' when my car came to pick me up. He almost caught me with his trick cigarette pack. Tea at Fuller's the very moment this silly war is over.

September 15, 1939

HRH is apparently not required to defend Wales after all. He's to be attached to the British Military Mission at Vincennes with the rank of major general. Fruity will be equerry. So it's back to France, as soon as a destroyer can be made available.

Lightfoot smelled of drink at eleven this morning. He said, 'I'm a goddamned wreck. I wish they'd left me to rot on Hill 666.'

His arm hurts him more now he doesn't have it than when he did. He said, 'I've become the completest shit to live with, Maybell. What am I? Flora?'

'The completest shit,' she said.

I've noticed a lot of people are starting to use language.

Doopie smiled, as always, but she had tears in her eyes. She said, 'Bedda gum home, Bayba. Bedda gum live here.'

I said, 'Can't they give Lightfoot something for the pain?'

'Wizgy,' she said. 'Lodsa wizgy.'

Flora came out with me to the car. She said, 'Mummy says I have to go to Drumcanna, in case of an invasion. It's too beastly. I haven't even seen any bombs yet.'

She's really getting to be quite pretty.

Freddie says passersby cheered HRH when he went to Downing Street to call on Mr Chamberlain.

Pips back late from Sussex. She says Wally's running the Metcalfes' elderly help ragged and compiling lists of things belonging to HRH that are still in storage and might usefully be taken to Paris. Pips predicts we'll be traveling back with a great deal more luggage than we brought.

September 19, 1939

There'll be a boat available to take us back to France tomorrow night. Wally sent Fruity to York House to liberate some of the wines left behind that are now ready for drinking. She said, 'May as well get something worthwhile out of the trip.' She's very upset because the New Bunch won't even give HRH back his old honorary colonelcy.

September 21, 1939, Hôtel Meurice, Paris
Pitched and tossed all the way back to Cherbourg and there was nowhere to lie down and die. If Adolf Hitler had sent a submarine to hunt us down they would have met no resistance from me. I hope Rory understands what he's letting himself in for.

September 30, 1939
We now have good supplies of stockings, soap, and hair color stored away. Wally says there's no point in stock-piling scent because it evaporates. Anyway, we may still get an early peace. Three weeks of war and we haven't heard a single shot fired.

October 3, 1939
Great excitement. Wally and I have volunteered for the Red Cross and Main Bocher is going to make our costumes. I must say war seems to suit HRH too. He looks very well in his uniform and Wally says he was up and gone by eight-thirty this morning even though he doesn't really need to be in till ten.

October 5, 1939
HRH has decided to put away his needlepoint for the duration and is knitting instead. Scarves for the troops. Next week he'll be away visiting fortifications. Fermont, Bois Karre, Thionville. It's all top secret.

Charlie and Fern to dinner. The Piston-LeRupins chucked. Winnie Gulliver thinks they've bolted for Switzerland. Winnie has signed up for the Red Cross too but at the moment she goes every day to help with Elsie Mendl's comfort-kit drive. Wally and I may go with her tomorrow.

October 8, 1939

Everyone was at Trianon with their sleeves rolled, even Sylvie Vieille-Soiffarde, and at an hour she's never normally conscious. Cigarettes, razor blades, socks, candy, all needing to be packed up for the soldier boys. It was the greatest fun.

October 18, 1939

Harry Gloucester is being sent all the way to France to inspect British troops. Wally's steaming. As she says, HRH should have been asked to do it. He's on the spot and he's senior. HRH says he may go along anyway. He doesn't have anything else much on next week.

October 23, 1939

Fruity's getting it in the neck from all quarters. From the Commander-in-Chief's people for allowing HRH to turn up at Arras uninvited. From Harry Gloucester's people for allowing HRH to elbow in and take a salute intended for his brother. And from Wally for allowing him to wear suede oxfords with his uniform. But nothing seems to ruffle him.

October 30, 1939

Our Red Cross uniforms are ready. Very fetching. Blue wool A-line skirt with a front pleat, belted jacket, white cotton shirt, and red necktie. We're going to be delivering supplies to hospitals and Winnie Gulliver has been assigned as our driver.

Wally got a letter from Ernest. He and Mary Kirk have had a baby boy. They've named him Henry. He was born in London but they're sending him to the States for safe-keeping until the war has blown over. I hope they've chosen their baby-minder with care. I hope Ernest remembers what happened to Thelma Furness's sister, Gloria.

November 3, 1939
Yesterday we did our first hospital run. Winnie picked us up before first light, six hours' driving, a two-hour break while the supplies were unloaded and we visited some French wounded, then six hours back. The roads are full of army convoys so it's very slow going. More of the same next week.

November 10, 1939
No sleep. We had two deliveries to make, one to a unit near Sedan, so even with Winnie's size 13 on the gas pedal we didn't have a hope of getting back to Paris before morning. They put us up in nurses' quarters. The guns were going all night. I didn't feel frightened though. We talked in the dark and Wally made us laugh with her impersonations of Queen Cotton Candy and King Bertie Bunny. It was rather like being back in the dormitory at Oldfields.

November 28, 1939
Three runs to the Line this week. Invalid potties and Christmas candy. Nothing much happening. Winnie says Hitler intends to bore us into surrendering.

December 20, 1939
The Lazslo Melchiors are giving a blackout party.

December 27, 1939
Such a dreary Christmas. We managed to get oysters but the girl Wally has cooking for her ruined the guinea fowl.

We had to fill up on cheese and almonds. Apparently, they're going to start rationing butter and sugar in England. Poor Flora. She's going to miss her 'gake'. I shall send her an emergency parcel. I wonder if Ladurée ship.

Kenny Opdyke still has a rash from wearing black boot polish to the Lazslo Melchiors'.

January 8, 1940

Snow. We were meant to do a Red Cross run but it was only pajamas so we're waiting for better conditions.

January 20, 1940

Colder yet. Have worn my Red Cross greatcoat all day. Even Wally's having difficulty getting fuel delivered. She says she may close up Boulevard Suchet and move back into the Meurice. I'm sure they'll get a good rate. No one is traveling.

February 10, 1940

They don't seem to have anything for HRH to do out at Vincennes anymore and he's run out of yarn for his scarves. He says he may resume writing his memoirs. Wally says if he wants to make himself useful he can get the French Army to give us back our chef. Nothing much seems to be happening in this foolish war so the man may as well be here where he's appreciated.

Fruity is very frustrated. He said, 'Frankly, Maybell, I'd like to be a good deal nearer to the Hun than a Paris drawing room.'

February 27, 1940

The French Army refuses to release our chef. Wally's told Fruity to resubmit the request at a higher level. Those army boys must be eating well. Meanwhile, no one in Paris has the means of putting on a decent dinner.

Winnie Gulliver is organizing a Red Cross benefit. It'll be at the Bobino Club and little Edith Piaf has promised to sing. Something to look forward to at last.

A letter from Violet mailed on December 29 to tell me she made First Officer and has a desk job at the Admiralty. Also that Flora and Doopie had just left for Drumcanna, to prepare it for use as a convalescent home. So I don't suppose Flora ever received her macaroons. Lightfoot is helping at a NAAFI canteen at Victoria station. Rory and Ulick both on active service so we're not allowed to know where they are.

March 9, 1940

Weak sunshine. HRH has been able to get in a little golf with Ambassador Bullitt.

We may go to La Croe for Easter. Fruity said, 'If that's the case I'd very much like to try and get to England, to see Baba.'

Wally said, 'Absolutely not. David needs you.'

Fruity looked so disappointed.

I said, 'Surely we can spare him?'

'We?' she said. 'No, *we* can't spare him. Things could flare up at any moment and the Duke of Windsor can't be caught without his ADC. Not that this is any of your business, Maybell.'

March 15, 1940

The Russians have taken Finland, and are expected to take Sweden too. Fruity says Germany will probably take Norway and Denmark, Italy will take Greece, and civilization as we know it will be dead. At this rate we'll all end up back in Baltimore.

The cherry blossom is out in the Bois de Boulogne.

April 12, 1940

Fruity was right. Germany has invaded Denmark. Winnie thinks our Red Cross runs will liven up now. We're not going to La Croe. Wally says she can't face seeing what the army have done to her lawns.

To Maxim's. Came, Sylvie Vieille-Soiffarde, the Esterhazys, and the Dimitri Shapaleffs, who are apparently not the same kind of Russians as the ones who betrayed us.

April 22, 1940

Easter Saturday but you'd never know. We took a station wagon full of plasma up to a depot near the Line yesterday and didn't get back till midnight. I nodded off after Epernay. When I woke up I heard Winnie saying, 'Maybell's jolly game, sticking with you through all your ups and downs. She must miss her people.'

Wally said, 'She doesn't really have any people. Just a pair of dreary sisters. She's had much more fun with me. Traveled. Met people she'd never have had a hope of meeting.'

Winnie said, 'But she's such a willing pair of hands. And such a cheerful attitude. You'd be lost without her, I'm sure.'

Wally said, 'Yes, good old Maybell. She has her uses.

490

And more money than she knows what to do with. I think of her as our little Paymaster-General. Always good for picking up the check.'

Paymaster-General indeed! And I do too have family. *She's* the one that has no one in the world except HRH and me, and if she doesn't watch out she won't even have good old Maybell.

They say things aren't going well for our sailor boys in the North Sea. I hope Salty Laird is keeping my Rory out of it.

May 11, 1940

Germany has invaded Holland and Belgium. Fruity says France will be next. Kitty Rothschild's gone, heading for Spain. So has Kenny Opdyke and without saying goodbye. Wally's been screeching all day. At HRH for taking the first job he was offered instead of sticking out for something in London. At Fruity for being Fruity. At me for not having twenty pairs of hands. Go to the bank. Find a new manicurist. Collect our furs. Call Maples about storage.

I said, 'We should just close the shutters and leave.'

She said, 'And leave our good things lying around? There'll be nothing left when we come back.'

I said, 'The Germans are collecting countries, not furniture.'

She said, 'It's not the Germans I'm concerned about. It's the French. They're all resentful little revolutionaries under the skin. We'll go when I've made my property secure.'

May 12, 1940

Mr Chamberlain has resigned and Winston Churchill is the new Prime Minister.

According to the wireless, the south coast of England was bombed last night. Wally said, 'Serve them right after the way they've treated us.'

I could see a vein throbbing in Fruity's temple. He left the room and HRH trotted after him, flicking a cigarette lighter on and off.

I said, 'That was an unforgivable thing to say. Fruity has family over there. I do. David does.'

She said, 'They have bomb shelters. Anyway, I've no time for sentimentality. If they hadn't forced David off the throne they wouldn't be at war now. If he'd still been King it would never have come to this. What goes around comes around, Maybell.'

I always hated that expression.

She said, 'Now why don't you do something useful? Go and draw out lots of cash. Get everything we have.'

I said, 'Do you mean everything *I* have?'

She gave me a very old-fashioned look.

May 16, 1940
Wally and I have parted company and on very bitter terms. Fruity came with the news that the Germans had broken through the Line which means that Paris is certain to fall. Wally was still in bed.

HRH called an emergency meeting. He said, 'Maybell, you and Fruity must take Wally and the dogs to safety. Go to La Croe, help her secure the house, and then proceed to Biarritz, ready for a fast getaway.'

Fruity studied his feet for a moment. He said, 'I'm sorry, sir, but for the first time in all our years together I'm unable to comply. I've decided to offer myself for active service.'

HRH said, 'What do you mean! You didn't ask me.'

492

Fruity said, 'No, sir. I decided on my way here. Things are hotting up and the army can surely find a better use for me than escorting Her Grace.'

HRH left the room without speaking.

Fruity said, 'I hope you understand, Maybell. I'll stay here with His Royal Highness until I get my orders but I'm really not cut out for watering dogs and burying Wally's silver. You'll have your detective with you and I'm sure your driver can handle himself. I don't think you'll be in any danger. I hope you get back to the States and have a decent war.'

I might still have gone with her, if she'd behaved halfway civilly to Fruity. If she hadn't screamed at the man from Maples after he'd been so obliging about storage, and if Pookie hadn't cocked his leg against my purse. But everything came to a head.

I said, 'I'm not coming, Wally. I'm going home.'

She said, 'You simpleton, the whole country is on the run. You won't get anywhere without my name to open doors.'

I said, 'I'll take my chances. Nothing's certain for any of us so I may as well go where I'm appreciated.'

She said, 'I've more than shown my appreciation. The places I've taken you. If it weren't for me you'd still be sitting in Wilton Place.'

I said, 'And if it weren't for your little Paymaster-General you'd still be in Marylebone with a veneer sideboard.'

HRH peered in to see what the shouting was about. He withdrew as soon as he saw her face.

She said, 'Off you go then, Maybell. It's really no more than I expected. I've grown accustomed to betrayal.'

I came back to the Meurice. Very strange to have no

duties all of a sudden, no little errands to run. The place is almost empty except for military. Winnie Gulliver is trying to get some gasoline. She thinks we can still make it to the coast.

May 20, 1940
They say Rheims has fallen. Fruity says my best bet is to try and get transport west. He and HRH have patched things up but he says the old warmth has gone. My name is now unmentionable.

Fruity said, 'You know David. Wally's happiness is paramount. Make an enemy of her and you're pretty much finished with him. But it's a loss I'm sure you can bear.'

May 21, 1940
Winnie still scouting for gas.

Fruity says Wally reached La Croe safely. Well, that's something. He'd quite expected a signal that the navy were on their way to pick up HRH and take him to England, but his hopes are now fading.

He said, 'He'd probably refuse to go without Wally anyway. I sometimes think all sense flew out the window the day he met her.'

May 22, 1940
No gasoline, but Winnie may have found a bicycle.

May 23, 1940
Fern Bedaux has a van leaving tomorrow carrying her linens across into Spain. There'll be room for me and Padmore if we take no more than one small bag each. Fruity says it's our best chance. The Germans are nearly

at Abbeville so if Fern's wagon doesn't turn up we'll just have to put out German flags and hope for the best.

Fruity himself is in a state of bafflement. When he called HRH for the day's orders the butler told him HRH had already left, for Biarritz. He kept saying, 'I must have misunderstood. He's still seconded to the British Mission after all. David would never have abandoned his post.'

Of course he would. He gave up an empire to chase after Wally so he'd certainly give up a little make-work army job. GHQ has told Fruity to fall back to the nearest port. Ever the gentleman, he offered to wait and see me safely away, but there's really no need. I can look after myself. I'm the great survivor.

January 8, 1946, Sweet Air, Baltimore
What a treat to crack open a nice clean copybook and resume my diary with happy news. Susan Violet Melhuish Smith was born on New Year's Day. Melhuish says Flora is doing well and the baby looks like Violet but men aren't good at judging these things. I hope for the child's sake she favors me a little. I've told Melhuish to make sure she's given cod liver oil and is kept to a routine. He says Doopie's back in her element with a baby in the house, but we can't allow another generation to grow up saying 'gake' and 'gustard' and I don't want Lightfoot cradling her with his gammy arm and dropping her on her head. The sooner I get there the better.

January 12, 1946
Randolph has pulled every string he knows but the earliest passage we can get is March 4. That damned war. It's supposed to be over but you'd never know it. Pips says the shortages are getting worse in England. Gasoline, clothing. Even bread's rationed now, and she hasn't seen an egg in months.

Good news for Wally though. I see the New York Dress Institute just named her as Best Dressed Woman of 1945. Well, now she's achieved that she'll stop at nothing to stay there. She and HRH have had a pretty good war of it, from what one hears, sitting it out in the Bahamas while the Germans kept guard over their silver. They say their houses came through unscathed, apart from a few land-mines in the lawns at La Croe. Well, they'll soon get some sappers in to clear those. Ethel Croker heard that Wenner-Gren, the Electrolux man, is their new best friend and he has billions. I'm sure he'll take care of everything.

January 28, 1946
Judson Erlanger is in town to bury his father.

January 30, 1946
Judson to tea. He says HRH has been in London, visiting his mother and angling for a new job, preferably Ambassador to Washington, but he's not going to get it.

February 3, 1946
Ethel Croker has written to Wally, hoping to rekindle the friendship when she and Boss resume their European vaca-tions. She says I should do the same and let bygones be bygones. She said, 'We all had a war, Maybell. Everyone's having to adjust to missing faces, even Wally. Charlie Bedaux's dead. Lily. Kenny Opdyke. Count Ciano.'

Well, Charlie took an overdose so that doesn't count and I doubt Wally'll be grieving for Ciano. He took a great big piece of her Chinese history with him when he went to the wall. Anyway, they were just people she knew. They're nothing compared to our losses.

Dear Rory on the *Repulse* off Malaya. He'd be twenty-three by now, just starting out. Looking forward to demo-bilization and a nice tea at Lyons Corner House with his Aunt Maybell. They say Violet never missed a day at her desk, not even the day the telegram came. She went right through to '44, till a rocket bomb hit the Air Ministry. It's all so unfair. She wasn't even working at the Air Ministry. She was just walking down the Aldwych minding her own business, then gone. She didn't even live to hear that Ulick won a gong.

So let Ethel pick up the threads if she must. I can't imagine what Wally and I would find to say to each other.

February 10, 1946
Pips says HRH was greeted by cheering crowds when he went to Marlborough House to see the old Queen. Probably all arranged by loyal old Fruity. Metcalfe's Rent-a-throng!

March 1, 1946
We sail on Monday and now it comes to it I feel quite apprehensive. Six years since I waved London goodbye. War seemed then like it might be rather an adventure. Pips says I'll hardly know the place. She says it's not just that London *looks* different, but the whole feeling of the place has changed too. The bombs have stopped but the gaiety hasn't returned. That will be because the Socialists are in.

But, as Randolph says, we're going because we're needed. Someone has to give some direction to Susan Violet's upbringing before the rot sets in.

March 10, 1946, Carlton Gardens, London
Susan Violet is adorable and has my nose. She has signs of the Melhuish coloring but we can hope for that to pass. Flora seems contented with motherhood, after a pixilated fashion. She goes for hours on end without visiting the nursery, as though it slips her mind that she has a baby,

but she'll get the hang of things eventually. At least she's not likely to turn out the kind of mother who keeps running out the door to Leper committees.

The husband is in Lancashire visiting with his people. As far as I'm concerned it will be no loss to us if he stays there. A convalescent home is no place to choose a husband. Either he'll remain an invalid, which will soon become boresome, or he'll recover and start throwing his weight around in all kinds of unforeseen ways. Melhuish says none of it matters if Flora's happy. He says the boy seems a decent type, although he doesn't have a penny to his name. Well, that's for me to worry about. I believe Melhuish has gone soft in the head without poor Violet.

Pips was right about London. Buildings gone, people tired and pinched, nothing in the shops. She's very cheery considering Freddie lost his seat. He has a few director-ships and may try his hand at pig-farming. All in all they got off rather lightly. Just a nephew of Freddie's killed at Arnhem and they hardly knew him. She and Freddie didn't try to see HRH when he was in town and he made no effort to see them. Wally apparently had the wisdom not to show her face in London. I'm sure I never want to see her again. Too much has happened. Violet dead. Rory dead. And no matter which way I look at it I can't help but think it all comes back to Wally.

If she hadn't been so anxious to escape from Baltimore and put her boarding-house days behind her she'd never have married Win Spencer, never have gone to Coronado, never met Benny Thaw, never happened upon him again in London. No Benny, no Connie, no Thelma, no Prince of Wales, no abdication. And that could have made all the difference. One thing about HRH, he got along well with Hitler. If he'd still been King something could have been worked out, he'd have kept us out of that terrible war. But Bessie Wallis Warfield pulled one stick from the pile and then everything came tumbling down.

We've all had to pay for it, but Wally and David always were slow to reach for the check. Still, as Randolph says, we have to look ahead. We have a new generation to think of now.

When Great-Aunt Maybell left Paris on 24 May 1940, she joined the flood of refugees trying to stay ahead of the advancing German Army. She rode in a laundry van as far as La Rochelle and then reached Santander on the north coast of Spain by coal boat. In Santander she was advised that her best chance was to make for Lisbon, where she arrived, almost penniless, on the last day of July. It was only thanks to the help of her friend, Kitty Rothschild, and a timely wire to Pan Am from Great-Uncle Randolph that she was able to secure a seat on a Dixie Clipper bound for New York.

As she learned later, nearing the Azores they passed directly overhead the steamship that was carrying the Duke and Duchess of Windsor to Bermuda, en route to his new job as Governor of the Bahamas. It was the closest she ever came to being in their company again. When she eventually got back to Baltimore, Great-Aunt Maybell rewarded Randolph Putnam for his patience and loyalty. She married him, the day before Pearl Harbor. She once told me it had been no great love match and she'd done it as much as anything to spite her stepson, Junior, but that with time she'd grown very fond of Randolph.

She said, 'He wouldn't have suited me when I was younger, but after fifty different things matter. And of course, *he* got a very good deal. He couldn't run a place like Sweet Air without me. A man on his own. It was ridiculous. And if I hadn't taken charge after you were born, he'd never have known what is was to have a family.'

I don't remember a single summer of my childhood when Great-Aunt Maybell wasn't around from May to September, browbeating my mother and infuriating my Uncle Ulick. Wherever we were, London, Drumcanna, or later, after we had to let Drumcanna go, at Canna Lodge, it was Great-Aunt Maybell who had colour televisions installed, who ordered pork ribs when we had a larder full of grouse, who sent out to Harrold's, as she always insisted on calling it, for one bottle of Tabasco. Great-Uncle Randolph, Grandpa Melhuish, Great-Aunt Doopie and Great-Uncle Lightfoot would just hunker down some-where with a bottle of whisky and hope she'd forgotten them. Uncle Ulick always said it was a pity we couldn't choose our relations and Great-Aunt Maybell said it was the only point on which they had ever agreed.

She had just arrived for her annual visit when we heard that the Duke of Windsor had died in Paris. That was 1972, the year I was expecting my first baby and Great-Aunt Maybell was revving up for yet another attempt at raising the perfect child. There was some difficulty over the date of the Duke's funeral, I remember, because Trooping the Colour couldn't be postponed, even for a man who had once been King.

Grandpa Melhuish went to Windsor to pay his respects, one of the last outings he made, and Great-Aunt Maybell gave him a letter of sympathy to deliver to the Duchess. She studied the photos in the next day's newspaper very closely and noted that the Duchess was wearing Givenchy and looked the very picture of grief. 'Poor Wally,' I remember her saying. 'She looks so lost. I suppose she did love him after all.'

Great-Aunt Maybell herself died on 24 May 1986, one month to the day after the Duchess.

She was in her eighty-ninth year. Her eyesight was poor, her heart was no longer strong and she kept mainly to her rooms, but one of her greatest pleasures was to have a few choice obituaries read to her each evening and news of the Duchess's death seemed to give her a new lease of life. In fact, she lost interest in any new deaths and preferred just to hear the Duchess's obituaries read over and over.

'Lies!' she said, when the year of the Duchess's birth was given as 1896. 'More lies!' she cried, when it was said that the Duchess never gave a fig for titles. It was as though with each repetition she was hammering another nail in the coffin lid.

I read to her later than usual the evening of 23 May but she said she didn't feel ready for sleep. She wanted things brought to her from the drawers and dressers in her sitting room. Photographs she could no longer make out but knew by their different frames: she and two friends, all in feathered hats, taking a sleigh ride in Garmisch; my Grandma Violet in her debutante gown; me on my first birthday. Then a crystal egg she'd shown me many times before, souvenir of some long past house party.

She said, 'Philip Sassoon gave me this. He hung it from an orange tree for me to find. Now *there* was a man who knew how to do Easter.'

Silly things too. A trick cigarette pack, once the property of my Uncle Rory; a threadbare, unidentifiable hand puppet, a pig, according to family legend and one of my mother's childhood favourites, and finally, an assortment of exercise books filled with Great-Aunt Maybell's loopy writing. They contained her diary begun in 1932 and kept faithfully until the war interrupted it. She had only taken it up again in 1946 to record my birth and make a few final entries.

'Susan,' she said, 'these are for you. These are history. But don't let your Uncle Ulick get his hands on them. He'll throw them on the fire.'

I asked her if she wanted me to read to her from them.

'Oh no, honey,' she said, 'I already know how it goes. I was there.'

She died peacefully in the early hours of the next morning.

Susan Melhuish Smith
Canna Lodge, Aberdeenshire